a   season of knives

Books by P. F. Chisholm

The Sir Robert Carey Mysteries
A Famine of Horses
A Season of Knives
A Surfeit of Guns
A Plague of Angels
A Murder of Crows
An Air of Treason

Writing as Patricia Finney

Lady Grace Mysteries
Assassin
Betrayal
Conspiracy
Feud

Children's Books
I, Jack
Jack and Rebel the Police Dog
Jack and the Ghosts

Other Novels
A Shadow of Gulls
The Crow Goddess
Gloriana's Torch
Unicorn's Blood
Firedrake's Eye

a season of knives

a sir robert carey mystery

P. F. CHISHOLM

Poisoned Pen Press

Trade Paperback Editions 2000, 2013

10 9 8 7 6 5 4 3

Library of Congress Catalog Card Number: 99-068784

ISBN: 9781890208325   Trade Paperback

Poisoned Pen Press
6962 E. First Ave. Ste 103
Scottsdale, AZ 85251
www.poisonedpenpress.com
info@poisonedpenpress.com

Printed in the United States of America

To Melanie, with many thanks

Historical Note

Anyone who wants to know the true history of the Anglo-Scottish Borders in the Sixteenth Century should read George MacDonald Fraser's superbly lucid and entertaining account: "The Steel Bonnets" (1971). Those who wish to meet the real Sir Robert Carey can read his Memoirs (edited by F.H. Mares, 1972) and some of his letters in the Calendar of Border Papers.

foreword

P.F. Chisholm writes You-Are-THERE! books.

A You-Are-THERE! book is a book that can make you feel the nap of Sir Robert Carey's black velvet doublet beneath your fingertips. A You-Are-THERE! book can make you smell the sewer in the streets of Elizabethan Carlisle. A You-Are-THERE! book can make you taste the ale at Bessie Storey's alehouse outside the Captain's Gate at Berwick garrison, and a You-Are-THERE! book can make you hear the arquebuses firing at Netherby tower. A You-Are-THERE! book can make you feel like you're ready to pack up and move THERE, if only you had a time machine.

THERE, in the case of P.F. Chisholm, is the nebulous and ever-changing border between Scotland and England in 1592, the thirty-fourth year of the reign of Good Queen Bess, five years after the Spanish Armada, fifty-one years after Henry VIII beheaded his last queen. Reivers with a high disregard for the allegiance or for that matter, the nationality of their victims roved freely back and forth across this border during this time, pillaging, plundering, assaulting and killing as they went.

Into this scene of mayhem and murder gallops Sir Robert Carey, the central figure of the mystery novels by P.F. Chisholm, including *A Famine of Horses*, *A Season of Knives*, *A Surfeit of Guns* and *A Plague of Angels*, brought to America (at last!) in paperback by Barbara Peters and the Poisoned Pen Press.

Sir Robert is the Deputy Warden of the West March, and his duty is to enforce the peace on the Border. Since everyone on the English side is first cousin once removed to everyone on the Scottish side, it is frequently difficult to tell his men which way to shoot. The first in the series, *A Famine of Horses*, begins with Sir Robert's first day on the job and the murder of Sweetmilk Geordie Graham. In *A Season of Knives* Sir Robert is framed and tried for the murder of paymaster Jemmy Atkinson. On night patrol in *A Surfeit of Guns*, he uncovers a plot to smuggle arms across the Border. In the fourth book (and why hasn't there been a fifth since, pray tell?), *A Plague of Angels*, Chisholm removes Sir Robert to London, where he encounters a bit player named Will Shakespeare involved in a plot that gives a whole new meaning to the phrase "bad actor."

Sir Robert is as delightful a character as any who ever thrust and parried his way into the pages of a work of fiction, in this century or out of it. He is handsome, intelligent, charming, capable, as quick with a laugh as he is with a sword. He puts the buckle into swash. He puts the court into courtier; in fact, his men's nickname for him is the Courtier.

The ensemble surrounding him is equally engaging. There is Sergeant Henry Dodd, Sir Robert's second-in-command, who does "his best to look honest but thick." There is Lord Scrope, Sir Robert's brother-in law and feckless superior, who sits "hunched like a heron in his carved chair." There is Philadelphia, Sir Robert's sister, "a pleasing small creature with black ringlets making ciphers on her white skin." There is Barnabus Cooke, Sir Robert's manservant, who thinks longingly of the time when he "raked in fees from the unwary who thought, mistakenly, that the Queen's favourite cousin might be able to put a good work in her ear." And there is the Lady Elizabeth Widdrington, Sir Robert's love and the wife of another man, who is "hard put to it to keep her mind on her prayers: Philadelphia's brother would keep marching into her thoughts." There is hand-to-hilt combat with villains rejoicing in names like Jock of the Peartree, and brushes with royalty in the appearance of King James of Scotland, who's a little in love with Sir Robert himself.

And who can blame him? Sir Robert is imminently lovable, and these four books are a rollicking, roistering revelation of a time long gone, recaptured for us in vivid and intense detail in this series.

What is a You-Are-THERE! book?

It's a book by P.F. Chisholm.

Dana Stabenow
www.stabenow.com

introduction

Anyone who has read any history at all about the reign of Queen Elizabeth I has heard of at least one of Sir Robert Carey's exploits—he was
the man who rode 400 miles in two days from London to Edinburgh
to tell King James of Scotland that Elizabeth was dead and that he was
finally King of England. Carey's affectionate and vivid description of
the Queen in her last days is often quoted from his memoirs.

However, I first met Sir Robert Carey by name in the pages of
George MacDonald Fraser's marvellous history of the Anglo-Scottish
borders, *The Steel Bonnets*. GMF quoted Carey's description of the
tricky situation he got himself into when he had just come to the
Border as Deputy Warden, while chasing some men who had killed
a churchman in Scotland.

"...about two o'clock in the morning I took horse in Carlisle, and
not above twenty-five in my company, thinking to surprise the house on
a sudden. Before I could surround the house, the two Scots were gotten
into the strong tower, and I might see a boy riding from the house as fast
as his horse would carry him, I little suspecting what it meant: but Thomas Carleton... told me that if I did not...prevent it, both myself and
all my company would be either slain or taken prisoners."

Perhaps you need to have read as much turgid 16th century prose
as I have to realise how marvellously fresh and frank this is, quite apart
from it being a cracking tale involving a siege, a standoff, and some
extremely fast talking by Carey. And it really happened, nobody made
it up; references in the *Calendar of Border Papers* suggest that Carey
made his name with his handling of the incident.

It's all the more surprising then that Robert Carey was the youngest
son of Henry Carey, Lord Hunsdon. Hunsdon was Queen Elizabeth's
cousin because Ann Boleyn's older sister Mary was his mother. He

was also probably Elizabeth's half-brother through Henry VIII, whose official mistress Mary Boleyn was before the King clapped eyes on young Ann. (I have to say that one of the attractions of history to me is the glorious soap opera plots it contains.)

The nondescript William Carey who had supplied the family name by marrying the ex-official mistress, quite clearly did not supply the family genes. Lord Hunsdon was very much Henry VIII's son—he was also, incidentally, Elizabeth's Lord Chamberlain and patron to one William Shakespeare.

Robert Carey was (probably) born in 1560, given the normal education of a gentleman from which he says he did not much benefit, went to France for polishing in his teens, and then served at Court for ten years as a well-connected but landless sprig of the aristocracy might be expected to do.

Then in 1592 something made him decide to switch to full-time soldiering. Perhaps he was bored. Perhaps the moneylenders were getting impatient.

Perhaps he had personal reasons for wanting to be in the north. At any rate, Carey accepted the offer from his brother-in-law, Lord Scrope, Warden of the English West March, to be his Deputy Warden.

This was irresistible to me. In anachronistic terms, here was this fancy-dressing, fancy-talking Court dude turning up in England's Wild West. The Anglo-Scottish Border at that time made Dodge City look like a health farm. It was the most chaotic part of the kingdom and was full of cattle-rustlers, murderers, arsonists, horse-thieves, kidnappers and general all-purpose outlaws. This was where they invented the word "gang"—or the men "ye gang oot wi'"—and also the word "blackmail" which then simply meant protection money.

Carey was the Sheriff and Her Majesty's Marshall rolled into one—of course, I had to give him a pair of pistols or dags, but they only fired one shot at a time. He was expected to enforce the law with a handful of horsemen and very little official co-operation. About the only thing he had going for him was that he could hang men on his own authority if he caught them raiding—something he seems to have done remarkably rarely considering the rough justice normally meted out on the feud-happy Border.

Even more fascinating, he seems to have done extremely well—and here I rely on reports and letters written by men who hated his guts.

By 1603 he had spent ten years on the Border in various capacities, and got it quiet enough so he could take a trip down to London to see how his cousin the Queen was doing. Unfortunately for him, Carey also seems to have been too busy doing his job to rake in the cash the way most Elizabethan office-holders did.

So when Carey made his famous ride, he was a man of 42 with a wife and three kids, no assets or resources, facing immediate redundancy and possible bankruptcy. As he puts it himself with disarming honesty, "I could not but think in what a wretched estate I should be left... I did assure myself it was neither unjust nor unhonest for me to do for myself.... Hereupon I wrote to the King of Scots."

What Carey did after his ride will have to wait for future books—or you could read his memoirs, of course. As GMF says, "Later generations of writers who had never heard of Carey found it necessary to invent him... for he was the living image of the gallant young Elizabethan."

Based on a few portraits, I think he was quite good-looking—as he had to be to serve at Court at all, since Queen Elizabeth had firm views on the sort of human scenery she wanted around her. As he admits himself, he was a serious fashion victim. Nobody wears a satin doublet AND a sash of pearls unless that's what they are, which is how he's peacocking it in one of his portraits. Most remarkable of all, he married for love not money—and was evidently thought very odd for it, since he was perpetually broke.

And that's it, the original man, an absolute charmer I have lifted practically undiluted from his own writings. The various stories I tell are mostly made up, though all are based on actual incidents in the history of the Borders. About half of the characters (and most of the bad guys) really lived and were often even worse than I have described. As I say in most of the historical talks I give, we like to think we're terribly violent and dangerous people but really we're a bunch of wusses. The murder rate has dropped to a tenth of what it was in the Middle Ages—and they didn't have automatic pistols. It took real work to kill somebody then.

And yes, I'm afraid I have fallen, hook, line and sinker, for the elegant and charming Sir Robert Carey. I hope you do too.

—*Patricia Finney*
Cornwall, 1999

introduction

Anyone who has read any history at all about the reign of Queen Elizabeth I has heard of at least one of Sir Robert Carey's exploits—he was the man who rode 400 miles in two days from London to Edinburgh to tell King James of Scotland that Elizabeth was dead and that he was finally King of England. Carey's affectionate and vivid description of the Queen in her last days is often quoted from his memoirs.

However, I first met Sir Robert Carey by name in the pages of George MacDonald Fraser's marvellous history of the Anglo-Scottish borders, *The Steel Bonnets*. GMF quoted Carey's description of the tricky situation he got himself into when he had just come to the Border as Deputy Warden, while chasing some men who had killed a churchman in Scotland.

"…about two o'clock in the morning I took horse in Carlisle, and not above twenty-five in my company, thinking to surprise the house on a sudden. Before I could surround the house, the two Scots were gotten into the strong tower, and I might see a boy riding from the house as fast as his horse would carry him, I little suspecting what it meant: but Thomas Carleton… told me that if I did not…prevent it, both myself and all my company would be either slain or taken prisoners."

Perhaps you need to have read as much turgid 16th century prose as I have to realise how marvellously fresh and frank this is, quite apart from it being a cracking tale involving a siege, a standoff, and some extremely fast talking by Carey. And it really happened, nobody made it up; references in the *Calendar of Border Papers* suggest that Carey made his name with his handling of the incident.

It's all the more surprising then that Robert Carey was the youngest son of Henry Carey, Lord Hunsdon. Hunsdon was Queen Elizabeth's cousin because Ann Boleyn's older sister Mary was his mother. He was also probably Elizabeth's half-brother through Henry VIII, whose official mistress Mary Boleyn was before the King clapped eyes on young Ann. (I have to say that one of the attractions of history to me is the glorious soap opera plots it contains.)

The nondescript William Carey who had supplied the family name by marrying the ex-official mistress, quite clearly did not supply the family genes. Lord Hunsdon was very much Henry VIII's son—he was also, incidentally, Elizabeth's Lord Chamberlain and patron to one William Shakespeare.

Robert Carey was (probably) born in 1560, given the normal education of a gentleman from which he says he did not much benefit, went to France for polishing in his teens, and then served at Court for ten years as a well-connected but landless sprig of the aristocracy might be expected to do.

Then in 1592 something made him decide to switch to full-time soldiering. Perhaps he was bored. Perhaps the moneylenders were getting impatient.

Perhaps he had personal reasons for wanting to be in the north. At any rate, Carey accepted the offer from his brother-in-law, Lord Scrope, Warden of the English West March, to be his Deputy Warden.

This was irresistable to me. In anachronistic terms, here was this fancy-dressing, fancy-talking Court dude turning up in England's Wild West. The Anglo-Scottish Border at that time made Dodge City look like a health farm. It was the most chaotic part of the kingdom and was full of cattle-rustlers, murderers, arsonists, horse-thieves, kidnappers and general all-purpose outlaws. This was where they invented the word "gang"—or the men "ye gang oot wi'"—and also the word "blackmail" which then simply meant protection money.

Carey was the Sheriff and Her Majesty's Marshall rolled into one—of course, I had to give him a pair of pistols or dags, but they only fired one shot at a time. He was expected to enforce the law with a handful of horsemen and very little official co-operation. About the only thing he had going for him was that he could hang men on his own authority if he caught them raiding—something he seems to have done remarkably rarely considering the rough justice normally meted out on the feud-happy Border.

Even more fascinating, he seems to have done extremely well—and here I rely on reports and letters written by men who hated his guts.

By 1603 he had spent ten years on the Border in various capacities, and got it quiet enough so he could take a trip down to London to see how his cousin the Queen was doing. Unfortunately for him, Carey also seems to have been too busy doing his job to rake in the cash the way most Elizabethan office-holders did.

So when Carey made his famous ride, he was a man of 42 with a wife and three kids, no assets or resources, facing immediate redundancy and possible bankruptcy. As he puts it himself with disarming honesty, "I could not but think in what a wretched estate I should be left... I did assure myself it was neither unjust nor unhonest for me to do for myself.... Hereupon I wrote to the King of Scots."

What Carey did after his ride will have to wait for future books—or you could read his memoirs, of course. As GMF says, "Later generations of writers who had never heard of Carey found it necessary to invent him... for he was the living image of the gallant young Elizabethan."

Based on a few portraits, I think he was quite good-looking—as he had to be to serve at Court at all, since Queen Elizabeth had firm views on the sort of human scenery she wanted around her. As he admits himself, he was a serious fashion victim. Nobody wears a satin doublet AND a sash of pearls unless that's what they are, which is how he's peacocking it in one of his portraits. Most remarkable of all, he married for love not money—and was evidently thought very odd for it, since he was perpetually broke.

And that's it, the original man, an absolute charmer I have lifted practically undiluted from his own writings. The various stories I tell are mostly made up, though all are based on actual incidents in the history of the Borders. About half of the characters (and most of the bad guys) really lived and were often even worse than I have described. As I say in most of the historical talks I give, we like to think we're terribly violent and dangerous people but really we're a bunch of wusses. The murder rate has dropped to a tenth of what it was in the Middle Ages—and they didn't have automatic pistols. It took real work to kill somebody then.

And yes, I'm afraid I have fallen, hook, line and sinker, for the elegant and charming Sir Robert Carey. I hope you do too.

—*Patricia Finney*
Cornwall, 1999

sunday 2nd july 1592, evening

If he had been doing his duty as a husband and a father, Long George Little would not have been in Carlisle town at all that evening. All the other men of his troop were out on their family farms, frantically trying to get the hay made while the good weather lasted. Some of them were also taking delivery of very tall handsome-looking horses recently raided by their less respectable relatives from the King of Scotland's stables.

Long George hated haymaking. It wasn't his fault, he reflected gloomily, as he came out of the alehouse by the castle wall and ambled down through the orchards and into Castlegate street in the warm and shining dusk. There was something in hay which disagreed with him. It was fine while the grass was growing, and he could even mow with impunity, but put him in a hayfield among neat rows of drying grass, and within minutes he was wheezing and sneezing, his eyes had swollen, his nose was running and his chest felt tight. His wife refused to believe in these summer colds. It stood to reason, she would snap, that you got colds in the cold weather, not the hot. That was logic. It didn't matter; whatever the logic of it, haymaking made him ill and if he started pitchforking the hay onto a wagon, he would also come up in a bright red rash that made his life a misery for another week at least.

On the other hand, his wife was going to make his life a misery as well because there were two fields to mow, and none of the children were old enough to do more than bind and stack. Without her man the whole weight of it fell on her alone since she had no brothers and Long George's family were busy with their own fields.

Long George didn't even want to leave the town. His nose was running already: if he went out into the countryside, it wouldn't be as awful as if he were haymaking, but it would be bad enough. Life was unfair. He didn't want to be a bad husband…

He paused, his hair prickling upright on the back of his neck. Perhaps unwisely he had been taking a shortcut through an alleyway called St. Alban's vennel between Fisher street and Scotch street. The thatched rooves hung over, within an easy arm's reach of each other and although it was light enough outside, in the alley night had already fallen. A tabby cat was watching with interest from a yard wall.

And he could smell sweat and leather and just make out the ominous shapes of three men hiding in various doorways.

Long George drew his dagger and picked up a half-brick, began backing away. His heart was pounding and he wished he had on better protection than a leather jerkin and his blue wool statute cap. He took a glance over his shoulder to check if there was someone coming up behind him, tensed himself ready to make a dash for Fisher street.

'Andy Nixon, is that you?' came a low growl.

'No. No, it's not. It's me, Long George Little.'

'Och,' said someone else in a mixture of relief and disgust. Long George recognised the voice and let his breath out again.

His brother detached himself from the shadows and came towards him. He had a cloth wrapped round the bottom half of his face.

'What's going on?' Long George asked.

The cat blinked and sat up. The smell of an imminent fight faded as the three other men came out of their hiding places and joined Long George. Their voices growled and muttered for a while, arguing at first and then gradually came to some agreement. Long George grinned and wiped his nose triumphantly on his shirt sleeve. All four of them went back into hiding, with Long George putting his knife away and climbing over the cat's wall, to hide behind the rainbarrel there.

The cat blinked again, licked a paw. Her ears swivelled to the familiar sound of whistling from the other end of the alley and her whiskers twitched as all four of the waiting men tensed to attack.

On a warm Sunday night, a little the worse for drink, Andy Nixon was in a good mood as he turned into St. Alban's vennel, thinking of his bed and the various jobs he had to do in the morning. He still had bits of hay in his hair from his usual Sunday night tryst with his mistress and the smug warmth that came from making the two of them happy. He savoured the memory of her again as he ambled along the alley, picking his way instinctively between the small piles of dung left by a neighbour's pig and the old broken henhouse quietly rotting against a wall, replaying the feel of his woman's thighs entwined with his own and...

Two heavy shadows jumped out behind him, grabbed for his arms. Andy tried to dodge them, managed to punch one on the nose and knock him over, swung about and tried to run back into Fisher Street.

Another shape vaulted the wall and got in his way as he ran, both of them went over, wrestling against the henhouse and breaking it. Andy tried a headbutt and missed, almost got free from the other man's grip and then felt his arms caught again and locked painfully behind him. He took breath to yell but one of the attackers clamped a large horny palm over his mouth.

'We've a message for ye fra Mr Jemmy Atkinson, Andy,' said the muffled voice. 'Ye're to leave his wife alone. Understand?'

Andy's eyes widened as he realised what was coming. He heaved convulsively, throwing one man into the wall and almost getting away, but by then the one whose nose was bleeding had picked himself up, waiting his moment, and punched Andy vengefully several times in the stomach.

Andy doubled over and fought to breathe, but before he could, somebody else drove the toe of a boot deep into his groin and he toppled over into a black pit of pain. More pain exploded in his right hand as someone trod on it; he put his arms up to protect his head and his knees up to protect his stomach. He was walled in by boots that thudded into his back and shins and pounded his bones to jelly and faded the world into a distant island in a sea of hurt.

From far away he realised one of the men was pulling the others off, spoiling their fun. He could just make out the words of the man who had given him the reason for the beating.

'He isnae supposed to be deid,' snarled the man. 'So leave off when I tell ye. Ay, and ye, for God's sake, what d'ye think ye're doin' wi' a rock? Mr Atkinson said to warn him, no' kill him.'

There were mutinous grumbles and whining. Somebody felt inside the front of his jerkin.

'An' he's no' to be robbed,' came the imperious voice. 'Get off, will ye.'

They caught their breaths while he lay there in a heap, gradually coming back to the sickening pain all through his body, and trying not to moan in case they started again. There was a sound of them brushing each other down.

'Mind,' said another, lighter voice, 'It wasnae a fair fight, four on one.'

'It wasnae meant to be,' grunted the man giving the orders. 'Did ye mind the lad in the wrestling at the last Day of Truce?'

'Ay. I won a shilling, thanks to him.'

'Well, that's thirty-one shillings he's earned ye,' said a third, cheerful voice. 'And Pennycook's one rent-collector the less for a bit.'

They laughed and gave him a couple more kicks in the back for luck as they passed by, going on to Scotch street.

Andy Nixon lay still for a long long time, waves of blackness passing through him every so often and moving the stars round the heavens above him. He waited between them for the simple act of breathing to hurt a bit less and nursed his swelling right hand, sick with anger and humiliation and fear for Kate Atkinson, his mistress. The cat jumped down and sniffed curiously at his ear, but then trotted silently off and left him in peace.

A serving girl had lit the wax candles in the Mayor of Carlisle's dining room, although the long dusk was still burning in the west. The combination of lights fell about the card players, complicating the shadows and flattering the ladies outrageously. Sir Robert Carey, the new Deputy Warden of the English West March, had glanced at his own four cards, known immediately that he had the makings of a chorus and put them down again with an instinctive caution he had learned at Queen Elizabeth's Court. He looked around idly.

His sister Philadelphia, Lady Scrope, was as pert and tousled as ever in black velvet and burgundy taffeta. She was frowning at her cards. Laboriously she totted up her primero points, while her husband watched her, his gaunt, beaky, under-chinned face quite softened for that moment. Even the Lord Warden of the English West March could lose his heart to a woman and it was right that the woman was his wife. Unfortunately, his wife did not return the sentiment.

To Carey's left sat Sir Richard Lowther, his enemy and rival for the Deputy Wardenship. Sir Richard was glowering at his cards as if they were reivers he planned to hang, but might be persuaded to let go for a bribe.

Nothing interesting would happen for a while, Carey thought, and let his attention wander again. Two of the players in the second game at the other end of the table were not very well known to him. There was Edward Aglionby, the Mayor, who had invited them to the card party and whose house this was. He was a handsome solidly-built man with fine wavy grey hair under his hat and a grave pleasant manner. There was a local merchant, John Leigh, like Aglionby a Carlisle draper and grocer. He was not paying proper attention to his cards and had lost heavily. Now he was blinking at them again, but clearly not seeing them. Then there was Young Henry Widdrington, heir to the headship of one of the major English East March surnames, painfully spotted. And the one Carey knew so well, who had methodically been taking John Leigh's money off him all evening, was sitting upright and alert on the bench beside him, with the rose-tinted light from the window falling just so on her face and making her beautiful.

She isn't beautiful, Carey thought to himself while he waited for his sister to finish counting under her breath. Not even the most maddened poet in the world could say Elizabeth Widdrington was like Cynthia or Diana or Thetis or whoever. She had a long nose and an extremely determined chin and there was no question but that age would make her even beakier. Her hair was a wavy brown, her eyes were the blue-grey of a steel helmet and her mouth would never ever be a rosebud. Wisely she didn't put red lead on it to make it something it wasn't.

She felt the warmth of his stare, looked up, caught his eyes and coloured. He smiled, and her cheeks became rosy and her eyes sparkled. It delighted him privately that she blushed when she saw him, more prized in her because otherwise she was distressingly self-possessed. He wondered idly where the blush started and how far down it went and from there went on to his perennial speculations about what he would see when he finally lifted her smock over her head and...

'Honestly, Robin, you should pay attention to the game.' He looked round to see his sister grinning at him naughtily. Young Henry Widdrington on Elizabeth's right was gazing elaborately into space so as not to see the byplay between his young step-mother and Carey. What little skin that could be seen between his outrageous collection of spots was redder than Elizabeth's. He had folded.

Carey coughed and pushed five shillings into the middle of the table. Sir Richard Lowther breathed hard through his nose and put in his own five shillings with a resolute thump of his hand. He gave Carey what Carey mentally tagged as the bad gambler's glare and upped the stake by two shillings. Equably Carey shoved his own two shillings into the pot and waited for Lord Scrope, who was dealing, to make his decision. Philly, he knew, was trying to mature her flush and so would stay in for the draw and then fold when she didn't get it. Nobody could fathom what Lord Scrope thought he was doing at the best of times, and Carey wasn't going to start now.

Elizabeth was watching him and he looked steadily back at her. Her eyes were still sparkling and she lifted her chin, her mouth curving. Carey moved his padded hose on the bench, the ruff round his neck suddenly feeling tight and uncomfortable. Lord, Lord, her husband, Sir Henry, was a lucky man. Damn the old villain for marrying her; damn Carey's own father for arranging the match; and damn Elizabeth too for being a great deal more high-principled than most of the married women he had met at Court.

'Er...' said Scrope, and pushed his stake into the middle. Philly exchanged three cards—what on earth does she think she's doing, Carey wondered briefly, as he dropped one card on the table for replacement. Lowther exchanged two, glanced at the cards, and his bushy grey eyebrows almost met in the effort to look disappointed. His fingers started drumming on his thigh. Scrope took two cards, squinted and humphed.

Carey got his new card which was a bit of a long shot, looked at it and relaxed. Most of the time he played strictly on the odds but every so often he gambled wildly on an unlikely hand, just to keep people guessing. On this occasion his gamble had suddenly turned into a much better bet. He was holding all of the fives—a chorus, with a point score of sixty. There were only three hands that could better it: a chorus of aces, sixes or sevens. Naturally it was possible somebody had one—he hadn't seen any aces, sixes or sevens discarded. The next stage in the game was the vying; it was a peculiarity of primero that you must announce how many points you held in your hand and while you could exaggerate your score, you couldn't understate it.

'As I have sixty points I think I'll raise you,' said Scrope, with his habitual nervous smile. Philadelphia looked annoyed and folded.

'Have you indeed?' sniffed Lowther, 'I've seventy two and I'll see you and raise you.'

Carey smiled lazily. 'Eighty four,' he said, as he often did, and raised the both of them. As they had all folded on the last deal, there were now about three pounds in the pot. Philly tutted under her breath and frowned, while Scrope looked from him to Lowther and back again, trying to read their minds. It was Lowther that Scrope was really worried about, Carey noted with interest; obviously Lowther's overbid was likely to mean something.

After a lot of hesitation, Scrope folded as well. Lowther glowered at Carey who looked back, still smiling. He scratched the itch on his cheekbone of the glorious green and yellow remnants of a black eye he had got a week before. A prominent local reiver had given it to him, along with many other grazes and bruises and a couple of cracked ribs, but the fault lay entirely with Sir Richard Lowther, who had once been Deputy Warden of the West March and intended to be so again, soon. Carey found that baiting Lowther had added greatly to his enjoyment of the evening; otherwise the play was too slow for him and too inept.

For ten years he had attended at Court and occasionally played cards with his cousin and aunt, the Queen; tense high-stake sessions lasting past midnight, sometimes with the Earl of Leicester, before his death; more recently with the magnificent and prickly Sir Walter Raleigh and Carey's own patron the Earl of Essex. Nothing could be more different from Carlisle. The hot faintly honeyed smell of expensive beeswax candles had brought it all back to him. At Court there were also occasional yawns from dozing maids-in-waiting and men-at-arms, the rustle of silk and velvet around the table, and the soft clatter of the Queen's pearl-ropes as she moved to bet. To his surprise he felt wistful for it: the brilliant colours and decorous smells, the sense of finding the edge of himself, every nerve stretched with the necessity for being witty as well as playing cleverly. The Queen was an excellent player with a good memory for the cards and absolute intolerance of hesitation or ineptitude. She expected to win much of the time but she also despised cheating to make sure she would and could spot it better than many coney-catchers in the City. Carey generally found it took five or six sessions with less dangerous courtiers in order to finance one evening playing the Queen.

He brought himself back to the present because Lowther had raised him again by two pounds, so he thought of his bed and of the walk back to the castle postern gate with Elizabeth.

'Well, Sir Richard,' he mused. 'What should I do?'

'You could try folding,' suggested Sir Richard.

Carey shook his head. Sir Richard had misunderstood the reasons why he had folded most of his hands in the first part of the evening; he had been betting only on the odds and very cautiously at that, in order to build himself up. Carey was flat broke again, needed to buy a new suit and pay for a new sword, and had borrowed three pounds off his own servant Barnabus in order to joint the game.

'I'll have to hurry you, I'm afraid, Robin,' said Scrope's reedy voice.

Suppressing his instant irritation at Scrope's use of his nickname which he preferred to restrict to relatives and women, Carey nodded and continued to pretend indecision.

'I have a number of letters which need urgent attention,' Scrope continued in an injured tone. 'And a message from the King of Scotland too.'

That was portentously spoken. Quite happy to let Lowther's tension build, Carey looked up at his brother-in-law and raised an eyebrow.

'What does His Majesty want, my lord?' he asked.

'Well, as you know, he's bringing an army of three thousand men into Jedburgh soon to try and hunt down the Earl of Bothwell,' said Scrope, looking at his fingernails. 'He's asked me to hold a muster for the defensible gentlemen of the March, to support him if he needs it during his justice raid.'

From the other end of the table Young Henry Widdrington whistled. 'Won't three thousand men be enough?' he asked naively.

Lowther barked a laugh. 'Not if he's going into Liddesdale after the Earl.'

'Mm,' said Carey casually. 'Of course, he'll be disappointed. The Earl's not there.'

'Oh?' That took Scrope's attention from his fingers. 'Where is he? Not in England, I hope?'

Carey shook his head. 'I understand he's gone north to the Highlands.'

'And how d'ye know that, Sir Robert?' rumbled Lowther.

'I have my sources,' said Carey blandly.

'Of course, he's also after the horses he lost to the raiders on Falkland Palace,' Scrope continued after a pause. 'I can't tell you how many letters of complaint we've had about it. Practically everyone in Scotland seems to have lost the best horse in the country.'

Carey had been distracted by Elizabeth again. The other card game seemed to have finished for the moment. They were drinking spiced beer brought by John Leigh's ugly little Scottish whippet of a servant and Elizabeth was listening gravely to some involved story from John Leigh while she counted her money. One of the two footmen standing by the door yawned suddenly and looked embarrassed.

'Half of the horses are in England at any rate,' said Philadelphia. 'Thirlwall Castle's captain had to go off in an awful hurry and I'm sure it's because his steward told him he had the chance of some superb horseflesh while the going was good. It's quite lucky really, because it means Lady Widdrington can stay with him on her way home.' She stopped. 'Oh, no, she can't,' she contradicted herself. 'The packtrain's due. Isn't it, Mr Aglionby?'

The Mayor smiled tightly across at her.

'Well, Lady Scrope, we try not tae gossip about the packtrains too much.'

There was a movement over by the window where Mrs Aglionby was sitting stitching at a frame underneath a candle. The woman was sitting up and looking worried.

Philadelphia's expression became very sweet and innocent which Carey knew from experience meant that the Mayor had annoyed her.

'I'm sure we're all friends here,' she said. 'And your dear wife told me she thought I would be able to get some black velvet to mend my old bodice by Saturday.'

The dear wife shut her eyes and bit her lip. Aglionby cast a single glance at her before he answered Philadelphia.

'Ay,' said the Mayor, just as sweetly. 'There's nae doubt we'll have a piece in the warehouse for ye when we've turned it out, and a pleasure to make a gift of it to the Warden's Lady.'

'How very kind,' said Philadelphia. 'So Lady Widdrington will be able to stay at Thirlwall?'

'I dinna ken, alas, my lady,' said the Mayor through his fixed smile.

Carey glanced under the table to be sure of his aim and then kicked his sister hard on the shin.

'Quite right, Mr Aglionby,' he said to cover her yelp and to have an excuse to move his own legs right out of her way. 'It must be a constant struggle to stop the local surnames from disrupting commerce.'

'Ay,' said the Mayor heavily. 'It is.'

Carey was glaring gimlet-eyed at his sister who was glaring back. Get the point, Philly, he was thinking; you weren't this thick-headed in London, but then you were drinking less. With King James expected in the area and prices already high in Carlisle, the old Roman road from Newcastle is probably choked with plodding ponies, heavy-laden with temptation.

'Are you going to bet, Sir Robert?' demanded Lowther, losing patience at last.

Elizabeth was giving back half her winnings to John Leigh and receiving his note of debt in return.

'Sir Robert?' said Lowther with emphasis.

Carey smiled sunnily at him. 'Sir Richard,' he said and pushed every penny in front of him into the middle of the table. A very pregnant silence fell.

'I'm raising you,' he explained, unnecessarily. 'Er...' he waved a negligent hand, causing the engraved garnet ring he had once won off the Queen to flash in the candlelight, '...however much that is.'

Lowther breathed very hard. He looked at the small pile of money in front of him, checked his cards again and breathed harder.

The others round the table abruptly remembered their jaw muscles and shut their mouths, with the exception of Philadelphia who solemnly studied the embroidery of her petticoat's false front. She had forgotten her annoyance and her face was suspiciously pink. Carey prayed she wouldn't explode into excited giggles as she had a couple times at Court. The Queen found it charming, but he didn't because it gave the game away.

Young Henry Widdrington came over, helpfully pulled the pile of coins towards him and counted them out and there was silence while he did it. The other players watched. Elizabeth took in the scene, looked amused and whispered into Aglionby's ear. He glanced at her astutely and shook his head, so she whispered to John Leigh and got a nod. Carey felt light-headed with that glorious cold fizzing in the pit of the stomach which could be found only at the gaming tables and in the moment of charging into battle. Elizabeth had seen him play at the peak of his abilities at Court when she was there with Philadelphia in the Armada year and she knew what she was about when she placed her side-bet. Carey hoped Lowther hadn't noticed. He hadn't. He was watching Henry count Carey's winnings of the evening, quite a lot of it originally his money.

'Twenty-one pounds fifteen shillings and sixpence,' announced Henry with a slight quaver in his voice.

'All of it?' queried Scrope.

'Yes, my lord,' said Carey simply.

Everybody was looking at Lowther. He checked his cards again—surely he must know what his points were by now, Carey thought. He was scowling heavily.

'What did you say your points were?' he asked again.

'Eighty-four,' said Carey. It was the point-score of the highest possible hand in primero: four sevens, each worth twenty-one points.

'You always say that.'

'No, I don't. Not always. Are you going to see me?'

Oh, it was agony to watch him. His hand came up to rub his moustache. The sensible thing for him to do, of course, and what Carey himself would infallibly have done, was to fold gracefully. Unless he actually had a chorus of aces, sixes or sevens.

'Well?' asked Scrope tetchily. 'I must get back to my bed before midnight, Sir Richard, if I'm putting out a muster in the morning.'

Carey felt the outlines of his new goatee beard which was just at the itchy stage, tapped his fingers on his teeth and hummed a little tune. He had decided to shave it in the morning because it was a different colour from his hair at the moment. Lowther had started to sweat. Couldn't he afford to play? Then he should learn to do it better, thought Carey unsympathetically, who had never been able to afford bad card-playing in his life. Philadelphia had got a grip on herself and was beckoning over John Leigh's servant.

'Jock Burn,' she said, 'is there any spiced beer left?'

'Ainly the wine, my lady,' said Burn after checking the flagons.

'Oh well, I suppose it'll have to do,' said Philadelphia, holding out her goblet imperiously.

Jock Burn came over into the pool of silence that had formed around them and poured for Philadelphia and then for everybody else. He was a dour enough man, and strictly should not have been employed south of the Border at all, since he was a Scot. It was a law everybody flouted since the Scots would work for half the cost of an English servant.

John Leigh was watching the play anxiously, with occasional glances at the window.

'Sir Richard?' whined Scrope again.

'My Lord Warden,' reproved Carey gently. 'Take all the time you want, Sir Richard,' he added generously to Lowther.

Lowther made a strangulated noise.

'Will ye accept my note of debt, Sir Robert?' he asked in the tone of a man telling a tooth-drawer to do his job.

'Of course,' beamed Carey.

Lowther snapped his fingers irritably at Jock Burn who came over with paper and pens. Lowther scribbled for a moment and then added the note to the pot along with the remnants of his cash.

Carey reached across, picked it up, checked it, nodded and put it back.

'Just making sure you haven't raised me,' he explained to Lowther who seemed close to explosion.

'Get on with it.'

'You first, Sir Richard,' Carey said courteously, wondering for a single icy moment whether Lowther had fooled him.

Lowther laid down a chorus of kings, with a total point score of forty.

Carey laid down his own hand showing sixty points. Everyone, including Philadelphia, sighed and Lowther let out a high little whine. Thought you had me there, did you, you old pillock, Carey thought with savage satisfaction as he scooped in his large pile of cash. There was actually too much to fit in his purse, but Jock Burn was at his elbow with a velvet bag, supplied like magic from under his sister's kirtle. Elizabeth Widdrington was also receiving a sum of money from John Leigh and smiling triumphantly across at him. Carey smiled back, wanting to laugh.

'Well,' said Philadelphia almost truthfully, 'this has been a very exciting evening.' She was standing up, shaking out her petticoats and farthingale and smoothing down the back of her kirtle where it had rumpled. Lady Widdrington was doing the same as she rose from her own padded stool. 'Mr Mayor, Mrs Aglionby, thank you so much for a delightful dinner and some splendid play.' Tactfully, Philadelphia did not mention the wine which had been terrible. Carey had left all of his, although Philadelphia had finished hers, he noticed. Philly was curtseying to Aglionby and his wife, who curtseyed back in mute distress.

'Ah, yes, indeed,' said Scrope benignly. 'Most excellent. Greatly enjoyed myself.'

Edward Aglionby bowed to both of them and then slightly less deeply to Carey and Lowther. Carey returned the courtesy, Lowther hadn't noticed since he was staring into space looking very green above his ruff.

It seemed John Leigh was in a hurry to go and had already made his bows while Philadelphia was speaking and left the room, followed by Jock Burn.

Down the stairs and into the darkened street where two yawning, blinking servants were waiting for them with torches to see them back into the Castle. The main gate had long shut but of course Scrope had the key to the postern gate. Carey looked around in irritation.

'Where's my man Barnabus?' he demanded of the oldest torchman.

'Ah dinna ken, sir,' came the answer. 'When we were having our dinners in the kitchen, he said he knew a place he could get better fare and went off, sir.'

'Blast him,' said Carey, who had the ingrained caution about walking around with a large sum of money acquired by anyone who had lived in London for any time at all. 'Oh, well. We should look dangerous enough.'

Lowther said goodnight to Scrope and departed to his home, and the rest of them set off up the side of the market place, past the stocks and into Castle street. The town was empty so close to midnight, even in summer when the sky never really darkened down to black but hung above, a canopy of deepest royal blue, studded with stars.

All about them the scent of haymaking thrust its way across the usual town smells of horse dung and kitchen refuse and the butchers' shambles on their right. Carey breathed deep and happily before offering Lady Widdrington his arm.

'You truly like Carlisle, don't you, Sir Robert?' she said.

He paused, looked at her and put his own hand on her firm square one.

'My lady,' he said. 'I have won enough money to pay for my new sword and buy me a suit; I have infuriated Sir Richard Lowther; I am away from London and best, best of all, I have your arm in mine.'

She smiled quickly and then looked down.

'It would take very little more to make me the happiest man in England,' he hinted delicately and found himself skewered by a grey glare.

'I don't think you should tease Sir Richard Lowther,' she said after an awful pause. 'You should know by now how dangerous he is.'

This was sensible; Lowther had almost succeeded in getting Carey killed the week before, although Scrope had insisted on an insincere reconciliation. Lowther had been Deputy Warden under the old Lord Warden and had run the March pretty much as he liked. After the Warden's death, he had confidently expected old Scrope's son Thomas to make him Deputy Warden in turn and had been very displeased to find that Scrope had asked his brother-in-law to do the job instead. The five hundred pounds per year that the office was worth was only the beginning of the financial loss this had caused Lowther, never mind the set-down to his prestige and power.

'I can't help it,' said Carey trying to look contrite and failing. 'He's so eminently teasable. Blast and damn Barnabus! I was looking forward to returning the money I borrowed off him so Lowther could see that even if he didn't have a better hand, he only had to raise me again and I'd have had to fold.'

Elizabeth snorted, trying not to laugh.

Barnabus had been drinking happily in the company of six beautiful women, when they weren't busy, and playing dice with some of their few customers. He rolled out of the door having drunk all his money, sad to be leaving the common room still bright with rush dips and a good singsong just beginning. Madam Hetherington had a policy which forbade credit and so he had to leave. Anyway, he remembered that he was supposed to help light his master home from his card-party. He waved goodbye to the juiciest trollop who was leaning out of the window in her smock, and started down the street humming to himself.

Unlike London, Carlisle was dead at night, most of the crime taking place outside its walls rather than inside. And with the hay harvest even the reivers were working hard. If there was a footpad in Carlisle with more practical experience than Barnabus, then Barnabus thought it would be interesting to meet him. He was like a cat at night, automatically silent and stealthy, even when seriously over-oiled and not actively looking for trouble.

It so happened that he took a shortcut through St. Alban's vennel between Scotch street and Fisher street and tripped on a soft bundle that moaned.

Knowing one of the nastier games played in London, he drew his dagger and looked carefully all about him. There were no bulky shadows lurking that he could see. He bent down again and squinted at the man at his feet, whistled softly.

'You bin done over good and proper, ain't you?' he said.

As Carey said later, if Barnabus had ever in his life paid attention to the Gospel on the Sundays when he had to attend church, he might have behaved differently. As it was, he did at least see the door the beaten man was feebly trying to crawl through, and he lifted the latch and pushed it open, even hefted the man through it. Unfortunately, that was an excuse for him to find the man's purse on his belt and quietly cut it.

Leaving whoever it was in a heap on the other side of his door, Barnabus turned on his heel and hurried back to Madam Hetherington's bawdy-house.

What story did John Leigh tell you that persuaded you to let him have his money back?' Carey asked Elizabeth conversationally as they walked slowly back to the Castle.

'Oh, a tediously long tale about roof mending and the cost of litigation. He has to pay the thatchers in the morning and a barrister in London is bleeding him dry over a suit in Chancery for some property of his wife's.'

'What's the property?'

'I really can't remember the details, Robin, but I think it's the house next door to his own in Carlisle, which was apparently supposed to be inherited by his wife and instead was somehow wrongly inherited by her half-brother. He wants it because he has five children and another on the way. Also, it's prime property and he could expand his business conveniently into the shop-front on the ground floor.'

'What did you say to him?' Carey led her around a large soft patch where the market beasts were usually tethered near the Cathedral. Ahead of them walked Young Henry Widdrington, being very tactful; before him were Lord and Lady Scrope, and at the tail and head of the little procession, the two torchbearers.

'I said there was no substitute for overseeing litigation personally and that when Michaelmas Term begins he should post down to London and deal with it himself.'

'Have you been in Westminster Hall?'

'You know I was, Robert. In 1588 I dealt with that problem over the chantry lands Sir Henry was supposed to get from the man who murdered his brother.'

'What happened?'

'We won.'

Carey hid a smile.

'That must have been when I was ill,' he said.

'No, you were convalescing by then, but you weren't very interested.'

This time he had to laugh a little. 'I could have been a barrister, you know.'

Elizabeth turned her face to him and looked disbelieving, the Castle looming behind her shoulder.

'It's true. Father suggested it to me; he said he'd pay for me to go to one of the Inns of Court if I wanted and he would find me a good pupil-master. After that I would be on my own, naturally.'

'They say it's a good way to office at court,' Elizabeth said neutrally.

'Hmf. Is it indeed? Take that catamite, Francis Bacon. They say Bacon's the best lawyer of his generation but he gets nowhere because the Queen doesn't like him, so what good was all his studying? I went to Paris and learnt to dress well and play cards.' And make love to women, he thought privately, but didn't say.

'Besides,' added Elizabeth, 'put you in Westminster with some jowelly lawyer insinuating that you must be either insane or lying, while his father-in-law the judge agrees with him, and your sword would be out in a moment.'

'Nonsense,' said Carey, quite offended. 'I can orate, if I must. It's the studying law that would have been hopeless. The only Latin I ever learned was Catullus and that was because my brother told me what it meant. *Vivamus, mea Lesbia, atque amemus...*'

'Good Lord,' said Elizabeth, curiously. 'Are you trying to impress me with Latin poetry? I'm not the Queen, I know hardly any Latin.'

'Yes,' said Carey truculently. 'Why not? I even remember what it means. *"Let us live and love, my...Elizabeth...And judge the jealous rumours of old men worth but a penny".*'

That was a little too apposite, given the age of Sir Henry Widdrington. Elizabeth turned away and sniffed briefly. Carey touched her hand with his to draw her attention, and went on insistently. Damn it, the beatings his tutor had inflicted in his youth to try and drive at least one declension into his head must be good for something! Besides, this was a crib he had learned by heart for some much-feared lesson long ago, and miraculously it had stuck, perhaps because it was scandalous. And God knew he was no hand at making up stuff like that for himself; he had learned not to embarrass himself that way before he was twenty. Other men's plumage would do for him. He smiled and recited softly, like the very gentlest passage of a madrigal.

'"*The sun may set and return again, but when our brief light is doused, we sleep in endless night. So give me a thousand kisses, and then a hundred more, and a thousand yet again, and a further hundred, and then when we have kissed so many thousand times, let us tumble them together, that neither we nor evil jealousy may ever tell, how very many were our kisses".'*

She was watching him steadily with those clear grey eyes, and as they walked, Carey leaned over and down a little, and kissed her lips.

'One,' he said and smiled for sheer delight at the taste of her, for all it had been quite a decorous kiss. Her chin trembled for a moment before she set it firmly.

'Did the Queen's maids-in-waiting find your Latin impressive?' she asked. The harshness of the words was a little tempered by the softness in her voice. He couldn't take offence; why should he? He wanted her in his bed that night, he was determined on it and she knew it.

'Of course not,' he laughed. 'There are far better Latinists than me about the Queen. Hundreds of them. I expect her laundress knows more than I do.'

'Card-players?'

'No. There, I'm the best.'

Again the dubious snort. He found it charming. But, as he had to admit, he found everything about her unreasonably charming.

'Why did you leave?'

'To be closer to you.'

'I don't think so,' said Elizabeth Widdrington with that same hard grey stare. 'I think you were bored.'

He gestured with his free hand. 'That too, of course. But I could have gone back to the Netherlands. I could have gone to Ireland...'

'What?'

'Well, no; perhaps not Ireland—but France. I could have wangled a place with the King of Navarre. I know the man and he likes me.'

'Oh, don't be silly, Robin. This is all very flattering, but you're here on the Border because it's closer to the King of Scots, and you know Burghley and his son want King James on the Queen's throne when she dies.'

For a moment he examined her face quite seriously. As a younger man he might have been annoyed at her unwomanly astuteness; now he thought how refreshing she was after the greedy empty-headed girls of the Court.

They had passed the orchards and the sweet smell of the Castle's physic garden, and had come, very unhelpfully, to the postern in the main gate which Scrope was trying to unlock. Young Henry Widdrington took his leave of them and ambled off to his lodgings. Carey drew Elizabeth aside a little.

'Are you offended with me, my heart?' he asked softly. 'There's no need to try and create a quarrel. I love you. If you don't love me, say so now, and I will leave you in peace.'

Elizabeth frowned and looked down. 'I am...I am only offended because...I'm married.'

'To an old bully with the gout.'

'It's easy to despise the old when you're young and healthy.'

'I'm not that young and I...'

'Robin, even if I were a widow you would be mad to marry me.' Her voice had taken a metallic tinge as she cut across his words. 'No friend of yours would let you. I've no more than four hundred pounds in jointure; Young Henry gets the land and houses when his father dies. You should marry some rich lady of the Court and settle your fortunes properly.'

It would have hurt less if she had slapped him. They were the last to go through the postern gate, so Carey shut and locked it and threw the keys to Lord Scrope, who dropped them.

Philadelphia whisked the keys off the ground, took her husband's arm in hers and practically frogmarched him to the rooms in the dilapidated old Keep where they were living while the Warden's Lodgings at the Castle Gate were being cleaned and refurbished.

'I'm sorry you think so little of me,' Carey managed to say to Elizabeth, without sounding as bad as he felt.

'Be sensible. I think very well of you, too well to think you'd let yourself be carried away by romantic nonsense.' She hadn't been looking at him, but now she did. 'How much do you owe?' He didn't answer because he wasn't quite sure himself. 'Thousands, I'll be bound. You're neither rich enough nor poor enough to marry for love, and it's a very fickle foundation for a proper marriage anyway. You've been at Court listening to silly poets vapouring about their goddesses for too long.'

Now they were facing each other, suddenly turned to adversaries, wasting a still summer night designed for dalliance. Elizabeth no longer had her arm in his.

For a moment Carey couldn't think of anything to say, since she was completely right about his finances, and what she said was no more than what all his friends and his father had told him often. He didn't care.

'You haven't told me you don't love me,' he said stubbornly.

'That's got nothing to do with anything,' she said. 'I'm married. Not to you, but to a...a rightful husband called Sir Henry Widdrington. That's the beginning and end of it.'

She turned away, to follow the Scropes up to the Keep. Carey thought of his bed, with its musty curtains and its expanse of emptiness, and put his hand on her arm to hold her, turn her to him and kiss her until he relit the passion in her...She slapped his hand away and hissed, 'Will you stop?'

She picked up her skirts and ran.

Carey went blindly after her through the covered way, through the Captain's gate and under the starclad night to the Queen Mary Tower. He climbed the stairs feeling heavy and tired, found his bedchamber dark and empty. He lit a rush-dip from the one lighting the stair, poured himself some wine and sat looking at the pewter tankard for a long time. He had never seen tears on Elizabeth Widdrington's face before.

At the Red Bull, Jemmy Atkinson counted out the money in front of the men he had employed to beat up his wife's lover. Billy Little's brother Long George had somehow come into the matter as well. Never mind, they weren't asking any more for him.

'You told him, Sergeant?'

'Ay,' said Ill-Willit Daniel Nixon.

Atkinson's thin lips pursed with satisfaction.

'Mr Atkinson?' said Long George. 'What happens if Andy Nixon remembers who we are and sues for assault and battery?'

'You didn't let him get a look at you?'

'Not much of one. But he heard Sergeant Nixon's voice at least.'

'Don't worry,' said Atkinson. 'All of this has been arranged through Sir Richard Lowther. If there's a court case Sir Richard will be your good lord and see to the jury, and Nixon knows he'll not get off so lightly next time.'

They looked at each other and nodded, but Long George was still frowning worriedly. He wiped his runny nose on his sleeve again.

'Well, but, master,' he said, 'Sir Richard's not Deputy Warden any more.'

Atkinson's face grew pinched and mean. The actual Deputy Warden, Sir Robert Carey, had wanted to sack him from his office as Armoury Clerk on discovering that most of the weapons in the Carlisle armoury had disappeared, to be replaced with wooden dummies. The Warden had been Atkinson's good lord on that occasion, protesting that they didn't have anyone else in Carlisle capable of dealing with the armoury. Carey had in fact sacked Atkinson from his other, even more lucrative, office of Paymaster to the Garrison, after somehow getting hold of and reading the garrison account books.

'I have every confidence in Sir Richard's ability to send that nosy long-shanked prick of a courtier running back to London crying for his mother,' he said venomously.

'Mm,' said Long George. He started to say something and then thought better of it.

'And in addition no one else will be witnesses, will they?'

'No,' said Ill-Willit Daniel.

Long George and his brother stayed in the common room until late, playing dice for pennies with their new-gotten wealth. Atkinson too seemed to be waiting for something, and sat drinking in solitary splendour. At last Billy touched Long George's arm and he turned to see Lowther advancing towards Atkinson. Long George stayed still and hoped he'd be invisible.

Lowther was in a dour mood, greeted Atkinson and sat down in the booth with him. They talked quietly for a while and Atkinson finally beckoned Mick the Crow over from the knot of drinkers by the empty fireplace. Lowther had sent the potboy for pens and paper and was writing. Mick pulled his forelock to Lowther and went out with him into the yard. Lowther didn't come back in again, but Mick the Crow did, nervously checking something he had inside his shirt. Long George opened his mouth to ask what was going on but Billy kicked him and they went out the back to the dormitory to sleep.

Atkinson went home to one of the few two-storey houses in Carlisle, in a row facing the marketplace and the end of Scotch street. He was savouring the sour pleasure of revenge. His wife had not waited up for him, so he drank home-brewed beer from the cask by himself in the downstairs living room until wife, lawyers, lovers, brothers-in-law all faded away, until he felt the horns on his head a little less sore, and he staggered up the narrow stairs, pulling his boots off on the way, and dropping his doublet and hose at the door to his bedchamber. Then hiccupping slightly he ripped the curtains aside and toppled into bed next to his bitch of a wife. For a while the room and the little watchlight on the bedhead whirled, so he sat up on his elbow and waited for it to settle. His wife was on her back, her smock pulled down off her shoulder to show her pitiful little pointed dug, her mouth half-open and snoring. The best you could say for her was that she had a reasonable dowry. What Andy Nixon saw in her was beyond him. For a moment he thought of waking her and telling her what he had done. Perhaps she would weep; certainly the bitch would deny everything. And then he could slap her, pull up her smock and have his rights there and then, but it was too much trouble and he was too drunk.

He passed out without even bothering to shut the bed-curtains or douse the candle, looking forward to telling her in the morning.

sunday 2nd july 1592, midnight

Solomon Musgrave was a big fat man with one arm and no teeth; he had lost an arm in action under Lord Hunsdon during the Rising of the Northern Earls, and so he had a permanent position in the Carlisle garrison despite being useless for fighting. He generally kept the gate and slept happily through the day, living as nocturnally as the Castle cats. He was usually the first to see the beacons that told of reivers over the Border and had the job of waking the bellringer who lived permanently up at the keep. Occasionally he bribed one of the boys to do his job, but as a general rule he liked it. It was peaceful in the night and his eyes were so adjusted to darkness that he found daylight often too bright for him and hard-edged.

And he saw a great deal. To his private satisfaction, he knew more about what happened in the Castle than anyone else. He had watched the new Deputy try and coax his ladylove to bed and receive his setdown. He had heard the Scropes in their usual arguments as their yawning maid and manservant got them undressed and he knew that Young Hutchin Graham was doing his best to bed one of the scullery maids, with no success whatever.

He stood at his sentrypost, admiring the stars as they wheeled across the sky, and heard somebody approaching the barred main gate.

Solomon Musgrave tilted his halberd against the stone quietly and leaned over the battlements. There was a hiccup and a loud belch, followed by the noise of puking. The words that floated up to him were too slurred and distorted for understanding, though he recognised the voice and grinned.

Looking across at the Queen Mary Tower, which still had the shutters on the window open, he saw the faint light of a rush-dip still burning. The lusty and fire-eating young Deputy could wait all night for his servant. Barnabus Cooke had had a skinful: more than a skinful. Singing floated up in the silence, something mucky about a Hatter's Daughter of Islington, wherever that was, and then more swearing.

'Shut that noise,' he called down. 'Folks wantae sleep.'

'Lemme in,' came the answer. 'C'mon, or I'll sing.'

Solomon Musgrave grinned. 'Ye can sleep there or find a bed. Ah dinnae care which, but if ye sing I'll spear ye like a fish.'

There was another loud belch. 'Come on,' whined the Londoner below, 'I've…got to shee to hish honour Sir Robert Carey inna morning.'

'Then I'll do his honour a right favour and keep ye out. Ye'd fell him with yer breath the way ye are, I can smell it from here. Go to sleep.'

'He'll beat me if I'm abess…abs…not there,' came the pathetic bleat.

'And nae more than ye deserve,' said Solomon Musgrave primly. 'Shame on ye, to be so drunk. Go to sleep.'

'She was only a 'atter's dooooorter an' she…'

Quietly Solomon went along the sentry walk, picked a slim javelin from its sheaf, went back and listened to the adventures of the Hatter's Daughter for a few seconds until he was sure of his aim, then threw. There was a satisfying whipchunk sound, and the vibration of the wooden shaft. The caterwauling stopped. After a moment, Barnabus's voice came again.

'Wotcher do that for?'

'I said I would.'

'You could've killed me.'

'Ay. Next time I willnae miss. Go to sleep.'

There was more sullen muttering and cursing, then shuffling and rustling sounds. Solomon Musgrave squinted down and saw that, from the look of it, Barnabus had picked up the javelin, rolled himself up in his cloak with his back against the wood of the door, pulled his hat over his eyes and gone to sleep. A noise that combined the music of a pigpen and the regularity of a sawpit rolled up towards him.

Solomon Musgrave sighed. 'Ah wish Ah'd known the man sounded better drunk and awake.'

Feeling sorry for the Deputy who presumably shared a room with that awful noise, he went back to his contemplation of the heavens.

monday 3rd july 1592, early morning

By the time Jemmy Atkinson's wife Kate had tired of shrieking up the stairs to wake him, the sun was well up and her two eldest boys had eaten their porridge, fed the chickens in the yard and gone off to school. Her cousin Julia Coldale had been late arriving that morning and late starting work. At last she was in the scullery at the back of the house, plunging the paddle methodically in the butterchurn, trying to get the butter to come. By the sound it would be a while yet, because the girl would keep stopping for breath. Kate's daughter Mary was sitting on a window seat in a patch of sunlight, blinking perplexedly at her sampler and occasionally putting her needle in as she held her breath and stuck out her tongue with the effort to do it right. The mousy ends of her hair hung out under her little white cap and her kirtle was a fine rose wool, with her petticoat showing crooked underneath. Kate Atkinson smiled at her fondly; after two boys, who spent most of their time finding new ways of almost killing themselves, her small girl's anxiety to be good was lovable. Mary looked up at her mother and smiled back.

'I'll fetch your father his porridge,' said Kate Atkinson. 'And then I'll come and show you a new stitch.' She sighed. She needed more help in the house, but her husband refused to allow her to waste his money on idle girls so she could sit by a window and plot like his bitch of a half-sister.

'I done this one almost straight,' said little Mary proudly. 'Look.'

Kate Atkinson looked and agreed that it was much straighter than the one above and in a little while all her stitching would be completely straight. The child wasn't likely to be a beauty, with her mousy hair and sallow complexion, but she would have a good dowry and unimpeachable skills in housewifery; she should make a good enough match.

Suppressing the knowledge that her own marriage had been a good enough match according to her mother, Mrs Atkinson took the bowl of porridge, sprinkled salt on it, laid it on a tray with a mug of small ale and steeled herself to the unpleasantness that awaited her upstairs. He had been drinking half the night. She knew he had; she had woken in the dark to the pungent smell of beer and the lolling body of James half shoving her out of bed. The watch-light had burned down wastefully and he hadn't even drawn the curtains to keep out the dangerous bad airs of the summer. She muttered to herself about it as she climbed the stairs carefully.

It was a long time before she came down again, and when she did she was as white as linen. Her hands shook as she found her husband's black bottle of aqua vitae in the lock-up cupboard and took a couple of painful swallows.

Ten minutes later, Mary Atkinson trotted self-importantly through the broad streets of Carlisle, carefully lifting her kirtle away from the little midden heaps all around. Mrs Leigh their next door neighbour waved to her and asked how she was, and she explained that she was very well as her mam had told her to do, before trotting on. She avoided the courtyard with the Fierce Pig in it and said hallo to three cats and a friendly dog, which took a little time. She also waved to Susie Talyer but couldn't stop to skip with her because she was taking a Message.

She was picturing herself walking up St. Alban's vennel to Mr Nixon's door and banging on it and explaining her Message, when she was very disappointed to see Mr Nixon coming down the street towards her. He looked funny; his mouth was all swollen, his eyes were bruised and he was walking with a limp and his arm in a sling. It was sad she wouldn't be able to knock on his door now, but she could still take her Message and she liked him, so she squealed his name and when he looked, she ran straight for him and cannoned into his legs.

Mr Nixon made an odd little squeak-grunting noise and held onto her tightly.

'Don't do that!' he growled at her.

Her face crumpled and puckered and tears started into her eyes.

Mr Nixon sighed, let go of her arms and patted her head.

'There,' he said awkwardly and rather hoarsely. 'Dinna cry, Mary my sweet, I'm not angry at ye, only ye hurt ma legs which is sore this morning.'

She might get a penny off him to quiet her, so she cried all the harder.

'Is yer father in?' he asked her cautiously, without taking proper notice of her tears.

A bit surprised that her magic power hadn't worked this time, she nodded and gulped. 'But me mam said for ye to come anyway, she said ye mun come right now and never mind what ye're at, she said she needs ye bad.'

Mr Nixon's face looked very odd and he stood still for a long while. He looked angry and afraid at the same time.

'Me dad's still asleep,' she said helpfully. 'He wouldna wake when mam yelled for him. She said he'd drunk too much last night.'

'Did he, by God?' said Mr Nixon in a nasty voice. He put his left hand on his dagger hilt and made the lift and drop movement that even Mary knew was the prelude to a fight. She took the arm that wasn't in a sling and started pulling him after her.

'Ye must come, Mr Nixon, please,' she said. 'Me mam's very upset, her face is as white as her apron, it is so, and she wouldna show me the new stitch like she promised, so please come.'

Mr Nixon's face took on a new set of lines under the bruising, his lips went all thin and into a straight line.

'Ay,' he said. 'I will.'

In the end, she couldn't keep up with him because he strode ahead of her forgetting her short legs and petticoats. She scooped them all up in an immodest bunch and ran as fast as she could and reached their door just as he did, completely out of breath.

Her mam opened the door without him knocking and let him in without a word, putting down a big basket of soiled sheets.

'I did it, mam,' she said plaintively. 'I did the Message.'

Her mam looked at her vaguely as if not seeing her. 'Go help Julia with the buttermaking,' she said, as if Mary had not just delivered an important message for her. Mary was thinking about crying again, but Mr Nixon did a sort of smile for her and nodded. 'I'll give ye the money for a penny bun if ye go off like a good lass now,' he said, so she held out her hand and after a pause he put the penny in it and she trotted off to the scullery where the paddle in the milk was finally beginning to make the *plunk plunk* noises that heralded butter. Perhaps she could get some buttermilk to drink as well.

Kate Atkinson blinked at Andy Nixon for several seconds after her daughter had gone. Her mind seemed not to be working properly, or at least it was some while behind what her eyes saw. She didn't look as if Atkinson had beaten her, or he had kept away from her face if he had. She frowned suddenly.

'Andy, what happened to your face…and your arm?' she asked.

'What d'ye think, Kate?'

'I…don't know.'

'Och, work it out, woman.'

'Did something fall on you?'

Andy Nixon managed a mirthless smile. 'In a manner of speaking. Four men, if ye want to know.'

'What?'

'Your husband paid four men to beat me last night.'

It seemed impossible but her face grew whiter. Both hands went to her mouth.

'Oh,' she said.

'Ay,' agreed Andy. 'Ah was comin' to tell ye we canna go on; I willnae come to see ye any more. Not for a while, any road. I'm going back to my father.'

Well, he hadn't expected her to like it, but whatever he had expected it wasn't a peculiar high-pitched little laugh.

She saw it frightened him, so she swallowed hard and took a deep breath.

'Come and see him,' she said, taking his good arm and leading him to the stairs.

'Kate, are ye mad? I dinna wantae see him. After what he had done to me last night, I willna be responsible for what I...'

'Oh, shut yer clamour and come wi' me,' snapped Kate. 'Ye'll understand when ye see him.'

He did indeed. While Mary had done her message, Kate had already stripped the sheets off the bed, but left her husband half wrapped in the worst-stained blanket. Dead bodies were nothing new to Andy Nixon, but he had never before seen anyone grinning so nastily from his throat, with all severed tubes and the like showing as if he were a slaughtered pig.

Kate bolted the door behind him as he took in the scene. It was all too much for his aching head and aching body. He sat down on the clothes chest beside a tray of cold porridge, and put his face in his hand.

'Oh, good Christ,' he croaked.

'Ay,' she said. 'What am I to do?'

'What happened?' he asked eventually, with a horrible cold suspicion fully formed in his heart. Atkinson had boasted of what he had done to his wife's lover and his wife had taken a knife and...

'Why? D'ye think I did it?' Kate's voice was shaking. 'I left him as alive as you are, and after I'd milked the cow and skimmed the cream for Julia and made the porridge and seen to the children and sent them off to school, I came back and this is what I saw. And...and the blood all over everywhere.'

He was still staring at her and for all his trying, she saw the doubt in his eyes. Her hands clenched into her apron.

'As God is my witness,' she said, very low and intense. 'I did not kill my husband.'

'Ay,' he said, still not able to deal with it. Kate laughed that high silly noise again.

'I was going to ask ye if ye'd done it yourself,' she said.

Andy's mouth fell open and he felt sick. He hadn't thought of that, but there was no denying the fact that he had wanted the little bastard dead as well.

'But I didna,' he said.

'No more did I,' she told him.

The two of them stared at each other while each could see the other wondering and wondering. Finally, Kate Atkinson made a helpless gesture and turned back to the corpse.

'Well, he's dead now. What's to be done?'

'I…I suppose I'd best get Sir Richard Lowther, and tell Fenwick to come for the body and…'

She whirled back to face him with her fists clenched. 'For God's sake, Andy, think!' she hissed at him. 'Who d'ye think they'll say did it? You and me, for sure. You think the women round about here havenae seen us? Well, they have and they'll delight in making sure Lowther knows the lot, and the Warden too. They won't know how it was done for sure, but they'll know I was in the house and that ye would likely be angry with him. What do ye think will happen? We're not reivers, ye're only Mr Pennycook's rent collector and I'm just a woman. You'll hang and I'll burn.'

'Burn?' he said stupidly.

'Ay. Burn. For petty treason. If you kill a man, Andy Nixon, and ye're caught, that's murder and you'll hang for it. If a woman kills her husband, that's no' just murder, it's petty treason. They hang, draw and quarter you for high treason and they burn ye for petty treason. So now.'

Andy Nixon was not a bad man, but neither was he a very clever one. He was broad and strong and quick in a fight, and he could withstand injuries that would have put a weaker man in bed, which was the only reason he could walk at all that morning. But thinking was not what he was paid to do by Mr Pennycook and, generally speaking, he left that to his betters. He gazed at the corpse and his mind was utterly blank.

'Well?' asked Kate Atkinson. 'We canna leave him there. What shall we do?'

'I don't know.' He blinked and bit the hard skin of his knuckles. 'I could likely say it was me did it, and ye knew nothing of it and then I'd hang but ye wouldna burn,' he offered as the best he could come up with.

Kate Atkinson looked at him for a moment with her mouth open. He shrugged and tried to smile.

'I canna think of anything else,' he explained sadly. 'I don't know what to do.'

She suddenly put her arms round him and held him tight. He put his good arm about her shoulders and felt the juddering as she wept into his shoulder, but she was holding him too hard and it hurt his bruises, so he whispered, 'Mind me ribs, Kate. I'm not feeling myself this morning.'

She lifted her head up and wiped her tears with her apron. 'You're Mr Pennycook's man,' she said, still sniffling. 'Would he be a good lord to ye, d'ye think?'

'He's no' bad to work for,' Andy allowed, trying to think it out. 'And he's rich and he has men to do his bidding.'

'Would he turn you over to the Warden?'

'I dinna think so.'

'Could we buy him?'

'Oh ay,' said Andy. 'He's always ready to be bought, is Mr Pennycook.'

'Well, I'll pay him a blackrent of five pounds in silver plate, if he'll find a way out.'

Andy nodded. 'He might listen at that. And five pounds would keep him quiet in hopes of getting more. It's worth trying.'

'Good,' she said, and patted at the shoulder of his jerkin with her apron to dry the wet there. She used one of the keys from the bunch at her belt to open the small plate chest under the bed and gave him a couple of chased silver goblets to use as a sweetener. 'Off you go to Mr Pennycook then, Andy, and say nothing to anyone…'

'Do you take me for a fool?' he demanded, and she managed to smile at him demurely.

'No, Andy.'

Just for a moment he felt a stab of happiness, because if they could only slip clear of the noose and the stake, she was a widow now and he could marry her at last. No more skulking about in the cowshed. He forgot about his ribs and put his good hand on her shoulder, pulled her close and hurt his mouth kissing her.

'There now, sweetheart. Pennycook will see us right. Dinna fret, Kate.'

monday 3rd july 1592, dawn

Barnabus Cooke awoke from a dreamless sleep into the belief that someone was beating him over the head with a padded club and kicking him in the ribs. The first was untrue, the second was true. It was Solomon Musgrave waking him into the worst hangover he had had since…Well, since his last hangover.

'Laddie,' said Solomon patiently, 'ye're blocking the gate.'

'Urrr...' said Barnabus self-pityingly, rolled onto his hands and knees and stayed there for a moment with his head about to fall off, his tongue furred with something that tasted of pig manure, and his stomach roiling. He was collecting the courage to stand. His clothes were all damp with dew, as was his cloak, and he had tangled himself up with a javelin.

'Wha...what 'appened?'

'Some enemy o' yourn must have poured too much beer and aquavita down your poor neck,' said Solomon drily.

The soft mother-of-pearl light in the sky was stabbing his eyes, his body ached, he needed to piss, and he was shaking.

'Oh God.'

'Ay,' said Solomon. 'That'll be him. Will ye get out of my way, Barnabus, or shall I kick ye again?'

'Give me a minute, will you?'

'Ye see, laddie, I would, but there's a powerful number of people waiting for the gates to open and it's no' my place to keep them waiting, so...'

Solomon's foot drew back and Barnabus scuttled out of range, hurting his hands and knees on the cobbles and stones. He reached the corner of the wall and used it to climb himself to his feet, then stood there swaying while Solomon completed his duties.

'Ye'd best go see after your master,' suggested Solomon kindly. 'Ah heard him roaring for ye a minute or two back, now.'

Very carefully and gently Barnabus walked to the Queen Mary Tower. He was still climbing the stairs like an old man, one tread at a time, when he was almost knocked flying by Carey trotting down them. Carey was one of those appalling people who wake refreshed and ready for anything every morning about an hour before everyone else, and then bounce around whistling happily, avoiding death only because they move faster than the people who want to kill them. This morning he wasn't whistling and was looking very bad-tempered, but otherwise he was his usual horribly active self.

Barnabus flailed helplessly on the step until Carey's long hand caught his doublet-front and steadied him.

'Where the devil were you last night...?' Carey began, and then caught the reek of Barnabus's breath. He looked critically at his shaking, swallowing pockmarked, servant and shook his head. 'By rights I should give you a thrashing,' he said conversationally, 'for drunkenness, venery and abscondment.'

'Wha...'

'And it's evident I don't work you hard enough.'

'But, sir...'

'*Shut up!*' Barnabus winced, though Carey hadn't shouted very loudly. 'What the bloody hell do you think you are? If I had wanted some idle beer-sodden fool without the wits of a caterpillar, who hasn't even the sense to be where he's ordered to be, when he's ordered to be there, I could have hired me some brainless wonder from the Court. Couldn't I?'

'Sir.' Briefly Barnabus wondered if a thrashing would be half as painful as Carey's loud voice in the confines of the stairwell, and then decided it would. Definitely. He swallowed hard. Puking on Carey's boots would not be a tactful thing to do, even if he hadn't much left in his stomach to do it with.

'And where the hell did you sleep last night? You're soaking wet.'

'I...er...I think I slept by the gate, sir.'

'Passed out there?'

'No, I...'

'Get upstairs. I want my chambers immaculate; I want my clothes in order; I want my jack and fighting hose ready to wear, and I want my spare boots cleaned.'

'Yes, sir,' said Barnabus despairingly. 'I'm not very well, sir. I'm sorry sir...'

'And,' added Carey venomously, using Barnabus's doublet front to pull him nose to nose, 'if I find you snoring in bed when I come back, I'll bloody well kick you out of it. Understand?'

Barnabus nodded, scurried past, up the stairs and through the door. Carey scowled and was heading for the stables when his sister caught sight of him.

'Robin,' she called. 'Robin, can I talk to you for a moment?'

Carey wanted only to get in the saddle and ride out of the city so he could be away from crowds of people and do some thinking. He pretended not to hear.

'Robin! I know you heard me.'

He stopped and sighed. 'What can I do for you, Philadelphia?' he asked politely. Philly came up to him looking very businesslike in a claret-coloured wool kirtle and bodice of black velvet, a lace-trimmed linen apron skewed halfway under her arm. She wrinkled her brow at him.

'What's wrong with you this morning?' she demanded, clearly in no very good temper herself. 'You didn't drink enough to have a hangover, and you wrung Lowther dry as well. Why aren't you happy?'

He wasn't going to answer that question, which he saw too late was as good as a complete exposition to his sister.

'Oh,' she said, a little regretfully. 'I see. I hoped Elizabeth might...Well, serve you right. I've got a great big bruise on my shin. You'll be wanting something to take your mind off things. Come with me.'

'Why?'

'I want you to help me...do some persuading. You used to be fairly persuasive, as I recall.'

Carey harumphed, which almost made his sister grin despite her sore leg and sorer head, because it was so exactly the noise their father made.

Perhaps because he had a long list of muster-letters to write to gentlemen of the county, and a teetering pile of complaints from Scotland about the recent large raid on Falkland Palace, Carey went along with her meekly enough, until she took him round the back of the Keep into the scurry of sheds and old buildings there. Finally he protested.

'What am I doing?' repeated Philadelphia with fine rhetoric. 'Why, nothing, Robin. Except assisting my husband in his duties,' she said over her shoulder as she stalked ahead of him through the cool dim dairy to the cheese store at the back. Out of a corner she got a cheese that was never of her making, being stamped with a large C. Carey recognised it at once.

'That one's got weevils in it,' he told her helpfully. 'All the Castle ration cheeses have weevils, or worse. Why don't you...'

She glared at him, hauled it onto the cutting board and gave him a knife.

'You cut it, then. I want about half a pound.'

'But, Philly...'

'Go on, if you want to find out what I'm doing. I hate the way they wriggle even after you've cut their heads off.'

Carey did too, but he manfully cut the required piece and lifted it gingerly onto a platter. Philadelphia arranged nasturtium leaves and dill around it and looked about for somebody to carry it. One of her maidens hurried past in the passage, carrying a newly scoured butterchurn.

'Nelly,' she shouted. The girl was a round-faced doe-eyed creature with a wonderful crop of spots and the faint cheesy odour of all dairymaids. She blenched at the sight of what she was supposed to hold.

'Don't drop it,' Philly ordered the horrified girl, as she swept into the wet larder by the Castle wall. She went purposefully to a barrel of salt beef in the corner of the room, this one with a no less ominous JP for James Pennycook on it, and used the tongs to fish up a piece of meat that managed to be as hard as wood and still stank, with a decorative light green sheen. Slicing it with great effort and her breath held, she arranged the whole on another platter, with some loaves of gritty bread and a dish of rancid butter, grabbed Carey's youngest servant Simon Barnet as he wandered past still rubbing straw off his hose, and had him form a procession up to the Keep. She herself took a pewter jug, dived into the buttery, and filled it from the ale barrel that was shunned by anyone with a nose.

'Robin,' she said brightly as they walked back to the draughty Keep. 'Do you remember what you were telling me the other day about victualling contracts?'

'Er...yes.'

'Good,' she said, tweaking Simon's blue cap straight. 'I'll go first. Then Simon and Nelly, then you, Robin. Then agree with everything I say and back me up.'

Eyebrows raised dubiously, Carey followed them all up the narrow stone stairs. Scrope was in the dining chamber that doubled as a council chamber, sitting in a meeting with a long-nosed high-nostrilled Scot by the name of James Pennycook and a couple of his employees. Scrope smiled as they processed in with the repast.

'A little refreshment for you, gentlemen,' said Philadelphia, with a grave curtsey to her husband and his guests and a dazzling smile. Simon was grinning. He laid his platter on the table between them, bowed and went to fetch the goblets and plates. Nelly did the same and backed away, picking nervously at a blackhead.

'Philadelphia...' began Scrope in a strained voice as the combined smells hit him.

'Yes, my lord?' said Philadelphia sweetly, turning back.

'My lady, we can't serve this to our guests...'

Her face crumpled with concern. 'Oh my lord, I'm so sorry. It's their own supplies. I thought they'd be interested to see the quality of them. But if the food's too rotten to eat, I'll go down and fetch something better...'

Carey coughed with the effort of keeping a straight face. Four pairs of male eyes were glaring at his sister.

'Madam,' intoned Michael Kerr, Pennycook's factor and son-in-law, 'surely these gentlemen should not be expected to eat the same food as the common soldiers of the garrison?'

'No?' asked Philadelphia, greatly surprised. 'Why not? It costs as much as our own food from our estates. More, in fact. And my brother eats it, don't you, Sir Robert?'

'Yes, yes, I do.' Carey had his face under control now. 'When it's edible.'

'Ye eat with the men?' asked Pennycook, disbelievingly. 'But Ah thocht ye were the Deputy Warden.'

'It's good practice for a Captain to do so sometimes,' said Carey blandly. 'That way, he and his men get to know each other better, which is important in a fight.'

This was certainly true, as far as it went. However, he generally ate with them at one of the many Carlisle inns, not in the Keep hall where this rubbish was served up to those of the garrison who had spent or gambled all their pay.

Scrope was watching hypnotised as a maggot broke from the safety of the cheese and began exploring the rest of the platter. No doubt it was in search of its friends still hiding in the meat. Perhaps they could have a little party...Get a grip on yourself, man, Carey told himself, as he sat down beside Michael Kerr and drew his eating knife to cut the bread. Simon came rushing back with the goblets and plates, laid them out and Philadelphia served them all from the jug, curtseyed again and swept from the room, followed by Simon and Nelly.

Carey was enjoying the row of stunned expressions. Lord Scrope had been told often enough about the appalling quality of the garrison rations and he had in fact carried out a short inspection. But clearly it had taken the sight of the muck laid out on plates ready to eat to bring home to him just how badly he and the Queen were being cheated.

The junior clerk swallowed stickily. With a flourish straight from the Queen's Court, Carey offered the platter to James Pennycook, who flinched back.

Scrope coughed. 'I think we're in agreement then, gentlemen,' he said lamely. 'The old contract is renewed for the following year. I'll have Bell draw up the notice...'

'Excuse me, my lord,' said Carey very politely. 'I was wondering if you'd had a chance to sort out the question of wastage?'

'Wastage?'

'Yes, my lord. When I was in the Netherlands...'

'My brother-in-law has served with the Earl of Essex in the Low Countries,' explained Scrope. 'He's an experienced soldier.'

'The Earl of Essex, eh?' said Pennycook. 'Is he the Queen's minion...er...favourite?'

'Yes,' said Carey pleasantly. 'I received my knighthood from him. The Queen was very put out; she said she had wanted to knight me herself since I'm her cousin.'

There, you Scotch bastard, he though. Chew on that.

'Do have some of this meat, sir,' he added. Pennycook smiled feebly, held up his hand and Carey, deliberately misinterpreting, gave him two generous slices. Oh dear, he'd got some severed weevils as well.

'While I was fighting the Spaniards, I learned a great deal,' he continued, taking some of the food onto his own plate. No help for it, he had to do it, thanks to Philadelphia. 'Particularly from Sir Roger Williams, a most reverent and experienced soldier.' They weren't really listening; they were watching him cut a slice of cheese that was veined with blue mould, tap out the foreigners. 'He always got on very well with his purveyors.' He ate the cheese while the men who had supplied it watched in fascination, realising to their dismay that if he ate their food, common courtesy dictated that they must too. There was an acrid musty tang to the cheese, not too bad, really, he thought to himself. It was actually better than the frightful stuff they'd eaten on board ship when fighting the Armada. He swallowed and continued. 'The contracts were generous—as yours are—but always included a clause stipulating that any food that was unfit to eat was sent back to the purveyors and its price subtracted from the next payment.'

'That's a good idea,' said Scrope, with an air of pleased surprise. Pennycook picked up a piece of bread, nibbled on it. Carey could hear his teeth grating on the grit, sand, sawdust, ground bones and God knew what else these thieves adulterated the flour with. Pennycook put it down. Michael Kerr had eaten a piece of cheese and was blinking unhappily at the crock of butter. The junior clerk looked at the meat and wisely decided to nibble on some bread. Thank the Lord, Philadelphia hadn't seen fit to offer them any of the salt herring as well; Carey had recognised the barrels as ones that had been condemned as unfit for the English fleet in the Armada year, four years ago.

Scrope put down his knife with a bright smile. 'You'd have no objection to a clause like that in our agreement, would you, gentlemen?'

Carey thought about braving the meat, but decided to stick with the cheese since the bellyache you got from that rarely killed you.

'But the food we supply is of the verra highest quality,' protested Pennycook automatically, falling straight into the trap. Michael Kerr choked on his ale.

'Of course it is,' said Carey smoothly. 'I'm sure that, as with Sir Roger, we will hardly need to use the wastage clause. The Queen will approve as well. She was very concerned at some of the troubles my brother has had with his victuallers in Berwick. Can I offer you some cheese, Mr Pennycook?' Mr Pennycook, who was, as Carey knew, one of the victuallers to the Berwick garrison, shut his eyes, shook his head.

'That's settled then,' said Scrope, who sometimes behaved as if he were not quite so foolish as he looked. 'We'll include the clause in the new agreement. A splendid idea, Sir Robert; thank you.'

Pennycook and his men glowered at him in unison and he favoured them with a particularly sweet smile.

'Ehm,' said Pennycook, his voice rather higher than normal. 'This is all verra weel, Sir Robert, my Lord Warden, but we canna go about putting in new clauses to the victualling contracts wi' nae mair than a wave of a hand…The advocates to draft it will cost a fair sum, d'ye not think?'

'Of course, Mr Pennycook,' said Carey, while Scrope dithered and looked worried. 'I was thinking of sending to Newcastle and briefing an English lawyer to check over those contracts as well while we're at it. Might as well make them as watertight as possible, don't you think? Litigation is such an expensive game.'

Mr Pennycook had small brown watery eyes and a pale bony face gone very waxy. There was a pause while he seemed to be struggling for words. 'Sir Robert?' he said, drawing his rich brocade gown tight about him. 'Surely ye canna be threatening me wi' legal action?'

'Threatening you, Mr Pennycook?' Carey laughed artificially. 'Nothing could be further from my mind. I was only agreeing that while we're briefing lawyers to draw up the new wastage clauses in the victualling contracts, we should get our money's worth and have them look at the contracts as a whole as well. Wasn't that what you said?'

Mr Pennycook had in fact paid good money to the young lord Scrope's father and Sir Richard Lowther to keep the contracts unexamined. He made a little rattle in his throat.

'After all,' Carey added confidingly, 'clerical errors do creep in, don't they, what with copying and recopying.'

For a horrible moment Mr Pennycook wondered if this strange creature had actually read the contracts, and then decided it was impossible. Nobody except a lawyer could understand a word of them. He fixed on high indignation as the only possible escape.

'And now ye're dooting ma word.'

'Far from it, Mr Pennycook,' Carey said affably. 'Why would I do that? Have some more ale.'

'I'll not sit here and be insulted,' Pennycook said, rising to his feet with dignity. 'Good day to ye, my Lord Warden, Deputy.' He fixed the thoughtful Michael Kerr with a glare and said, 'Are ye with me, Michael?'

Kerr stood, made his own bows and followed Pennycook from the chamber in a rush of dark brocade and velvet. Scrope sat staring at the green meat before him and frowned worriedly.

'Was that wise, Robin?' he asked and began twiddling his knife in and out of his spidery fingers. 'Our stores are nearly empty.'

'Well, my lord,' Carey said. 'Sir Roger told me that until the contract's signed, you have them at a disadvantage. They need you more than you need them. Pennycook has warehouses full of food that no one can sell anywhere else, bought dirt cheap, and harvests paid for in advance. If his contract is not renewed, then he's a ruined man.'

'Hm. I never thought of that. So you think he'll come round?'

'Definitely.'

'There isn't more in this, is there, Robin?'

I wish you wouldn't call me by that name, Carey thought, but shrugged.

'What do you mean?'

'You're not after the victualling contract yourself, are you? Or for somebody you...heh...know?'

Carey made a little shake of his head. He hadn't in fact thought of it that way, but it was an interesting idea. Everyone knew victualling contracts were pure gold...

'I don't know, my lord,' he said honestly. 'But it's a thought, isn't it?'

Scrope beamed at him. 'Get Simon to clear this dreadful rubbish away,' he said. 'I'm not at all hungry.'

monday 3rd july 1592, morning

Pennycook walked speedily away from the Castle, trailing his factor and junior clerk, collected two further henchmen at the gate and went to his house.

'How much d'ye think the new Deputy Warden wants?' Pennycook asked Michael Kerr as they sat with spiced wine and wafers to settle their stomachs. Michael was his son-in-law and he valued the young man's advice.

Kerr shook his head. 'I don't think it's so simple as that,' he said. 'I heard Thomas the Merchant offered him the usual pension and he turned it down flat.'

Pennycook half choked on his wine. 'Eh? But he's a courtier, is he no'?'

Michael Kerr shrugged. 'He is, but that's what I heard.'

'Good...Heavens.'

'Perhaps it's Lord Scrope putting him up to it. Perhaps he's turning the screw on the price.'

Pennycook sat back in the carved chair, looking relieved. 'Ay,' he said. 'That must be it. He'll get the difference between what the Queen pays and what we ask, and he'll have put his Deputy up to the game…I dinna like this talk of lawyers, though.'

'Well, you started it,' Kerr pointed out. He was pacing up and down, looking very worried. 'I wish ye hadnae. That young Deputy's mad…'

'Don't trouble your head, Michael. It's Lord Scrope.'

'No, but…' Michael Kerr was rethinking his own theory. 'It must have been a surprise to him, when he saw the…the…er, vittles brought in. I saw his face. He's not that good an actor, and he was angry wi' his little wife as well. No. It's the Deputy. And I know what he's up to.'

'What?'

'See, if it was just a bribe he was after, he would have come to you privately and said, this is what I'll do unless…And you would have argued a bit and then paid it. This was too public. If he suddenly changed his tune, him or Scrope, and says the vittles is fine, well, it's an embarrassment.'

'So?' asked Pennycook warily.

Michael Kerr drank some wine.

'He's after the victualling contract himself,' Kerr said grimly. 'Or he's doing it for some big London merchant.'

Pennycook screwed up his face in horror. 'But they canna supply from London…'

'Or in Newcastle or where he grew up in Berwick. Anyway, they only back him. He insists on the wastage clauses and that gives him the way out of renewing. Then Scrope will give him the contract and then…'

He didn't have to explain it. The two of them were as deep in the business as they could be. There were ships already on their way from further down the coast and packtrains from Scotland, all of which would need paying soon—and with what, if not the Queen's money?

Pennycook's face was a bony mask and Kerr felt sick.

A servingman knocked at the door and then slid round it.

'Mr Pennycook, sir,' he said, cap in hand, 'Andy Nixon's waiting downstairs. He's desperate to see ye, sir.'

'What does he want?'

'Willna say, sir. Only he has to see ye now.'

Elizabeth Widdrington regretted having to leave Carlisle, in a way, but in another way it was a relief to have the decision taken from her. She would have liked to give her poor horses more rest—after all they had been from Netherby to Falkland Palace and back in a week—but she would take the journey to Widdrington very gently and spend four days on it, rather than the two it had taken her coming the other way.

She sighed, signalled for her menservants to carry the packs down from her chamber in the Keep, and followed after them hoping she would find the two men-at-arms Scrope was lending her, but not Philadelphia's persistent brother.

Like them, he was waiting for her at the stables. She paused by the muck heap before he saw her, and watched him for a while. It was likely to be her last good stare at him, so she took her time. Cramoisie wool for his suit was a dangerous colour for him, but this was the right shade of purple red: his hose were paned and padded but not foolishly so, and made his long legs very elegant; his doublet had a slight peascod belly for fashion's sake, the kind a man could only get away with if his own stomach was as flat as a pancake. The fit was perfect across his broad shoulders. It was trimmed with black braid and had a row of carved jet buttons down the front that caught the light. She found it horrifying to think what the buttons alone might have cost, never mind the London tailoring that shrieked from every line of his clothes. He was wearing a plain linen collar on his shirt, rather than a ruff.

She smiled a little. There was no question he was vain, but she couldn't help forgiving him for it. He had evidently changed his mind about regrowing his little Court beard because he had shaved that morning. His hair was still dyed black though showing dark chestnut at the roots. She had saved his face quite consciously for last, his long mobile face with that jutting Tudor nose, his blue eyes which could make her laugh only by dancing and quirking an eyebrow...Oh, for goodness sake, he was only flesh and blood and she was mooning like a lovelorn girl.

She ignored those tediously sensible thoughts and stayed where she was, watching. At the moment he was talking to one of the grooms; now he went and greeted his charger, a large black beautiful creature completely out of place among the scrawny tough little hobbies. He smiled, patted the shining arched neck affectionately, gave him some salt from his hand. It hurt her deep inside her chest—where her heart was, she assumed—to see the casualness of that affection. If only he knew it, she valued that in him far more than his unconcealed passion for her. Passion, she believed, could only be fleeting, no matter what silly poets might say, but kindness…That was built into a man, or it wasn't. She had never seen her husband show kindness to any creature: from his horses, his dogs, his servants, his son, his wife, from all of them he simply expected obedience, in exchange for not beating them or humiliating them.

And that memory brought her back to earth with a vengeance. She took a deep breath, let it out again to quell any foolish tremors, and forced herself to march forwards.

Her grooms had prepared the horses. Young Henry was there checking hooves and legs. Carey turned to face her, one long hand still at his favourite horse's neck. He bowed to her, she curtseyed. Young Henry straightened up, patted the hobby's neck and shook his head.

'I'm not happy, ma'am,' he said to her in his surprisingly deep voice. 'They're still not recovered.'

'Why the haste, my lady?' asked Carey.

For a moment there was a flood of words in her mouth, battering at her teeth to be let out. Because if I stay in Carlisle much longer, Robin, you'll have me in your bed and that would not only mean ruin for both of us, it would be a wicked sin in the face of God. The words were so bright in the forefront of her mind, for a second she thought she had said them, but his expression didn't change the way it would have. She swallowed hard and the nonsense subsided. For answer, because her throat wasn't working properly, she took a letter from her sleeve and gave it to him.

Carey took it; his eyes narrowed at the seal. He opened it, and read it. The blue stare scanned the curt lines from her husband, and then lifted to hers.

'I see,' he said. 'You told him what you had done to help me at Netherby. Was that wise, my lady?'

A week before she had lent him the Widdrington horses to provide cover for his masquerade as a pedlar, knowing full well it would take a miracle if she was to see them again. Although the miracle had happened, wrought by Carey somehow, still...

'It would have been foolish to do anything else,' she said coldly, 'since his friend Lowther would have told him the full tale, with embellishments. At least this way, I cannot be accused of dishonesty.'

'Yes,' he said.

'But you understand, I simply cannot stay here against my husband's clear orders.'

'You told him the horses would be overtired?'

'At the time I wrote to him, I didn't know whether I would get them back.'

'I wish you would stay a day or two more,' he said. 'I could give you a proper escort then, when my men come back from haymaking.'

'We have our own hay to get in,' Elizabeth said. 'That's partly why he's...angry. And the reivers will be busy too.'

'Not the broken men,' said Carey. 'They can steal what others mow and stack.'

Elizabeth shrugged. There was no help for it and she saw no point in putting it off. 'I'm sure my husband's name will be some protection,' she said.

'Not in this March. In the East March, certainly, the Middle March perhaps, but not...'

'Sir Robert, there is simply nothing to discuss. I must start for home today. Are the horses ready, Henry?'

'Yes,' he said. 'As ready as they'll be without a couple of days' more rest.'

She clicked her fingers at one of the grooms, and he led her horse up to the mounting block. He would have offered her his arm to mount, but Carey was there first. The flourish he gave the simple act of helping her into the saddle could have been meant for the Queen of England, and she knew perfectly well he did it that way on purpose.

She hooked her leg over the sidesaddle, found the stirrup and rearranged her skirts, took the reins and her whip from the groom.

'Do you never ride pillion?' Carey asked, smiling up at her.

'I prefer to make my own mistakes,' she told him severely and he smiled wider. 'Goodbye Sir Robert,' she managed to say, without the least wobble in her voice, and felt quite proud of herself for doing it.

Young Henry was in the saddle as were the other four men, all of them wearing their jacks and carrying lances. Henry's jack betrayed him by its new pale leather. Nominally, Young Henry was in command as her husband's heir and those who wished to think it true, could do so. Elizabeth nodded at him, checked that her hat was well pinned to her cap and hair, and let him take the lead out of the stable yard.

She had already embraced Philadelphia and exchanged courtesies with Lord Scrope, though the two of them were in the main castle yard to see her off. She rode with her back so straight that her horse skittered sideways uneasily, catching the desperation she was cramming down tight inside herself. She breathed deeply, took the mare in hand and forced her to behave herself.

She simply would not—she refused to—look over her shoulder, though she knew that Carey was there, staring at her departing back as she passed the gate and started down through Castlegate on the long road for Newcastle.

About fifteen minutes later, the large handsome charger was trotting down English street as well. When he was through Botchergate and past the Citadel, Carey put his heels in. The sheer pleasure of feeling the power in Thunder, as he made the transition faultlessly to a gallop, almost broke his dark mood. The sun was shining bright and the meadows round about were alive with men and women and carts, the women raking the golden hay into piles, the men flinging them up onto the tops of the wagons where boys and girls raked it all into shape. Every so often, a cart would rumble along the ruts to a barn or haystack and the same activity would start again in reverse. The pace seemed very hectic and Carey wondered why as he galloped past, given the warmth of the day and the clear harebell blue of the sky with a few clouds floating in from the west.

He caught up with them quickly and reined in, let Thunder get over his customary side-stepping and pawing as he came back to a sedate walk.

The look Elizabeth Widdrington gave him was not what he would have wished. Carey swept his hat off and bowed low in the saddle to her and tried to smile. He found that the steadiness of her grey glare was making him feel like a schoolboy in the middle of an escapade and for a moment he felt awkward. Then he had to grin.

'Do tell me the joke, Sir Robert,' Elizabeth said frostily.

He waved an arm expansively. 'I was thinking that only the Queen and yourself can take me back to my schooldays so easily.'

Elizabeth faced forwards and said, 'Humph.'

'Thunder needed exercise,' Carey explained innocently. 'I thought I'd bring him along the Roman road for a while.'

She said 'humph' again. Thunder snorted and tried to speed up to go past, but Carey hauled him back. Young Henry Widdrington was pretending he hadn't noticed Carey's arrival but the wide neck at the base of his helmet was bright red and not from the sun.

'Have I offended you again, my lady?' he asked Elizabeth.

'Do you understand the meaning of the word *discretion*?' she asked very haughtily. Never mind, at least she was talking to him.

'No, my lady,' he said. 'Please explain it to me.'

'Oh, for goodness' sake, you're making a public exhibition of yourself. What do you expect me to do? Welcome you with a kiss?'

'That would be nice,' he said wistfully and wondered if she would slap him. She didn't, but it looked like a near thing.

'Haven't you got anything better to do than make a nuisance of yourself?' Elizabeth asked in tones that would have withered a tree. Lord, he liked looking at her when she was in a temper.

'Yes, I have,' he said. 'I have piles of tedious papers to deal with and Scrope won't let me have Bell to be my clerk today, so I have to write all the damn letters myself.'

'It sounds as if you had best get back to work then.'

'On the other hand, the sun is shining and Thunder…'

'Needed exercise. So you said. You haven't raised a sweat on him yet, so we'll move aside for you and you can give him a good run. Then you can get back to your papers.'

'To hell with the papers,' Carey said conversationally, 'I wanted to ride with you for a while.'

'Why do you insist on making this so difficult for me?' she asked, and for a moment he felt guilty. Only for a moment, though.

'How am I making it difficult?' he asked, deliberately obtuse. 'I'm not in your way. I'm riding alongside in a perfectly proper manner. I thought you might like to be entertained with some conversation for a little of your long journey.'

'I really don't want to talk,' she said, looking straight between her mare's ears.

'Then I shall ride beside you in silence, my lady.'

'Hmf.'

He did manage to stay silent for several miles, so they could hear the shouts from the hayfields. They got stuck for a while behind a haywagon screeling along behind two yoke of oxen, so Carey trotted ahead and asked the driver to stop while they squeezed past at a wider place. With the road clear ahead of them he let Thunder have a run and then came back to the Widdringtons. Young Henry looked as if he was trying to decide whether to say anything to the scandalous Deputy Warden but, as Carey knew, Young Henry was a likeable young man and far more sympathetic to his step-mother than he was to his unpleasant father. On the other hand, he took his responsibilities as heir very seriously.

Carey took Thunder alongside Henry and tipped his hat in courtesy. Henry bent his head a little and flushed.

'How badly tired are the horses, Mr Widdrington?' he asked and Young Henry frowned.

'We shouldn't be travelling at all, Sir Robert,' he said. 'If none of the horses goes lame, it'll be a miracle. We should have rested for two more days.'

'I quite agree,' Carey said. 'Did you explain this to Lady Widdrington?'

'Yes,' said Henry unhappily. 'I did, and she said my father had ordered us home and so home we would go.'

'It's a pity none of the horses went lame in Carlisle,' said Carey innocently. Young Henry looked at him sideways and then quietly swore.

'I never thought of that,' he admitted.

'Nor did I until this minute,' Carey said candidly. 'Never mind, we'll know better next time.'

'And she would spot it,' Henry added.

'Of course she would. But what could she do about it?'

Young Henry sighed.

'I daren't try it now,' he said. 'She'd know.'

'I'm not happy about you travelling at the moment, with the Debateable Land so stirred up,' Carey went on. 'I wish you could stay in Carlisle.'

'If I turned back to the Castle now, I wouldn't put it past her to carry on by herself. And my cousins would obey her, I think, not me. So might the Castle men.'

Carey looked at the two large Widdrington menservants critically. He knew the other two slightly, both Carlislers and often used for dispatches. They would take Lady Widdrington to Newcastle and then wait there for the next dispatch bag from Burghley down in London.

'Well, they look dangerous enough to keep off any chancers,' he admitted. 'And so do you. But what happens if a horse goes lame while you're in the middle of some waste?'

'Have you heard anything, Sir Robert?'

'No. But I'm not happy.'

Henry looked at him with his jaw set square. 'There could be another reason for that,' he said after a moment.

'Well, there is,' said Carey lightly. 'But I'm making allowances for selfishness and I'm still not happy.'

Henry gestured with his lance. 'Go and talk to Lady Widdrington. You know my opinion; I'd willingly turn back to Carlisle and stay there, but my lady…'

'Your father's letter was certainly very…peremptory.'

Henry set his jaw again and suddenly looked like the man he would be in a few years' time. Then he swallowed and broke the illusion of maturity.

'I wish you were a reiver, Sir Robert,' he burst out. 'I wish you could sweep down on us with all your men and carry her back to your peel tower.'

Then he shut his lips very firmly and looked as if he expected Carey to laugh at him for his romantic notions.

'I won't deny the thought had crossed my mind,' Carey said slowly. 'But why do *you* wish that? Is she so unhappy with Sir Henry?'

Henry had the peculiar expression of someone who is longing to explain a great deal but can't bring himself to the necessary disloyalty.

'What's she going back to, and why is she in such a hurry about it?' Carey hadn't meant to sound so peremptory but his heart had gone cold.

Young Henry stared ahead for a few moments longer and then said, in a rush, 'Well, Sir Robert, you know if someone has to have a tooth pulled, they're either one way or the other. Some people put it off for as long as possible, and others get it over with as quick as possible.'

For a moment Carey didn't understand. 'But she...Oh.'

Even Henry's spots were glowing red and he looked quite wretched.

'It's his right,' he mumbled. 'And he's a very suspicious man. It took him a long time to...to calm down when she came back from Court. And now...'

Carey understood perfectly. His voice became remote.

'Is he likely to kill her?'

'Well...'

'Widdrington, I want to know what she's facing.'

'Well...I don't think he'd kill her. You see, he needs her to nurse him when he's having one of his attacks of the gravel in his bladder.'

'Couldn't he marry again?'

'I don't think any of the families near us would give him one of their daughters. And none of the widows would take him either,' Henry explained damningly. 'He had to send all the way to Cornwall to get her, remember.'

With some part of his mind, Carey planned to have a great many words with his father the next time they met. But for Lord Hunsdon, Elizabeth would never have married Sir Henry. On the other hand, then they might never have met.

'How did your mother die?' Carey demanded, too angry to be tactful.

Young Henry said nothing which was much worse than an answer. Carey took a deep breath, looked back over his shoulder at Elizabeth riding sedately along. Her face was perfectly normal, though she still looked thoroughly annoyed.

He now understood another reason why she was so coy, for all his sister's machinations. At Court, surrounded by temptation, he had not been a seducer—but he had certainly been very easy to seduce. Like any sensible man, he had avoided the unmarried girls whom the Queen guarded with the ferocity of an Ancient Greek dragon, although occasionally he made mistakes. Married women were much safer, unless their husbands were no longer fit for the marriage bed. In which case the green venom of jealousy was inflamed by the black bile of envy and the whole enterprise became too dangerous for the woman to be fun. Poor Elizabeth.

Certainly Philadelphia could have no idea. It hadn't really occurred to him, although he had no quarrel with a man exercising proper authority over his wife. Obviously, what Young Henry was alluding to was more than that. Coldness trickled down his spine as he wondered if Sir Henry had the brainsickness he knew that Walsingham's inquisitor Topcliffe certainly had. He couldn't ask Young Henry, he wouldn't understand.

Henry was speaking again, in a low mumble.

'What?' he asked.

'I was saying, my father might make her do penance if she's… er…if he thinks she's committed adultery.'

'What, spend Sunday standing outside the church in a white sheet with a candle?'

Henry nodded. Carey looked over his shoulder again. Elizabeth was watching him now, so he turned back in case she saw his face. Considering her pride, he suspected she would prefer to be beaten.

Young Henry was screwing up his face as if he was trying to find the courage to ask something insolent. Carey knew immediately what that was and pre-empted it.

'Your stepmother, Mr Widdrington,' he said coldly and clearly, 'is the most virtuous woman I have ever met. I won't deny I've been laying siege to her with every…every device I have, and I have got nowhere. Nowhere at all.'

Despite the beetroot colour of Henry's face he seemed happier. He nodded.

'But I suppose, given Sir Henry's nature, he isn't likely to believe it, even without Lowther to poison the well for us.'

Henry nodded again. Carey rode along for a moment.

'Christ, what a bloody mess.'

Abruptly he swung Thunder away from Henry's horse and put his heels in again. Thunder exploded straight into a gallop, catching his rider's mood. Carey let him have his head, though he got no pleasure from it now, and then brought him to a stop under a shady tree where he dismounted and walked Thunder up and down to let him cool more slowly, and waited for the Widdringtons. He stood watching them as they came up and cursed himself for being so obtuse, for thinking he was playing a game with Elizabeth when she was in fact gambling with her life. She reined in beside him and he came to her stirrup and looked up at her.

'My lady,' he said gently. 'I'll leave you here.'

'What were you talking about with Henry?'

He also wondered how much she knew of what was in his mind, but she wasn't a witch, only a woman.

'We were agreeing with each other about the dangers of travelling in this March with horses that need more rest,' he lied bluntly. It wasn't a lie. He was worried about it.

'We shall be well enough,' said Elizabeth sedately. 'Thank you for your concern, Sir Robert.'

'Good day to you, Lady Widdrington,' said Carey, uncovering to her as they continued past. 'God speed.'

Barnabus knew better than to say anything to his master when Carey slammed into his chambers with a face as dark as ditchwater and went straight to the smaller room he used as an office. He sat down at the desk, opened the penner and took out pens and ink. Summer sunlight like honey streamed in through the window and he looked up at it once and sighed, then drew paper towards him and dipped his pen.

There was silence as the pile of muster letters grew steadily on one side of the desk. Barnabus finished mending netherstocks that had gone at the heels and canion-hose that had been unequal to the strain of being worn by Carey. For all he liked to look so fine, he was terribly hard on his clothes—one reason why he was so heavily in debt—and it had got a great deal worse since they moved north.

Somewhere around noon they had a visitor. James Pennycook and his son-in-law knocked tentatively at the door and, after wine had been brought, Barnabus and Michael Kerr were told to leave and shut the door.

'What's Mr Pennycook after?' Barnabus asked Kerr as they sat on the stairs, waiting to be called back. Michael Kerr fiddled with one of the tassels on his purse, looked up at the arched roof and said, 'Och, it's the usual. Mr Pennycook wants to know his price.'

'What for?'

'For not interfering with the victualling contracts.'

Barnabus sucked his teeth. 'What a pity Mr Pennycook didn't send you to me first,' he said meaningfully.

Kerr looked knowing. 'Oh,' he said. 'Expensive, is he?'

'Very,' said Barnabus. 'And very unpredictable. He's got to be approached just right, has Sir Robert.'

The low muttering inside had stopped suddenly. Barnabus braced himself.

'Barnabu-u-us,' came the roar.

Barnabus opened the door and went in. Mr Pennycook was standing in the middle of the floor, looking pinched about the nostrils.

Carey was by the fireplace with his back turned.

'Barnabus, escort Mr Pennycook to the gate, if you please.'

'Yessir,' said Barnabus briskly and came forward. 'This way sir,' he said confidingly. 'Best to leave now.'

'But...' said Pennycook.

'Good day to you, Mr Pennycook,' said Carey curtly and walked through into his office, where he sat down.

Barnabus sighed heavily at more riches unnecessarily thrown away—after all, it wasn't as if Carey had yet seen a penny of his legendary five hundred pounds per annum.

'See,' he said to Michael Kerr, as he led the two of them down the stairs again. 'He's a bit touchy, is my master.'

Pennycook was looking ill as he walked unseeing through the gate and into Carlisle town. Barnabus made no haste on his way back and by the time he got up the stairs again, Carey had finished the pile of muster letters and put them to one side. He paused, wiped and put down the pen, stretched his fingers and brushed stray sand from the desk in front of him. He looked as if he was fighting a battle with his conscience again, then he sighed and turned to the pile of complaints that were flooding in about the horses reived in the previous weeks—both those that Jock of the Peartree Graham had stolen as his remounts, and those he and the other Grahams had successfully lifted from the King's stables at Falkland. Carey considered for a moment and then started painstakingly compiling two lists of victims, booty, victims' surnames or affiliations, value of horse stolen (generally very high, by their owners' accounts) and area. The pen whispered softly across the paper, with the occasional rhythmic dip and tap on the ink bottle while the light coloured into the slow afternoon of high summer.

Barnabus finished polishing Carey's helmet and sword, his boots and other tack, then gathered up yesterday's shirt and moved to the door. He suddenly thought of something and coughed. What was the betting Carey hadn't eaten all day? Perhaps some vittles might mend his mood.

Barnabus coughed again gently and when that got no response said, 'Sir, shall I bring up something to eat?'

'What?' The voice was irritable. Carey was recutting the nib of his pen which had worn down.

'Food sir. For you, sir?'

Carey waved a hand dismissively. 'I'm not hungry. Get me some beer.'

'Yes sir,' said Barnabus, confirmed in his suspicions.

The shirt went into the Castle laundry with the other linen and Barnabus wandered to the kitchens where the idle little cook had his domain. He had gathered together a tray of bread, cheese, raised oxtongue pie, sallet and pickle and was going to the buttery for beer, when a boy stopped him in the corridor.

It was Young Hutchin Graham, his boots and jerkin dusty and his blond hair plastered to his head with sweat.

'Mr Cooke,' said Young Hutchin in an urgent hiss. 'I wantae speak to the Deputy.'

'Well, you can't,' said Barnabus pompously. 'He's very busy.'

'I must, it's verra important.'

'What's wrong?'

Young Hutchin looked furtive and unhappy and then shook his head. 'Ah'll tell it to the Deputy and naebody else.'

'You can give me the message and I will ask the Deputy if he wants...'

'Mr Cooke, Ah can tell ye, he'll wantae hear what I have to say, but I'll say it to him only.'

Barnabus looked shrewdly at the boy's anxious face and could see no more dishonesty than usual in the long-lashed blue eyes.

'Very well,' he said. 'Come up to the Queen Mary Tower with me and you can…'

'Nay, I'll not go there. Ask him if he'll please come down here so I'm not seen wi' him.'

Barnabus gave Hutchin a very hard stare and then shrugged.

'I'll pass it on, my son, but I doubt he'll…'

Young Hutchin bit his lip and then whispered, 'It's concernin' Lady Widdrington.'

'Hm,' said Barnabus. 'I'll tell him.'

In fact he let Carey eat what he wanted of the food he'd brought before he mentioned Young Hutchin's anxiety. Carey was preoccupied and it took Lady Widdrington's name to get him to leave his careful list-making and go down the stairs and across the yard to the buttery beside the keep, Barnabus following behind him out of plain nosiness.

Once in privacy by the huge casks of beer and the ample sweet smell of the malt, Young Hutchin gabbled out his tale.

Young Hutchin had seen Mick the Crow Salkeld at dawn in the Castle stables, taking one of the hobbies and asking about the best route to Netherby that avoided the road. When somebody wanted to know why he was sneaking into the Debateable Land, he had tapped his nose and said something about Lady Widdrington.

'What did he say?' demanded Carey.

'Ah dinna like to repeat it, sir, it were…rude,' answered Hutchin primly. 'It were along the lines o' my uncle…er…takin' your place, so to speak.'

Carey breathed deeply through his nose for a moment and then nodded. 'Go on.'

Young Hutchin had been greatly taken with Lady Widdrington, so he had decided to go to Netherby himself and see what was up.

'Ah dinna trust Uncle Wattie, see,' explained his treacherous nephew. 'It's costing him a fortune to mend Netherby an' there isnae a man he's met since it happened that isnae jestin' ower the way ye pulled the wool over his eyes and got the better of him.'

Carey's eyes had narrowed down to slits.

'You didn't run all the way there and back again? It's ten miles.'

Young Hutchin coloured. 'Nay sir. Ah ran a couple of miles to the further horse paddock and…er…borrowed a hobby and a remount. I brung 'em back too,' he added with proud rectitude.

Carey nodded.

'So, anyway, sir, I got to Netherby an' it were full up wi' me cousins and the like, and Skinabake Armstrong and his gang. Ah couldnae get close enough to hear what Mick the Crow's message was, but half an hour after he arrived he was back on the road south again and the place was boiling out like an overturned beeskep.'

'Which way did they go?'

'South east. Across the Bewcastle Waste, sir.'

'How many?'

Young Hutchin squinted at the roofbeams and thought hard. 'By my guess he'd have fifty men or thereabouts, fra the look of them.'

'Armed?'

'Oh aye, sir. Well armed.'

'Who was leading them?'

'My Uncle Wattie, sir, nae mistaking it. Only, Ah wouldnae tell ye if it were nobbut a raid, but my thinking is that Mick's tellt Wattie which way my Lady Widdrington's gone an' he's intending to lift her and ransome her to ye. He'll have heard by now how she helped ye.'

Carey said nothing for a moment and looked as if he was thinking furiously, which surprised Barnabus who had expected immediate fireworks. He was thinking regretfully about all the hard cleaning work he had put in on Carey's fighting harness which would now no doubt be wasted.

'Barnabus,' said Carey eventually. 'I know you're there, skulking in the corner. Go and find Long George and Bessie's Andrew and tell them to come to my chambers in an hour. Young Hutchin, thank you for telling me this. I'm indebted to you. Only I'd like to know why you did it.'

Young Hutchin went pink about the ears.

'It wasnae for ye, sir,' he said gruffly. 'Only, I like the Lady, see.'

Carey looked shrewdly at Young Hutchin for a moment, causing further reddening around the ears, and then smiled.

'All the better,' he said. 'That's a perfectly honourable reason.'

Barnabus came hurrying back to the Queen Mary Tower from his errand and was surprised to see Carey still wearing his ordinary clothes. He would have expected the Deputy to be in helmet and harness and chafing to ride to rescue his beloved, knowing the man. Carey grinned at his obvious shock.

'Barnabus, think,' he said. 'I've got no men around here; they're all at the haymaking and even if they weren't, seven certainly is not enough to match fifty riders. And we don't know for sure what's going on.'

'But if Wattie Graham's after Lady Widdrington, shouldn't we get after 'im, sir...?'

'You're a bit rash, Barnabus.' Barnabus blinked at this outrageous instance of a kettle calling a brass warming-pan black. 'I said, think. Nothing's going to happen to her today because unless she's been extraordinarily unlucky, she'll be into Thirlwall Castle by now.'

'Ain't you going to send a message? Or talk to the Warden?'

'No, I'm going to talk to Lowther first, he's due to take the patrol tonight.'

Barnabus trotted after Carey as he strode out of the Castle and into the town where Sir Richard had a small town house on Abbey street.

monday 3rd July 1592, afternoon

Carey was magnificently languid as he was ushered into the Lowther house and bowed to the dumpling-faced nervous creature who was Lady Lowther. Sir Richard came out and his face hardened with suspicion. After a few exchanges of airy courtesy, Sir Richard growled, 'What can I do for you, Sir Robert?'

'I would like to take your patrol out tonight.'

'Eh?'

'I've heard a rumour about where some of the King of Scotland's horses are being kept and I'd like to investigate. Unfortunately, most of my men are out making hay and as it's your patrol night tonight, I thought I'd ask you.'

He smiled guilelessly, looking remarkably dense for one so intelligent. Barnabus wondered uneasily what elaborate lunacy he was maturing now.

Lowther grunted with suspicion. Barnabus watched him considering the suggestion. Discourteous as ever, Lowther hadn't even offered his master anything to drink, but Carey was standing there playing with his rings as if he hadn't noticed, looking benignly enthusiastic.

Carey reached into his belt pouch and took out a folded sheet of paper. 'I could…er…give you this back,' he offered. It was Lowther's note of debt for fifteen pounds.

Uh oh, thought Barnabus, he's overdone it. Lowther will want to know why he's so eager to take somebody else's patrol.

Lowther did want to know. 'That's very handsome of ye, Sir Robert,' he said. 'Why are ye willing to say goodbye to so much money for such a minor thing?'

Carey smiled. 'King James is offering a large reward for his horses,' he explained. 'If I can find those horses and bring them in, I might make ten times that, besides pleasing the King.'

'Ah.' Lowther's expression lightened slowly. This he understood, and he was only too happy to tear up his large losses at primero. 'I'll speak to Sergeant Nixon then.'

He reached for the paper but Carey put it away again.

'You can have it when I get back,' he said.

Aggravatingly, when they returned to the Queen Mary Tower, Barnabus was sent to find Young Hutchin and make sure he stayed near the stables where Carey could find him, though out of sight.

Carey arrived a little later with Long George and Bessie's Andrew, all three of them wearing their helmets and jacks. Long George's pink-rimmed eyes were looking amused and Bessie's Andrew was swallowing nervously and biting his fingernails, whereas Carey was humming something complicated and irritating about springtime and birds going hey dingalingaling.

'Barnabus,' he said as he passed by. 'Don't try and wander off; I want your help as well.'

'Yes, sir,' said Barnabus resignedly, making sure he had his dagger and the throwing knife behind his neck. The one he usually kept up his left sleeve was currently in pledge with Lisa at the bawdy-house. Then he climbed up one side of a box partition and sat on top of it with his legs dangling.

Lowther arrived, followed by his troop of men, including Sergeant Ill-Willit Daniel Nixon, Billy Little and Mick the Crow Salkeld.

All the men bunched up in a disorderly rabble and stood picking their teeth while Lowther made a short speech explaining that

Sir Robert Carey would take them out in search of some of King James's horses and they were to render to him all the assistance they would to himself, etcetera and so on. Touching, Barnabus called it. Then Lowther departed, quite pleased with himself, while Carey looked them over. Considering the state of them, Barnabus wondered what he would say, but all he did was to ask, 'Where are your bows, gentlemen?'

They looked at each other. Sergeant Nixon spoke up.

'We havenae got none.'

'Ah,' said Carey. 'Well, I want you to get some. I assume you can use them? Good. Sergeant Nixon, take your men down to the armourer's in Scotch street and buy them all bows and a dozen arrows each.'

He tossed Sergeant Nixon three pounds to pay for them and nodded at him to be off.

'If I'm not here when you get back, wait for me. You can drink the change, by the way, gentlemen, but not tonight. Fair enough?'

This seemed to thaw even Ill-Willit Daniel's heart. He touched his hand to his helmet as he led his troop back out of the stables. Carey watched them pass and then said. 'Mick the Crow.'

'Ay, sir,' answered the one with greasy black hair hanging out under his steel cap, a sallow skin and a lamentable jack.

'I've got another errand for you, Mick; wait here a moment.'

'Ay, sir.'

They waited, while Barnabus learned from Carey's humming that springtime was also the only pretty ring time. The excited chatter of Lowther's troop faded in the direction of the gate and out of earshot.

'Well, Mick,' Carey said in a friendly fashion, and nodded meaningfully at Long George and Bessie's Andrew. Long George had moved behind Mick the Crow, examining a hobby's forehoof. Now he whisked about and put his long arm round Mick the Crow's neck. Bessie's Andrew was slower but managed to catch Mick's right arm before it reached his sword and twist it behind his back. Mick kicked wildly at Carey, so Barnabus leaned down from his perch and put his dagger point under Mick's nose. Mick squinted at it and took breath to yell.

''Course you could get along wivout a nose, mate,' said Barnabus conversationally. 'But it wouldn't arf' urt your chances wiv women.'

'Eh?' gasped Mick the Crow. 'What the hell are ye doin'? Lemme go...'

Carey leaned forward and pulled Mick's sword out of its sheath, looked at it distastefully and dropped it in the straw. The dagger went the same way. Carey handed Bessie's Andrew some halter rope and he and Long George tied Mick's hands behind him.

'What the...what's goin' on...'

'Shut up,' said Barnabus. 'Think of your nose, mate.'

'But I...Owch!'

'Oh. Sorry.'

Carey pointed at Mick the Crow's chest. 'You're under arrest, Mick the Crow Salkeld,' he said. 'For March treason.'

'What? Wha' are ye talkin' about...?'

'Question is, which March is the treason in?'

'You'll swing for his one,' said Long George regretfully. Mick the Crow was beginning to look worried. He licked some blood off his moustache. March treason was the catch-all charge: if you couldn't think what else to hang a man for, you hanged him for 'bringing in of raiders'—helping raiders to cross the Border.

'Ah've done nothin'...'

'Shut up,' said Carey. 'All I want to know from you is where the Grahams are setting their ambush. They'll have to lift her before she reaches Tynedale, because there are too many surnames there at feud with the Grahams to risk it. So where are they doing it?'

Mick's eyes bulged. He croaked a couple of times.

'My guess is by the Wall somewhere, because they can hide behind it, but I want to know the exact place.'

Mick the Crow was a good rider and a bonny fighter, but he hadn't the brains for a traitor, Barnabus decided. His brow knitted and his lips moved as he tried to catch up.

'Look,' Barnabus whispered to Mick from his perch on top of the partition. 'I know you're wondering how he knows so much, but you'd be much better off wondering how you're going to stop him making you look forward to your hanging. Right? I mean, he learned a lot from Walsingham's boys, you know.'

'That's enough, Barnabus.' Carey's voice was curt.

'Yessir,' cringed Barnabus, enjoying himself greatly.

'Also, Mick, I want to know who they're planning to hit on their way back to make the trip worthwhile.'

'But I dinna ken that, sir. How could I? All I did was, I took the message, that's all.'

'What message?'

Carey had pulled his dagger from the sheath hanging from his belt at the small of his back. It was a fashionable London duelling poignard, nine inches long, with a pretty jewelled hilt and an eye-wateringly sharp point, and he was using it to clean his nails. Mick the Crow watched him and licked his lips.

'Ahh...he said Wattie could fetch himself a good ransom if he would foray out to the Roman Wall and catch...er...'

'Catch whom?'

'Er...Lady Widdrington, sir.'

Carey trimmed his thumbnail carefully and then fixed Mick the Crow with a blue considering stare. He tossed the poignard up in the air while Barnabus winced a little. As far as he was concerned, showing off with blades like that was a good way to get religious-looking holes in your palms.

'Who sent you?'

Mick licked his lips again. 'Er...who, sir?'

'Yes,' said Carey with dangerous patience. 'Who sent you?'

Mick's face twisted in panic. 'I canna say, sir.'

'Why not?'

'Ah...' Inspiration struck him. 'I didna ken who he was, sir. It were dark.'

'You took a message into the Debateable Land, for a man you don't know?'

'Ay, sir. He give me a shilling for it.'

There was an awful pause while Carey considered this. Mick was shaking like a mouse in a cat's mouth.

'Give me the message,' Carey said at last.

Mick shook harder. 'It was writing and Wattie burnt it.'

'What was in it?'

'I dinna ken, sir. I canna read.'

Carey was tossing the dagger again. 'You carried a letter to Netherby for a man you don't know.'

'Ay, sir.' Mick the Crow was sweating.

Carey squinted at him in the light from the open top door and the poignard flashed and slapped hilt-first back in his hand. 'If it makes you feel happier, I'll regard any obscenity dealing with my Lady Widdrington as being of other authorship.'

Mick's eyes bulged again with bewilderment.

'He's saying, he won't kill you for being rude about the lady; he'll kill the man what sent you,' translated Barnabus helpfully.

'But I canna tell ye what was in it, I dinna...' There was a rising note of panic in Mick's voice.

'You knew they were planning to take Lady Widdrington,' snapped Carey.

'Ay, sir, he let it slip an'...an' they could call in on Archibald Bell by the way, sir, for he hasnae paid his blackrent. That's all. As God's my witness.'

Carey stared coldly at the shaking sweating creature before him, and his mouth made a small twitch of distaste.

'You're very frightened of this man, aren't you, Mick? The one you don't know.'

'Ay, sir,' said Mick hoarsely, licking blood off his lip again. 'I'm a married man, see ye, and I've three small weans.'

'It seems to me,' said Carey remotely, 'that entirely too many of you are married men. Will you tell the Lord Warden what you've just told me?'

Mick closed his eyes and moaned softly. 'They're ainly little, sir,' he said pleadingly.

Carey sighed and put his poignard back in its sheath.

'Would it help if I put you in gaol for refusing to tell me the man's name?'

Mick opened his eyes again.

'Oh, ay,' he said pathetically. 'It would so. Only not the Lickingstone cell, please, sir. It's sae dark in there.'

'Come along,' said Carey sadly. 'We'll do it before I see the Warden.

The really damnable nuisance of it, Carey thought, as he rode out of Carlisle with Sergeant Nixon and the others (except for Mick the Crow) in a bunch behind him, was that this wasn't even the raiding season. July was one of the few times of year when you could be fairly secure from raiding because the nights were too short and too light and any sensible man with a square foot of meadow was out getting his hay in. There was never enough hay for the number of horses on the borders, although the hobbies could get by on about half of what Thunder needed to survive. The Borderers sent cattle skins and salt beef and cheeses south and north to pay for the horsefeed they needed, but it was expensive bringing it in, so whatever you could grow was pure profit. Despite what he had said, even reivers made hay because while cows, sheep and horses had legs and could run, haystacks did not. All this activity in high summer was most irregular.

The result of the unseasonable nature of Wattie Graham's raid was that Carey had practically no men to meet it with and not enough horses. Carlisle was almost a ghost town. Carleton's troop of men were with Carleton and his relatives in Thirlwall; they certainly weren't in Carlisle. Carey's men were scattered to the four winds, on condition they turned up at the Keep by tomorrow night when he was officially due to take a patrol out. Lowther's men...well, they were at least with him and might possibly fight for him, but he had a private bet with himself that Sergeant Ill-Willit Daniel had been given strict instructions to put a lance through his spine if he ever turned his back on the man for long enough.

After deep consideration and with some worry, he had sent Young Hutchin Graham on a fast pony out ahead of him on the road with a letter for Captain Carleton in Thirlwall, telling him on no account to let Lady Widdrington out of the gates the next morning. He thought it very unlikely the boy would get through in time to stop her, assuming—which was highly unlikely— Hutchin's Uncle Wattie hadn't put fore riders in place around the castle to guard against such things. At least if the Grahams caught Young Hutchin, they wouldn't kill him as they might Long George and certainly would Bessie's Andrew Storey, with whose surname they had a feud. Young Hutchin could say convincingly that he had no idea what was in the letter he was carrying since he couldn't read and would probably end up at Wattie's side during the raid. That might even give Carey a card to play if everything went horribly wrong. He would have liked to send Long George off with a letter for the Middle March Warden, Sir John Forster, since the raid was actually due to happen on his ground, but he didn't dare. Firstly, Long George was more than likely to end with his throat slit, and secondly, Carey didn't like the thought of being alone on the road with Sergeant Nixon and his thugs and no one to guard his back but Bessie's Andrew.

The situation was actually worse for him than it would have been for Lowther or Carleton because he didn't know the ground well enough. He was beginning to get a rough shape of it in his mind from his hunting expeditions of the previous week, but nothing like the detailed knowledge of someone born there. He knew the land round Berwick far better from living there as a boy; in Carlisle he was a foreigner. As a result he didn't know what route Wattie Graham would take from Netherby, nor where he would lie up for the night, nor where on the old road he might be planning to take Lady Widdrington.

Take Lady Widdrington. Damn it, how dare they! How dare Graham try to salve his wounded pride with a raid of fifty riders against one woman and five men? God damn them all for bloody cowards, if he could catch them red-handed he'd string them up on the nearest trees, by God he would, and to hell with giving them a fair trial...

He pulled his mind back from that train of thought, simply because he knew that if he followed it he would end up too enraged to think straight.

Sergeant Nixon was riding beside him with an ingratiating expression on his face. Carey looked sideways at him; he was a strongly built ugly man with bulging cheeks like a water-rat's and a long pointed nose, and the blackest beard on a pale face Carey had ever seen. He was not a man you would willingly buy a horse from, nor anything else, and the surly competence in the way he rode and carried his lance implied that you would be wise not to fight him. Which made him probably near enough to Lowther's ideal of a henchman.

'Did you want to ask something, Sergeant?'

'Ay, sir.' Unlike Sergeant Dodd's miserable drone, Sergeant Nixon's voice was the most attractive part of him. 'I was wonderin' how ye got word of the twenty horses ye say are at Brampton.'

'Ah,' said Carey opaquely. 'Now, that would be telling, wouldn't it, Sergeant?' He had in fact deduced it from the fact that nobody at Brampton had rendered a complaint about horses reived from them. He wasn't sure there were twenty there, but it was as many as he thought their pasturage could stand.

'Would we be getting any of your fee, sir?'

'You might.'

'Only we heard ye'd paid Dodd and his men their backwages...'

And you thought I might be a soft touch, Carey thought but didn't say. 'Perhaps you had better talk to Sir Richard Lowther about that.'

Sergeant Nixon sniffed. 'Ay, sir.'

Sunset was coming, a slow beacon setting light to half the sky and turning the clouds to purple. There were still people working in the fields, which astonished Carey. He asked the Sergeant about it.

'Well, sir,' said Nixon, seeming surprised. 'It's going to rain soon; can ye not feel it hanging in the air?'

Now he mentioned it, the air was sultry and heavy and the warmth was oppressive. Carey had only his shirt on under his padded jack but was still feeling sticky. He sniffed the air. If it rained Wattie Graham's trail would be a great deal harder to follow back...But then Lady Widdrington might even stay at Thirlwall for an extra day...No, she wouldn't; he was fooling himself.

'Yonder's the road to Brampton,' said Nixon after a long straight canter.

'I know, Sergeant,' said Carey. 'We're going to Gilsland first.'

'Why?'

Carey stared at him for a while. Eventually Nixon got the message and coughed.

'Why, sir?'

'Because I want to talk to Dodd about something.'

Sergeant Nixon was frowning heavily, but then he shrugged. There was no love lost between him and Dodd, but neither were they enemies and nor were their families at feud.

Even so, Carey nodded at Long George and Bessie's Andrew. Long George let his horse fall behind until he was at the rear of the men, while Bessie's Andrew came up to Carey's left shoulder and looked thoroughly nervous. God help me if Sergeant Nixon gets suspicious, Carey thought, then dismissed the thought from his mind. Sergeant Nixon wouldn't get suspicious, that was all there was to it.

As Carey's body swung rhythmically with the horse's stride, he turned over and over in his mind the various loose combinations of ideas he was trying to form into a sensible plan. Scrope had been willing enough to let him try and deal with Wattie Graham's raid, but was as hamstrung by lack of men as he was himself. He had barely ten men in the place and all of them were needed. He hadn't even let Carey send off his clerk, Richard Bell, with a message to Forster because, as he pointed out, the Bells were yet another surname at feud with the Grahams and he didn't want to lose the one man in the West March who had a thorough grasp of March Law. He had promised to send for a few of the gentlemen to the south of Carlisle, but had opined that they were unlikely to be reliable in a fight against the Grahams.

'Most of 'em pay blackrent to Richard Graham of Brackenhill,' Scrope had said, looking tired. 'None of them want any trouble with that family.' Brackenhill was the acknowledged Graham headman and wealthy enough to arm most of his own men with guns.

What I need in this Godforsaken country is at least a hundred men I can trust and some decent ordnance, Carey thought bitterly. And pigs will fly before the Queen gives me the money to find them.

monday 3rd july 1592, evening

Sergeant Henry Dodd nodded at his brother Red Sandy, and the laden cart creaked off towards their main hay barn. The two small English Armstrongs, cousins of Janet, who had been helping him load, sat quietly together on top. One of the sandy heads was nodding.

'Lizzy,' called Dodd, and a freckled face under a mucky white cap peeked over. 'Stop your brother from sleeping or he'll fall off.'

'Ay, Mr Dodd,' she said, hiding a yawn. 'Will ye be wanting us back again?'

He did really, but hadn't the heart. 'No, sweeting, get to your bed.'

Red Sandy touched up the oxen and the cart creaked away, a plaintive yell floating from the top as Lizzy obediently pinched her brother to wake him up.

The sun was down and there was another field to get in, but after that, it was done. Janet was coming towards him across the stubbly meadow with bits of hay stuck to her cap and a large earthenware jug on her hip. She smiled at him, and the back of his throat, which felt as if it had glazed over with the haydust stuck to it, opened a little involuntarily in anticipation. He put his hands behind the collar of his working shirt and eased the hemp cloth off the sunburn he'd collected a few days before while mowing this same field. He resisted the urge to have a go at the itchy bits of skin that were coming off because if he started scratching, all the little bits of dust that had got inside his clothes and stuck to his skin would start itching too and drive him insane.

Janet arrived where he stood leaning on his pitchfork, gave him the leather quart mug she had in her other hand and filled it with mild beer. He croaked his thanks, put it to his lips, tilted his head and forgot to swallow for a while. It almost hurt, it felt so good. He finished two thirds of it before he came up for air.

'Ahhh,' he said, and leered at her. Janet had untied her smock and loosened the laces of her old blue bodice to free her arms for raking and there was a fine deep valley there, just begging for exploration. Not in a stubbly field though, and they were both too old and respectable now to bundle about in the haystack, but a marriage bed would do fine, later, if he wasn't too tired. And if he was, well, there was the morning too before he had to set off for Carlisle. She leered back at him and took breath to say something that never was said.

'Och, God damn him to hell,' moaned Dodd, seeing movement, men on horseback breasting the hill in the distance over her shoulder, and instantly recognising the man in the fancy morion helmet at the head of the patrol riding towards them along the Roman road. 'God rot his bloody bowels...'

'Eh?' said Janet, startled. She turned to look in the same direction as her husband, and her eyes narrowed.

'But those are Lowther's men he's with.'

Dodd knew with awful clarity exactly what the thrice damned Deputy Warden was doing out at Gilsland with Lowther's Sergeant and Lowther's bunch of hard bargains. Full of wordless ill-usage, he picked up his pitchfork and drove it tines first into the ground, narrowly missing his own foot.

'Make yerself decent, woman,' he growled unfairly at his wife, who had only been behaving as a good wife should to her hardworking husband. She gave him a glint of a stare and he handed her what was left of his beer by way of apology. Still, she tied her old smock again, pulled up her bodice lacings and the curves of her breasts went back into their secret armour.

Dodd folded his arms and waited for the Deputy to come to him. There was some satisfaction in the thought that he must be hot wearing a jack and morion in this weather, followed by a gloomier memory of just how miserable a jack could be in summer.

Carey left Lowther's men at the wall and came trotting over.

'Good evening, Sergeant. How's the haymaking?'

The bloody Courtier had probably been sitting on his arse all afternoon, unlike Dodd, who could only bring himself to grunt.

'Well enow.'

'Have you finished yet?'

Resisting the urge to snarl that if he was finished he wouldna be standing in a field like a lummock, he'd be at table stuffing his face, Dodd gestured in the direction of a long triangle of land which still had its neat rows of gold. Carey's face clouded over.

'Ah,' he said.

'What's the trouble, Sir Robert?' asked Janet. 'Is it a raid?'

Carey sighed and slid from his horse. 'In a manner of speaking, Mrs Dodd,' he said. 'I'm sorry to trouble you when you're so busy, Sergeant; if I had any other choice I wouldn't be here.'

Dodd grunted again, only slightly mollified, jerked his pitchfork out of the ground, straightened the bent tine with his clog heel, put it on his shoulder and set off for the last field. Janet picked his abandoned jerkin off the ground, and her own rake, and went with him. The Courtier went too, leading his horse.

As they went he talked, and in Dodd's mind a picture formed of what was happening. At the end of it, he commented, 'Wattie Graham must be fair annoyed to be risking a foray into the Middle March and so close to Tynedale. Who put him up to it?'

'I've no idea, though I could guess.'

'Well, ye canna take fifty assorted Grahams and broken men with that lot over there.'

Carey half-smiled. 'I'm aware of it, Sergeant.'

'What's she...what's Lady Widdrington worth at ransom, then?'

'I haven't the faintest idea and I have no intention of paying it in any case.'

'No,' agreed Dodd. 'That'd be for her husband to do.'

'Dodd,' said Carey with a certain amount of effort. 'I am not going to allow her to be taken.'

That's what being at Court and listening to all them poets did for you, Dodd thought savagely; it rotted your brain.

'I dinna ken what ye can do about it, sir,' said Dodd, looking about for the other cart which should have finished and come back by now. Oh yes, there it was, being driven by Willie's Simon with his bandaged arm. Janet had already set down her jug and his jerkin and started in on the furthest row to pile it up. Two of the other girls came down off the wall where they had been waiting and drinking, and started on two other rows. The cart creaked in at the gate and lined up, ready for him. Normally Willie's Simon would have been helping Dodd pitch the hay, but the wound from an arrow in his arm ten days before was still not healed enough so Dodd had it all to do himself. Janet raked ferociously, muttering under her breath; Dodd knew she was calculating how much more food Sergeant Nixon and the others would require, when she was already feeding too many mouths.

'How long would this normally take?' Carey asked fatuously, waving at the field.

'I'd leave it till the morrow, but it looks like rain,' said Dodd, driving his pitchfork into a bundle and twisting to lift and throw. 'It'll be fair dark by the time we finish.'

'How many pitchforks have you got?'

What was the Courtier blethering about now?

'Four. Three over by the barn.'

Carey waved his arm at the men still sitting like puddings and letting their hobbies crop wildflowers from the wall's base.

'Sergeant *Nixon*,' he roared. '*Over here!*'

Nixon came trotting over, looking very wary.

'Send a man over to Sergeant Dodd's barn and fetch the spare pitchforks.'

Nixon's face became mutinous. 'We're on patrol,' he said. 'We didnae come here to help wi' Sergeant Dodd's...'

Carey didn't appear to have heard him.

'I will pay an extra sixpence to each man that gives a hand with a pitchfork,' he said. 'You can draw straws to decide which will be the lucky ones. The others can help rake if they want sixpence too.'

'I done my own fields yesterday...' whined Sergeant Nixon and then seemed to forget what he was going to say when Carey glared at him.

'Nixon, either you can do what you're told or you can go back to Carlisle, with no sixpence for a little bit of extra sweat and no chance of what's at Brampton.'

Dodd pricked up his ears at that and exchanged glances with Janet. Sergeant Nixon's mouth tightened, he turned his hobby and cantered sullenly off to his men. A chorus of whines and moans rose from them and then stopped, presumably at news of the sixpence which was a full day's pay for haymaking.

'Right,' Carey said to Dodd. 'I want your professional advice and I want men, and I can see I'll get neither if you're worrying about your hay.'

For a wonder, the men did come over, although not Sergeant Nixon who clearly regarded this as beneath his dignity, nor the Lowther cousin. Billy Little came back shortly after with the pitchforks. Then there was an argument over who would stand on the wagon to pack the cart. Willie's Simon couldn't do it because of his arm and the girls were busy raking with Janet. The others felt it was beneath their dignity to do a wean's job and said so at length. Carey listened impatiently for a while, then tethered his hobby to a bush and started undoing the fastenings of his morion helmet and the lacings of his jack. What the devil was the man playing at, Dodd wondered, in the middle of explaining that as the head of the household he couldn't possibly stand on the cart...

Carey took his morion off, scratched his hair and put the helmet down carefully on the wall. His sword belt he laid down beside it, followed by his knife-belt, then he slid his shoulders out of his jack, revealing a darned but very fine linen shirt. Janet was staring at him open-mouthed as he hung his armour over a stone, turned and grinned at Dodd who was just beginning to suspect what the madman had in mind.

'I'm afraid I'd be a danger to man and beast with a pitchfork,' he said. 'But I know how to pack a cart, so I'll do that.'

He turned and jumped up onto the empty cart, took the small rake lying in it.

Dodd made a short rattle in his throat. Carey was rolling up his sleeves.

'Barnabus will want to kill me,' he muttered to himself. 'What's the problem, Sergeant?'

What Dodd wanted to say was that he had never in all his life heard of a Courtier to the Queen helping to load a haywagon like a child. In fact his mouth was open to say it but no words came out.

Janet was better with her tongue. She came over to the cart and looked up at him severely.

'Sir,' she said. 'It's not fitting. You're the Queen's cousin.'

Carey raised his eyebrows at her. 'Yes,' he said down his nose. 'I am. That's why I can do what I bloody well choose.'

Sergeant Nixon and the Lowther cousin, who were looking after the horses leaned on their saddle horns and openly gawked at the insanity of the Deputy Warden. Carey was telling the truth; he coped perfectly well with the forkfuls of hay being tossed up to him and didn't trample it down too much. Nor did he fall off when Willie's Simon was too busy staring to warn him when the oxen moved on along the rows. In fact, the lunatic looked as if he was enjoying himself. Certainly he was whistling something irritating.

Dodd shook his head to clear it and bent to his work. After a while he began to see the funny side, and his ribs almost burst with the effort not to laugh. The last field was cleared in record time with so many helpers, and as Willie's Simon goaded the oxen through the gate, Carey slotted his rake in behind the seat and jumped down.

'What's the joke, Sergeant?' he asked as he came over, brushing bits of hay off himself.

Dodd snorted and put his pitchfork on his shoulder to follow the cart back behind the barnekin wall.

'Only I was thinkin' I'd be willin' to take ye on for the harvest, sir, if ye was free,' he said grudgingly while Carey hefted up his jack and put it back on again.

'Thank you, Sergeant,' said Carey deadpan. 'I'll certainly consider your offer.'

Janet had already gone back to their peel tower ready to welcome them in with the best beer and lead them to their suppers. The trestle tables were packed tight with friends and neighbours in the hall of the tower and Dodd presided over the lot of them at the head of the top table. He had offered the place to Carey but Carey had courteously refused and sat at his right instead. Once Dodd had swallowed enough pudding to quiet his empty stomach, he banged mugs with Carey and laughed again.

'I'll have to ride wi' ye against the Grahams now,' he said, not feeling as miserable about it as he might otherwise have done.

'Yes,' answered Carey equably. 'I know.' He finished his beer and sighed. 'God, that's good.'

He lifted his mug in salute to Janet who tilted her neck to him in acknowledgement. Dodd poured himself some more before the Courtier could finish the lot.

Janet always served the strongest beer for this supper, unless you included what she gave to the harvesters after the last sheaf was in, which could knock you over. She was sitting at the next table which was packed with local girls who had been helping with the raking and the stacking. Word had evidently gone round about the Courtier. Many of them were wearing ribbons in their hair and craning their necks to stare at the Deputy Warden. At least half had forgotten to tighten their bodice lacings which offered a very pleasing view. Dodd saw that Carey was human enough to be admiring it. After all, it was very distracting.

'So what would you advise, Sergeant?' Carey asked after a moment's thoughtful pause.

'I'd advise not mixing it wi' them,' said Dodd, wiping beer off his mouth and digging into his food again. 'Wi' the Grahams, I mean,' he clarified round a lump of beef, and Carey grinned perfect understanding. 'But what would be the use?'

'Come on, Dodd,' said Carey. 'Be reasonable. I can't let Wattie Graham lift Lady Widdrington. I couldn't hold my head up again in this March.'

'Ay, he's puttin' a bit of a brave on ye,' agreed Dodd. 'The cheeky bastard.' He snorted again at the memory of the elegant Deputy sweating on his hay cart. That would be something to think of on his deathbed, he decided; it would cheer him up no end. 'Well, sir, if it was me running the rode, and I had the start that he's got, I'd steer well clear of Bewcastle itself and lie up by Hen Hill or Blackshaws in the forest for tonight. I'd give it till the sun was up to let the lady get well on her way, then I'd cross the Irthing above the gorge and use the rough ground and the Giant's Wall as cover until I got to the Faery Fort at Chesterholm, and I'd nip her out there.'

'Right,' said Carey. 'Now, how many men do you think we could scrape up overnight?'

'If we ring the bell...'

'No, I don't want to do that; he might hear it. I want to stop Wattie quietly if I can.'

'Quietly,' repeated Dodd. 'Well, it doesnae make so much odds because we've got the night. Have ye not tried to warn Captain Carleton what's afoot?'

'Of course I have,' Carey said. 'But I'm not betting on my messenger getting through. It would only be sensible for Wattie to send some men out to Thirlwall Castle overnight to keep an eye on what's going on and make sure Carleton hasn't convinced Lady Widdrington to let him send some men with her.'

'Ay,' nodded the Sergeant. 'Ye're right. I'd do it.'

'So would I.'

'Well, then, it's nobbut a couple of miles to Thirlwall. We get the men together, we deal with Wattie's lads and we warn the Castle what's afoot. Then we escort her along the road to Hexham.'

'Of course, there's the possibility that Captain Carleton's in on it as well.'

Dodd thought of the barrel-shaped Captain with the loud laugh, and decided it wasn't so unlikely as all that.

'And if Wattie's loose on Thirlwall Common with fifty men, there will be a pitched battle when he hits us on the road, with us at a disadvantage. We don't know he'll be at Chesterholm; there must be other places.'

'What's wrong wi' a pitched battle?' Dodd wanted to know, made confident by the beer. 'Bloody murdering Grahams.'

'With a woman in the middle of it.'

'So?' said Dodd, wondering if they were talking about the same Lady Widdrington. 'She'd likely grab a pike and do for Wattie Graham herself.'

Carey sighed. 'Listen, Henry. I've no quarrel with a pitched battle, I just like to choose my own ground. And getting to the Castle isn't simply a case of dealing with some lads. You know what the ground around it is like; it's horribly steep, there are earthworks everywhere. You could hold off an army if you placed your men right, that's why they built it there. I can't even be sure Wattie's got no more than fifty riders. I only know what left Netherby, not what he might have picked up along the way.'

'Ay,' allowed Dodd, beginning to wonder if Carey had some other pressing reason for not wanting to meet Lady Widdrington face to face.

'And there's the question of authority,' Carey added with a sigh. 'Once Wattie's over the Irthing and into the Middle March he's supposedly out of my jurisdiction and into Sir John Forster's. I don't want to start up any inter-Wardenry feuding if I can help it and Sir John's known to be difficult.'

Dodd nodded, appreciating the Deputy Warden's talents at understatement. Sir John Forster was irascible, deeply corrupt, as old as the century and far into his dotage. Unfortunately, he also seemed to be indestructible.

'Anyway,' Carey went on, 'I want to teach Wattie a lesson. Who the hell does he think he is, running a raid that size across the March at haymaking?'

He thinks he's a Graham and one of the lords of creation, Dodd thought but didn't bother to say. After all, Carey was convinced he was a lord of creation too, wasn't he? That was half the trouble between him and Lowther who had the same opinion of himself. The other half was money and politics, of course, but there was plenty of room for the pure animosity of two bulls in the same field.

'Well,' said Dodd slowly after some more thought and a lot of cheese. 'We could surely come up with twenty or thirty good men from hereabouts, especially if we went to Archibald Bell and warned him, and in any case the Bells are always willing to give the Grahams a bloody nose when they can. That's all, I'm afraid, sir. Ye could get double the number inside the hour at a different time of year, but...'

'I know, I know. It'll have to do. All the more reason not to tangle with Wattie on the road.'

Dodd was thinking hard and sucking his teeth. 'We should be able to get over to north of the road and maybe shadow them, but it'll be a long ride and hard country, and the horses will be tired and...'

Carey shook his head. He swallowed one of Janet's eyewatering pickled onions half-chewed and drank some beer.

'No,' he said. 'I'm not prancing about in Sir John Forster's March with a mixed bunch of...of men, if I can help it. I want to stop Wattie quick and clean before he goes near Lady Widdrington. In fact I want to ambush him on the way and send him back to Netherby with his tail between his legs.'

Dodd's heart started to warm to the Courtier a bit more. It seemed he had some sense after all.

'Hm,' he said. 'Ay.'

'What about when he's crossing the Irthing? Where will he do that? There can't be more than a couple of places, it's too steep.'

'Ay,' said Dodd. 'He'll go over the ford at Horseholme and then there's the Wou bog, so he'll likely take the path that runs north of it round by Burn Divot and Whiteside. But then he'll strike off eastwards away and there's any number of roads he could go after that...Ay, the ford would be the place to find him for sure.'

A horrible thought struck him. 'By God,' growled Dodd, 'He'll be in among my own shielings as well. I've forty head of cattle at the summering up there, and nobbut a man and a boy to guard them. If that bastard bloody Graham...'

'Absolutely,' said Carey cheerfully. 'I agree, we must stop them there.' He was making messy puddles with his finger on the table. 'Is this what the country looks like?' he asked. Dodd squinted at the puddles and wondered what he was jabbering about. Carey explained patiently. 'If this was the Irthing and that was the bog...'

'Och,' said Dodd, having difficulty converting his instinctive knowledge of the land into a picture. 'Ah. Maybe,' he allowed cautiously.

With the aid of some bits of bread, Carey explained what he wanted to do, and Dodd put in his notions to which Carey listened gravely. Although Dodd was being deprived of the dancing and the singing in order to go and fetch out the Bells, he didn't mind as much as he would have thought. It was a pity really, that Carey had had the misfortune to be born on the right side of such a very high-class blanket; he had the makings of a decent reiver in him.

tuesday 4th july 1592, dawn

Wattie Graham was in the middle of an argument with the outlaw Skinabake Armstrong while they waited for the rest of their party to cross over the Irthing ford in the damp grey dawn. Skinabake wanted to hit a nearby Dodd for his cows; Wattie wanted to concentrate on taking Lady Widdrington first before indulging in private enterprise. He had a couple of foreriders out, from sheer habit, but nothing else. The land was empty of anything but a medium sized herd of likely-looking cattle and horses and a tumble-down shieling a few hundred yards away. They had another good eight miles to go before they came near the Stanegate road, and most of them had their helmets hanging on their saddles and their jacks open in the heat. The dawn sky was dull and stifling, armoured with cloud that promised ruin for anyone who hadn't got his hay in. Not a single man among them had loaded a caliver; their bows were still unstrung across their backs.

The first he knew was when one of Skinabake's broken men yelped and clutched his leg. Wattie Graham looked at the place and at first refused to believe what his eyes told him, that there was a feathered arrow shaft sticking out of it. Another arrow zipped by his nose and a third stuck in the hindquarters of one of the horses in the ford who promptly went berserk, reared up, stood kicking on its head and then crashed through the press of other horses and up the bank. Its rider was in the water, spitting mud and weed and looking astonished.

Wattie grabbed for his gun out of its case, pulled out the small ramrod, tried charging it, but more arrows were flying from the low hill. Men who had been lying down in the bracken on the slope were standing, shooting at them. They were at too great a range to do much damage, but the panic they were causing among the horses was bad enough. The cattle in the field lowed unhappily. Some of the broken men who had already come across trampled back down into the ford, trying to run away, and added to the thrashing, shouting, swearing confusion.

Wattie fumbled and dropped his ramrod, cursed, slammed the gun back in its case and drew his sword.

'Come on, ye fools, get on out of the water,' he roared. A few of them managed to do what he ordered and bunched around him looking scared, while the men on the hill continued to shoot judiciously. There was the sound of hooves from their right, men and horses boiling like bees from the little shieling, more men swinging themselves up onto their horses' bare backs from where they had been hiding in amongst the cattle, joining with the riders pounding down from the shieling.

Wattie swung round to face the threat, saw lances, hobbies, and at the head of them a long man in a morion pointing a dag straight for his chest. Unthinkingly, he slid sideways clinging to his horse's neck and actually heard the crack as the bullet passed through where he had been. Then the men hit them, and he found himself cutting and slicing against the press of bodies; it was all Bells at first, Archibald Bell at their head roaring something obscene about blackrent. He glimpsed Sergeant Dodd in there, riding bareback, with a face like a winter's day and blood on his sword, and then it was the man with the fancy morion battering at him with a bright new broadsword, and he recognised Sir Robert Carey.

'Shame on you, Wattie,' roared the Courtier. 'Attacking a defenceless woman.'

Somebody backed a horse between them, and Wattie managed to collect himself. Half his men had scrambled back across the ford; he could see a few horses' rumps galloping away in the distance. More broke from the right as they worked their way to the edges.

'Skinabake!' he yelled in a sudden breathing space, catching sight of the Armstrong reiver. 'Back across the ford; we'll have them if they follow.'

He felt something behind him, ducked; steel whistled over his shoulder and nicked his hobby which promptly squealed and tried to run away. He managed to turn about to face his attacker and found Carey must have been pursuing him because there he was again, sword in one hand, dag in the other and its wheel-lock spinning sparks. He froze, staring at death like a rabbit. It misfired. He swung his sword down on Carey, hoping he would be distracted by his gun, but the bastard Deputy parried and slashed sideways, still shouting something incomprehensible.

Another plunging riderless horse banged into the other side of Wattie, bruising his leg against his own mount. Carey was coping with another rider on his other side, crossed swords a couple of times and knocked that man out of the saddle. Wattie disentangled himself from the terror-crazed nag, just in time to face the Deputy as he turned again and came after Wattie.

Nobody would dare call any Graham a coward, but it was unnerving to see Carey dismissing all the dangerous mayhem around him while he tried to attack only Wattie. Skinabake was

already across the ford, shouting at him. There were a few Grahams
left on this side and in a second they would be surrounded, perhaps
captured. The Deputy Warden looked to be in a hanging mood.

'Liddesdale, to me!' yelled Wattie, standing up in his stirrups.
When as many as could were around him he launched his horse
down the bank again, through the water, up the other side and
turned about, breathing hard.

Let them follow us and we'll have them the way they had us,
he thought, but Dodd and Archibald Bell were wise to that and so
were the others with them, too wise to try crossing a ford opposed.
Only the lunatic Deputy Warden seemed eager to try, but Dodd
caught his horse's bridle and snarled at him and he seemed to
calm down.

The two sides stared at each other, those of the Grahams who
had bows stringing them frantically on their stirrups and
awkwardly nocking arrows. It was very hard to use a longbow on
horseback, but it could be done if you twisted sideways and leaned
over a little. The bowmen on the hill came jogging across and
lined up facing them over the water.

Wattie looked about at his men. A number of them were
bleeding somewhere, there were five still shapes over on the other
bank and three men surrounded. A couple of the ones who had
fallen off during the melee in the water were climbing out again
as fast as they could, cursing. Several horses were down, others
galloping away squealing.

Skinabake came up beside him, shaking his head.

'We're out of it,' he said without preamble.

'Ay,' said Wattie heavily, knowing a lost cause when he saw it.
He shook his fist impotently at the Deputy Warden. 'Ye'll regret
this, Carey,' he shouted. 'I'm no' forgetting this.'

'Ah, go home and cry, Wattie,' sneered the Courtier. 'I'll give
you a long neck one of these days, you bloody coward.'

Wattie's neck swelled and his eyes almost bugged out of his
head. He took a firm grip on his sword, kicked his horse forward
to the water.

Skinabake got in his way and the hobby was anyway not
inclined to go near the blood-tinged water.

'Come on, Wattie,' said Skinabake, highly amused. 'Put a lance
through him some other time.'

Wattie was shaking with rage. 'Did you hear...' he sputtered. 'Did ye hear what he called me?'

'Och,' said Skinabake negligently, in a voice that carried. 'He only said it to bring ye back in range of the bowmen there.'

Carey's head went up. He had heard, as he was meant to. But Dodd had already shifted his horse in front of the Deputy Warden's nag and had changed grip on his lance to bar his path.

'*Any time!*' Carey bellowed, his horse backing and prancing under him. 'Any time, Graham, I'll meet you. Any weapons, any time.'

Wattie spat over his shoulder, and began riding away north west, his men lightly gathered around him, the ones who had lost their mounts running at their friends' stirrups. Skinabake's outlaws were already breaking northwards for the Debateable Land.

The men who had come out for Carey were shaking hands and congratulating each other. They had gained the loose horses who were trotting about shaking themselves, if they could catch them. Some were wounded, but hobbies were notoriously hard to kill. They had three reivers as captives, who could be ransomed once Sergeant Dodd had talked some sense into the hotheaded Deputy Warden who wanted to hang them immediately. They had what could be got from the five corpses, which included some nice swords and a good new jack or two. Also their cows were safe. They agreed with the Deputy Warden that it would be as well for them to stay by the ford and make sure Wattie didn't return, though it wasn't any reiver's way to keep on after something had gone wrong.

Sergeant Dodd decided he might as well go to Carlisle with Carey and they all rode back to his tower where most people, including Sergeant Nixon and Lowther's other men, were just waking up with sore heads. Carey collected them together, paid them, then insisted on returning by way of Brampton where Dodd's father-in-law lived. Dodd might have worried about this if Janet were not such a jewel of a woman. He knew she would send to her father to warn him that the Deputy had somehow got wind of the stolen horses he was keeping. Sure enough, the only horses left in Will the Tod's paddocks were stumpy rough-coated animals that had every right in the world to be there. Afterwards Carey seemed morose, which was natural enough since he had got very little sleep that night and about halfway back to Carlisle the heavens finally opened with a rolling cannonade of thunder and a downpour of fat grey drops.

Behind them, the heavy-laden packtrain owned by Edward Aglionby paced northwest along the road, miraculously unmolested.

tuesday 4th july 1592, morning

The roofbeams of the Carlisle Castle stables vibrated with the already legendary Carey roar.

'*He's what?*'

Bangtail winced and stepped back a few paces. All the horses stamped and shifted and some of them neighed protestingly. Dodd had to hold the headstall of the hobby he was rubbing down, to stop himself being knocked over.

'He…he's in the dungeon, sir,' Bangtail repeated. 'Lowther put him there on a charge of murder.'

Carey advanced on him, still in his sodden jack and wet morion. His fists were clenched tight and two spots of colour flamed below the incipient bags under his eyes.

'It wasna me, sir,' yelled Bangtail, dodging behind one of the stall posts. 'It was Lowther.'

Carey seemed to catch himself and stop. He breathed deeply, carefully unfisted his hands and folded them across his chest.

'Start at the beginning, Bangtail, and tell me exactly what happened.'

'Ay, well. It were Atkinson, ye see, sir, Jemmy Atkinson, the Armoury clerk, that used to be paymaster until you…'

'I think I remember him.'

'Well, what I heard was, he was found deid this morning, in an alley, with his gizzard slit, see ye, and so his wife sent for Lowther because he's known to be Lowther's man.'

'Clear so far.'

'An' Lowther's up to the Castle in a fearful bate just afore ye come in, sir, and I'd just arrived, see, and he says, it's bound to be ye that did him in, because ye didna want him fer armoury clerk, but ye werena there and nor was Dodd, so then he says, ye must have set the thief that serves ye on to dae it, and so he's gone up to the Queen Mary Tower and haled yer man out and thrown him in the dungeon and he's making a complaint out against ye now, forbye.'

'Is that it, that's the full tale?'

'Ay, sir, so far as I know.'

'Well then, thank you for coming to tell me of it so promptly.'

Bangtail smiled. 'We drew straws for it, sir, an' I got the short one.'

Carey coughed. 'Where's Lowther now?'

'He's still in with the Lord Warden.'

'Is he, by God! Well, go and keep an eye on him and try and see he doesn't find out that I'm back yet. Go on, off with you.'

'Ay, sir.'

As Bangtail trotted off on his mission, Dodd wondered what the Deputy Warden would do. For a moment as his colour faded he looked tired and thoughtful, and to be sure, his position was bad. Dodd knew that it wasn't so much the question of whether or not Barnabus had actually slit Atkinson's throat, it was whether Lowther could get the bill fouled against him and so hang him. Barnabus might even decide to turn Queen's evidence to save his own neck and say that Carey had ordered him to do the killing. In London or in Berwick, Dodd didn't doubt that Carey could muster enough influence to clear himself of such an accusation, but they were in Carlisle where his only important relative was Lord Scrope. And Lord Scrope was notoriously easy to persuade if got at right. It was unlikely but not completely beyond the bounds of possibility that Lowther might see Carey swing for the death of Atkinson, despite the Queen's liking for him, whether he had anything to do with it or not. Or no: as a nobleman, he would face the axe. At best, with his servant hanged for murder, the blow to his prestige meant Carey would have very little chance of commanding obedience in the March.

Carey set his back against the loose-box wall, one leg bent, took his helmet off and with his eyes shut, rubbed the red marks left by the leather padding and the chin strap.

'What'll ye do, sir?' asked Dodd morbidly, wondering if he should begin making overtures to Lowther. No, it would be a waste of time.

'Hm? See Barnabus first.'

Carey guessed Lowther would have put Barnabus into the worst prison in the Castle and so they fetched lanterns and the Castle Gaoler and went cautiously through the door that led past the wine cellar to the dungeon in the base of the Carlisle Keep. He wasn't in the outer room, but in the one behind it, black as pitch and dank from the nearness of the Castle well. It was called the Lickingstone cell because if a prisoner was left there and no water brought for him, he could live by spending most of his time licking the moisture from the dampest part of the wall. Some men had survived a surprisingly long time that way, given that their tongues would swell and bleed from the rough stone. Families paid their fines faster if they knew their man was in that dungeon, Scrope had explained to Carey when he suggested the room be used for something else.

Carey didn't have the keys to the inner door, but he gave Dodd his helmet, pulled aside the Judas hole and called softly, 'Barnabus. Wake up.'

There were a couple of grunts and an adenoidal 'Yes, sir.'

Carey was silent for a moment as his lantern light hit Barnabus's face. 'Did Lowther do that to you?'

A long liquid sniff. 'Yes, sir. It's a good one, isn't it?'

'Any particular reason, or was it just high spirits?'

Another sniff. 'Yes, sir. He wanted me to confess to killing Atkinson.'

'And did you?'

The sniff that followed was offended. 'No, sir. I'm not that stupid. Even if I dun it, which I din't, I'd never say I did, would I?'

'Was that all he wanted from you?'

'Er…no, sir.'

'Well?'

'He wanted me to say you'd ordered it and forced me to do it, sir.'

Carey nodded. He didn't look surprised. Evidently he had thought along the same lines as Dodd.

'I din't admit that either, sir.'

'I'm glad to hear it.' Carey's voice was dry.

'What do you want me to do, sir?'

'Where were you last night?'

There was an apologetic cough. 'Well, you wasn't 'ere sir, so…'

'You were at Madame Hetherington's?'

'Er…yessir.'

'All night?'

'After I'd been in Bessie's for a bit, I was there till this morning when the Castle gate opened and I come in. So I'd be here to serve you when you finished your patrol,' he added virtuously.

'Would Madame Hetherington testify that you were with her?'

'I dunno, sir. She might.' And then, complacently, 'Maria will, though.'

'Unfortunately a notorious French whore is not the best of alibi witnesses.'

'Well, if I'd known I'd need one, I'd've got a better one, wouldn't I, sir?'

Carey treated that impudence with a measured pause that said he was making allowances, but would not make them indefinitely.

'Did anybody else see you at Madame Hetherington's?'

'I don't think so, sir, that'd speak for me... Oh, bloody hell, it's started again.'

'Try pinching the bridge of your nose, see if that stops it.'

'I can't, sir. It's broken.'

Carey was silent for a moment. 'I'm sorry, I can't get you out yet, Barnabus,' he said. 'I haven't the authority. It probably wouldn't be a good idea anyway.'

'I know that, sir. Lowther's on the up and up, in'e?'

'For the moment.'

'You'll be able to sort it, though, won't you, sir? I mean, the juries round here won't be any more expensive than London ones, will they?'

Eh? thought Dodd. Carey had winced.

'Barnabus,' he asked gently. 'You didn't do it, did you?'

Barnabus's voice was an outraged adenoidal whine. 'Sir! You know me better'n that!'

'I seem to recall a fight at the Cock tavern...'

'That was different. I never done nuffing like this, sir, never, not that I haven't 'ad offers, mind, I just never would. 'S stupid. There's better ways of doing it than slittin' 'is throat in an alley. Besides, it's wrong.'

'Quite.'

'So what do you want me to do, sir?'

'Keep your mouth shut. That's all. Are you cold?'

'Yes, sir, freezing. I bin in Clink afore now, of course, but this ain't what I'm used to and Lowther's bastards took me jerkin and doublet off lookin' to see if I had a bloody knife, which they didn't find, I might add.'

'I'll get my sister to bring you some clothes and food.'

'Yes sir,' said Barnabus gloomily.

Dodd trailed after him as Carey marched from the dungeon, rounded the side of the Keep and was pounced on by his sister. She had her cap on crooked, her ruff under one ear, and her damask apron sideways, with a bundle of Barnabus's clothes under her arm. She took one look at her brother and said, 'You've heard then, Robin.'

'I have. How did you stop Lowther searching my office?'

Her heart-shaped face became very forbidding. 'Simon threw the key for your office in the fire and said you had it with you. I got there just after and when he wouldn't go I drew my dagger on him and told him I'd stick him if he moved a step nearer, and he believed me.'

Carey embraced her, but she pushed him off.

'What are you going to do about it, Robin?' she said. 'Lowther's out for your blood. He's telling everyone that Barnabus did it and he's half got Scrope believing you ordered him to.'

'How? I wasn't even here.'

'Well, that hardly matters, does it? Anyway, Lowther found one of Barnabus's knives and a glove of yours by the corpse.'

'*What?*'

'Don't shout, Robin, and don't grab me like that, you're all wet and muddy.'

'Jesus Christ.'

'Don't swear. It doesn't help. And I would get out of the Castle, if I were you. My lord might even have signed a warrant for your arrest by now.'

Carey was staring at her as if unable to believe what he was hearing.

'How do you know all this?'

Philadelphia lowered her eyes demurely. 'Lowther has a very carrying voice,' she said.

Carey smiled faintly at her tone. Then he shook his head.

'Well, my sweet, if he does issue a warrant for me, block it any way you can.'

Philly scowled ferociously. 'I'll steal it if I have to, silly man. Where are you going?'

Carey chucked her under the chin. 'If I don't tell you, then you can tell the truth to your husband if he asks.'

'I wish you'd take your jack off; it's sodden.'

'I haven't got time.'

'And you haven't even got a hat...'

Dodd gave Carey the morion he'd been carrying, which Carey put on.

'Better?'

Philly's brow wrinkled. 'No, you look tired.'

'At least if I have to ride for the Debateable Land, I'll be properly dressed,' Carey said with a crooked smile.

Philly swallowed very hard. 'Do you really think it'll be all right? I mean, the Queen's an awfully long way away.'

'Yes. God looks after me always, remember?'

Philly snorted. 'Hmf. He didn't look after Jemmy Atkinson very well, did he?'

'Philly, you're being heretical. Anyway, Jemmy Atkinson was a bad corrupt man and I'm not.' He kissed her bunched up forehead and tried unsuccessfully to straighten her cap which had been pinned on crooked. She batted him off and marched away across the courtyard.

Dodd kept on at Carey's heels as he lengthened his stride to pass through the Castle gate and down the covered way, his hands clasped behind his back and his head thrust forward.

'Where are we going, sir?'

'Hm? You still there, Sergeant?'

'Ay, sir.'

'It might be better for you if you got back to the Castle.'

Dodd considered this. 'Nay, sir,' he said. 'If Lowther's gonnae foul a bill against me, I'd rather it was in my absence.'

'Why should he?'

Dodd was surprised to hear Carey being so naive. 'He reckons I'm one o' yourn now.'

'Ah. Of course.'

'Any road, I've always had a fancy to live in the Debateable Land.'

'Have you? I haven't.'

'Oh, it's no' sae bad, sir. Skinabake Armstrong, that's my brother-in-law, Janet's half-brother...'

'You're related to Skinabake Armstrong?'

'Oh ay, sir. Or Janet is.'

'Why didn't you say?'

'Och, sir. If I told ye all the reivers I'm related to through Janet, we'd be all day about it. Besides, what difference does it make?'

'Was that why you wouldn't let me fight Wattie Graham at the ford?'

'Ay, of course. I know Skinabake. He'd ha' put a lance in yer back the minute ye was busy with Wattie. I know him, he's no' a very nice man. That's why he likes it in the Debateable Land. He says he'd never live anywhere else, even if he wasnae at the horn in both countries.'

'Lowther might not include you in his feud.'

'Only if I turned Queen's evidence and swore ye ordered Barnabus to dae it, sir.'

'Ah. Well, let's see what we can do to prove I didn't order it and Barnabus didn't do it.'

'Ye didnae, did ye, sir?'

'I beg your pardon?'

'Well, he wasnae what ye could call a good armoury clerk and Scrope wouldnae let ye sack him, if ye see…'

Carey had stopped and he was an odd greyish colour. 'If you think I'm stupid enough to set my own servant on to cut someone's throat for me…'

'I wouldna hold it against ye, sir. I've known others do the like.'

'Who?'

'Lowther for one.'

'When?'

Dodd shrugged. 'When somebody didna pay him blackrent and give him cheek when he went round to collect. He had some of the Grahams drop by and kill the man. It's no' so unusual, ye ken.'

Carey took one of those deep breaths that signalled he was holding on to his anger. Then he laughed and carried on walking.

'Christ's guts, Dodd, I'm a bloody innocent in this place. Will you believe me if I give ye my word that, aside from a couple of hangings, I never killed nobody in my life without it was me holding the weapon?'

Dodd nodded gravely, noting with interest how Carey's voice had changed to pure Berwick.

'Ay,' he said. 'I know ye're a man of your word, Courtier. Ye're a bloody hen's tooth in Carlisle and no mistake.'

tuesday 4th july 1592, late morning

The hen's tooth had several lines of inquiry in mind and was in a fever of impatience to follow all of them. Carey knew he had to be able to present an alternative theory to Scrope. After some thought, he sent Dodd to Bessie's to find out what he could of Barnabus's movements the night before, while he himself went to the two-storey house by the market that had belonged to Atkinson.

He knocked at the door, poked his head round it into the ground floor living room. She was surrounded by her gossips: one was making bread and milk for the children by the fire, while two others held her hands and talked in low voices.

'What d'ye want, Deputy?' demanded the largest of Mrs Atkinson's gossips, looming up before him.

'I want to find out who cut Mr Atkinson's throat,' said Carey, politely taking off his morion and putting it on a bench as he came in. His head was crammed against the ceiling beams even without it on.

'Oh, ay?' said another, a middle-aged woman with a withered hand. 'From what I heard, ye should be asking yerself the question.'

Carey looked at her in silence for a while, without anger. He had spent much of the night before with Dodd riding about Gilsland, calling individually on the local Bell and Musgrave headmen. They had mustered two hours before dawn in order to catch Wattie when he crossed the Irthing. Perhaps he had slept for two hours in total. His thinking was slower than usual, that was all, but the women read threat into his lack of reaction. They all fell silent as well and the one who had spoken shrank back.

'Who are you, goodwife?' he asked.

'I am Mrs Maggie Mulcaster, Mrs Atkinson's sister,' she said stoutly.

'Well, you heard wrong, Mrs Mulcaster,' he said mildly. 'Who did you hear it from?'

'Lowther,' she admitted.

'You should know better than to trust a man that kills anyone who won't pay him blackrent.'

The women muttered between each other and Mrs Atkinson stood up, curtseyed and wiped her hands in her apron.

'What can I do for you, sir?' she asked, civilly enough.

'My condolences for your loss, Mrs Atkinson. Will you be good enough to tell me when you last saw your husband?'

She wiped her hands in her apron again. 'I…I saw him yesterday morning. He went out about the middle of the morning, to deal with some business, he said, and that's the last I saw of him.'

'Weren't you worried when he didn't come home last night?'

She looked studiously at the fresh rushes on the floor. 'He often stays out all night. I didn't think anything of it, and then the man came to…to tell me this morning.'

A well-built girl, fresh-faced and cheerful with red hair streaming down her back, came in carrying a large empty basket.

'I've put them back out again, mistress, but them sheets will take all week to dry with the way the sky…Oh.'

The girl looked at Carey and her mouth dropped open.

'It's all right, Julia,' said Mrs Atkinson. 'Go and see after Mary and the boys.'

'Oh, she's well enough,' said Julia putting the basket down and picking up the empty pewter mugs. 'She's rolling dough for me in the scullery and the boys are feeding Clover.'

'Did you want to know anything else, sir?' demanded Mrs Mulcaster.

'Has anyone here seen Mr Atkinson since yesterday morning?'

They all looked at each other and shook their heads.

'Can you tell me which undertaker…'

There was a spasm in Mrs Atkinson's face, but she controlled herself.

'Fenwick,' she said shortly, naming the most expensive undertaker in Carlisle, and then stood there waiting.

Carey sighed. He hadn't expected to be very welcome. 'Thank you for your help, goodwives,' he said, picked up his morion and went out. The buzz of talk followed him out as he instantly became the prime subject of conversation.

Mr Fenwick was one of the most prosperous traders in Carlisle, with a large house on English street facing the gardens where the old Greyfriars monastery had been. He had a long yard out the back where he kept two different hearses, grew funeral flowers and ran a joinery business on the side for when business was slack. It seldom was. He himself was a large comfortably plump man, balding under his velvet hat, who wore black brocades of impressive richness and had a deep pleasant voice.

'Well, Sir Robert,' he said thoughtfully, after Carey had been seated in his sitting room and brought wine to drink. 'I hadn't expected to see ye. What can I do for you?'

'I want to see Mr Atkinson's body.'

'Ah.' There was a pause while Mr Fenwick's chins dropped onto his snowy ruff and he clasped his hands across his stomach. 'May I ask why, sir?'

Carey at first wasn't sure why. It had been an instinctive feeling that he should look at the corpse he was being accused of making. He wasn't sure how to deal with Fenwick either and in the end decided on honesty.

'You know how I'm placed here,' he said, 'My servant is falsely accused of killing the man and I am wrongly under suspicion for ordering him to do it. I am trying to understand what actually happened.'

'How will viewing the corpse help you?'

'I don't know, Mr Fenwick. I don't even know if it will. I haven't got a warrant with me, I am simply asking this as a favour.'

Fenwick had soft brown eyes which suddenly looked very shrewd.

'We are in the midst of preparing him for his funeral,' he said. 'If you are willing...'

'Of course.'

Fenwick stood and motioned Carey to follow him. There was a shed in the brightly blossoming garden where bodies could be laid out if there were not room for them at home or while they were waiting for an inquest. Atkinson lay there in his shirt and hose, while a slender woman sewed the gaping wound on his neck with white thread. Carey was not particularly squeamish but he looked away from that: it was ugly the way the needle pulled and tugged at the edges of flesh and no blood came.

'Where did you bring him from?' Carey asked. 'Where was he killed.'

'He was found,' said Fenwick carefully, 'in Frank's vennel, off Botchergate.'

'Found?' Carey lifted his eyebrows. Fenwick hesitated.

'There wasna hardly any blood about,' he said. 'In fact, there was none; my litter was hardly marked. He had his clothes on but not his boots. It was...' Fenwick stopped suddenly.

Carey turned to him urgently. 'Please, Mr Fenwick,' he said. 'I know you must be experienced in these things. If anything struck you as odd about Mr Atkinson, please will you tell me?'

Fenwick hesitated again, searching Carey's face. Whatever it was he found there, he nodded and led the way quietly back to his sitting room.

'Well, Sir Robert,' he said. 'The whole thing was odd and no mistake. The distribution of blood for one...None in the alley. None on the outside of his clothes, but his shirt soaked with it. No boots to his feet, but his feet not broken to take them off. I have collected men's mortal remains in many different circumstances and, yes, these were odd.'

'Are you saying that Atkinson was not killed where he lay?'

'It is not my place to say such things,' Fenwick remarked heavily. 'I can only speak of what I saw. I saw too little blood in the alley...'

'Yes, but it rained,' Carey objected. 'Couldn't the blood have been washed away?'

'The rain came on after we brought the body within. There was no rain last night.'

Carey nodded. He had been out in it and his jack was clammy from it, but there had indeed been no rain until after dawn.

Fenwick was silent again. He looked sympathetically at Carey who caught the look and found it didn't irritate him as it would normally. He stood up and found his morion.

'If you think of any other odd thing, will you let me know, Mr Fenwick?' he asked.

Fenwick nodded, and came to show him out. 'Frank's vennel?' Carey asked, to be sure.

'Ay.' The undertaker sighed. 'Poor fellow. Nobody seems sorry to see him go.'

Carey found the alley without much trouble and walked up and down, not knowing at all what he was looking for. Certainly Fenwick was right, there was no blood to speak of in the mud. The mark of where the body had lain could be seen, and the scuff marks of Lowther and his men, sightseers and Fenwick's men as well. The wheels of Fenwick's handcart were clearly printed in the soft combination of rush sweepings and animal dung that floored the alley, though they had turned into little runnels with the rain.

Carey stared at them for a long time, trying to make his brain work and then cursed softly. He walked out of the alley and back along up English street.

Mrs John Leigh had three serving girls to help her in the house, and a boy and a man to serve in the draper's shop on the ground floor. Of her children, two were boys and old enough to go to the City grammar school by the Cathedral; the other three were girls, two of whom trotted around in their little kirtles and caps getting into fights, skipping rope in their yard and occasionally getting in her way when they decided to be helpful. The youngest girl was fourteen months old, not long out of swaddling clothes and with no more sense than a puppy. She was in her baby-walker at the moment, a round sausage of cloth tied about her head to cushion it when she fell over or bumped herself and currently her favourite game was making her wheeled wooden babywalker go as fast as it could over the expensive rush-matting until it rammed into one of the walls. All the new oak panelling was dented along the bottom where the babywalker had bashed it. Each time she made an earsplitting crash she crowed 'Waaarrrgh', and the noise went through Mrs Leigh's head like an awl. It was worse than the steady hammering from the men working on the roof now the rain had stopped. She had come into the small room over the shop at the front of the house to rest and do some sewing. However, rest was impossible. She was in too great a state of tension and there was too much noise in the children's room next door where Jeanie the wetnurse was with the baby. Why didn't the silly girl take the baby into the garden?

Somebody knocked at the street door. One of the lazy creatures finally went down the stairs and opened it. There was a mutter of voices and a man's boots on the stair. The girl came fluttering into the sitting room where Mrs Leigh had her feet up, followed by the long-legged new Deputy Warden. He was so tall he had to keep his head tilted to be clear of the ceiling beams. Evidently he had just come in from the Border since he was in his damp leather jack and carrying his helmet. Mrs Leigh hadn't seen him before, but had heard a great deal about him from those who had. None of them had lied and Mrs Leigh wistfully wished she were not in the last month of pregnancy and wearing her oldest English-cut gown. He bowed to her, saw her shifting her swollen feet to the floor to stand up and return the courtesy, and waved a long hand at her.

'Please, Mrs Leigh, don't tire yourself. May I ask you a few questions about the tragic murder that happened this morning?'

Mrs Leigh went pale and her hand flew to her mouth.

'Murder? This morning?' she trembled.

'Of Mr Atkinson,' Carey told her kindly. 'Had you not heard? I'm sorry, I would have…'

'N…no, no. I…well. Poor James.'

'He was found in an alley with his throat slit this morning,' Carey explained.

'In an…alley,' repeated Mrs Leigh, still white-faced and shaking. 'I…I…what a terrible thing. He…he was my half-brother.'

'I'm sorry indeed,' Carey was serious. 'I had forgotten that. If this distresses you too much, I can return at another time…'

'No. I would…like to help. What did you wish to know?'

There was the squeak and rattle of wheels in the next room, followed by a crash and a delighted 'Waauuugh!'

Carey turned his head at the noise. 'What's that?'

Mrs Leigh winced. Her headache was much worse. 'My daughter. She likes crashing her babywalker into walls…'

Carey grinned. 'According to my mother, I had a habit of diving out of mine, preferably into the fire.'

Mrs Leigh smiled back at him wanly. 'It is…very wearing, but she screams if we prevent her.'

'I won't keep you, Mrs Leigh; I can see you need your rest. All I wanted to ask you was whether you had happened to see Mr Atkinson leave his house yesterday morning on business. Nobody else seems to have done so.'

'No, I didn't.'

'Can you tell me anything else about the Atkinsons?'

Mrs Leigh lifted her head and sniffed. 'I have nothing to do with either of them.'

'But you are neighbours and kin.'

'He is...was my youngest half-brother. Unfortunately he made a bad marriage. We have not spoken for several years. I did not wish to have anything to do with him or...her.'

'Why not?'

Mrs Leigh's small pink mouth pouched in at the corners in disapproval.

'Mrs Atkinson is a disgrace to the family.'

Carey's eyebrows went up and he waited.

'She is...er...she is fraudulently preventing me from inheriting her house which was clearly intended to be mine and she is also a wicked unchaste woman.'

'Oh?'

Mrs Leigh looked prim. 'It's too disgraceful to repeat.'

'That's a pity. Any little information, no matter how... disgraceful, might help me clear my servant.'

Squeak, squeak, rattle, rattle, crash! 'Waaauuugh!'

Mrs Leigh stayed silent looking out of the little diamond-paned window beside her. She had a baby's nightshirt on her lap and was stitching at it desultorily.

'My husband, you know,' she said, 'is John Leigh, brother to Henry Leigh who holds Rockcliffe Castle for my Lord Scrope.'

'I know,' said Carey. 'I was playing cards with him the other night—at the same card party, I mean, not actually with him.'

'Yes,' said Mrs Leigh distantly, obviously not knowing or not wishing to think about John Leigh's losses. 'He is a prominent citizen and has a position to maintain. We are impossibly crowded in this house, what with the children and the servants, and the warehouse and showroom downstairs. My aunt always intended me to have the house next door, though she leased it to...my half-brother out of charity. Perhaps *he* would have let us have the house, but *she* has taken wicked advantage and the case is in Chancery at the moment.'

Carey tutted sympathetically. 'Legal disputes are very wearing,' he said. 'I have one rumbling along myself with one of my brothers.'

'And very expensive,' agreed Mrs Leigh. 'What the barrister charges is...criminal.'

Carey nodded with a straight face. Sometimes he wished he had become a lawyer, but he soon came to his senses again.

'I hope he's a good one?' he said.

'Very good, I understand,' said Mrs Leigh unhappily. 'Or he should be. Unfortunately, that woman has managed to get the services of a young man who has just become the judge's son-in-law.'

'Oh dear.'

Mrs Leigh nodded at him. 'It seems very hard. We are not unreasonable. We even offered the Atkinsons another house, a better house, that we own on Scotch street, but she will not see reason. And she keeps a cow in her yard.'

'Oh,' said Carey, not knowing if he was supposed to be shocked about something so normal.

'That's where she meets her lover,' said Mrs Leigh.

'Ah…?'

'In the cow byre. He creeps in from the garden backing on behind, she goes out in the morning and evening and that's where they meet, the dirty sinful…Anyway, she disgraces the whole street.'

'Do her other neighbours know about this.'

'Of course they do. It's common knowledge she's got no use for her rightful husband and wants to marry Andy Nixon.'

Carey blinked a little at the venom in Mrs Leigh's voice. 'Are you saying that Mrs Atkinson might have killed her own husband?'

Mrs Leigh looked away. 'I would not wish to lay such accusations against anyone,' she said primly. 'However, it's a fact that she has a lover.'

'Is it, by God?' said Carey thoughtfully. 'Well, well.'

Squeak, rattle, rattle, crash…*crash!* 'Waah! Waah! *Mama!*'

'She's fallen over,' Carey explained helpfully. Mrs Leigh wearily moved her sore feet to the floor and started the rocking movements that would get her out of her chair. The Deputy Warden offered her his arm which she took gratefully.

'I'll see to her,' she said. 'The idiot girls are useless besoms. Did you want to know anything else, Sir Robert?'

He was looking satisfactorily thoughtful and absent-mindedly helped her to the door.

'I may do later,' he said. 'May I come back some time, Mrs Leigh?'

She smiled at him. 'Of course, Sir Robert,' she said. 'Whatever I can do to help.'

He smiled in return and clattered down the narrow stairs, leaning back and ducking his head to avoid the low ceiling beams. He went through the shop where Jock Burn was serving. Mrs Leigh longed to shout down and send the man for her husband so she could talk to him, but she couldn't yet. She waddled off to see after her smallest daughter who was still screeching.

Carey was deep in thought as he walked up Castlegate towards Bessie's alehouse, at last noticing properly how clammy and uncomfortable his jack was. The outer leather was beginning to dry, but the inner padding still squelched whenever he moved his arms. He was supposed to be out on patrol tonight as well and he refused to think about going to bed for a nap as he had planned. He simply didn't have the time if he wanted to find out as much as he could before the trail went cold. Also, he was putting off going back to his chambers in the Castle. He didn't know what he might find there, whether Scrope would believe Lowther against him or give him the benefit of the doubt. The whole thing was ridiculous, but still very dangerous. He didn't seriously think Scrope would dare to execute him on such a trumped-up charge, for all Philadelphia's worries. But he might well find himself in gaol with no ability to help Barnabus, while evil tales galloped down the roads to London and the Queen. The whole thing could ruin him, in which case he might as well be dead, because if he went back to London with no prospect of office and no hope of favour from the Queen, his creditors would certainly put him in the Fleet prison for his mountainous debts. And there he would rot.

He paused to look unseeingly at one of the shops, a cobbler's, with a bright striped awning over the counter to keep the rain off the samples of leather and made shoes displayed there.

He heard his own voice out of the past, assuring Scrope that he could deal with Lowther when they had been talking the day after he arrived. Evidently he had seriously underestimated the man and his influence. That had been stupid of him.

'Can I help you, sir?' asked the man behind the counter hopefully.

'Er...no. Thank you.'

He left the shop behind him and carried on to where Bessie's alehouse squatted, unofficial but tolerated, by the wall of the Castle, feeling a thousand years old and heavier than a cannon. For a moment he thought about simply going into the inn courtyard, fetching a horse out of Bessie's stables and heading north for the Debateable Land. Jock of the Peartree would receive him, might even take him in; they had come to an odd sort of understanding at the top of Netherby tower, despite the old reiver's deplorable character. He had his sword and his harness, he could hire out as one of the many broken men of the area…

It was a fantasy. It wasn't that he was too brave to do it, rather the reverse: he was afraid to turn his back on everything he knew, on his cousin the Queen, on his sister…And furthermore he was feeling too tired, he'd probably fall asleep on his horse and wander into a bog.

Bessie's was packed, with no sign of Dodd or anyone else of Carey's troop. As he stood in the doorway, peering into the smoky shadows, Carey knew that every eye in the place was on him and that conversations were stopping in each direction. He smiled faintly and shouldered his way through the throng to the bar.

'A quart of double-double,' he said to Bessie, who looked at him slitty-eyed. 'On the slate.'

She snorted. 'I want your bill paid, Sir Robert,' she said. 'It's getting on for eleven shillings now.'

'I've no money on me, though I've plenty up at the Castle,' said Carey humbly, wondering why things could never let up and be simple. 'Can you not extend my credit until this evening?'

She folded her arms and glared at him. 'I give credit to the men I know will come back,' she said as if she had been reading his mind. No doubt about it, Atkinson's murder and Lowther's accusations were all over Carlisle and probably well into Scotland by now.

'Och, for the love of God,' boomed a rasping voice beside him. 'Give the man a drink, woman, he needs it. Put in on my tab if ye must.'

Bessie snorted again, flounced off to draw the beer. Carey turned to see Will the Tod Armstrong beaming up at him, his girth clearing three struggling would-be drinkers away from the bar. The beer slammed down beside him. Carey picked up the tankard and swallowed. It went down a treat; he'd forgotten how long it was since he'd put anything in his belly, and his headache and weariness started to recede.

'Thank you, Mr Armstrong.'

'And we'll have another quart in the booth over there when ye've a minute, Bessie,' Will the Tod added to Bessie's departing back as she went to mark up the English Armstrong's heroically long slate. 'Now then, Deputy, ye come along wi' me, we'll see ye right.'

Carey was borne along in Will the Tod's wake by sheer force of personality, to the booth where Dodd was sitting with a large jug in front of him and a plate of bread and cheese. Carey found his mouth watering at the sight.

Carey lifted his pewter mug to Will the Tod as he slid in beside Dodd, and put his morion down on the bench beside him.

'Thanks for coming to my rescue yet again, Will.'

Will the Tod laughed. 'Ay, I like to see my friends treated well. Now then. What's all this I hear about you and Jemmy Atkinson?'

Carey shrugged. 'It seems the whole of Carlisle believes I told Barnabus to slit his throat.'

'And did ye?'

The headache came back with full force. 'Mr Armstrong, I could have had him hanged for March treason last week, if I'd wanted…'

'Ay, but that were last week. What about this week?'

'God damn it, if you think I'm…'

'Now there's no need to get in a bate, Deputy. Did ye or did ye no'? I know ye didna do it yersen, for ye were riding about the Middle March with a pack of Bells and Musgraves givin' Wattie Graham and Skinabake a good leatherin', but did ye set any other man on to it?'

'For the last time, Armstrong, and on my word of honour, I had nothing to do with Atkinson's murder.'

'Well, no need to bang on the table neither; if ye gi' me your word, that's good enough. Might Barnabus have done it by himself, thinking ye might want it but wi'out asking?'

'No. He knows I'd hand him over to be hanged.'

Will the Tod's eyebrows went up to where his bristling red hair flopped over his forehead.

'Ay, well enough,' he conceded. 'Well enough.'

'And you, Will. Why are you in town?'

'Och, that's easy. I came to warn Henry here.'

'What about?'

Will the Tod harrumphed and took a long pull at his beer. Dodd spoke up.

'King James is coming to Dumfries on a justice raid,' he explained. 'He's looking for the horses that were reived from him last week.'

'I knew he was coming,' said Carey. 'But what's it got to do with you, Sergeant?'

Dodd was suddenly very thirsty as well.

'Nothing, Deputy, nothing,' boomed Will the Tod. 'Only a matter of public interest, that's all.'

Nancy Storey, who was known by the nickname of Bessie's Wife, came over with a jug on her hip and her fair hair loose down her neck. All the northern girls wore their hair loose and uncovered until they married, and it was a delightful sight, Carey thought appreciatively. On the other hand, there were rumours that Bessie had been seen to kiss her on the mouth when tipsy, hence her nickname.

'So where was Barnabus last night?' Will the Tod asked, finishing his own beer and holding out the massive leather mug to be refilled. Bessie's Wife tipped the heavy jug off her hip and poured for both him and Carey, while Dodd demolished his plate of food.

'I'll have some bread and cheese too, Nancy,' Carey said to her.

She lifted her fair eyebrows. 'Who's paying?'

'I am,' said Will the Tod. 'Get on with it, girl; the man's like to die, he's so famished.' Carey didn't know how he knew, but with the double-strength beer hitting his empty stomach, his head was reeling.

'It's encouraging to see how opposed Bessie's household is to murder,' Carey said sardonically as Nancy swayed her hips through the crowd.

Will the Tod quivered with laughter. 'Nay, Deputy,' he said. 'If she were worried by such trifles, she'd have nae customers. It's your position she's worriting about: if ye're no' the Deputy Warden any more, what are ye and where's yer money to come from? Ye've no family hereabouts, bar your sister, and no land and no men neither, bar the garrison men that have been given to ye and can be taken off ye again. So if ye're a broken man, how will ye pay your debts? And if ye go back to London, why should ye pay them at all? That's her concern.'

Carey grunted. There was nothing wrong with Bessie's assessment of his situation, unfortunately. He had to remind himself that to a Borderer, a broken man was simply a man without a master. He didn't like the sound of it; he had always thought of himself as the Queen's man first, and the Earl of Essex's second. But it was true at the moment: if Scrope took his office away, that was what he would be—broken.

'How did you do with your enquiries, Sergeant?' he asked. 'Did Bessie see him in here last night?'

'I only just got here,' said Dodd mournfully, swallowing his last piece of cheese. 'Ye can but ask. Hey, Nancy?'

Nancy put a wooden platter in front of Carey with the heel of a loaf and some cheese on it, with a couple of pickled onions rolling about beside the little crock of butter.

'Ay, what is it, Sergeant Dodd?'

Carey pulled out his eating knife and started engulfing the food. He wondered privately why Sergeant Dodd could not simply do as he had been told. What had he been doing all morning if he had only just got here?

'Did ye see Barnabus in here last night?'

She sniffed and tossed her head. 'I did. He was here all evening playing dice.'

'Where did he go when you closed?'

'Out the door with the rest of them.'

'Do you know where he was headed?'

'It's none o' my affair. Now if you'll excuse me, sir, we're that busy...'

'Thank you, Goodwife.'

Dodd and Will the Tod exchanged glances.

'Ah know how ye can solve yer troubles, Deputy,' said Will the Tod as he finished his second quart.

'How?'

'Find Solomon the gateguard and get him to say he saw Barnabus coming in for the night.'

'Barnabus says he was at Madame Hetherington's.'

Will the Tod guffawed. 'Ye could speak to the women, I suppose,' he said. 'For a' the good that'll do ye.'

'No doubt they'll lie,' said Dodd.

Carey looked at him properly for the first time. Dodd's long dour face was always hard to read, but at the moment he looked happy. That meant he was uncommonly pleased with himself.

'What have you been doing, Sergeant?' he asked. 'Before you came here, I mean.'

Dodd sniffed. 'I was looking for Simon Barnet.'

Simon Barnet was Barnabus's nephew and was supposed to help Barnabus look after his master. In fact, Carey had been seeing less and less of him as he was sucked into the gang of boys that hung around the Castle, nominally working in the stables and kitchens. His speech had changed with lightning speed until now Barnabus often complained he couldn't understand the lad at all.

'Why?' asked Carey.

Dodd gave another sniff and drank some more beer. He looked as if he was having one of his perennial internal struggles. At about thirty two years Dodd was the same age as Carey himself, although he looked older, and he had spent most of that time hiding a surprising intelligence. Whatever was going on under the miserable carapace would decide whether Dodd grunted something noncommittal or whether he actually explained what he was up to. Carey had already learned from experience not to interfere with his thought processes, and so he waited as patiently as he could.

'Ye see, sir,' Dodd began, 'Begging your pardon, but I didna think what Barnabus was at last night was so important.'

Carey didn't like being told his orders were unimportant but he kept his mouth shut.

'Ye see,' Dodd said again, staring at the lees in his mug. 'I thought it stood to reason, if he'd had a good alibi for last night he would have said so to us. And he'd have said so earlier, and not even Lowther would have put him in the dungeon.'

'Go on.'

'So he hadnae got none or couldnae remember. So then I thought of what your lady sister said and I wondered, sir.'

'What Philadelphia said?'

'Ay sir. Lady Scrope.'

Carey tried to remember. Come to think of it, there had been something…

'She said they found Barnabus's dagger and one of my gloves by the corpse.'

'Ay, sir. That was it. So that set me to wondering. How they got the dagger—well, if Barnabus was at Madam Hetherington's it's no mystery, but how did the murderer lay hands on one o' your gloves?'

Carey laughed. 'By God, how did I miss that? Excellent, Dodd, of course.'

'Ay,' said Dodd smugly, 'So I said, the one to ask is Simon Barnet. But I havena found him.'

'Damn.'

'No bother, sir; the lads are in town now and I've set them to searching for him. He'll turn up. And then,' Dodd said ominously, 'we'll ask him.'

They had finished eating by the time Bangtail Graham and Red Sandy Dodd arrived, looking about for them. Red Sandy went straight up to Carey and handed him a piece of paper. Carey looked at it with awful foreboding; it was an official-looking letter sealed by Scrope's signet ring. He put it down by his trencher and finished his beer, his heart beating hard. The seal was in the nature of a Rubicon: once opened...He thought about it.

'Now why would the Warden do that?' asked Will the Tod's voice, fascinated.

'Hm?' Carey asked.

'Send for ye by letter? He only has to tell Red Sandy to tell ye...'

'Och,' said Dodd. 'It's quite friendly, really.'

Carey had worked it out but was a little surprised that Dodd had.

'See,' explained Dodd patronisingly to his father in law. 'If he's made a warrant out for Sir Robert, an' he tells him by letter, he's covered but Sir Robert can still...er...get away and no one the wiser. Or not, as he chooses.'

'Trouble is,' Carey said, putting his tankard down again with a decisive tap, 'where the hell would I go?'

'The Netherlands?' suggested Will the Tod, with all the impersonal ingenuity of one who was quite secure in his position. 'There's always room for right fighting men there.'

The Netherlands were fast becoming a sink hole for the unemployable young gentlemen of Europe. All of them went in the hope of sacking a town and making a fortune; most of them died within six months of fever, wounds or, occasionally, starvation.

'Or Ireland?' put in Dodd with ghoulish interest.

Carey shuddered slightly. He had heard descriptions of that particular hellhole from Sir Walter Raleigh, one of those unfortunate enough to have served there, of malarial bogs and half-savage but extremely intelligent and ferocious Wild Irish.

'Not if I can help it,' he said to the both of them as he picked up the letter and used his eating knife to break the seal.

Aggravatingly, Scrope had not seen fit to be clear when he wrote. All it said was, 'Sir Robert, I require to speak to you immediately. Please come up to the Keep at your earliest convenience.'

Carey sighed. The only possible indication was the signature, which was Thomas, Lord Scrope. If a warrant had already been issued, it would more likely have been Lord Scrope, Warden. However, there was no question but that he was right about its meaning.

He stood up and took his morion. The bloody thing was more of a nuisance than his jack, whose weight he hardly noticed any more. But the helmet weighed several pounds and was too expensive to lose.

'Where are ye going, sir?' asked Dodd.

'Up to the Castle,' Carey answered, putting his helmet on.

Dodd gave a dour nod. 'I'll keep asking for ye,' he said as if it were a foregone conclusion that Carey would end up in the Lickingstone cell next to Barnabus.

Red Sandy came with him, not precisely as an escort, more likely out of nosiness.

'Will ye be taking the patrol tonight, sir?' he asked.

Carey had forgotten all about it and looked up at the sky. It was promising rain.

'I don't know yet,' he said. 'I hope so.'

'Ay,' said Red Sandy happily. 'Who d'ye think killed Atkinson, then?'

'I don't know.' Carey looked curiously at Red Sandy, who was Dodd's younger brother but took life much less seriously. 'You're the first man who hasn't asked me whether I'm sure I didn't do it.'

'Ay sir,' said Red Sandy. 'See, I wouldna say ye wouldnae do it, sir, of course not, but by my thinking ye'd ha' done it better.'

'Thank you, Red Sandy.'

'H'hm. Your usual hobby's in the stables by the way, sir, wi' his tack on. In case ye'll be needing him for...for patrol, sir.'

Carey nodded. It was very touching really, their consideration for him. And it gave an insight into the Borderers. Carey had spotted Dodd's intelligence, but had thought Red Sandy the same as any others of the garrison, much better at fighting than thinking. But there it was: he must have tacked up the hobby himself as soon as Scrope gave him the letter, which suggested he understood its meaning too. Given their intelligence, why on earth did so many of them spend most of their time raiding and killing each other?

tuesday 4th july 1592, early afternoon

Scrope and Lowther were waiting for him in the sitting room on the top floor of the Keep that Scrope was also using as his office, where Carey had first met both Dodd and Lowther. As Carey put his hand to the axemarked door, he heard Lowther's voice growling dubiously, 'He'll never come.'

That was enough to make him pause. Carey eavesdropped shamelessly, having learnt the skill at Court and been grateful for it on several occasions.

'I don't know, Sir Richard,' came Scrope's reedy voice. 'I hear what you say, but I still don't believe it.'

'What more do you need, my lord?'

'I admit, the evidence is…er…damning, but you see, you've ignored one very important factor.'

'Which is?'

'Character. It doesn't make any sense, you see. I know the Careys. I can't claim to know Sir Robert as well as I know my lady wife, but…er…nothing I've seen from him since he got here has changed my mind.'

This was fascinating. Carey held his breath, wondering what would come next. Lowther grumbled something inaudible.

'Of course, I understand your point of view, Sir Richard, but even so…They're all extremely arrogant, of course, despite being upstarts. The cousinship with the Queen is the reason for their prominence, that and…er…my Lord Hunsdon's paternity.'

'I heard there was a bastardy in there somewhere,' said Lowther who was obviously not well up on Court gossip.

'Ah, well,' said Scrope. Being of an ancient family himself, he found lineage in men, horses or hounds deeply interesting. 'Y' see, Mary Boleyn, Lord Hunsdon's mother, was Anne Boleyn's older sister and thus Her Majesty's aunt.'

'Ay,' said Lowther. 'He's her cousin. I know that.'

'But also...' said Scrope's voice, rising with extra scholarly interest, 'Mary Boleyn was King Henry VIII's official mistress *before* Anne Boleyn...er...came to Court. She was married off to William Carey in a bit of a hurry.'

'Oh ay?' said Lowther, catching the implication.

'Yes,' said Scrope gleefully. 'And she called her first son, her rather...er...*premature* first son, Henry. And the King let her. You see? You've never met Carey's father, then?'

'I have,' said Lowther. 'Twenty years ago at the Rising of the Northern Earls. But he was a younger man. Loud, I recall, and a bonny fighter too, the way he did for Lord Dacre.'

'The resemblance to his...er...natural father has become more marked as he got older,' agreed Scrope. 'But you can see the Tudor blood coming out in my Lord Hunsdon's sons, and indeed in Sir Robert—arrogance, vanity, impatience and terrible tempers—but generally speaking they do not arrange for their servants to cut the throats of functionaries. It isn't their...style.'

Carey, who had been listening with rising irritation to this catalogue, nodded sourly. He supposed there was a little truth in it; he knew well enough he had a short temper, after all. He wasn't arrogant, though. Look at the way he had helped Dodd with his haymaking. As for vanity—what the Devil did Scrope think he was on about? Just because Carey knew the importance of a smart turnout and Scrope looked like an expensive haystack...

Lowther was saying something dubious about there being a villain in every family.

'True, true,' said Scrope. 'But although I wouldn't put multiple murder in some berserk rage past Sir Robert, I would put backstreet assassination.'

Carey decided he had heard enough. Berserk rage, indeed! He went down the stairs quietly and came up them again, gave a cough as he did so and pushed the door open.

Lowther had one fist on his hip and the other on his sword hilt, with a scowl on his face as threatening as the sky outside.

Scrope was also wearing a sword and his velvet official gown and pompous anxiety in every bony inch of him.

If he hadn't been listening to Scrope's opinion of his faults, Carey would have felt sorry for the man. As it was, he had decided that there was no point shilly-shallying; it would only confuse the overbred nitwit. He advanced on Lord Scrope who was behind a table he used as a spare desk, undoing his sword belt as he came. Then he bowed deeply and laid it with a clatter of buckles on the table in front of the Warden.

'I assume I am under arrest, my lord,' he said quietly, and waited.

Lowther snorted, and Scrope looked down at Carey's new sword with alarm. It had only been properly blooded that morning, Carey thought, a hundred years ago or so. Scrope would know nothing about that, of course.

'Well...er...not so fast, Sir Robert,' faltered Scrope. 'I...er... must ask you some questions, but...er...'

'My servant is in the Castle dungeon on a charge of murder,' Carey interrupted. 'I understand from him and...others...that I am suspected of ordering him to kill Mr Atkinson.'

'You deny it, of course,' scoffed Lowther.

Carey looked at him. 'Of course,' he said evenly.

Scrope sat down behind the table, but did not invite Carey to be seated. 'If you don't mind, Sir Robert,' he said, 'I must ask you to account for your actions since yesterday afternoon.'

With an effort Carey thought back. He told the story baldly. He had learned from a good source of a large Graham raid out of Netherby, threatening Archibald Bell and also Lady Widdrington who would be vulnerable on the Stanegate road.

'I take it that Mick the Crow is still in the Gatehouse gaol,' Carey commented at this point. 'I put him there because he wouldn't tell me the name of the man that sent the letter to Wattie.'

Lowther's heavy face was unmoved.

'He's not there now.'

'Did you release him, Sir Richard?' asked Carey innocently.

'Ay, I did. There was no charge and no need to keep him when he's wanted at home for haymaking.'

'There was a charge. It was a charge of March treason for bringing in raiders.'

'Pah,' said Sir Richard. 'He'd done nothing; I let him go.'

'Do continue,' said Scrope.

As a younger man, Carey would have argued about this but now he only gave Sir Richard a hard stare before telling how he had asked to borrow Lowther's patrol and had done so.

'Speaking of which, ye offered me my note of debt back, did ye not?' said Lowther offensively.

Silently Carey took the paper out of his belt pouch and handed it over. It was no loss, he reflected, since it was very unlikely Lowther was the kind who worried overmuch about paying his gambling debts. Lowther took it, squinted at it and tore it in pieces.

'Ye said you knew where to find some of King James's horses,' he accused. 'Well, did ye find 'em?'

'No,' admitted Carey. 'I didn't.'

'Hah,' said Lowther, rather theatrically, Carey thought.

'Go on,' put in Scrope.

'I'm fairly sure the horses were there, my lord,' he added. 'But obviously the people holding them got word I was on my way and hid them.'

It suddenly struck him how that could have happened and he mentally cursed himself for a fool as he continued, 'I didn't want to take Lowther's men into a fight against the Grahams…'

'And why not?' Lowther had the infernal impudence to demand.

'Because, Sir Richard, I didn't trust them,' Carey said as insolently as he dared. Lowther's bushy eyebrows were already almost meeting; he couldn't scowl any more deeply. 'So I went to my own Sergeant Dodd at Gilsland and he helped me call out the Bells and Musgraves. With their help, we met Wattie Graham and Skinabake Armstrong at the Irthing ford early this morning and put them to flight.'

'Well done,' said Scrope. 'It seems you have had a busy time of it.'

'Yes, my lord.'

'Doesna mean nothing,' said Lowther. 'It only shows he was anxious to be out of Carlisle last night. He could have given his order any time in the past week.'

Carey was itching to punch the evil old bastard, but he kept reminding himself that this was no time to lose his temper. He had had a swordmaster once, a big dark heavy man with wonderful lightness of foot, who deliberately goaded him into a fury, then disarmed him and knocked him on his arse in the mud to demonstrate how temper could undo him. Occasionally he remembered the lesson in time.

'On what evidence, Sir Richard, do you base your accusations?' he demanded, hearing his voice brittle with the effort not to shout.

'On the evidence of a knife owned by your servant and a glove owned by yerself that I found by the body.'

'How frightfully convenient for you,' Carey drawled. 'Did you have much trouble stealing one of my gloves?'

'Are you suggesting that *I put them there?*' roared Lowther, the veins standing out on his neck.

'Really, Sir Robert...' began Scrope.

'With respect, my lord,' Carey said through his teeth, 'I'm sorry to find you have such a low opinion of my intelligence.'

'How dare ye, sir? I never was so insulted in all my...'

'For God's sake, Sir Richard,' Carey shouted back at him, temper finally gone. 'What kind of fool do you think I am? Leave one of my *gloves* beside a *corpse*? Why not simply sign my name on his face and leave it at that? Or didn't you think of it when you watched them cutting his throat, you old traitor?'

That did it. Lowther drew his sword and put himself between Carey and the table where his own weapon lay. Carey backed hurriedly into a fighting crouch, pulling his poignard from its sheath behind his back and his little eating knife from the one by his belt pouch.

'Gentlemen, gentlemen...' said Scrope, jumping to his feet. 'Sir Richard, I insist you put up your weapon...'

Lowther ignored him. 'Call me traitor, would ye, you ignorant puppy...?' he hissed. 'Ye prancing courtier, ye...You had his throat cut and ye know it, because the poor wee clerk was an obstacle to ye and ye couldnae see another way to it...'

Carey circled, part of him vividly aware Lowther was trying to put him in one of the corners of the room. That same part was looking at Lowther's stance and the very experienced way he held his sword, and furthermore its length compared to a poignard, and not liking what it saw. Surely Scrope would do something. He did.

'Sir Richard,' he wailed. 'I will not have my officers duelling...'

'He's ignoring you, my lord,' Carey said. 'You'd better...'

'Your officers,' snarled Lowther sideways to Scrope, but not taking his eyes off Carey. '*I'm* the Deputy Warden in this March.

What was good enough for yer father is good enough for ye, boy, and don't you forget it.'

Of course, thought the part of Carey that was getting ready to fight for his life, I'm wearing a jack and morion and he isn't; that's something, isn't it?

'Put your sword away, Sir Richard,' pleaded Scrope. 'I order you to stop.'

Don't order him, you fucking fool, Carey thought; make him. Your father would have killed him just for drawing blade in a council chamber.

There was a faint creak of hinges behind Carey. He didn't dare turn his head to look. Then came a long clearing of somebody's throat.

'Sir Robert,' said Sergeant Dodd's doleful moan. 'We've found Simon Barnet for ye. If ye're busy, we can come back.'

Much of the murderous rage went out of Lowther's face to be replaced by something resembling embarrassment. Carey straightened a little, moved sideways so he could look at both Lowther and the door. Dodd was wearing his most stolid expression, but he had his stillsheathed sword in his hand, ready to throw to Carey. By God, Carey thought affectionately, I was in luck the day Scrope put you under my command.

To Carey's surprise, the presence of Dodd alone tipped the scales for Lowther. Belatedly, he realised what he was doing, put his weapon back in its sheath and folded his arms.

'Thank you,' said Scrope with unwarranted dignity. 'Sir Robert?'

Carey put his own blades away meekly enough, not sure what he felt nor why he was shaking. Was it anger or fear or relief? All of them, probably. He wondered a little at the shake since it never happened after he had been in a proper fight. Dodd rebuckled his sword belt, still looking dismal.

'We are...ahem...somewhat busy,' Scrope said to Dodd. 'Why have you brought the boy here?'

'Because he has a tale to tell I thought ye might wish to hear, my lord,' said Dodd.

'What on earth could a boy...'

'It's a tale about a glove, sir,' said Dodd. 'Which was found by Atkinson's corpse, sir.'

Scrope sat down again. 'Oh,' he said. 'Well, bring him in then.'

Simon Barnet came into view, an unremarkable snub-nosed lad of twelve with brown curly hair and brown eyes. He looked dusty and miserable, as if he had been hiding in a loft somewhere. There were muddy tear stains down his face, but he didn't look as if Dodd had beaten him.

Lowther drew a deep breath and glowered.

'Hiding behind a boy...' he muttered disdainfully. Carey chose not to hear him.

'Well, Sir Robert,' Scrope said. 'What does your boy have to say?'

'I haven't the faintest idea, my lord,' said Carey. 'I haven't seen him since...When did I see you last, Simon?'

'Yesterday morning, sir.'

'Ah.'

'Get on with it,' said Lowther.

Carey looked at him again and smiled. 'I think you should question him, Sir Richard, not me. That way you can't accuse me of coaching him to lie.'

Simon Barnet looked very scared and moved closer to Carey, like a chick to a mother hen.

'It's all right,' Carey said to him. 'Tell the truth, so my lord Warden can hear you.'

'Ay sir,' said Simon, still rolling his eyes at Lowther. Lowther advanced on him and he shrank back.

'Please don't threaten him with your sword, Sir Richard,' Carey put in. 'It wouldn't be fair. He's only young.'

Lowther gave Carey the kind of stare usually seen during the arrangements for a duel, and harrumphed at Simon Barnet.

'How much is Sir Robert paying you to say this?' he demanded.

'Er...p...paying me, sir? As his s...servant?'

'Perhaps, Sir Richard, we should hear the tale before we go around accusing people of lying,' suggested Carey icily.

'Ah, yes, er...quite. Be fair, Sir Richard.'

'What tale have ye brought, then?'

Simon Barnet stared wretchedly at Dodd, took his cap off, squeezed it, stared at the floor, stretched the cap out. 'Sergeant Dodd said I wouldnae be beaten for it,' he said in a small thin voice.

'I said I would ask the Deputy to go easy on ye. I made no promises.'

Carey sighed. The boy wasn't a fool either. 'There'll be no beating provided you tell the truth,' he said.

'A...ay sir.' Simon Barnet sighed wretchedly and continued to stare at the floor while he mumbled out his sorry tale. He had been approached by a man the day before. No, he had never seen the man before. The man asked him if he was servant to the new Deputy Warden. Simon had said he was. The man had said, he wasn't. Simon had said he was. The man had said, he bet anything Simon couldn't get hold of one of the Deputy Warden's gloves for him. Simon had taken the bet, which was large, and waited until Carey had gone out with Sergeant Nixon and Barnabus had gone down to Bessie's. He had lifted Carey's oldest glove, taken it to the man behind the stables and the man had laughed and said it could have come from anyone.

'I said it were London work,' Simon was aggrieved. 'He said he didna believe me, and then he said he would ask yer honour himself, and pretend he'd found it, but because I had an honest face he paid my bet anyway. And he went off wi' it.'

Carey sighed and shook his head. 'You're Barnabus Cooke's nephew, and you fell for that?'

Simon compressed his lips and scraped his boot toe in a circle round his other foot.

It had dawned on Simon what the man had wanted the glove for when Lowther had come storming into Carey's chambers in the Queen Mary Tower with two of his relatives and arrested Barnabus. This had given the boy the courage of outrage to lock the door to Carey's office and throw the key in the fire quickly enough to be able to claim Carey had it with him. Lowther had boxed his ears and kicked him for that, and after Lady Scrope arrived he had gone away again. Simon Barnet had been terrified and had run away to hide in the only place he could think of, the loft above the new barracks where Dodd had found him.

There was a silence as Simon came to the end of his story. Carey was frowning in puzzlement, and Lowther's expression remained grim.

'You may have to swear to that story in court, on the Holy Bible,' Scrope said. 'Will you do it, Simon?'

'Oh yes sir,' said Simon. 'Of course I will.'

'Do you know what swearing on the Bible means?' demanded Lowther. Simon turned to him. He had gained some courage from confession and managed to face Lowther squarely.

'Yes sir,' he said. 'It means if I swear and lie I'll go to hell.'

'Would you recognise this man if you saw him again?' Carey asked.

'I think so, sir.'

'What did he look like?'

'Well, big and wide.'

'Was he a gentleman?'

'No sir. He had a leather jack on and an arm in a sling and his face was bruised, sir.'

'No name?'

'No sir. He's not one of the garrison. I've not seen him about the Keep.'

'If you spot him again, Simon, try and make sure he doesn't see you. If you can, find out his name and come and tell me or Sergeant Dodd, understand?'

Simon nodded. 'Can I go now, sir? Only I havena eaten nothing today.'

He was at the age when one missed meal was a serious thing and two threatened instant starvation. Carey nodded.

'You're to stay in the Castle. Don't leave it for any reason.'

'Ay sir.'

'What did you do with the money?'

Simon looked even more woebegone. 'Och, sir. Ian Ogle had most of it off me at dice.'

Carey was careful not to laugh. 'Some advice for you, Simon,' he said. 'When you get a windfall, pay your debts first, then gamble with what's left.'

'Ay sir,' said Simon, who wasn't listening. 'May I go now, sir? They'll be ringing the bell...'

Carey looked at Scrope who nodded. Dodd was still there, busily pretending to be a piece of furniture.

'My lord,' Carey said intently. 'I'm beginning to have an idea of what's been happening. Will you hear me out?'

Scrope was squinting unhappily between his two hands at something on the table before him, underneath Carey's sword.

'Go on, Sir Robert,' he said.

Carey paced up to the table and back again. 'We have the corpse of Mr Atkinson, whose throat was cut, and which was found in Frank's vennel, off Botchergate. I've seen the corpse, I've talked to Mr Fenwick the undertaker and also to Mrs Atkinson and her neighbour Mrs Leigh.'

Lowther looked sour, but kept his mouth shut.

'Now then, firstly Fenwick's suspicious about it and he's seen more dead bodies than most. There was no blood in the alley where the corpse was found and although Atkinson's shirt was soaked, his clothes were unmarked on the outside and he had no boots on. That argues he must have had his throat cut when he was wearing only his shirt, and his killers then dressed him in his clothes. They couldn't get his boots on because his feet had stiffened by then. Somebody brought something heavy into Frank's vennel last night. There are clear tracks of a handcart in the alley, I've seen them.'

'It could have been there for another reason,' objected Lowther. 'Or Fenwick could have brought it to take the body away.'

'It could,' agreed Carey. 'But it's suspicious, especially as Fenwick used a litter; he told me so. Next, there's a knife and glove from Barnabus and myself. Respectfully, my lord, would you be so careless? Do you really think I would be? Would Barnabus? Anybody at all? The knife could have been lifted from Barnabus in Bessie's yesterday evening while he was drunk or at Madam Hetherington's which was where he went after Bessie closed for the night. As for my glove...You've heard Simon Barnet's story.'

'He could have made it up,' said Lowther.

'No,' said Scrope positively. 'The boy's not...er...enterprising enough. If it were Young Hutchin Graham standing there with that tale, I wouldn't believe a word of it, but I think Simon was speaking the truth.'

'So?' demanded Lowther. 'What are ye getting at, Sir Robert?'

You can't be that obtuse, Carey thought, but he answered evenly enough. 'Atkinson was not killed in the alley but somewhere else.'

'Where?'

'I don't know where, Sir Richard, since I didn't do it. But somewhere else in Carlisle his throat was cut. I expect, unless whoever did it was clever enough to choose a butcher's shambles for it, there will have been a great deal of blood about the place. No doubt, if you could find the blood, you could find the killers.

Whoever killed him then put his clothes on, wrapped him in something, piled him on a handcart and trundled him into the alley where they dumped him. Then, to make it look as if it was Barnabus and I that did it, they left what they thought would be clinching evidence. Which means I would very much like to talk to this mysterious man who made the bet with Simon Barnet.'

Lowther growled something completely inaudible. He looked from Scrope to Carey and back to Scrope again.

'Ye'll not do it? He's convinced you with that smooth courtier's tongue of his, hasn't he?'

Scrope frowned. 'If you recall, I had my doubts from the beginning,' he said. 'I'm certainly not…er…going to take any rash steps simply because you want to believe that your political rival would kill your man.'

This time Carey heard what Lowther said about brothers-in-law needing to stick together. It annoyed him, but he held his peace. Scrope heard as well and was more angered.

'I think you had better go, Sir Richard,' he said, sounding more genuinely the Lord Warden than Carey had heard him before. 'I may be related to Sir Robert, but if necessary I would arrest him, try him and execute him on a foul bill. I'll have no favourites here as my father did.'

Lowther was even more surprised than Carey at the determination in Scrope's voice. He looked down, put his fist on his hip again, took a breath to speak. Evidently he thought better of whatever he had been about to say because he let it out again and marched out of the room. Scrope picked up the paper he had been glancing at, folded it sideways and tore it into pieces. Carey's heart turned over to see how very close he had been to ruin. He smiled and was about to make some comment to Scrope about Lowther being a bad loser and to ask if Barnabus could have bail, when his brother-in-law fixed him with a fishy look.

'I may be satisfied you didn't do this, Sir Robert,' said Scrope. 'But I'm not at all satisfied about Barnabus. I may as well…er…tell you that I'm setting the Coroner's inquest for Thursday, since, thanks to the muster, we'll be able to empanel a good jury that will have some hope of not being entirely under Lowther's thumb. Oh, and there's a problem of jurisdiction here; whether I should…er…sit, or whether it should be the Carlisle Coroner.

After all, Atkinson was a townsman and was killed in the town. We will have to see. You did manage to write the muster letters before haring off after Wattie Graham?'

'Yes, my lord,' said Carey virtuously. 'Barnabus should have taken them to Richard Bell yesterday evening.'

Scrope seemed surprised by this.

'Oh...er...good. I'm glad to...see you're not neglecting your paperwork. I want a report about this Graham raid, by the way.'

'Yes, my lord. Ah...my lord, about Barnabus...'

'No, certainly not, he can't have bail. It's a capital charge.'

'No, I realise that. But could he not be locked up in the gaol under the Warden's Lodgings rather than the Lickingstone cell?'

'Ah.' Scrope seemed more co-operative. 'Don't see why not. I'll talk to Barker and have him moved.'

'Thank you, my lord.'

'It's supposed to be your patrol tonight.'

'Yes, my lord.'

'Are you going to take it?'

Carey hesitated. 'I think so, my lord. Unless you want me to stay in Carlisle.'

'I'd prefer it if you didn't go too far away.'

'No, my lord. I give you my word I'll be at the inquest.'

'See if you can find some of King James's horses. I'm getting letters every day from his courtiers about them.'

'Yes, my lord.' Carey waited politely.

'Er...yes, well, that's all then, Sir Robert. Oh, and you'd better take this back.' Scrope gestured at the weapon before him.

Carey picked his sword up again, bowed and left the room, feeling puzzled on top of his perennial annoyance with his brother-in-law. How was it that Scrope could be such a dithering idiot one moment and then the next moment act like the old Lord Scrope in his heyday? Dodd followed him quietly down the stairs, for which Carey was grateful. Halfway down it hit him that he had been wearing his jack and helmet all day and he was going to be up much of the night. The energy that had kept him going up to now suddenly deserted him and weariness fell on him like a cloak. He sat down heavily on a bench in the gloomy Keep hall, took his helmet off and rubbed his aching forehead, wishing he had time for a nap. His eyes were feeling sandy.

A heavily pregnant lymer bitch spotted him and came over to plump herself at his feet. Absent-mindedly he reached down to rub her stomach and she panted happily.

'Do you know whether it's true that Mrs Atkinson had a lover?' he asked Dodd. The Sergeant sucked his teeth noncommittally.

'Janet could likely answer the question better. They're old friends.'

'Oh,' One more complication to add to the many surrounding him. 'Do you think Lowther did it?'

Dodd looked taken aback. 'I couldna say, sir,' he answered cautiously.

'It's all right, Sergeant, I won't hold you to it. I thought he might have, but when I let it slip out in front of the Warden, he was in such a rage it could have been genuine. I'm just interested to know what you think. Sit down and tell me.'

Sergeant Dodd sat down on the bench facing Carey and leaned his elbows on the trestle table behind him. He looked up at the roof with its dusty martial banners and grinned suddenly.

'What's so funny?'

The bitch was restless. She rolled herself back onto her legs and put her muzzle on Carey's leg, dribbling a little.

'Only, I recall Lowther telling me more than once that I wasna paid to think.'

'More fool him, then. Come on. I'm not paying you extra to think, by the way; I expect that as part of your ordinary duties. Anyway, I can't afford it.'

Dodd smiled again. Two in ten minutes, Carey thought, what is the world coming to?

'An' that's another thing I cannae understand, sir. There ye are, ye're wearing more money in ironware on yer belts than I see from one year's end to the next and ye say ye cannae afford this or that. Then ye go throwing money around: three pounds for Sergeant Nixon to buy bows; sixpence each for them to help with my haymaking.'

'Oh.' For the first time in his life it occurred to Carey to wonder if the way he spent money might have something to do with his debts.

'It makes me curious, sir,' said Dodd, quite loquacious now he'd been asked for his opinion. 'I thought all courtiers were rolling in money. Are ye not rich?'

Carey could not be offended with him, his curiosity was so naked. Instead he sighed again.

'Dodd, do you recall me telling you that the last time I was out of debt was in '89 after I walked from London to Berwick in twelve days for a bet of two thousand pounds.'

'Ay sir. I remember. You were taking one of my faggots off me.'

'Oh yes,' said Carey. 'That reminds me, we haven't recruited anybody for that place yet, have we?'

'No sir,' said Dodd, dourly.

'I expect I'll get round to it. Well, that was the last time I paid my various creditors. Since then...I'm a younger son, Dodd, as you are yourself. I get nothing from my father except the occasional loan and a good lecture. I've got no land and no assets at all, except my relatives and the people I know in London and Berwick.'

'How d'ye live at Court, sir?'

'The Queen likes me and she gives me money occasionally. Sometimes I can help someone get an office, or they believe I can.'

'Is that all? I heard it was very expensive, living at Court.'

'Oh Lord, Dodd, it is, it is. It's crippling.'

'So ye must have some means of earning money, sir; it stands to reason.'

'I'll tell you if you promise not to tell anyone else.'

'Ay. My word on it.'

'Gambling.'

'Eh?'

'I gamble. I play cards. Not dice, and I don't bet on bears or dogs. Just cards.'

Dodd was fascinated. 'Can ye win enough that way, sir?'

'Yes, usually. There are plenty of people with more money than sense at Court, and a lot of them want to play me because I'm the Queen's cousin and they're snobs and want to boast about it, or they've heard I'm...good, and they want to beat me.'

'And you get enough that way, sir?'

'Yes. I paid Sergeant Nixon out of my winnings on Sunday night. Most of it was originally Lowther's money anyway.'

Dodd laughed, an odd suppressed creaking noise. 'No wonder he's out for your blood.'

'He would be anyway.'

'No, but see, sir, he's used to winning against your sister and my lord Scrope.'

'Of course he is. They're both appalling players.'

'How about horses, sir? D'ye ever bet on them?'

'What tournaments and suchlike? Yes, on myself to win, to try and cover the cost of it.'

'Nay, racing.'

'No. Cards are more reliable.'

'That's where I lose my money,' confided Dodd. 'At cards too, but on the horses as well. Will ye teach me to play, sir?'

Carey looked at him, astonished that the stiff-necked Sergeant could admit that he needed to learn. But then the only other person who had done that had been the famously proud Sir Walter Raleigh.

'I expect so, I learnt it myself from a book. I'm afraid I don't play seriously with you and the men, though, because you can't afford to lose enough.'

'Och, I'm happy to hear it. Take yer living off Lowther by all means. So why did ye leave London, sir, if ye could support yourself at play?'

'Well, unless you cheat, which I don't unless somebody's trying to cheat me, it's still fairly precarious. You can always have a run of bad luck. And things were getting a little…tense.'

Dodd had the tact not to ask directly. 'Ye felt like a change?'

The lymer bitch was nudging at Carey's leg and whining again. 'I felt like not going to the Fleet prison, which was looking more and more likely. I could finish there yet, if Lowther hangs Barnabus.'

'Ay,' said Dodd. 'Ye couldna keep on as Deputy then.'

'Quite.'

'Seems like ye'll need to marry money or land, sir, like I did.'

Carey sighed again, cracked his knuckles. 'That's what everybody keeps telling me.'

But ye've lost your heart to Lady Widdrington, who's married to someone else and not likely to inherit much either, thought Dodd sympathetically, though he didn't say it.

'So what do you think about who murdered Atkinson?' Carey asked abruptly, obviously forcing his mind away from depressing thoughts and back to puzzles.

Dodd hesitated a moment longer and then answered slowly.

'All I can say is, by my thinking there's two kinds of murder. There's the kind that happens in a right temper when ye go after a man that insulted you with a rock in yer hand and beat out his brains. Or there's the kind where ye think about it beforehand and then do it when he's not expecting ye. That's the kind of murder that happened to Atkinson.'

'Yes. Throat cut. I couldn't see any signs on him that he'd fought at all.'

'He wouldn't know how any road. What about the man that got your glove off of Simon Barnet?'

Carey nodded, scratching the lymer bitch around her ears. She moaned with pleasure and rubbed her chin on his leg. A couple of the Keep servants came in and began laying the tables ready for the second of the two meals they served daily.

'Either the murderer or his servant.'

'Arm in a sling and bruised face. Shouldna be too hard to find if he's in Carlisle still.'

'If.' Carey yawned jaw-crackingly. 'It's no good Sergeant, I've simply got to get some rest or I'll fall asleep in the saddle tonight.'

'Did ye not sleep well last night, then?' Dodd asked solicitously. Once they had returned from talking to the Bell and Musgrave headmen, he had given Carey the best bed and he himself had taken Rowan's truckle bed with his wife. After waking her up for his marital rights, he had slept like the dead until Carey woke him in the dark before dawn.

'Not really,' Carey admitted, not intending to explain that Dodd and his wife had kept him awake for the first half hour and then sea-green envy and a miserable worried longing for Elizabeth had wound him up too tight to do much more than doze after that. He came to his feet and the lymer bitch gazed up at him hopefully so he bent down and patted her broad yellow flank. 'I'll snatch an hour now before it's time to gather the men together.'

'Ay sir,' said Dodd cheerily. 'I'll have a wander round the town and see if I canna find this man wi' his arm in a sling for ye.'

Carey nodded, put his helmet under his arm and walked out of the Keep door, down the steps and across to the Queen Mary Tower where he was lodging. There was no Barnabus in his bedchamber to help him, and Simon Barnet was doubtless about to start stuffing his face with poor quality boiled salt beef and bread across in the Keep's hall. The yellow lymer bitch had followed him all the way across and up the stairs and he hadn't the heart to throw her out. He put his helmet and swordbelt on the top of his jackstand, wearily took his jack off, hung it up. He hadn't the energy to struggle with his riding boots, so he drew the curtains of his bed to keep out the sunlight and threw himself full length on it as he was. The big lymer bitch whined a couple of times and lumbered up on to the bed next to him. Ancient strapping creaked alarmingly under their combined weights.

'Oh, for God's sake,' Carey moaned, and tried to push her off, but she licked his face lovingly, turned round a couple of times and settled down against his stomach. He shoved her a couple of times, but she became a warm furry lump of immovability. If he wanted her off his bed, he knew he would have to get up and haul her off by the collar and he couldn't be bothered. 'You are not the kind of woman I want in my bed,' he told her severely and she yawned and panted and licked at his nose, so he held her muzzle with his hand and told her severely to be still. She put her nose down between her paws and watched him with her soulful brown eyes until his own eyes blurred and he pitched into sleep.

Dodd stepped out into the sunlit courtyard and walked whistling out through the Captain's gate and the covered way into the town. He couldn't have explained why, but the discovery that Carey the elegant courtier was only one step ahead of a warrant for debt in London made him like the man much more. Carey had the indefinable assets of birth and influence and the Queen's favour; Dodd had a good solid tower, a hundred pounds' worth of land at lease, and kin who would follow him if he asked them.

For a while Dodd quartered the town and then changed direction and went back to Bessie's. There, as he had expected, he found the rest of his men. He explained his quest to them and they were happy to join in.

Eventually Bangtail came hurrying up, trailing a boy whom Dodd recognised as Ian Ogle, the steward's young son.

'Tell him,' Bangtail encouraged the lad, who squinted up at Dodd and wanted to know what was in it for him.

Feeling inspired, Dodd resisted the impulse to shake the information out of the boy, and instead handed over a penny. Ian Ogle squinted at it ungratefully.

'Ay,' he said. 'He were in here yesterday askin' which lad was it served the Deputy Warden, so I tellt him. Why'd ye want to know?'

'Who was?'

'Who was what?'

'Who was asking which lad…?'

'Andy Nixon, Mr Pennycook's rent-collector,' said Ian Ogle with a contemptuous sneer. 'And he'd had an argument he lost with somebody, by my reckoning.'

'Andy Nixon,' breathed Dodd, who knew more about Mrs Atkinson's private life from Janet than he had let on to Carey.

'Ay.'

'Have you seen him today?'

'No.'

'Well then, be off wi' ye. By God, Andy Nixon. I wouldnae have thought it.'

By the time Carey woke up to the sound of the yellow lymer bitch's echoing snores, the light filtering through his curtains was as yellow as her coat. He got up, feeling irritable and aching, mainly the effect of being stupid enough to sleep in his hose and boots, but there was no point in taking them off now.

Dodd knocked on the door just as Carey drank the remains of the beer in the jug and wished Barnabus was around to bring him food. He would have to talk to Scrope about finding another servant to look after him while Barnabus was in jail.

Dodd's face was unrecognisable because it had a broad grin on it. That faded when he saw the frowstiness of the Deputy.

'I wouldna recommend sleeping in your boots,' he said helpfully.

'Thank you, Dodd.'

Carey scratched his hair, smoothed it down again, put on his morion and finished buckling his swordbelt.

'Well, we've got his name, sir,' said Dodd, full of happiness and bonhomie.

'Eh?'

'The man that bribed Simon Barnet for your glove. We know his name.'

That woke him up properly. 'Do you, by God?'

'Ay, sir. His name's Andy Nixon.'

Where had he heard that name before? He remembered the extremely pregnant Mrs Leigh with her nasty particles of gossip.

'Andy Nixon?'

'Ay. Mr Pennycook's rent-collector.'

That fitted. That all fitted nicely into place. Carey's jaw set. 'He's Mrs Atkinson's lover, isn't he?'

Dodd sighed regretfully. 'Ay sir. They was childhood sweethearts, but Kate Coldale's mother wouldna let her marry a man wi' no land and no prospects, seeing she had a good dowry in property, and she was married off to Jemmy Atkinson instead. But I canna see Kate…'

'It looks bad for her, though. If she conspired with her lover to kill her husband, that's a wicked crime. It's petty treason. She…'

Dodd was looking at Carey with peculiar directness. Go on, thought Dodd, tell me you've never at least toyed with the notion of shooting Sir Henry Widdrington, tell me you haven't.

Carey's voice did trail off and he looked at the floor. Up again. 'It's a crime,' he said more quietly. 'It has to be a crime. If it wasn't, none of us could sleep easy in our beds.'

'Depends how ye treat yer wife, though, sir,' said Dodd with all the smugness of the happily married. 'And what her lover thinks of it and what kind of a man he is.'

Carey studiously ignored the personal implications of all this.

'You think Andy Nixon's capable of slitting Atkinson's throat?'

'Oh ay, sir. Andy Nixon wouldnae do the job he does if he couldnae use a blade.'

'And Mrs Atkinson? Do you think she knew?'

Dodd shrugged. 'I dinna ken sir.'

'Well, let's go and find out.'

'We need a warrant, sir…'

'I'll get the bloody warrant,' Carey growled. 'Fetch the men.'

Kate Atkinson was just about to lock up her house for the night when there came an almighty hammering on her door. She opened it and was faced with a waking nightmare: the tall Deputy Warden with a piece of paper in his hand that gave him the right to search her house, and behind him six men to do it. At the tail of them all was Janet Armstrong's bad-tempered husband looking very uneasy.

They tramped their muddy boots up the stairs and into her bedroom; she hadn't been sleeping on her marriage bed, but on the truckle bed beside it, as she told them. Two of them went out into the back yard and started gingerly raking through her midden heap. She didn't go with them but sat on the window seat in the downstairs living room and looked at her clenched fists. When little Mary started to wail because she was frightened by the high comb of the Deputy's helmet, she did nothing because there was really nothing comforting she could say to her. Occasionally wisps of thought would gust through her mind. I should have gone to Lowther. I should never have told Andy. What can I say?

'Mrs Atkinson,' came a powerful voice from upstairs. 'Will you come here, please?'

She went and found the Deputy Warden and Henry Dodd staring at the mattress of her marriage bed. They had stripped the clean sheet off it and turned it up the other way again. The Deputy reached down a long glittering hand, prodded the large brown stain. It was still a little sticky, and he sniffed his fingers.

'Where are the other sheets to this bed?' he demanded.

'Downstairs, in the yard,' she said. 'Hanging out to dry.'

'And the blankets?'

'The same.'

'The hangings?'

'Ay.'

'Did all the blood come off?'

She looked down at her apron, which was greasy, and twisted her hands together.

'This is blood. You won't tell me, I hope, that you've been killing a chicken in your marriage bed?'

If he was making a joke, she didn't find it funny.

'Mrs Atkinson, look at me.' The Deputy's voice had an impersonal sound: not angry at all, which surprised her for Lowther would have been bellowing at her by now. She looked at him and oh, the bonny blue eyes he had; it was hard to concentrate, the way they looked into you.

'Mrs Atkinson, did you murder your husband?'

At least she could answer that question honestly and yet she didn't. She said nothing.

'Do you know who did?'

She shook her head.

The blue eyes narrowed; a little surprise, a lot of cynicism, more contempt.

'I think you do know.'

'I dinna, sir.'

Janet Armstrong's husband was staring at her in plain astonishment. Also suspicion. She must seem like every married man's nightmare, she supposed, as they were hers.

'I think either you or your lover Andy Nixon slit your husband's throat. You and he then conspired to dump the body in an alley and lay the blame on me, for whatever reason, though heaven knows I've done nothing against you that I know of.' The Deputy's voice was heavy with authority.

Yes, that was the sin of it, to lay the blame on an innocent man. But Pennycook had said somebody had to be blamed, and it might as well be the upstart southerner who was interfering with business and had no kin around Carlisle to back him up.

'We...er...' She stopped speaking. How could she possibly explain? She didn't even know for certain that Andy Nixon hadn't done it. And she had helped to dump the body. Which made her guilty of something, she supposed. She couldn't speak for the number of things she needed to say.

'You know what happens if ye refuse to plead, Kate,' said Dodd anxiously. 'Ye must answer.'

At least she was able to speak to him, if not to the terrifying Deputy. 'Ay,' she whispered. 'Pressing to death. Well, I didna kill my husband and nor did I plot with anybody to kill him. I dinna ken how he came to be dead. So now.' There, it was done. When they found her guilty, she would burn.

Carey took a deep breath. 'I'm afraid I must arrest you, Mrs Atkinson, for the crime of petty treason.' he said formally. 'Come with us.'

'No, wait.'

'What for?'

'The children,' she said wildly. 'I must get someone in to see after the children.'

'Oh,' said the Deputy with the surprise of the bachelor. 'Yes, I suppose you must.'

The next half hour passed in more chaos than the worst night terrors, Mary howling as her mother tried to explain, and the boys' faces white and scared; this was a terrible thing for them on top of their father's death. The Deputy Warden and his men stood around like lumps, getting in her way while she tried to sort things out. Of course, she couldn't go to her sister-in-law, Mrs Leigh next door, so Sergeant Dodd accompanied her to her sister, Maggie Mulcaster over the road, who came bustling across, full of excited goodwill. Telling her what was happening was akin to using the Carlisle town crier, but it couldn't be helped. Julia had gone home but she would go across to Mrs Mulcaster as well when she arrived in the morning to find the house shut. She could get in at the wynd to milk the cow and deal with the cream put to rise for today in the tiny dairy. Kate had to leave the plate-chest where it was under the bed and hope no one would find it. She closed and bolted the shutters. While they were all downstairs two of the men came in triumphantly from the midden heap, carrying sticky clumps of rushes that she had swept out of the bedroom, dropping bits of them on the new clean rushes.

At last they were organised, and Maggie herded the crying children across to her house in their shirts, carrying their day clothes in a bag over her arm. She paused to give Kate Atkinson's shoulders a squeeze and then hurried away.

'I can come with ye now, sir,' she said, noticing that the Deputy was at least looking less triumphant, though still severe. Henry Dodd was upset, which he should be. Perhaps Janet could help her?

'Take your cloak, Mrs Atkinson,' said the Deputy, snagging it off its peg and handing it to her. 'It's cold in the gaol.'

That nearly did for her. She choked and bit her knuckle, but swallowed her tears. How to save Andy, that was the question now, since it seemed she was a dead woman. No doubt God was punishing her for her sin of adultery, though she had thought her dead baby of last year punishment enough. Clearly it was only a warning. Unseeing, she tied the cloak and put its hood up.

Everyone would know from Maggie, but she wanted to hide her face all the same. The Deputy asked for the key to the house and locked the door.

Dodd nodded to the other men of the guard who were staring at her in shock as if she had suddenly grown a viper's head, and they surrounded her. It was kindly of them, she thought, hiding her like that, since she was not likely to run away from them, but she almost had to run to keep up with them as they tramped her into the Castle gate, through the righthand door and up the tiny stairs into the upper of the two prison rooms there.

Mrs Atkinson refused point-blank to tell Carey where Andy Nixon lodged, but it didn't matter because Sergeant Ill-Willit Daniel Nixon was willing to say where he was. His landlady answered the door to their knocking and said distractedly that he had gone, taken his baggage and left an hour earlier and she didn't know where, and the rent not paid.

Running Sergeant Nixon to earth again took time since he had gone to an alehouse in Fisher street where he could drink in peace, as he put it. It cost a sixpence from Carey, but he finally admitted that while Andy was likely headed for the Debateable Land, as any sensible man would be, he might stay until nightfall at his father's farm a couple of miles out of Carlisle where he could get horses and food. Nay, he wouldna simply leg it there, not in his condition. Oh ay, he had cousins aplenty in the Debateable Land; once he got in they'd never winkle him out, and good luck to him. No, Sergeant Nixon would not come with them to help; Dodd knew the place well enough. Who the hell cared if somebody cut Atkinson's throat, it was no loss to man nor beast...

Carey and his men took horse and galloped from Carlisle, heading for a long low farmhouse with a surrounding brushwood fence, the walls made of stone halfway and wattle and daub the rest. It was close enough to Carlisle not to need its own peel tower, though there was a place on the next hill that was likely the Nixons' refuge if necessary.

The Deputy Warden spoke to Andy Nixon's father at the gate, a broad grizzled man with the habitual worried expression of someone who had to pay blackrent to Thomas Carleton as well as to the Grahams. John Nixon took the Deputy's warrant and looked at it upside down, which was lucky since it only referred to Mrs Atkinson's house.

'He's not here,' said John Nixon. 'He's gone to the Debateable Land.'

Carey peered over the gate at a saddled and bridled hobby standing at a hitching post, a remount already tethered behind it.

'I must make sure,' said Carey charmingly. 'You won't object, will you, Mr Nixon?'

Carey had given Dodd one of his wheellock dags, ready wound, with orders not to point it unless necessary. The other men he had already told to station themselves all about the fence, in case Andy tried making a break for it.

At this point Carey simply walked past John Nixon and into the small yard, stood with one hand negligently on his swordhilt and his other dag under his arm and looked around.

'Sergeant,' he said.

'Ay sir,'

'You and Red Sandy start searching the way I told you.'

'Ay sir.'

Carey settled himself with his back to the wall of the house, perched on the edge of a water trough, watching John Nixon's face. As Dodd and Red Sandy trampled noisily around the farm and outbuildings, Carey quietly sat and watched, privately laying a bet with himself. Dodd had left the pigpen till last and sure enough as he went in, there was a flicker of John Nixon's eyelids.

Carey stood upright, took the dag in his gauntleted hand and put it behind his back. Seconds later there came a lot of shouting from the stye, and a crunching sound. Dodd came reeling out to land in the mud. Andy Nixon charged past him, grabbed the dag out of his unresisting hand, vaulted two sows and the fence and then slowed. He advanced on Carey pointing the gun squarely at his chest. Carey smiled.

'Well, Andy Nixon,' he said, 'I must arrest you in the name of the Queen for the murder of Jemmy Atkinson.'

'I didna do it,' said Nixon, still advancing. 'Now get out of my way.'

Carey brought his gun out and levelled it at Nixon. 'This dag is loaded. That one is not. Do you think the Sergeant would let you get your hands on a loaded gun so easily? Shame on you, Andy.'

He and Dodd had spent ten minutes discussing ways of arresting Andy Nixon without having to fight him, something Dodd was keen to avoid. It was the best they could come up with.

Andy growled inarticulately and threw the useless dag at Carey's face. He jerked back, fired and missed at pointblank range, shooting one of the unfortunate pigs instead. It went berserk, charging round its pen and biting anything that got in its way, which included Dodd who was just trying to get to his feet.

Carey stayed upright, dropped his gun, pulled out his sword.

'Carlisle garrison to me!' he roared, and Andy Nixon looked over his shoulder to see Bangtail Graham and Long George crowding the gate, their lances ready. However, he could see that wave them though they might, neither of them were anxious to come and help. Andy drew his sword awkwardly, then transferred it to his left hand. Carey drew his poignard lefthanded and advanced on the man, his blades en garde before him: Dodd had been very insistent about the importance of not getting to close-quarters with Andy Nixon. On the other hand, Carey wanted him alive to confess, be tried and hanged, a scruple that Dodd clearly thought insane.

Dodd had managed to struggle stinking out of the pigpen and was menacing Andy's father with his sword, in case he got excited. The wounded pig continued to buck round the pen squealing like a human child.

Andy Nixon and Carey moved around each other, Carey trying to keep himself between Nixon and the horses. Nixon, who was desperate, moved in swinging his sword awkwardly. Carey parried with his two crossed blades and tried a quick underarm stab with the poignard, but Nixon skipped backwards too fast. Not in fact left-handed, then, but holding his sword in his left hand because his right was hurt somehow. Simon Barnet had said something about his hand in a sling. And his face wasn't only smudged with pig dirt but also badly bruised about the cheeks and jaw. It was a square young-looking face on a square barrel-chested body, solid all through and very determined. Now after the fizzing excitement of anticipation Carey felt that cold narrowing down of focus, the hard beat of his heart and the strange sensation of everything being very slow and crystal clear, which was there whenever he fought. He liked it. That feeling was one reason why he had come to the north.

Andy Nixon's face tightened, the betraying flicker. Carey waited for him, caught the rhythm of his attack, slipped sideways and struck backhanded with his sword at Nixon's. Metal screeched as the blades slid past each other, he flicked his wrist, and Andy's sword was on the ground. Andy stared at it, panting slightly.

'Now, Andy,' Carey said reprovingly. 'Why don't you...?'

Andy cannoned into him frontally from low down and Carey was knocked backwards onto the ground practically under the hobbies' hooves. He had dropped his sword with the shock. The horses skittered nervously backwards and forwards, hooves coming and going, distractingly enormous right next to his face, while Carey found himself held down by immensely strong shoulders. He could have used his poignard, which he still had, but he wanted Andy Nixon alive, and anyway, Andy was holding his left wrist down. There was something flawed in that grip; Carey couldn't move the rest of him—where the hell was Dodd?—but he twisted his arm, jerked up on his elbow, reversed the poignard and managed to hit Andy across the head with the pommel.

He didn't even notice, except to land a punch on Carey's face which sent stars whirling through the sky. The horrible weight came off Carey's shoulders; Andy Nixon was getting into the saddle of one of the hobbies. Carey gasped some air into his lungs, heaved himself up still blind, grabbed Nixon's foot and shoved him up and off the horses's back on the other side. Nixon landed with a crunch on the ground. Carey ducked under the horse's head to grab him and was met with a kick like a mule which he saw coming just in time to turn and take it on his hip instead of his crotch. The force of it knocked him back and into the hobby which whinnied and swung about until stopped by the tether. Somehow he had dropped the poignard. Andy was on his feet again, rocking, gasping for breath, but up. Jesus, the man wasn't human, what was he made of—and where the bloody *hell* was Dodd? Carey dimly heard a sound of cheering...Cheering? Were his troop of useless scum enjoying this?

More enraged by that thought than by anything Andy Nixon had done, Carey forgot all about not coming to close-quarters with Nixon and launched himself at him. There was a confused moment, during which his legs and Andy's seemed to become mysteriously tangled, and then the ground was leaping up; he had landed bruisingly on his stomach and Andy was about to break his arm backwards over his shoulder. Carey kicked and bucked, there was a second when he thought he might get free at the cost of dislocating his arm and then there was a brisk movement above him, a dull thud and Nixon was keeling over with a sigh. Carey lay for a moment, cawing for breath, and then levered himself up off the ground with his hands, came to his knees. Dodd was there, a large rock in one hand, offering him the other. He took it and climbed back onto his feet. He stood for a moment while he concentrated on breathing and felt his wrenched arm and his incompletely healed ribs. Then he looked at Nixon who was lying there, bleeding from a graze on his head.

'Where the…hell…were you…, Sergeant?' he rasped.

Bangtail and Archie-Give-It-Them came forward with care, picked up the floppy Andy Nixon and tied his hands before him as fast as they could. Then they hefted him up over the lead hobby's saddle just as he began to mutter and connected his bound hands with a rope under the horse's belly to his feet.

Sergeant Dodd was grinning inanely. 'Och, I thought ye were making such a bonny fight of it wi' Nixon, ya didna need my help.'

If he had had the energy he would have punched Henry Dodd.

'B…bonny fight…' he got out, 'The…bastard…nearly broke my arm.'

'Ay,' said Dodd, not at all abashed. 'Ye did verra well, sir. Andy Nixon won the wrestling last summer for a' Cumberland, knocked Archie-Give-It-Them out cold, and beat three Scots after.'

Carey sat on the edge of the water trough and spat some blood out. Nixon's punch to his face had cut the inside of his mouth against his teeth.

'The…the bastard nearly…broke my arm,' he said to Dodd again, still unable to believe such perfidy.

'Ay,' said Dodd. 'He beat ye right enough. I've won half a crown off Bangtail and…'

'Wait a minute. You…you bet on me to lose?'

'Ay sir. It were a safe bet.'

'Jesus Christ! I am going to kill you, Dodd.'

'In that state? I wouldna bet on it, sir,' said Dodd with great good humour.

Carey shook his head to clear it and picked up his morion whose chin strap had broken at some stage in the fight. He looked round at his men who were settling bets and nodding approvingly at him, then saw John Nixon who was being held by Red Sandy and Long George.

'Mr Nixon,' he croaked. 'I'm arresting your son Andrew on the charge of conspiracy and premeditated murder. If I have any trouble on the way home, I'll cut his head off. Understand?

John Nixon nodded.

Weapons were scattered all over the yard. Dodd had already retrieved both of his valuable Tower armoury dags; Carey himself picked up his sword and poignard, sheathed them, went over to Dodd to take his guns and reeled at the smell.

'Do something about the pigshit, Dodd,' he said drily. Dodd went to the water trough, picked up a bucket and poured the water over himself, which helped a little.

They mounted up. Red Sandy took the reins of the hobby carrying Andy Nixon because Long George was in the middle of a sneezing fit, and they started back to Carlisle. At the Eden bridge Carey told Dodd to begin the patrol and wait for him at the Gelt ford. He led the hobby himself as he turned the horses in towards Carlisle town with the sun dying in fire behind the Castle and the clouds. He had Archie-Give-It-Them Musgrave on the other side to help if Nixon should get free.

Andy Nixon was conscious again, turning his face sideways to keep his graze away from the horse's flank and wriggling occasionally when the horse jerked. He had already been sick, there were traces of it on the horse's belly. Carey supposed the head-down position, the motion and the smell would make you sick, come to think of it. Good. Serve the bastard right. Not a scratch on him after fighting fifty-odd Grahams and outlaws that morning—and then he went to arrest one rent-collector and ended up feeling as if he had been run over by a cart and nursed by the Spanish Inquisition. His whole shoulder was aching with pulled muscles, his ribs were griping him again, his hip was sore though his jack had softened some of the force of the kick, and his face was bruised which made him talk out of one side of his mouth.

He doubted there was an inch of his body which didn't have some complaint and he sincerely hoped Nixon was feeling much worse.

Nixon croaked something inaudible.

'What was that?' Carey asked.

Nixon lifted his head and yelled. 'I didna do it.'

Carey rode along in silence for a moment, thinking. 'I'm disappointed in you, Nixon,' he said flatly. 'I wouldn't have thought you were the kind of man that would let a woman face burning alone.'

The head flopped to hang downwards again. 'Ah Christ,' came a muffled groan.

There was no more chat until they got back into Carlisle and tethered their horses at the Keep. Carey had to keep fighting the illusion caused by taking an afternoon nap, that in fact he had fought the Grahams the day before.

A young man called William Barker was keeping the dungeons for Scrope, deputy to his grandfather who was officially the Gaoler. He stared with surprise as they rode into the inner yard and Archie-Give-It-Them heaved Andy Nixon down from the horse.

'Fetch the irons, Barker,' Carey said.

The youth fetched them out of the little locker. Carey put them on Nixon's wrists before he cut the ropes binding him. Nixon's eyes looked like a cow at the slaughter. When he cut the rope, Carey saw the puffiness of Nixon's right hand.

'What happened there?' he asked.

Nixon's lip lifted. 'Some whore's get trod on it in an alley, Sunday night,' he said. He looked down and shifted his feet; Archie was putting leg irons round his boots.

Carey took the keys from Barker in the passage by the wine cellar, opened up the heavy door to the outer dungeon and Nixon shuffled clankingly inside, sat down on the stone bench. He looked at Carey hopelessly.

'Where's Kate?' he asked.

'In the Gatehouse prison,' Carey said as he swung the door shut and locked it. 'You can't see her.'

Leaving Barker in charge, Carey and Archie-Give-It-Them changed horses and hurried back to the gate which was just closing. They cantered out of Carlisle and over the Eden bridge to catch up with Dodd for the patrol. Carey squinted up at the sky as he rode. The roof of clouds had an ugly grey bulbous look and the sun's last rays squeezed under its lower fringes.

'More rain, Archie,' he said conversationally.

'Ay,' said Archie. 'At least Dodd will get his jack cleaned for him.'

The clouds were as good as their promise: halfway through their patrol it began to pour and continued until they came back to Carlisle in the pitch darkness well after midnight. Carey thought that at least he now knew for certain where King James's horses were not, since neither hide nor hair of them had they seen anywhere. Long George kept up a monotonous sneezing, wheezing and snortling all through the patrol. Carey was sure nobody could be fool enough to be raiding in that kind of rain, so they turned for home early and after some argument with the City gate guard came in by the postern gate. Solomon Musgrave was more co-operative, trotting down to open up the Keep gate and let the soaked men and horses in.

'Ay, sir,' he said, as Carey came through. 'It's a foul night.' Carey remembered him from when he was a boy, but was too depressed to do more than nod. Generally speaking he was not a worrier, so the way thoughts and imaginings about Elizabeth Widdrington kept attacking him was a new experience for him. It happened whenever he was not positively thinking of something different: his thoughts wandered down a well-beaten path that began with what Elizabeth might be doing or thinking about now, continued with plans for the future that were always stumped by the fact of her husband, and then came to a new juddering halt with the certainty that Sir Henry Widdrington was ill-treating his wife and that Carey could do nothing whatsoever about it.

They dealt with the horses, drying them off as well as possible, picking mud out of their feet, feeding and watering them. Carey was not sure he could feel his own feet as he left his men at the barracks door and headed through the dark for the Queen Mary Tower. Upstairs in his chamber, somebody had left a watch-light burning for him and put out a clean shirt—probably Goodwife Biltock, with Barnabus in quod. For a while Carey simply stared at it, too stupid to think what to do next.

'Ye'll not be sleepin' in yer boots again,' nagged Dodd's voice from the door. He was standing there, stinking only slightly now, holding a trencher of bread and cheese and a jug of beer and looking embarrassed.

'Er…no, Sergeant,' said Carey, starting to undo his laces slowly.

'Ay,' said Dodd dubiously. 'Well, I brung ye some vittles, seeing ye dinna have the sense of a child that way.'

'Well, I…'

'Nobbut a fool sleeps in his boots if he doesnae have to,' continued Dodd in an aggressively sulky tone. 'And even a fool will eat occasionally.'

He put the food on the largest chest, came over and helped Carey take off his armour, shook it and hung it on the jackstand to drip. The feeling of lightness and freedom that came with the sudden removal from his body of about fifty pounds' weight of iron plates and leather padding, almost made Carey's head spin. With the dour expression that said he was a free man doing favours, Dodd helped Carey pull off his riding boots, always a two-man job if they fitted properly. Then he lit a couple of tapers off the watch-light, went to the bed and started to draw the still shut curtains aside.

'Och,' he said in a strangled tone of voice.

Carey was pulling off his smelly dank shirt streaked with brown from his wet jack. He went to look at what Dodd had found. Could it be worse than the corpse of Sweetmilk Graham which had welcomed him to Carlisle a couple of weeks ago?

It could. The yellow lymer bitch who had been his bedfellow earlier lifted her head and growled softly in her throat. She had pupped on the bed; there were three yellow naked ratlings squirming in the curve of her belly.

Carey looked at her and blinked. 'Oh God,' he sighed.

'Shall I have her off there?' asked Dodd, obviously working hard not to laugh.

Carey had to smile. It was funny, in a perverse sort of way.

'No. Leave her.'

He turned to put on his fresh shirt and then paused, looked again, having difficulty focusing his eyes. The bitch was whining softly, nosing at her tail end. Her flanks heaved, but nothing happened.

'There's something wrong here,' he said.

Dodd frowned and looked closer. 'Ay,' he said. 'She's havin' difficulty.'

He put out his hand to touch her and the bitch snapped at him warningly. Carey came close and tried as well, but she only sniffed at him and whined heartrendingly.

'There, there,' he muttered. 'It's all right, sweeting.'

Dodd brought a lit taper and put it on the watch-light shelf in the bedhead.

'Bring me another taper, an unlit one,' Carey said, kneeling down and peering at the bitch's rear end. That was another counterpane ruined, he thought absently—would Philadelphia have a replacement?

He could see something in her birth passage, but another heaving effort from the bitch moved it no further out. Dodd gave him the unlit taper and had a cautious look.

'It's stuck,' he said.

Carey nodded. He had seen what you did when that happened because he had spent a great deal of his boyhood in Berwick earning beatings for running away from his tutor to play with his father's hunting dogs in the kennels.

'Shell I fetch the kennelman?' Dodd asked.

Carey was using the tallow from the taper to grease his fingers. He yawned and shook his head to try and wake himself up a bit more.

'I'll have a try. She looks as if she's been straining for hours,' he said. 'Would you hold her head in case she snaps at me?'

Dodd did as he was asked. Carey lifted her tail and gently put his fingers in. The pup had a big head which was the reason for the trouble. Very carefully, he slid his fingers round the head, waited for the next straining heave from the bitch, and pulled. For a moment his fingers were being crushed and then the pup's nose came free and straight, and the little body shot out onto the bed. The bitch panted and sighed and licked Dodd's hand, then turned and started licking the puppy. It looked dead. Carey felt in its mouth, cleared out the bits of caul and the pup hiccupped and started to breathe. Its mother carried on licking it firmly while Carey had another feel in her birth passage.

'I think that was the last one,' he said, standing up and wiping his hands on his mucky shirt which he dropped in the rushes. 'Bring the taper out and shut the curtains for her; she can stay there and I'll have the truckle bed.'

Dodd had shut the curtains; now he went and brought the food to Carey.

'Eat,' he said.

'I'm not hungry.'

'Ay, well, I canna make ye,' said Dodd, putting the trencher on the chest again. 'Never mind. I'll see ye in the morning, sir, and we can talk to Andy Nixon. Good night.'

Dodd walked to the door looking mightily offended.

'Er…Dodd,' said Carey, ashamed of himself. 'Thank you.'

'Iphm.' Dodd nodded and clattered down the stairs.

Wondering what on earth had given Dodd the idea he needed cosseting like a baby, Carey put his clean shirt on, absent-mindedly drank some of the beer and munched down most of the bread and cheese. Barnabus's truckle bed was too short for him by several inches, and smelled pungently of Barnabus, but Carey finished undressing and climbed in anyway. Seconds later he was fast asleep.

weдnesдay 5th july 1592, дawn

When the light in his chamber began to change with dawn, Carey's eyes opened and he looked straight up at the ceiling beams, instead of the tester of a four-post bed. His legs were sticking unrestfully over the end of a musty straw mattress. For a moment he was confused, wondering if he was at Court or on progress, and then he remembered the dreamlike incident of the puppies. Although he could hear the shouts of the stable boys as they began work, the bedchamber was quiet. How peculiar to be the only person sleeping in it. He got up, scratching at a lot of new flea bites, yawned jaw-crackingly, finished the beer from last night and padded across the rushes in his bare feet to have a look between the bedcurtains at the bitch. She was fast asleep with her tumble of four puppies, the biggest one lying on his back with his paws in the air. As Carey watched he whined and twitched.

'You're mine,' Carey told him. 'As rent.'

'Eh, sir?' came a boy's voice from the door. It was Ian Ogle, the steward's eldest son, standing with a tray and looking alarmed.

'It's all right,' Carey said to the boy. 'Where's Simon Barnet?'

'He's coming, sir, only I was up before and he asked me.'

'Well, go and get him; I want him to help me dress.'

'Ay sir.'

Simon, when he arrived, had to be told what to do, which was irritating since he had watched his uncle attend Carey so many times before. It appeared he had paid no attention, and he fumbled maddeningly with the points at the back of Carey's green velvet doublet until Carey pushed him away with a growl and did them up himself. Neither the doublet nor the wide padded green brocade Venetians were quite fashionable, being a year and a half old, but as they hadn't been paid for yet, Carey felt obliged to wear them. When they were finished, Carey gave him a long list of things to do which included taking his shirt to the laundry and his leather fighting breeches to be brushed, finding sponges and cloths to dry and clean his jack and polish his helmet after he'd taken it to the armoury for a new chinstrap, and further bringing the kennelman in to inspect the bitch and her puppies and also making sure there was food and water for her.

Carey listened patiently while Simon falteringly repeated his list. 'Simon,' he said gently. 'You weren't paying attention. What would you do if I asked you to take a message for me? You'd forget it. You missed out cleaning my jack and morion, which is one of your jobs anyway.'

'Sorry, sir,' said Simon, still looking longingly at the rising sunlight outside.

'Go through it again.'

Screwing up his face with the effort, Simon managed to repeat it correctly.

'That's better. Off you go then.'

Carey went into the second room he used as his office and sat down. He had to write the report for Scrope about his actions against the Graham raid the day before. And that was before he even began to deal with the sudden muster asked for by King James of Scotland. The depressing prospect daunted him far more than a mere half-hundred armed Grahams. Considering the amount of paperwork generated by a simple muster, Carey's heart failed him at the thought of how much might be involved in a full Day of Truce. There was food and beer to be organised, although Philly and Ogle, Scrope's steward, did most of that, lodgings urgently needed for the more prominent and remote gentlemen, the Carlisle racecourse made ready for the purpose and a few races arranged as entertainment, horsefeed and troughs to be provided. Someone also had to sort out the keeping of order, which meant careful attention paid to the sequence in which surnames were mustered to make sure no two families at feud were too close to each other. He hoped there was no question of keeping the men there overnight; it beggared belief what could happen in the dark between all those long-experienced and accomplished reivers.

He picked up his pen, wondered self-pityingly how much longer Richard Bell would take to find him a suitable clerk to be his secretary, and began writing his report.

He was halfway into his second paragraph when someone lumbered into the bed chamber and sneezed fruitily. He looked up in irritation. Long George was peering behind Carey's bed curtains at the lymer bitch.

'What the devil do you want?' Carey snapped.

Long George leapt back guiltily and touched his forelock, wiped his streaming nose on his sleeve, then took his blue statute cap off his round head and plumped it back and forth in his hands.

'Well?' growled Carey who hated being interrupted when he had settled down to paperwork—simply because he longed for an excuse to stop.

'Er...see, sir,' said Long George. 'Only I heard ye arrested Andy Nixon yesterday for killing of Jemmy Atkinson.'

'Yes?'

'I thought I'd best tell ye what we were at on Sunday night, see,' explained Long George.

'And what was that?'

'Ah...well, we give Andy Nixon the hiding of his life that very night round about midnight.' Long George sneezed again, apologetically.

'We?'

'Ay, sir. Me, my brother Billy Little, Sergeant Ill-Willit Daniel Nixon and Mick the Crow Salkeld. Y'see, Jemmy Atkinson paid my brother and his mates to gi' him a beating and warn him away from Kate Atkinson, an' I spotted them and joined in.'

'Where was this?'

'In the alley by his lodgings, St. Alban's vennel; ye ken, the wynd that's a shortcut between Fisher street and Scotch street.'

'Did he know who paid for the beating?'

Long George nodded and sniffed vigorously. 'Ay, sir. Ill-Willit Daniel tellt him and he wis to stay away from Kate or he'd get worse.'

Carey put his pen down. 'Well, that certainly is interesting, Long George. When did Jemmy Atkinson pay you off?'

'Right after, sir, at the Red Bull.'

'Who else was there?'

'Naebody but us. Lowther looked in for a couple of minutes, but he went off again.'

'Lowther?'

'Ay, sir.'

'What did he want?'

Long George shrugged and snortled again. 'I dinna ken, sir.'

'Did he quarrel with Atkinson?'

'Nay, 'twas all smiles. He gave Mick the Crow a message.'

'Hm.'

'So ye see, sir, mightn't that have made Andy Nixon want to take revenge on Atkinson?'

'It might. Was that when he hurt his hand?'

'Ay, I think I trod on it, sir, unintentionally.'

'Of course.'

'I thought I'd tell ye sir, in case there was a reward.' Long George's watery pink eyes peered at him hopefully.

Carey sighed. 'Long George,' he asked. 'Do you realise you have just admitted to assault, battery and riot?'

Long George's face with its inadequate frill of beard looked shifty. 'Er…well, we were working for Mr Atkinson,' he said.

'It's still against the law to beat people up.'

This was a novel idea to Long George. 'Oh,' he said, and thought. 'I wouldna like to speak to it in a court of law, sir, if y'see what I…'

'Never mind. Thank you for coming, Long George. It's useful information.'

Long George nodded, glanced fascinated at the bitch and her puppies who were suckling enthusiastically, crammed his hat back over his ears and clattered down the stairs, sneezing as he went.

Carey stood and peered out of the slit window down into the yard. There was Long George greeting Bangtail and Archie-Give-

It-Them who were waiting for him. And yes, as expected, Bangtail was clearly settling a bet with Archie.

Shaking his head, Carey returned to the duties which he really hated and dipped his pen again.

By the time he had finished the report Simon Barnet had come back with the kennelman and two bowls for the bitch's food and water.

The kennelman's face was bright red with emotion. 'I wis looking for her all night,' he said, his broad hand on the lymer dog's head. 'How did ye come by her, sir?'

'She followed me up here and pupped while I was out on patrol. She can stay there for the moment until she's ready to move down to the kennels again. Had a bit of trouble with the last one but we sorted it out.'

'Ay,' said the kennelman gently rubbing the bitch's ears. 'Ye're a stupid woman, Buttercup, and no mistake.' He nodded confidingly to Carey. 'She allus pups in somewhere strange. Last time it were the bakery and the time afore that she were in the tackroom. And there's a beautiful big pupping kennel all ready strawed for her, but she's a liking for luxury, this old girl...'

They set out the bowls for her on the rushes and she drank long and deep before jumping onto the bed and flopping herself down by her squirming blind little pups again. They squeaked and latched on greedily.

'I'll tell my lord she's turned up,' the kennelman said. 'He wis right worried about her. She's a good bitch and her pups are fine hunters.'

'Do you think he'd give me the big one?' Carey asked.

'Why not, sir? I'll ask him.'

Carey picked up the report and decided he could do some more letters later. He also took up a purse fat with money from his winnings of the Sunday and decanted some coins into his belt-pouch. The rest he put back in his heavy locked chest.

'I'll leave her in your capable hands,' he said to the kennelman. 'You can draw the curtains when you've finished so she isn't disturbed.'

Carey took Simon Barnet with him to see Andy Nixon in the dungeons, by which time Dodd had finally woken and appeared, scratching and yawning and foul-tempered for some reason. It passed Carey's understanding how anyone could oversleep past dawn unless they were ill or injured. They all went under the Keep steps and through the ironbound door.

Carey lifted Simon Barnet up to look through the Judas hole in the dungeon door. The boy stared gravely for a while until his eyes had adjusted to the small light from the lantern in his hands and nodded.

'Ay.'

'Is that the man that wanted my glove?' Carey asked, putting him down again.

'Ay, it's him, sir.'

'When? What time of day did he come to you?'

'Afternoon, sir, on Monday.'

'You're sure? I may want you to testify and swear on the Bible that it's him. Can you do that?'

'Ay. My word on it,' said Simon with dignity.

They went to check on Barnabus in the lower of the two gatehouse cells, looking through the barred window.

'At least Scrope had him moved,' Carey muttered.

'Is that you, sir?' came Barnabus's forlorn voice from inside. The effects of Lowther's persuasions the day before had flowered to a glorious purple riot across much of Barnabus's ugly little ferret face. The rest of it was worryingly sickly. Carey frowned.

'I don't like the look of you, Barnabus. Are you all right?'

'Don't feel very well, to tell you the truth, sir.'

Carey turned to Simon Barnet. 'Go and fetch my Lady Scrope and some food for your uncle,' he said. When the boy had gone, he called on William Barker the Gaoler on the other side of the Gatehouse. Carpenters refitting the place for the Scropes passed by him on the stairs with their bags of tools. Barker took him across unwillingly and let him into Barnabus's cell.

It smelled bad, and the floor was slimy although Barnabus had been careful to do his business as near to the drain as he could get. Carey frowned.

'Who chained you?' he demanded.

Barnabus looked dolefully at the chain from his ankles to the wall.

'Sir Richard Lowther.'

'I might have guessed. When did he do it?'

'Yesterday, after they moved me from the 'ole.'

Just after I had that argument with him, Carey thought, biting down hard on his anger; damn him. Barnabus was sitting on the wooden bench bolted to the wall which was the only other furniture of the cell, with his arms wrapped around his body.

'I'm working on getting you out but you must tell me everything you can. For a start, can you think of any reason why Andy Nixon might hate you enough to try and get you hanged for a murder he did?'

'I dunno, sir. Never met him.'

'All right, what about Sunday night.'

'Sunday night, sir?'

'Yes. Where were you at midnight on Sunday when you should have been lighting me home?'

'Oh well...er...' Barnabus looked shifty.

'How did you manage to get so stinking drunk you passed out by the gate until morning?'

'I...er...'

'You didn't rob someone, did you?'

Barnabus coughed and looked very shifty. Carey stared at him until he shrugged. 'In a manner of speaking, sir.'

'All right, what happened?'

'Well, I was coming back to you when I tripped on a...well, somebody who'd bin in a fight and got the worst of it, I'd say.'

'Where?'

'Down the alley between Scotch street and Fisher street.'

'And so you robbed him?'

'No, sir. First I helped him in his door, then I robbed him.'

Carey put his hands to his head. 'Barnabus, I have *told* you about footpadding...'

'I didn't footpad 'im, sir; 'e was already done over. I just...'

'You just bloody robbed a man who was lying there helpless. For God's sake, Barnabus, where's your Christian charity?'

'I was drunk, sir. It seemed like a good idea...'

'How much did you get?'

'Half a crown sir, and some pennies.'

'Well, you could hang for that half a crown, you silly bugger. You robbed Andy Nixon and I would imagine that's the reason why he went to the trouble of incriminating you.'

'Yes sir.'

'Which has indirectly caused me an immense amount of aggravation.'

'Yes, sir. I'm sorry, sir.'

'You damn well deserve to be in here, and that's the truth.'

Barnabus looked about him and evidently found this a bit hard, but he decided to say nothing, which was wise of him, Dodd thought, considering Carey's expression of disgust. At that moment there was a complicated rattle of keys and the gaoler let Lady Scrope into the cell. She looked around, sniffed and shouted over her shoulder. 'Mr Barker, bring a bucket and spade in here.'

Dodd helpfully moved out of the cell so there was room for Barker who came in eventually with a bucket and spade borrowed from the stables.

'Pick that up and take it out of here,' said Lady Scrope, pointing imperiously at the turds by the drain.

'That, my lady?' said the youth unhappily.

'Yes, that. It's causing bad airs. Quickest way to get gaol fever in a place, which you could catch as well, William Barker, and die of, what's more. So clean it up.'

'Me, my lady?'

Lady Scrope put her basket down on the wooden bench next to Barnabus and her hands on the bumroll padding out her hips.

'I'm not going to do it and nor is my brother. Barnabus can't because he's been chained. So that leaves you or Sergeant Dodd to fight it out between you, and personally, I'm backing Dodd.'

Dodd put his head round the door and fixed Barker with a glare that settled the matter. Mumbling that it wasnae his job and an insult forbye, Barker used the spade and bucket and slumped out of the door.

'I'll stand guard while you put that on the midden heap,' said Dodd, wondering briefly if this were some complex way of breaking Barnabus out of jail. No, why be so elaborate about it? If he was going to defy all of Scrope's authority and the law of the land into the bargain, the Deputy Warden could simply unlock the doors.

Philadelphia turned to Barnabus and briskly examined his eyes, mouth and ears, felt his forehead and wrist and demanded that he undo his doublet buttons and lift his shirt so she could inspect the bruises on his body.

Carey whistled with sympathy and muttered something about bringing a suit for assault against Lowther on Barnabus's behalf.

'Don't be ridiculous, Robin,' said Philadelphia tartly. 'It was perfectly normal interrogation of a murder suspect. Besides, Lowther owns or can terrorise almost any jury you could put together in these parts; it's one of our main problems with him.'

That made Carey look depressed and thoughtful for a moment. His sister took the cloth off her basket and brought out a couple of black leather bottles. Barnabus rolled his eyes as she poured two horn cupfuls of what looked like bogwater.

'Don't look so worried, Barnabus,' Philadelphia added. 'My lord Warden has already refused Lowther permission to put you to the question so nothing else is going to happen to you.' Barnabus swallowed stickily. 'Now what else is wrong with you?' she demanded, putting her hand on his forehead again. 'You're running a fever. Have you got a headache?'

'No, my lady,' croaked Barnabus. 'I'm sore, but...'

'Stick your tongue out.'

Barnabus did and Philadelphia squinted at it critically. 'Hm,' she said. 'Have you been vomiting or purging, or passing blood in your water?'

Barnabus hesitated and looked at Carey.

'Not blood, my lady.'

Philadelphia frowned. 'What then?'

'Er...nothing.'

'Barnabus,' growled Carey. 'If you've...'

'Shut up, please, Robin,' said Philadelphia to her brother. 'Now please don't play me for a fool, Barnabus. You're not well and you have to tell me everything that ails you. I'm worried you might be coming down with a gaol fever.'

Remembering the gaol fever he had caught on board ship after he had gone to fight the Armada in 1588, which had almost killed him, Carey looked carefully at Barnabus again, then shook his head.

'No. You see, Philly, he's been in gaol before.'

'Born there,' said Barnabus with some satisfaction. 'It can't be gaol fever, my lady. I've had both kinds and it's like the smallpox; you don't get it twice.'

'Well then, what's the matter with your water?'

'Er...' Barnabus looked at the ground. 'I'm pissing green, my lady. And...er...it hurts.'

There was a penetrating silence. 'I expect it's because of Lowther...' Carey began.

'Unless Lowther's a worse man than I take him for, that's not Lowther. That's the clap.'

Neither Carey nor Barnabus knew where to look, while Dodd by the door listened in fascination.

'It's that bawdy house, isn't it? Madam Hetherington's? The one Scrope sneaks off to occasionally?'

Both Barnabus and Carey made an extraordinary strangulated noise.

'And I suppose you've got a dose too, have you, Robin?' demanded Philadelphia in withering tones.

'No, I haven't,' said Carey with great emphasis. 'For God's sake, Philly...'

'Don't swear. Well, Barnabus, there is nothing whatever anybody can do for the clap, no matter what they say, except let nature take its course. You should drink as much mild beer as you can and eat plenty of garlic to clean your blood. You'll have to give him lighter duties until he's better, Robin. Anyway, he should rest for today and I think his nose may need resetting eventually. Drink this.'

Barnabus meekly drank down one cup of bogwater and looked relieved when the other cup turned out to be a lotion to put on his nose and face. Carey recognised the smell as the same stuff Philadelphia had been painting him with all the previous week. As far as he could tell it had done him no harm.

Baker came back from the midden and at Philadelphia's bidding, put the bucket inside the cell where Barnabus could reach it and use it. Carey snapped his fingers for the bunch of keys he carried, took it and unlocked the chains around Barnabus's ankles.

'Thank you, sir,' said Barnabus, rubbing his legs and stretching. 'I hate to scour the cramp-rings.'

'Nobody chains my servant,' said Carey ominously, 'except me. So watch it, Barnabus.'

They came out, Carey still carefully not meeting Philadelphia's eyes. Dodd was as straight faced as he knew how, though he thought that Barnabus was getting undeserved soft treatment.

'Have you fed the other two prisoners, Mr Barker?' he asked.

'Oh ay, sir. They got garrison food, same as Barnabus.'

Poor bastards, thought Dodd. When Janet turns up I'll send her in with some proper vittles.

'Did ye want to talk to 'em, sir?' he asked.

Carey thought about it. 'No, I don't think so, Sergeant,' he said. 'I need more information.'

And where was he proposing to get it if he didn't even want to talk to his prisoners, Dodd wondered sourly, but didn't ask. Philadelphia remained quiet as they walked out of the dungeons and into the silky morning sunlight, all washed clean by the rainstorms of the previous day. She looked about and sighed.

'You called me from checking over the flax harvest, Robin,' she said. 'So I'm going back to it.'

Carey nodded, with the expression of a man who wants to say something comforting but doesn't quite know how. He remembered the report he had written for Scrope and gave it to Philadelphia to pass on to her husband. She tossed her head, took it and marched off across the yard, trying to pull her apron straight as she went. Dodd felt he was not called upon to comment and so he followed Carey silently as he strode down to the Keep gate and past Bessie's into Carlisle town.

weðnesðay 5th july 1592, morning

Dodd was very shocked when he realised Carey was about to go straight into the house with red lattices and the sign of the Rainbow over the door down an alley off Scotch street.

'Sir,' he protested. 'I dinna...'

'You've got a mucky mind, Sergeant,' said Carey. 'I'm only making sure Barnabus was telling the truth about where he was.'

'Oh.'

From the way Madam Hetherington greeted the Deputy Warden with a curtsey and a kiss, it was obvious he had been there before, which further shocked Dodd's sense of propriety. It wasn't that he didn't know the bawdy house—he'd been there a couple of times himself, when drunk, and prayed Janet would never find out about it—only he felt it was a bad thing for an officer of the Crown to be seen entering the place in daylight.

Carey didn't seem to care; no doubt Londoners, courtiers and lunatics had different standards in these things.

'No, mistress,' said Carey courteously to the lady's enquiry. 'I want to talk to you about my servant Barnabus Cooke.'

They were led into her office and wine was brought for both of them. Dodd sipped his cautiously and then found to his surprise that it tasted quite good.

Carey smacked his lips as he put the goblet down.

'I now know who has managed to find the only decent wine in Carlisle.'

Madam Hetherington had sat down on a stool beside a table clear of anything except some embroidery and she smiled modestly.

'I have a special arrangement with my cousin, sir,' she said.

'Hm. You're aware of Barnabus Cooke's arrest.'

'Of course, sir.'

'Can you tell me where he was on Monday night?'

Madam Hetherington took her embroidery and began stitching like any lady of a house. Dodd stared about at her little solar; it was hung with painted cloths and floored with rushmats. When he looked closer at the painted cloths, he stretched his eyes: naked women abounded, were pinkly profuse in all directions. There was a naked woman with a lascivious-looking swan on her lap, and another naked woman riding a bull and a third who seemed to be very happy to receive a lot of gold coins tumbling down a sunbeam. Surely that would hurt, Dodd thought incoherently, all those pennies hitting your bare skin. He was mesmerised by the round pearly shapes and little red touches here and there on lips and nipples...In comparison with Janet's these were rounder and plumper and...

'What do you think, Dodd?' Carey asked.

'Ah,' said Dodd, caught out and he knew it. Carey seemed amused.

'I was saying that Barnabus was certainly here on Monday night after Bessie shut her doors,' repeated Madam Hetherington kindly. 'He left early on Tuesday morning in time to go in at the gate to attend Sir Robert.'

'Oh,' said Dodd.

'Madam Hetherington does not think one of her girls will be believed by a jury either.'

'Er...No, that's right,' Dodd said desperately, staring at Madam Hetherington's embroidery hoop. 'They wouldna. They'd say she was nae fit person to be in front of them and could be bribed and they couldnae place any confidence in her word.'

Madam Hetherington and Carey nodded.

'In fact,' said Madam Hetherington, stitching away at a shape that looked suspiciously like a buttock, 'Barnabus spends much of his free time here. He was here on Sunday night as well, twice.'

'Oh?' said Carey neutrally.

'Yes, he left at a reasonable time and not too drunk and then he returned a little while later with more money to spend, which he spent.'

'Yes,' said Carey. 'I know how that happened. Another thing I would like to know is how someone also managed to get hold of one of Barnabus's knives.'

Madam Hetherington was threading a needle and she said nothing.

'Mr Pennycook owns the freehold of this house, doesn't he?' pressed Carey.

'I'm sure I have no idea what you're talking about, sir,' said Madam Hetherington coldly. 'Will you or your henchman be wishing to take your pleasure with one of the girls now, sir?'

Carey rose to leave. 'I must be on my way, Madam Hetherington,' he said. 'Oh and by the way, Barnabus has the clap.'

She frowned and bit off a piece of thread. 'Not from my house,' she said.

'No?' asked Carey. 'Good day to you, Madam.'

She rose to see them to the door, curtseyed and gave no farewell kiss.

Dodd was quite glad to get out of the place with no more upsetting sight than one of the girls in her petticoat and bodice hurrying through with a bucket of water. He hoped no one had seen them. Janet was likely to be in town soon.

'Right,' said Carey to himself and set off again down Scotch street with that long bouncy stride of his.

Andy Nixon's landlady was a Goodwife Crawe, widowed a few years back in a raid, who lived precariously by spinning and letting out her loft. Her two tousle-headed young boys were at the football in the alley when Carey and Dodd arrived.

It was difficult to talk to Goody Crawe because she would not stay still, but kept turning the great wheel of her new-fangled spinning machine and walking backwards to twist the thread, then forwards again to wind it on the spindle, back and forth, back and forth like a child's toy. Spindles hung all about her small living room; Dodd tripped over one of the half-dozen baskets of carded wool lambstails on the floor and there was a pile of new sheep's fleece lying by the ladder to the loft, ready to be picked and carded.

'Tell me what Andy Nixon did on Monday, Goodwife Crawe,' said Carey formally.

'Well,' she said unhappily, 'I dinnae want to get him in any more trouble because he's a good lodger and a nice lad and pays his rent every other Monday and it's a pleasant thing to have a grown man about the house, for the boys, ye ken.'

'Only tell me the truth, Goodwife; that will help him best of all.'

'Hmf. Y'see, I heard he was accused of cutting Mr Atkinson's throat and I dinna see him doing it. In a fight, perhaps; he's a bonny fighter is Andy...'

'I know,' muttered Carey.

'...and sometimes doesnae ken his ain strength, but from behind with a knife—nay, he's not the type.'

'How about his...friendship with Mrs Atkinson?'

'Ay,' said Goodwife Crawe heavily. 'That was it, y'see. I couldnae blame them for it, but the Lord knows it's a sin and a scandal.'

'What happened on Sunday night, Goodwife?'

She sighed as she stepped backwards nimbly over the rushes, her fingers flying as she smoothed the wool into a taut thin thread.

'Some men jumped him in the alley as he came home,' she said. 'Poor lad, he was in a terrible state. He couldnae get up the ladder and his hand was all puffed up. And some dirty thieving bastard had cut his purse as well, which Andy took very hard because it had his rent in it and he knows well how I fare and that I need the money. He knew who it was too, sir, for he said he heard the man's voice and there was nobbut one voice like that in Carlisle.'

Carey nodded. 'Yes,' he said simply. 'It was my servant, Barnabus.' He felt in his belt pouch and brought out some money. 'Here's your rent, Goodwife Crawe,' he said. 'I'm sorry about it. I've told him often enough about footpadding, but some habits die hard.'

Don't give it to her yet, ye soft get, thought Dodd in despair, wait until she's told ye what she knows. Do ye not know anything?

Goody Crawe took the half crown and put it in her bodice looking thunderstruck, as well she might.

'Ay well,' she said. 'Once a reiver, allus a reiver, I say.'

'When did you find Nixon then, Goody?'

'Och, a while before dawn when I came down to milk the goat. He slept down here on the fleeces when he couldnae climb the steps in the night. I gave him milk to gi' him strength and put some cold water on his face and give him a sling for his arm, though he said it annoyed him. Then off he went when the sun was up and that's the last I saw of him that day, for he didnae come back until it was well dark and I was in bed, but I heard him at the door and going up the ladder.'

'That was Monday night.'

'Ay sir. A little before midnight, I hadnae heard the bell yet. And then yesterday, he was up as usual and looking a bit better though he hadnae much stomach to his meat for breakfast, and then he was off to see Mr Pennycook, the man he works for. And then he come home in the afternoon and he was in a terrible state o' fear, and he didnae tell me what it was but I think he heard ye'd gone to arrest Mrs Atkinson, and he packed his bags and promised me the back rent as soon as he could get it, and then he was off out the door as fast as he could go. And that's the last I saw of him, sir, as ye know, for I told ye yesterday.'

Carey smiled at her. 'Thank you, Goodwife. That's very clear.'

'Ah've done him nae good, have I sir?' She had actually stopped her toing and froing to look at Carey.

Ye've about hanged him, woman, Dodd thought but didn't say. Instead he handed her a fresh basket of lambstails for spinning and she gave him a distracted smile of thanks.

'We'll see what happens,' said Carey diplomatically. 'Nothing is certain yet.'

Goodwife Crawe screwed her face up anxiously. 'It'll be a sad thing for the boys if he hangs, for they like him.'

'If he did the murder, Goodwife, it's only right he should hang for it,' said Carey pompously.

She sniffed and started the wheel turning again. 'Ay, well,' she said. 'He's nobbut one man. He's no' rich nor a gentleman nor a gentleman's servant and his father's not strong enough to save him either, so nae doubt he'll hang whether he did it or no'. Poor lad.'

Carey looked annoyed. Why was he so touchy, Dodd wondered. Goodwife Crawe had only stated the obvious.

'I give you my word, Goodwife, if he isn't guilty I'll try and make sure he doesn't hang.'

'Hmf. But ye willna favour him over your ain servant, now will ye, sir?'

'I might,' Carey's voice was cold. He went to the door and opened it. Goodwife Crawe curtseyed as she walked with her spinning. 'Thank you for your help, Goodwife.'

Carey was looking thoughtful as they left the alley. He stopped in the middle of the way and Dodd nearly bumped into him.'

'You still there, Dodd?'

'Ay,' said Dodd.

'Why are you following me around?'

'It's no' fitting for the Deputy Warden to be wandering around Carlisle town wi'out any man of his ain to back him,' said Dodd, highly offended at this example of southern ignorance. 'And dangerous, what's more. D'ye think the Grahams willna kill ye if they have the chance?'

Carey had the grace to look embarrassed. 'To be honest, I hadn't thought I was in danger in Carlisle.'

'Ay, well,' said Dodd. 'Would ye go out unattended in London?'

'I might. If I didn't see any need to make a fuss.'

'Ye're not the Deputy Warden in London. Ye're but one o' thousands of rich courtiers milling about the place, nae doubt.'

'And you weren't trotting after me like a calf with his mother yesterday either.'

'Sir,' said Dodd patiently. 'The way ye flourish around upsetting folk, has it never crossed your mind that somebody might put a price on ye? Wattie Graham for sure; if he didnae after Netherby, he will now, and Sir Richard Lowther as well, I shouldn't wonder.'

'Good Lord,' said Carey, evidently rather taken with the idea. 'Do you really think they have? How much do you suppose it's for?'

The man was impossible. Dodd grunted and decided he would hold his tongue in future, no matter how charmingly Carey asked his opinion. And there was, according to Will the Tod, a strong rumour that somebody was offering ten pounds in cash for Carey's head.

Their next visit, Dodd was relieved to see, was to Bessie's alehouse because Dodd for one was parched from all the wool fluff filling the air of Goodwife Crawe's house. Carey asked Nancy if he could speak to Bessie and she came out from her brewing shed with smoke smuts on her face, wiping her hands on her apron, and curtseyed to him. In silence, Carey counted out the ten shillings and seven pence he had run up as his tab while Bessie watched him with an odd expression of mingled satisfaction and alarm on her broad red face. He turned to leave, which Dodd thought was a pity and Bessie called out to him. 'Will ye not take a quart before ye go, sir?

Carey turned and looked at her with his eyebrows raised.

'I don't usually go back to a place where I'm refused credit,' he said to Dodd's horror. Where else did the silly fool think he was going to get beer as good as Bessie's?

Bessie clearly wasn't thinking straight. She beamed at him as friendly as she knew how. 'Och no,' she said. 'That was all a mistake and a lot of gossip I was fool enough to believe. Sit down sir, and take a drink...on the...on the...' she nearly choked saying it, 'on the house, sir. A quart of my best double-double.'

'What will you have, Dodd?' Carey asked him.

'The same.' Dodd's mouth was watering.

'Two quarts of double-double on the house, Nancy,' cried Bessie with painful gaiety as she bustled back into the yard and Nancy served them in a booth.

'Cheers,' said Carey with a sly grin and lifted his tankard. Unwillingly Dodd found himself tempted to smile back so he drank quickly to hide it.

Carey was the first to break the companionable silence. 'It's all sounding very black for Andy Nixon,' he said.

'Ay sir,' said Dodd regretfully. Lord, how his wife would give him trouble for being part of the process that led to Andy Nixon on the end of a rope. Not to mention Kate Atkinson at the stake. Carey was drawing pictures again with beer spillage on the wooden table between them. The alehouse was almost empty at that time of the morning, but would be full by noon, full and bursting with all the men come in from the haymaking with their money burning holes in their purses.

'This is how I see it,' Carey went on more to himself than to Dodd. 'On Sunday night Long George, Sergeant Ill-Willit Daniel Nixon and two others of Lowther's troop waylay the unfortunate Andy Nixon in the alley and beat him up. They tell him to stay away from Atkinson's wife, because Atkinson paid for it.'

'How d'ye ken that, sir?'

'Long George told me.'

'Ah.' Long George was always a fool, Dodd thought; why did nobody know how to keep his mouth shut? And he had never liked Ill-Willit Daniel.

'Andy Nixon is helped into his doorway by my appalling servant, Barnabus Cooke, who completes Andy's happy evening by cutting his purse.'

'Ay.'

'Next morning, Andy Nixon is full of wrath and vengeance. He comes up with a plan for landing Barnabus in trouble and getting his own back on Atkinson. Probably he asks his master Pennycook for help, and Pennycook agrees to loan him a handcart and get hold of one of Barnabus's knives. Nixon himself comes up to the Keep to get one of my gloves—perhaps at Pennycook's suggestion, who has reason not to like me.'

'Why's that, sir?'

'Oh, I'm interfering with the smooth corrupting of the victualling contracts for Carlisle. He was very upset.'

'Oh.'

'Andy Nixon with Kate Atkinson's help then cuts Jemmy Atkinson's throat in his bedroom; they bundle the body onto the handcart after dark and take it to Frank's vennel, where they dump it along with Barnabus's knife and my glove, and there you are.'

Dodd sipped some more of his beer and thought for a while.

'Hm,' he said.

'Is that all? Hm? I think that's what happened, don't you?'

'Ay, perhaps.'

'Why don't you agree?'

'I didna say I dinnae agree.'

'You don't look as if you do.'

It occurred to Dodd that perhaps one of the things you learnt at Court was bald-headed persistence. Certainly Carey had that.

He gave up trying to keep his counsel. After all, the Deputy kept saying he wanted to know Dodd's opinion.

'Ay well, sir, it's in the character. He's no' a clever courtier like yourself, sir, Andy isnae. He's a fine wrestler and a bonny fighter…'

'So everybody keeps telling me.'

'But he's no' a clever man. If he was angered enough to kill Jemmy Atkinson then he wisnae cool enough to think out all yon about gloves and knives.'

'Perhaps Pennycook helped him.'

'Ay. Perhaps. Will ye ask him yet?'

'No, I want to find out what was going on at the Atkinsons' place.'

And the Deputy Warden swallowed down his beer at a sinful pace seeing how good it was and that it was on the house, came to his feet again. 'Come on Dodd, unless you want to sit there supping.'

Sighing deeply Dodd finished his quart and followed Carey on his self-imposed mission to prevent the Deputy getting a knife in the ribs before he had a chance to do for Lowther.

They went straight to Maggie Mulcaster's house, across the road from the shut-up Atkinsons' place, and found Kate's little girl Mary sitting by the door very slowly shelling peas. She had her tongue stuck out and she held her breath every time she pressed open a peapod which made her gasp occasionally when she forgot to breathe again.

Mary looked up at Carey and immediately flinched back. Her face crumpled up and she started to cry. The bowl slipped off her knees and Dodd bent down just in time to catch it from going into the mud.

Dodd squatted in front of her and put the bowl down on the doorstep.

'Mary, Mary,' he said gently, 'D'ye know me?'

She nodded, very big-eyed. 'You're Mrs Dodd's bad-tempered husband.'

Carey who had looked glum at finding the little maid frightened of him, grinned at this, though Dodd failed to see what was funny.

'I'm her husband, ay,' he said. 'Now, Mary, is Mrs Mulcaster in?'

She nodded and then shook her head. 'She's gone to fetch in Clover. She said it wis soft to leave her in our garden since there's nobody there and she's need of the milk as well for the extra pack of weans the Deputy put to her, the southern bugger, and what was he thinkin' of arresting Kate and her a poor widow and us poor orphans. And I'm shelling peas,' she finished with a sunny smile.

It faded and she shrank back again because the Deputy Warden had sat himself down on the step beside her. He took off his hat, put it beside him and scratched vigorously at his head. There wasn't room for Dodd so he leaned against the wall.

'Do you mind if I sit here and wait for her?' said Carey politely to the small girl. She shook her head. She was staring at him wide-eyed. What was the mad Courtier playing at now? For a few moments there was a silence until curiosity got the better of Mary's fear.

'Is it true you know the Queen, sir?' she asked.

'Yes,' said Carey simply. 'She's my aunt.'

Mary's mouth opened, revealing a gap where she had lost one of her teeth.

'What does she look like?'

Carey took a penny out of his belt-pouch, tossed it up and showed her the head.

'She looks like that only her skin is pink and white and her hair is red.'

'Does she really have a hundred smocks and kirtles and petticoats?'

'More like a thousand.'

Mary's mouth opened wider. 'Why?'

'People give them to her because they know she likes to look pretty.'

'What colours are they?'

'Most of them are black and white with some different coloured trimming, but some of them are cloth of gold or cloth of silver and a lot of them have pearls sewn on them loose enough to drop off when she walks.'

'Why?'

'So people will pick them up and keep them and remember her by them.'

'Will she come here?'

'It's very unlikely. She doesn't travel so much now she's…er…a little older.'

Dodd had learnt enough about the Queen from Carey by now to know that mentioning her age was skimming dangerously close to treason as far as Her Majesty was concerned.

'Is she very old?'

'She was already a grown woman and Queen when I was born. But she's still beautiful,' said Carey diplomatically.

'Will she die soon?'

'It isn't polite to talk about it.'

'How many gowns has she got?'

'A couple of hundred, most of them made of velvet.'

'Like your doublet?'

'Yes.'

'I like your clothes. They're pretty. Do you have lots of pretty clothes like the Queen?'

'Not nearly as many,' said Carey straightfaced. 'And not a tenth as pretty.'

'Why are your hose so fat?'

'Because it's fashionable.'

'Does it no' make it hard to walk?'

Carey grinned. 'A bit. But you get used to it.'

'Do you like pretty clothes?'

'Yes, very much.'

Now there's the truth, thought Dodd.

'*I* have a yellow kirtle with rose velvet trimmings,' said Mary proudly. '*And* a going-to-church petticoat with a false-front like your hose.'

'What, made of brocade?'

'Yes, only it's purple. Mrs Dodd gave the bits to me mam when she made hers. It's very beautiful.'

'It sounds it. You're a lucky girl.'

For God's sake, Dodd thought to himself, what is the Courtier on about, prattling over clothes with a child?

'And I am learning to sew. I made a purse for money.'

'Excellent.'

'Will ye give me the penny to remember the Queen by to put in my new purse?' asked the dimpled child artlessly.

Carey made a small choking sound which he turned into a cough and then smiled.

'I'll give you two pennies if you can show me you have a good memory.'

Eh? thought Dodd.

'I have a very good memory,' said Mary. 'Me mam says so. She says she canna speak her mind without I'll repeat it after.' Her face clouded over momentarily as she remembered how the Deputy had come and taken her mam away.

'I thought so. But I bet you can't remember what happened on Monday.'

What? Dodd stood up straight with outrage. This was going too far, questioning a little girl about her mother's crime. He took breath to speak and found himself on the receiving end of a very blue glare from Carey. He scowled back but held his peace.

'That was the day before me dad died?' said Mary anxiously.

'Yes,' said Carey simply. 'And I'm sorry for your dad dying.'

Mary blinked at him for a moment. 'Why? Ye didnae like him, ye sacked him.'

'Er...yes.'

'I didna like him neither,' Mary pronounced. 'Is he no' in heaven now?'

'I...expect so,' said Carey cautiously, who doubted it.

'Well, then, it's no' sad, is it? Because we dinna have to be sae quiet when he's about wi' a sore head and there's no sore heads in heaven. That's happy, is that.' Her face clouded and threatened rain. 'It's me mam I'm sad for,' she whispered.

'Do you think you can remember such a long time ago as the day before yesterday?' Carey prompted hurriedly.

Mary paused, thought for a moment. 'I can so,' she said complacently. 'Will ye gi' me the pennies now?'

'No. Prove it to me. What happened on Monday? Start with when you got up.'

She took a deep breath, frowned, closed her eyes and began. She had come downstairs when her mother called with her kirtle and petticoat already on, but her mother had to do up her laces because she couldn't do bows yet. Did the Deputy Warden think bows were pretty? He did; Her Majesty had a kirtle all covered over with them made in blue satin. What happened next? Well, the boys came down in a hurry and ran off to school with the reverend and she ate her porridge and Julia came in late and she went hurrying up the stairs to find a ribbon she lost and then she came down again and her mother told her to start making the butter before the day got too hot and where had she been and Julia said nowhere and her mother was kneading bread and she said oh ay, then ye'd best be at the butter. So Julia said humph and went to the dairy for the yesterday's cream to pour it in the churn and her mam said…

'What colour was Julia's ribbon?' asked Carey inanely.

'Oh,' said Mary, frowning. 'I dinna remember.'

'Never mind. What happened after you ate your porridge?'

Mary had got out her sewing and started making some stitches and her mam had promised to show her a new one when she came down from taking her dad's porridge and beer up to him and she went up with a full tray.

Mary paused here and frowned. 'She was up a long time,' she said. 'And she came down and she'd forgot all about my sewing and wouldnae teach me the stitch but she sent me with a Message to fetch Andy Nixon.'

Carey nodded. 'What was she wearing?'

'Och, what she allus wears, her blue kirtle and petticoat, with the black bodice, nothing fine.'

'What about her apron.'

'Ay, she allus has her apron.'

'Was it…was there anything different about her when she came down the stairs?'

Mary frowned again and shook her head. 'Nay, only her voice was soft, like a whisper.'

Off went Mary in her memory to fetch Mr Nixon, with a long digression on Susan Talyer and how fine she thought herself because she had black velvet trim on her everyday kirtle, found him in the street with his arm in a sling and brought him back and he almost forgot to give her a penny, but then he did, and he went up the stairs to see her dad.

'What did he say about your dad?'

'Och,' said Mary, frowning again. 'He said he didnae want to see him at all and me mam said it didna matter, he'd see anyway and up he went and I had the buttermilk from Julia in the kitchen while she washed the butter and she asked what was happening and I said I didnae ken. I like Mr Nixon,' she added.

'And then what happened?'

Andy Nixon had come running down the stairs and out the door.

'Ahah,' said Carey grimly. 'What did he look like? Was he dirty?'

Mary gave him a sidelong look of pity. 'A bit. He was in his working clothes, but he doesnae labour, he's a rent collector.'

'Was there anything on them? Like mud or…er…blood?'

Mary shook her head.

'Did you hear anything, a shout or a call?'

'Nay, they was talking quietly.'

'Can you remember seeing blood anywhere around?'

'Oh ay,' said Mary seriously. 'There was blood all over the sheets to me mam's bed, for she said she'd lost a wean in the night, and she was in a state about washing them before it could set worse.'

Carey frowned at this. 'Was the blood dry?'

'Ay, mostly.'

'When did she strip the bed?'

'While I wis running for Mr Nixon, see, she had them in the basket by the door when I come back with him. It took all day to wash them sheets, ye should have seen them, all stiff they were…' The ghoulish child sighed at the thought. 'Me mam gave me a penny for grating the soap for it.'

'And then what happened?'

The day was overwhelmed with sheet and blanket washing and Mary was sent out to play with Susan Talyer which she didn't want to do but went because her mother gave her another penny and they skipped and played at Queens and princesses and then Susan Talyer wanted to be the mam and have Mary as the child and Mary wanted to be the mam and when Susan Talyer pinched her she only tapped her a very little with her hand, hardly at all, and accidentally pulled a little of her hair and is wisnae fair…

'When did you go to bed?'

She had eaten her bread and milk with the boys when they came back from school and then they had all gone up to bed though it was still light and they had seen Andy Nixon coming out the back wynd from Clover's byre with a handcart with a whole lot of hay on it. And their mam had come in and told them a long story about Tam Lin and how the Queen of the Elves had taken him and Janet and gone to fetch him back—not Janet Dodd, another Janet—

and how he changed into all different things by magic...Did the Deputy Warden know the Queen of the Elves too?

'No,' said Carey thoughtfully. 'I've not met that Queen at all. Perhaps I will one day.'

'Ye mustnae eat nothing they give ye in Elfland,' said Mary seriously. 'If ye do ye'll be bound to serve for seven years and when ye come back all your kin will be dead and gone for they'll be seven hundred years here.'

'That's good advice,' said Carey.

'Can I have my pennies now?' said Mary and Carey handed them over. 'I've got five pennies to my dowry,' she said happily.

'Mary Atkinson, what are you doing there?' demanded the voice of Maggie Mulcaster. She was holding a very obstinate-looking cow by a halter and breathing hard. Carey unfolded himself to stand up, put his hat back on.

'We were waiting for you, Mrs Mulcaster,' he said mildly. 'I was telling Mary about the Queen's gowns.'

Maggie Mulcaster snorted and gave a mighty tug at the cow's halter.

'Give me five minutes and I'll have this thrawn beast into our yard. You get on wi' those peas, Mary; we're eating them tonight.'

'Ay, Aunt Maggie.'

'Get *on* wi' ye, Clover! *Will* ye get on...'

'Er...Sergeant,' said Carey with a meaningful look at the cow. Dodd sighed, slapped the beast's bony hindquarters and helped Maggie Mulcaster drive her round by the wynd and shut her up in their own small byre for the night. There was just room for Clover and Maggie Mulcaster's cow to stand in there.

'I dinna like to leave kine on their own at all. You never know what might happen to them,' she confided in him. 'This one's upset. Kate's the only one can do anything with her.' Her eyes narrowed as she remembered the last time she had seen him. 'Well?' she demanded. 'Have ye come to arrest me as well, Sergeant?'

'Nay, Mrs Mulcaster,' he said hurriedly. 'It's all some notion of the Deputy Warden's, none o' mine.'

'Hmf.'

Very pointedly, Maggie Mulcaster did not invite them over the threshold, but stood stalwart in her doorway with her arms folded, and little Mary shaded by her skirts, while Carey asked her what she remembered of the Monday. There wasn't much, a day like any other, in fact. It was the next day that stuck in her memory, she said heavily, what with Mr Atkinson found dead in Frank's vennel in the morning and Kate arrested after. Carey thanked and left her and went to her next-door neighbour.

He painstaking asked each of them the same question. One had helped Julia and Kate Atkinson with washing the sheets from Mrs Atkinson's miscarriage. She told of that only with much coaxing from Carey who was starting to look very puzzled indeed.

Mrs Leigh was at home, more enormous and lethargic than ever, and very pale. She pushed at wisps of her hair, shoving them back under her cap in such a way that they immediately came out again and whispered that she hadn't been watching.

Carey started back to the Castle as Dodd's stomach began growling for its dinner.

'What'll we do now sir?' he asked, hoping to hear the name Bessie in the answer.

'Hm? said Carey, still lost in thought. 'Oh, I think we'll talk to Andy Nixon now.'

Why not before we did all this prancing about the town and spending an hour prattling with little maids about pretty clothes, wondered Dodd. Aloud he said sadly, 'Ay sir.'

wednesday 5th july 1592, early afternoon

That was all the conversation they had as they walked back up to the Castle, while Dodd reflected that Carey wasn't deliberately keeping him from his meat; it was simply he was too caught up in thinking to remember food. At this rate Dodd would be reduced to eating garrison rations in the Keep hall simply to keep body and soul together.

Carey was frowning as he knocked on Barker's door.

'You know, up until I talked to the child I was quite certain what had happened,' he told Dodd quietly. 'Now I'm not so sure.'

'Ay, but ye willna put too much faith in what a little maid would say?' protested Dodd.

Barker unlocked the Keep door and led them into the passage full of the cool pungent smell of wine and then the throat-scraping stink of old piss from the dungeons.

'I don't think she was lying and there were a number of things she said which don't fit.' Carey opened the Judas hole for Andy Nixon's cell and saw he was lying perched uncomfortably on the narrow stone ledge.

'Well, she got them mixed up,' said Dodd. 'She's only small. Ye canna call her as a witness in any case.'

'Of course not.'

Their voices woke Andy Nixon, and he turned and sat up with a clank.

'Is that ye, Deputy?'

'It is.'

'I want tae confess.'

Carey's mood lightened at once although he was astonished. He had been wondering how to persuade the man. 'Excellent. Can you wait until I get witnesses and a clerk?'

'Willna make no odds, will it?'

At last they assembled in Scrope's council chamber, with Scrope behind his desk and Richard Bell taking notes behind him. Just as Andy Nixon was brought shuffling in, Sir Richard Lowther arrived with his usual foul-weather face. There was quite a crowd in there, including Dodd and Archie-Give-It-Them who were guarding the white-faced Nixon. Carey told Scrope briskly how he had discovered the name of the man who wanted his glove, gone after him and arrested him.

'What have you to say for yourself?' asked Scrope gravely.

Andy Nixon took a deep breath. 'That I killed Jemmy Atkinson. His missus didnae ken a thing about it until the deed was done.'

Lowther snorted disbelievingly.

'Then what did you do?'

'We hid the body under the bed. I'd asked a…friend what we should do, and he said, best thing was to dump it in an alley. So after nightfall we got it in a handcart covered wi' hay and that's what we did.'

'Explain to me about Barnabus's knife and my glove,' put in Carey.

'Ay, well,' Andy Nixon coughed and continued staring at the floor. 'My…er friend said it wasnae enough to dump the corpse, somebody had to take the blame, and it might as well be ye, sir, since ye hadnae kin here and ye were a gentleman so ye wouldnae swing for it but only go back to London, which would suit Mr Pe…my friend. So he arranged for your man's knife to be got at the bawdy house.'

'My glove?'

'Ay. Well, I thought it weren't enough to catch ye. so I thought I could get something of yourn to add to it, see, and I went by myself and found out which boy was your servant and then bet him he couldnae get me one o' your gloves, and he give it me, and then I put it with Jemmy's body as well. It was me own idea.'

Overegging the pudding, Carey thought; just as well for me you did that, you young fool.

Nixon looked contemplative. 'I'll hang for that glove, will I not?' he said.

'Yes,' said Carey. 'Tell me how you did the murder?'

'What's the point, sir? It's done now.'

'The point is that I want to know.'

Lowther tutted and rolled his eyes and Carey noticed that Long George had come up to the council chamber and was standing at the back, sniffling self-importantly. What's happened now, he wondered.

'Ay well, the murder, sir.' Nixon thought for a while. 'He were killed in bed, in his sleep, sir. I…er…I climbed up from the street and got in at the window, and then I…er…I cut his throat.'

Carey's eyes narrowed. 'How did you climb up from the street?'

'On the Leighs' shop awning and the scaffolding and then onto the eaves. And then back again when I'd done it.'

'And when was the murder done?'

'About dawn on Monday.'

There was a concerted gasp, though of course that had to be right. Scrope interrupted fussily.

'Wait a minute. Are you telling us that Jemmy Atkinson was killed early on Monday morning, not on Monday night?'

'Ay sir, of course. We hid the body through the day, first under the bed and then in Clover's byre and then I put it on a handcart and I…'

'Quite so, quite so. But his throat was slit on Monday morning.'

'Ay sir. Dawn or thereabouts.'

'Hmf.' said Lowther, 'Why should we believe you?'

Nixon shrugged. 'It's when he died, sir. I dinna ken how to prove it to ye.'

'After you climbed the awning and got through the upstairs window?' Carey asked again with a frown.

Nixon nodded. Scrope tutted. 'What is the point of repeating it, Sir Robert?'

'I'm not sure,' Carey admitted. 'I'd like…'

'Well then, don't interfere. Very well, Nixon, you can go back down to the cells for the moment and we'll consider what to do with you.'

Dodd and Archie marched him out and Long George came forward to whisper urgently in Carey's ear.

'One moment, my lord,' he said. 'Apparently the woman wishes to confess as well.'

Scrope looked pleased. The whole thing was turning out very neatly. With luck his wife would stop giving him trouble over the way he was treating her brother, as if that could be helped.

Her brother, however, was being aggravating, shaking his head and pacing up and down.

'That's not right, that can't be right,' he was saying.

'What on earth is troubling you, Robin?' Scrope demanded. 'Nixon has just exonerated Barnabus Cooke for you.'

Carey blinked at him as if he'd forgotten all about Barnabus.

'But, my lord,' he said in a voice tight with frustration. 'What Andy Nixon has told us makes no sense at all. I have the testimony of his landlady that she was with him from the dark before dawn until the sun was up.'

'Perhaps he mistook the time.'

'Hardly likely, my lord, if he's confessing. And it's hard to make a mistake about something like dawn. Noon perhaps, but not dawn. And in any case, I can't see Andy Nixon climbing any awning or scaffolding to get to a high window, not with his hand the way it still is. He was badly beaten up on Sunday night and his hand trodden on. I doubt he could do it now.'

Lowther was staring at Carey from under his bushy eyebrows, as if at some two-headed wild man of the New World. Carey ignored him and carried on pacing until Kate Atkinson was brought up from the prison by Dodd and Archie. She stood staring round at them and Carey saw she was ghostly white and shaking.

'Tell us what you want, Mrs Atkinson,' said Scrope.

'I...I want to confess to k...killing my husband.'

'In the name of God,' growled Lowther. 'This is a bloody farce.'

'Just a minute, Sir Richard,' said Carey. 'Are you getting this down, Mr Bell?'

'Ay sir.'

'Mrs Atkinson, tell us how you killed your husband?'

'I crept upstairs after I'd given the children their porridge, and he was still asleep, so I took a knife and I...I cut his throat like a pig's.'

'While he was in bed on the Monday morning?'

'Ay sir. And then I sent for Andy Nixon...'

'Your lover,' put in Lowther contemptuously.

'My friend,' said Mrs Atkinson firmly. 'I sent Mary for him and when she brought him, he said he would ask Mr Pennycook, who he works for, what to do.'

'Ahah,' said Carey, one suspicion confirmed.

'Yes sir. Mr Pennycook was busy at the Castle, sir, about the renewal of the victualling contracts and when he came back he was very upset. He told Andy and me to hide the body and pretend nothing had happened, so we put m...my husband under the bed while he finished his business wi' you, sir. I had to wash the sheets, though, or the blood would have set in them, so I told my gossips I'd miscarried of a wean in the night, to explain it, you see. When he came back again, he lent Andy his old handcart and when it was dark, we took the cart and Andy p...put Mr Atkinson's body on it, and he left it in Frank's vennel. Mr Pennycook sent his clerk Michael Kerr with your servant's knife as well as the cart and Andy had gone and gotten your glove and so that's how we left him, sir.'

She looked at the floor as the silence settled around her. Carey had stopped his pacing and was now staring at her with his arms folded and his eyes like chips of ice.

'Are ye satisfied wi' this, Sir Robert?' asked Lowther sarcastically.

'At least it's possible,' he said levelly in return. 'Which Andy Nixon's tale is not.'

Kate Atkinson looked up at that name and then returned to examining the toes of her boots.

'You are a very wicked woman,' said Scrope gravely. 'You have committed a most serious and terrible crime.'

'Ay sir, I know,' muttered Mrs Atkinson.

'Your husband is your rightful lord, according to the Holy Bible and all civilized laws. To murder your husband is more than murder, it is treason.'

'Ay sir, I know.' Tears were falling down Mrs Atkinson's face.

'Why did you commit this evil deed, Mrs Atkinson?' Carey asked her gently.

She stared at him wildly, with the tears still welling. 'Sir?'

'Did he treat you badly? How was he worse than other husbands?'

'Well, he wasna, sir. He beat me sometimes but no worse than any other man.'

'Why did you do it, then? You must have known what could happen.'

'For heaven's sake, Robin,' warbled Scrope. 'I expect she did it so she could marry her lover. She's only a woman, she probably didn't think what would happen to her.'

Mrs Atkinson had bright colour in her cheeks and she took breath to speak, but then let it out and stared at the floor again.

'Ay sir.'

'Is that why?' Carey pursued. 'So you could marry Andy Nixon?'

'Ay sir.'

Lowther let out a long derisory snort but held his peace.

'What were you wearing that morning?'

'Sir?'

'Sir Robert,' said Scrope. 'What is the point of all this?'

'Bear with me, my lord.'

'Oh, very well. But get on with it. I haven't had dinner yet.'

'What were you wearing that day, Mrs Atkinson?'

'What I always wear, except Sundays, sir. My black bodice and my blue kirtle and petticoat and my apron.' She was puzzled at that.

'What you wore when I came to speak to you yesterday.'

'Ay sir.'

'What you're wearing now, in fact?'

'Ay sir.' She looked down at herself and frowned.

'But Mrs Atkinson, your sheets were soaked and so was the mattress, and the rushes. How did you keep the blood off your clothes?'

She shut her eyes. 'I...I was careful, sir.'

Carey stood and stared at her for a moment, mainly with exasperation.

'But…'

'Ye may well ask,' muttered Lowther in general to the tapestries.

'I think we've had enough of this,' said Scrope. 'Take the woman back to the cells, Sergeant. You'd better chain her, I suppose.'

'Ay sir,' said Dodd stolidly, not looking at Kate. He jerked his head towards the door at her and she went in front of him with her hands clasped rigidly together at her waist, as if they were already manacled.

wednesday 5th july 1592, afternoon

Janet Dodd née Armstrong had ridden into Carlisle all the way from Gilsland that morning, on an errand of assistance. The previous day her father had sent her youngest half-brother with a message for her about the twenty horses from King James's stables that they were looking after for Will the Tod, who was hiding them for some of their disreputable relatives. That had caused her enough trouble, to scatter the horses among their friends the Pringles and Bells. He had added the information that Jemmy Atkinson had been killed, because he knew she and Kate had been friends when Janet was in service with the old Lord Scrope years before. And so once she was sure the Deputy Warden would not be able to find the horses and, if he did, he wouldn't connect them with herself and the Sergeant, she saddled Dodd's old hobby Shilling and brought her half-brother Cuddy Armstrong on Samson their new workhorse with her to Carlisle. To make the ride worthwhile she took some good spring cheeses, a basket of eggs, a basket of gooseberries and another of wild strawberries to sell to Lady Scrope and while she rode she thought of the price of hay and how much they might get for their surplus if she sold direct to the Deputy instead of going through Hetherington or Pennycook as a middleman. Her baskets would have cost her four pence toll at the City gate if she hadn't been married to a garrison man. Bringing in vittles on the Queen's prerogative was one of Dodd's few worthwhile perks.

The first thing she knew about the further disaster of Kate's arrest was when she arrived at the Atkinson's house to find it locked and empty. A couple of workmen on the scaffolding around the Leighs' roof called down to her that she should try the Leighs' door and they'd do their best to be of service too—with much winking and leering.

She was about to shout something suitable back at them when she saw a tight knot of women in their aprons gathered opposite, talking vigorously. Maggie Mulcaster with the withered arm called her over.

She was enfolded into a whitewater of talk and speculation and disapproval and after a quarter of an hour had the full tale as known to the local women. It passed belief that her own husband could have been so cloddish as to arrest Kate Atkinson for murdering her husband. You expected idiocy from a gentleman, but she had honestly thought Henry would have more sense. She was about to say this when she spotted Julia Coldale, Kate Atkinson's cousin and maidservant, standing at the back of the group, looking as knowing and superior as any sixteen year old maid can. She took Julia aside and cross-examined her and fifteen minutes later she mentally took her apron off, rolled up her sleeves and prepared for battle.

'Hush now,' she said to the girl. 'We'll go and see the Deputy Warden.' Julia flinched back in alarm. 'For goodness sake, ye goose, he willna bite you. Under all his finery, he's only a man.'

'Ay,' said Julia doubtfully.

And an uncommonly nicely-made one at that, thought Janet, who had greatly enjoyed watching him in his shirt and fighting hose on top of her own hay cart. By God, if Dodd got himself killed in a raid one of these days, leaving her a widow...

Get a grip on yourself, ye silly cow, she told herself sternly; this will not save Kate from burning.

'And that's a foul piece of slander too,' she snapped, having caught the tail end of a sneer from Mrs Leigh.

'Why?' demanded Mrs Leigh, one hand at her back and another at the prow of her belly. 'It *is* God's judgement on her. You may have lower standards, Goodwife Dodd, but she's a dirty bitch for keeping a fancyman as far as I'm concerned.'

Janet considered whether slapping her would bring on the wean and decided it might. 'Ay,' she said caustically. 'I'm sorry to find ye sae full of jealousy and so short of charity, Goodwife. All this virtue wouldnae have aught to do with your lawsuit over her house, now would it?'

'Nothing at all,' said Mrs Leigh with a toss of the head and a satisfactory reddening of her cheeks. 'Some of us know what's right.'

'Well, some of us might do more good looking over the Bible where it talks of judging not that ye be not judged,' said Maggie Mulcaster unexpectedly, who was able to read quite well. She looked significantly over at the next wynd where little Mary Atkinson was skipping with one of her friends.

There was a mutter of agreement. Mrs Leigh was less popular than she thought with the other women of the street.

'*If* you can read, that is,' said Alison Talyer, Kate Atkinson's other neighbour.

'Well, I'm very sure *you* cannot,' said Mrs Leigh snappily.

Alison Talyer heaved her large round shoulders with laughter. 'That's true, but then I dinna give meself so many airs, eh, Mistress Leigh, with three maidservants, and a man and a boy and a fine new roof to me house?'

'*Can* ye read?' pursued Janet. 'I'm learning it when I can find the time and it's no' so very hard, ye ken.' The kindness in her voice would have spitted a suckling pig.

'I'm sure I don't have time to stand gossiping here,' sniffed Mrs Leigh, quite defeated, and waddled back into her house, leaving the women behind to shred her character instead of Kate's. Since it was an emergency and she had always liked Maggie Mulcaster, Janet gave her one of the cheeses, six of the eggs and half the wild strawberries to tide her over with looking after three extra children. She left Cuddy with her as well, in case she could put the lad to some use, rather than have him wandering about the Keep and getting into trouble.

'Come along,' she said to Julia who had pulled a comb out of her purse, and was giving her long copper hair a good seeing to. 'And ye can pull yer bodice lacings up tight again, you young hussy. What do you think ye're at?' she added flintily as she took Shilling's bridle to lead him on. Julia blushed.

It was all terribly annoying, thought Scrope, gazing at the two contenders for the post of Deputy Warden of the English West March who were glaring at each other again. If these two fire-eaters could possibly bring themselves to agree, they might clean up the entire March between them and leave him with very little work to do. They would make a perfect team: his brother-in-law had energy and courage and a certain amount of wild ingenuity on his side, whereas Lowther had the local influence and vast experience. It was true that Lowther was deep in corruption and Carey was full of arrogance, but in the Lord's name, it was possible. The Queen had persuaded men more fundamentally at odds than they were to work in harness together. Wistfully, Scrope wondered how she had managed it.

'I don't like you insinuations, Sir Richard,' Carey was saying through his teeth.

Lowther was tapping the fingers of his left hand on his sword-hilt. 'Ay, d'ye not?' he said. 'Well, I dinna ken and I dinna care how ye got the silly woman to confess like that, but it's a poor thing to hide behind a woman, so it is.'

'Now, Sir Richard,' Scrope interrupted quickly before blades could be drawn again. 'You have no evidence for that suggestion at all.'

'Imprimis,' said Lowther, placing a square thumb on a square finger. 'Atkinson's body was found in Frank's vennel, not in his bed...'

'I explained that the mattress was stained with blood...'

'Item, his throat was cut and I've never heard of a woman killing anybody by cutting his throat; they haven't the strength, they haven't the height and forbye they havenae the courage. That's a footpad's trick, is that, and your man Barnabus is a footpad and well ye know it.'

Carey didn't say anything to that, because it was true.

'Item, we've only the woman's word for it his throat was cut on the Monday morning and I dinna believe her. And naebody knows where your man was on the Monday night when Atkinson was likely done to death. It's all a bit pat, is it no', the time she gives is the time when Cooke has an alibi from Solomon Musgrave.'

Carey was breathing hard through his nostrils.

'It's possible to twist the clearest evidence,' he said.

'Clear? I dinna think so. We've no witnesses, no nothing. So what have we got? Your man's knife and your glove by the body which is the next best thing. That'll do. And ye'll have wanted Atkinson out of your way, what's more, so there ye have it. Ye had the will; ye had the tool in Barnabus, and he could ha' done it. It's good enough for a rope.'

'I have explained about how his knife…'

'Och, and a cock and bull story it is too. A boy says Andy wanted yer glove. Ye say Pennycook got Cooke's knife fra the bawdy house. It's all very complicated, verra elaborate, Sir Robert, but it willna wash, for all ye've got a couple of fools in the gaol to swear out their lives for ye.'

'How the devil do you think I got them to do that, eh, Sir Richard? Your own methods of bribery or threats would hardly persuade anyone to die for me.'

'Hmf. It's no' so hard. I heard ye had a long chat wi' little Mary Atkinson, did ye no'?'

It was impossible to miss the implication, even without the heavy sneer across Lowther's jowelly face. Sir Robert's face took on the white masklike appearance of a Carey about to kill someone, and his hand fell on his swordhilt. Scrope leapt to his feet and put himself between them.

'Now, now,' he said. 'This is all complete speculation. And very offensive, Sir Richard, very offensive indeed. You have no call to go making that kind of accusation.'

'Me?' said Lowther. 'I'm not making accusations, my lord. If the boot fits him, let him wear it.'

'Yes, well, you know perfectly well what you're about. I think you should withdraw it.'

There was a moment of tension while Scrope wondered if he would, and then he growled, 'Ay, well, perhaps I let my tongue wander on a bit. I dinna believe the woman, though, and I willna without better reason to.'

'You withdraw your hints about Mary Atkinson?' pursued Scrope.

'Ay, I do,' said Lowther heavily. Carey bowed slightly in acknowledgment, obviously still too angry to speak. 'In fact, I'll go further,' Lowther added. 'I'll say that perhaps—perhaps, mark you—it was all a misunderstanding betwixt yerself, Sir Robert, and your servant. Was there no' a king I heard of once, that said he wanted to be rid of a priest and off his henchmen went and killed the man wi'out asking did he mean it? Now, I could see that happening here, Sir Robert; I could accept that.'

Carey was still silent which encouraged Lowther to expansiveness.

'There's always the risk of misunderstanding when ye've a quick tongue and a short fuse. And you've come up from London where perhaps they do things differently, and perhaps you and your man have made a mistake.'

'And?' enquired Carey very softly.

Lowther smiled as wide as a death's head on a church wall and waved a velvet clad arm.

'Och. It's only Barnabus Cooke that did the deed, especially if he did it on a misunderstanding. If you take yerself back down to London again, where you belong, we'll hang your little footpad and that'll be the end of it, for me.'

Was Lowther trying to drive Carey into a killing fury, or did he genuinely think the man would abandon his servant and take himself back to London again without a second glance? Scrope shook his head and put out one hand to touch Carey's right arm which had dropped across his body again, the fingers on his sword hilt.

'I'm sure you think that's very generous,' said Scrope quickly. 'But…ah, of course, it's a nonsensical suggestion and I'm certain you had no intention of further insulting Sir Robert, but I have to tell you that I think—quite objectively, mind—that you are wrong. I believe the woman, Mrs Atkinson. I think she did kill her husband, and conscience has very properly prompted her to confess to us at last.'

'Ha!' said Lowther, moving to the door. 'I see blood's thicker than water as usual. Ay well, it willna make no odds in the long run. Your footpad will hang, Sir Robert, and if it's aught to do with me, you'll face the axe on the same day.'

The door banged as he made his exit and Scrope turned nervously to Carey who was still standing there gazing into space.

'He's a very obstinate man,' he said, half in excuse for Lowther whom he had known since he was a boy and feared almost as long.

Carey gave a little jump and looked at him remotely as if not entirely seeing him there.

'Hm? Oh, Lowther. Yes. He's well dug in, isn't he? I expect he's got the inquest jury packed.'

Scrope sighed at this undeniable truth. 'I've done my best to find gentlemen who hate him too,' he said. 'Unfortunately, the reason why they hate him is generally that they're afraid of him and his Graham allies.'

Carey sighed. 'I suppose that's what I thought would happen. Never mind.' He turned to go, looking tired and depressed.

'You know,' said Scrope, just remembering something important in time. 'My lady wife is...er...very annoyed with me. She says I work you too hard and don't feed you properly; she wants you to have dinner with us this afternoon.'

Carey bowed. 'I am at your lordship's command,' he answered. 'Tell my lady sister I'll be delighted to come. Would you mind if I made some more enquiries into Atkinson's death?'

'Yes, I would,' said Scrope instantly. 'Firstly, I'm quite satisfied that Mrs Atkinson did it as she told us she did. And secondly, there are the letters to write concerning the muster, and the Coroner's jury to empanel, and I simply cannot ask Richard Bell to do all of it so you'll have to.'

Carey's face darkened again, though more with depression than with anger. It didn't take a genius to guess that he hated paperwork, even if he hadn't had some notion about poking around looking for yet another suspect for Atkinson's murderer.

'Yes, my lord,' Carey said meekly enough. 'I must take Thunder out for a run but then I'll deal with it.'

'Of course, of course, my dear fellow,' said Scrope, hugely relieved that he had escaped the whole interview without either blades or blood being drawn. 'I'll see you later then.'

Despite the sunlight, as soon as he had returned Thunder to the stables and told the head groom to fetch in the farrier for a new set of shoes, Carey conscientiously went to his office to work on the letters organising lodgings for the gentlemen coming in for the muster and the inquest. The simple act of riding Thunder had done a lot to relax him. Unfortunately, as soon as he re-entered the Queen Mary Tower his whole towering thundercloud of worries closed in on him again. Richard Bell was there waiting for him, with a list of people to write to and a couple of form letters to give him the style. It had not occurred to him, when he persuaded the Queen to let him come north, that he would spend so much of his time acting like one of her own blasted secretaries, but he darkly supposed she knew perfectly well and had found it funny.

He was a third of the way through the letters when there was a knock on the door to the stairs.

'Enter,' he said automatically, hoping Simon Barnet might have come with the beer, as ordered at least an hour ago. Barnabus was still in the gaol and would stay there at least until the inquest.

He heard the feminine rustle of petticoats in the rushes and looked up to see Janet Dodd, magnificent in her new hat and red gown, followed by a doe-eyed copper-haired creature in a blue-green kirtle who seemed vaguely familiar. Both of them curtseyed to him but Janet Dodd then folded her arms and gazed at him steadily. He looked back with considerable wariness.

'What can I do for you, Mrs Dodd?' he asked, his courtesy a little strained.

'Is it true what I hear about Kate Atkinson burning for killing of her husband?'

'Aahh…Has the Sergeant told you?'

'Nay, I've not seen him. I had word by my father that her husband was dead so I came in to help my old friend Kate. I heard it from her gossips. And why d'ye want to burn her?'

'She murdered her husband.'

'Hmf. Is it right what Julia says, that his throat was cut in his bed before dawn on Monday?'

Carey's eyes had suddenly gone intensely blue. 'That's when Mrs Atkinson confesses to having cut it.'

'Och God, the silly bitch,' said Janet disgustedly. 'She's saying she cut her own man's throat in their own marriage bed?'

'Yes.'

'Did ye have Andy Nixon under lock and key when she told you it?'

Carey smiled a little oddly. 'Yes, and in fact Andy had just finished telling us that it was him cut the man's throat and Mrs Atkinson knew nothing about it. Unfortunately, my Lord Scrope believes Mrs Atkinson.'

'And you?' demanded Janet. 'What do ye believe? Sir?' she added belatedly.

'Please, Mrs Dodd, be seated. And you too…er…'

'Julia,' simpered the girl, who had not in fact done her bodice up again. 'Julia Coldale, sir.'

'Julia.' And what a lovely warm smile the Deputy had for a girl with copper curls tumbling down her back and her bodice half-open, to be sure, even though it was clear he had a lot on his mind. Janet's own expression would have done credit to her husband.

There was only one joint stool in there which Carey was using to pile his completed letters upon. Janet removed them, put them carefully on the chest by the door and sat down. Julia perched herself at the other end of the chest, a little tilted forwards to make the best of herself.

'Well, sir?' Janet said. 'Which do you believe?'

'I don't believe Andy Nixon did the killing because my man Long George Little has confessed to beating him up in an alley along with three other men that very night and furthermore the window would be far too small for him to get in by. I doubt I could get through it myself and I'm narrower built than he is.'

'Just what I was going to say, sir,' said Janet, lightening slightly. 'And Kate?'

'Mrs Atkinson?' Carey looked stern. 'She's confessed to it.' Privately he was worried by Lowther's logic, but couldn't bring himself to admit it.

'And ye believe her?'

'Why shouldn't I?'

'Och God. Nobbut a man would believe she could do a thing like that,' said Janet springing to her feet and advancing on Carey's desk.

'Why?' he demanded. 'I don't believe a woman incapable of murder.'

Janet planted her hands on the desk and leaned towards him.

'Sir Robert,' she said. 'Have you ever washed a full set of sheets and blankets and bed-hangings?'

He was not amused at the suggestion, which he might have been under other circumstances.

'No, Mrs Dodd,' he said. 'I haven't.'

'Then ye dinna ken what backache is.'

Carey rather thought he did know what backache was, having spent up to twelve hours on his feet waiting on the Queen in one of her moods, and he disliked Janet's truculence, but he only lifted his eyebrows. This encouraged her.

'It's a full day's work, is that, on top of all the other—or you'd have to hire a woman and risk her telling the world. Ye'd needs be fighting for yer life or gone Bedlam mad to cut anything's throat in yer bed chamber.'

He looked away and then back at her. 'I admit, I hadn't thought of that.'

'Ay,' she said. 'Now, I'll not deny that a woman's capable of murder, though it's a harder thing for her against a man if he's awake and in his right mind, ye ken.'

'And besides being a crime, it's an appalling and wicked sin,' put in Carey.

'Ay,' agreed Janet unexpectedly. 'It is. There's rarely any need to murder your husband if ye've any men in your family at all.'

Carey coughed. It wasn't what he had meant.

'But...' Janet was sticking her finger under his nose which annoyed him. '*But* in your ain marriage bed so the blood gets all over the sheets and the blankets ye've woven, and the bed-hangings the price they are—no, never. In the jakes, perhaps, with a lance; or poison in his food; or get him drunk and put a pillow over his head...But cut his throat in the bedroom? It's a man did that, because he wouldnae think of the washing after.'

She finished triumphantly, removed the offensive finger and folded her arms again.

'Mrs Dodd,' said Carey allowing a little of his annoyance to show through in his voice. 'Please be seated.'

She sat, not abashed.

'Did you know Sir Richard Lowther thinks the same as you?' Carey asked.

She was stunned. 'Does he now?'

'He does. Mainly because he prefers to believe my servant Barnabus did it.' Or so he says, Carey thought, struck anew by an old suspicion.

'Oh.' Her thoughts were plain to be read on her face and typically she gave voice to them. 'Ay, well then, I expect poor Kate's a dead woman.'

Very few things annoyed Carey more about the whole business than everyone's bland assumption that it mattered not at all who had actually done the murder, it only mattered who could be brought to hang for it. They assumed he was as little interested in justice as any of them, and would find the weakest victim he could to blame. At the moment it passed his capacity to think of words to persuade them that if he genuinely thought Barnabus had slit Atkinson's throat, for whatever reason, he would hang the man himself. It was too outlandish a way of thinking for Borderers.

After a moment he said, 'I hear what you say, Mrs Dodd. Perhaps you're right. But the problem is, it's not enough. Andy Nixon, I think, is safe, but there is no denying that Mrs Atkinson was in the house at the time and had the opportunity of doing it. Now I'm not saying she did...' he went on hurriedly as Janet Dodd took breath again, '...I'm only saying that she'll have a hard job convincing the Coroner's jury she didn't even if she does withdraw her confession.'

'Ay,' said Janet thoughtfully. 'I see. The jury will a' be men, of course, and they'll know naught of washing sheets either.'

'Quite. And the confession will weigh heavy with them, unless I can convince them she was a woman distraught and unable to help herself. It weighs heavy with me and not only because I'm Barnabus's master. We did nothing to make her confess, you know, Mrs Dodd, she came to us of her own free will.'

'She was worriting about Andy Nixon, of course, the silly bitch,' said Janet.

'Do you think she should have let Nixon hang for her? He was willing to do it; that's why he lied to us.'

Janet looked at him as if he were mad.

'Ay, of course,' she said. 'He's a good man, is Andy, but she's got her bairns to think of. But then she allus was featherheaded, was Katy Coldale, and allus did think the sun and the moon and the seven stars shone out of Andy Nixon's...er...face.'

She looked over her shoulder at Julia Coldale who seemed mildly shocked at this ruthlessness.

'Well, go on,' she said. 'Tell him about the sheets anyway, Julia.'

Julia wriggled a bit and told the story of the Monday morning in a breathless voice. She had arrived and been set to make the butter while Mrs Atkinson kneaded the bread. Then Mrs Atkinson had fetched some bread and beer for her husband and gone up with it. She came down in a dreadful state and had sent Mary for Nixon, then gone up with a laundry basket. She brought all the sheets and blankets down and they were dirty with blood. They had put the sheets in to soak in cold water in the big brewing bucks they had in the yard sheds, and Mrs Atkinson had gone up to sweep up the rushes and then come back down again saying it was better to do it later, which had puzzled Julia. At the same time, Mrs Atkinson had told her she had had a sudden issue of blood in the night, though it seemed a bit much even for a miscarriage, and Mrs Atkinson didn't look ill enough for a woman who had had a miscarriage although she certainly was pale, and she hadn't sent for the apothecary nor the midwife neither. Then most of the day was taken with scrubbing and soaping and bringing out the triple-strained lye to soak the sheets in again. Julia had been kept busy going to the street conduit with buckets and back again, and once she was sent over to Maggie Mulcaster to borrow another scrubbing brush, but they had done the sheets and blankets by the evening, pretty much, and left them to soak in fair water until the morrow when they had wrung them and hung them out on the hurdles. It had ruined the day completely.

'Ye see,' said Janet significantly. 'Nobbut a man would make so much trouble.'

'Yes,' said Carey thoughtfully. 'Now, Julia, what was it you did at dawn on Monday which you haven't told us about?'

The effect of this simple question was very interesting. Julia gasped and put her hand to her mouth as if the Deputy Warden had struck her. Janet swivelled round and glared at her.

'Eh?' she said.

'You've left something out, haven't you?'

Julia put her hand down again. 'No sir,' she said quite calmly. 'I told you just as it happened.'

'How did you know that Mr Atkinson had his throat cut on Monday morning?'

'It were the sheets,' she said. 'I knew from the sheets.'

Carey gave her a very hard stare which she returned, quite recovered, and then lowered her eyes modestly to the rushes.

'Hm,' he said. 'If you saw anything, Julia, I strongly advise you to tell me.'

'Me, sir?' said Julia. 'I saw nothing, sir, only what I told you. I helped Mrs Atkinson with the bed covers and such.'

Doubt crept into Carey's mind; perhaps he had mistaken her reaction. She certainly seemed scared of him, which was a pity. He sighed, caught Janet Dodd's expression and tried to hide the thoughts and speculations chasing themselves across the surface of his mind.

There was a short awkward silence, of which only Julia seemed unconscious, for she picked up a letter she had knocked off the chest, smoothed it and put it back in a very distracting way.

Deputy, the sooner you're safely wed to Lady Widdrington the better for everyone, Janet thought to herself, wondering vaguely why there were soft squeaking noises coming from the curtained four poster bed; and as for you, Julia, you little hussy...

'We'll be off and out of your way, Sir Robert,' she said briskly, rising and waving at Julia to come with her. 'D'ye know where my husband is?'

Carey shook his head, not really paying attention to Janet at all as Julia went to the door. Janet make an impatient noise and began hustling the girl out, but Carey beckoned her to him.

'Ay sir?' she said suspiciously.

'Send Julia to find your husband,' he murmured. 'I want a word with you alone.'

Janet's expression cleared slightly. 'Ay sir.'

Julia went with a wiggle of her hips and a toss of her red curls while Janet darkly considered what she would do to the little bitch if she aimed her wiles at Henry while she was fetching him. Carey had a thoughtful expression on his face.

'Mrs Dodd,' he said. 'I'm worried about that girl.'

Me too, thought Janet, but she held her peace.

'I think she may have seen something which she isn't telling us because I've heard that she went upstairs at the Atkinson's house around dawn, to fetch a ribbon, she said, and she hasn't mentioned that although I invited her to.'

'She might have forgotten,' suggested Janet.

'Do you really think so?'

'No, I dinna. Where did you hear that from?'

'From Mary Atkinson, which means I can only wonder.'

'Ye've questioned the little girl?'

'We had a very long conversation. Dodd was there, he can tell you what she said, but she seemed to me to be a bright child and quite truthful.'

Janet examined his face thoughtfully. It surprised her that he could have coaxed Mary to give him anything like a coherent tale after he had arrested her mother.

'Don't look at me like that,' he said defensively. 'I've no need to bully maids to get them to talk to me.'

And isn't that the truth, thought Janet.

'Now, Mrs Dodd, I haven't the time to go enquiring about Jemmy Atkinson's death. My lord Warden considers the matter solved by Mrs Atkinson's confession and he has given me direct orders to get on with organising the muster for Sunday and the inquest for Thursday and as I have no clerk yet, I have to write the letters myself. But Sergeant Dodd is presumably at a loose end...'

That thought made her blood run cold. With money in his pocket and Bangtail in town...She nodded.

'First, I want him to subpoena Pennycook's clerk, Michael Kerr, to appear at the inquest tomorrow. Then I want him to enquire into the matter for me. Poke around a bit and see what he finds. And you too, Mrs Dodd. Mrs Atkinson's gossips will talk differently to you than they would to me.'

Janet's mouth fell open. Carey didn't seem to have noticed what he had said and now he was cocking his head to listen to the funny noises from the bed. Next minute he was on his feet and beckoning her over to it. She followed suspiciously. He drew back one of the faded curtains gently; she peered in and then started to laugh. The yellow bitch lying there with her pups nuzzling up against her flank lifted a lip and gave a low growl.

'Shame on you, Buttercup,' said Carey. 'Mrs Dodd, this is Buttercup and Buttercup this is Janet Dodd. Buttercup,' he said with the first proper smile she had seen from him that day, 'has evicted me from my own bed.'

He let the curtains fall again as Dodd came shambling lankily in, looking injured and sorrowful as usual. At least his long dour face brightened when he saw Janet who came over to kiss him and then he remembered what he had been doing recently and his expression became wary.

'Where's Julia Coldale?' she demanded.

'Och, the maid with the red hair?' he asked.

'Ay.'

'She said she had tae go back to the town again urgently and she didnae want to wait for ye, so I said she could go.'

'By herself?' sniffed Janet.

'Er…no,' admitted her husband. 'Bangtail and Red Sandy went with her to see she was all right.'

'They're both married men.'

'Ay, they'll protect her right enough.'

'*Quis custodiet ipsos custodes*,' said Carey suddenly.

'Eh, sir?' asked Dodd.

'"Who will protect her from the protectors?"' Carey translated, and Janet laughed.

'Now there's a piece of sense,' she said. 'Who said that?'

Carey thought for a moment. 'I can't remember,' he admitted. 'Some Roman or other.'

'Well, it's uncommon good sense for a foreigner,' said Janet patronisingly. 'Good afternoon to ye, sir.'

In later days, Mrs Leigh often thought about what she saw from the window that afternoon. She was sitting sewing a baby's nightshirt with the little window open as far as it would go to let in some cool air. It also let in pungent smells from the various yards round about and flies, despite the bunches of wormwood hanging from the ceiling, and the sounds of children playing. Her own brood were out in the garden at the back, apart from the boys who were at school still; the two big girls were playing with hoops and the baby was sitting happily with one of the maidservants gurgling as it ate a dandelion. It was too hot and she was too heavy and tired to go out. The night before she had dreamt of swimming in a river as she had when she was a child, but then a fierce pike had come along and bitten her stomach and she had woken up to the ghost pains that often rippled her stomach now. Mrs Croser, the midwife and apothecary, had attended her at noon and said that the babe was head-down and in the right place and it was only a matter of waiting on God's decision. At least she was happier than she had been the day before, despite the heat, and the men were no longer hammering the roof.

She saw Julia Coldale come along the street with two of the garrison men, one on each side, both of them as full of pride and preening as a couple of cock pheasants. The girl had a high colour and seemed to be enjoying herself. She left them outside as she went into the Leighs' own draper's shop.

And then she saw Janet Dodd and her husband, also coming along the street. Janet paused to talk to Alison Talyer who was shelling peas in her door while Dodd came on and disappeared under the scaffolding. She heard creaking and realised he was climbing the ladder, very cautiously, and she heard his voice drone as he spoke to the foreman.

Mrs Leigh put down her work, struggled herself off the window seat and went to the top of the stairs.

'Jock!' she yelled. 'Jock Burn!'

'Ay, mistress,' came the answering shout. 'I'll be with ye in a minute.'

It was quite a bit after a minute that the skinny little man finally came up the stairs and stood lowering at her in his greasy jerkin and the incongruous new blue suit her husband had given him. Julia left at the same time and could be seen through the window chatting and laughing with the garrison men.

'What did Julia Coldale want?' she demanded.

He looked shiftily away from her. 'Och,' he said. 'She was time-wastin', only wantin' to hear the price o' this and that.'

'Oh?'

He gave her the straight stare of the experienced liar.

'Where's the master, Mrs Leigh?' he asked.

'Over at the new warehouse. Why?'

'Ay,' said Jock, taking off his shop apron. 'I need to speak wi' him; will ye excuse me, mistress?'

She nodded, suddenly glad he could lie, and he turned and pattered down the stairs again. That perhaps was why she failed to notice that, when Dodd came creaking down the ladder again some time later, he was carrying a small bundle.

wednesday 5th july 1592, late afternoon

Carey was deep in the tedium of paperwork again, his mind nibbling frustratedly at the problem of Jemmy Atkinson as he worked, when he had another visitor. After the first flash of fury, he saw it was the Bell headman who had called out his family against Wattie Graham the day before.

'Mr Bell,' he said courteously, wondering when he would be finished with his damned letters. 'What can I do for you?'

Archibald Bell came stumping in through his chamber looking uncomfortably hot in a homespun green suit and a new high-crowned hat.

'Ah've come about the blackrent,' said Bell. 'To pay it, I mean.'

For a moment, Carey didn't understand.

'Er...Lowther's not here,' he said cautiously.

'Ay, I know that. I've come to pay it to ye, sir.'

Carey sat down again, wondering how to handle this. On the one hand he direly needed the money because his winnings from Lowther wouldn't last forever and he was sure nobody in Carlisle would make the mistake of playing primero for high stakes with him again. On the other hand, blackrent was one of the cankers of the Border, as poor men paid protection money to crooks like Lowther and Richie Graham of Brackenhill to keep their herds and houses safe from reivers. Since no one could live paying rent to two landlords, most of them got their living by reiving and demanding blackrent of their own.

Archibald Bell had his purse in his hand, ready to do the business. He was looking puzzled.

Carey stood again, went and poured two goblets of the diabolical wine which Goodwife Biltock had sent up by Simon Barnet who was, as usual, not around.

'Mr Bell,' he said, handing one to the headman, who looked astonished. 'How much blackrent was Sir Richard demanding?'

'Thirty shillings a quarter,' Bell answered promptly. 'But I havena paid it for a while, so I brung what we owe which is six pounds.'

That was no less than extortionate.

'I give you a toast,' said Carey, while he struggled with temptation. 'I give you, confusion to Richard Lowther and the Grahams.'

Bell lifted his goblet and drank the lot without noticeable strain.

'Ye willna be wanting more, sir?' he said anxiously. 'For we canna pay it.'

'No,' said Carey. 'I'm sure you can't. In fact, I'm not sure I should accept it.'

'Eh?' Bell was flabbergasted.

'Well,' said Carey reasonably, 'you give blackrent in return for protection from reivers, don't you?'

'Ay.'

'To be frank with you, Mr Bell, I'm not sure how much more protection I can offer you. I haven't Lowther's contacts or his family backing. I'm only an officer of the Queen.'

'Ye did well enough keeping my stock fra Wattie's clutches yesterday.'

'I have to admit it wasn't my prime consideration.'

'Nay, I ken that. I know well enough you was protecting Mr Aglionby's packtrain.'

Something in the pit of Carey's stomach gave a lurch of excitement. Now that made sense of a fifty man raid at hay-making. Carefully he drank more of the sloe-coloured vinegar in his good silver goblet.

'Ah,' he said wisely. 'And how did you find that out?'

'It was one o' the reivers we caught yesterday. He was in such a taking, yelling and shouting about what he'd lost by ye and how he hated ye, and the packtrain the heaviest to go into Carlisle for years and so on. So then I knew why ye were there, which was puzzling me; it was for the packtrain, to keep it fra Wattie Graham,' Bell explained.

Carey stared into space, his mind working furiously. He was remembering the cardgame at the Mayor's house. Suddenly he knew who had killed Jemmy Atkinson.

'I supposed you haven't got the reiver any more?'

'Nay, we ransomed all of them back, the minute Skinabake's man turned up wi' the money.'

'Do you know his name?'

'Ay, it was Fire the Braes Armstrong.'

'And where does he live?'

'The Debateable Land, seeing he's at the horn for murder and arson in two Marches.'

Carey came to a decision.

'Mr Bell,' he said. 'I'll be straight with you. I don't want to take blackrent, which is against the law, but I'll take my rightful Wardenry fee for protecting your cattle, which is two pounds.'

'Ay,' said Bell. 'But I want yer protection in the future.'

'You have that,' Carey explained. 'It's one of the duties of the office of Deputy Warden to protect you from raiders.' Dammit, thought Carey, really it's the only one. 'You shouldn't have to pay me rent for that; the Queen's supposed to do it.' Not that she did, or not regularly. 'You only pay me a fee for a particular raid.'

Bell was looking deeply suspicious.

'Are ye tellin' me to pay my blackrent to Lowther?'

'No, Mr Bell, I'm telling you to give me two pounds sterling and call it quits. Keep the money. Buy weapons or steel bonnets for your family or even a new plough or whatever. Just give me information when it comes to you and turn out to fight for me when I call and that's all the blackrent I want.'

Bell's mouth was hanging open. Carey was glad neither Dodd nor Barnabus were there to tell him he was mad turning down good cash; he even felt a little mad and reckless doing it. But he was grateful to Bell for solving Atkinson's murder for him and besides, if he himself took blackrent like Lowther, how could he stop anyone else from doing it?

Bell had a broad spreading grin of incredulity on his face.

'Are ye tellin' me ye willna set on anybody to raid me if I dinna pay ye off?'

'Yes,' said Carey, wondering if every Borderer would now think him soft, as well as Dodd, the garrison and Jock of the Peartree. 'I want my Wardenry fee, though. I have to live too.'

'Ay,' said Bell, still grinning. 'Ay, o' course ye do. Ay.'

He took two handfuls of crowns and shillings from his purse and carefully counted them out. Then he spat on the palm of his hand and held it out to Carey.

'Ah'll come out for ye, Deputy,' he said. 'There's ma hand, there's ma heart.'

Carey spat on his own palm and grasped Bell's firmly.

'And mine, Mr Bell,' he said. 'Pass the word, if you will.'

'Ay,' said Bell, still grinning as he put away his purse and moved to the door quickly before Carey could change his mind. 'Ay, I will. By God,' he added, shaking his head and Carey heard him laugh as his hobnails clattered down the stairs.

Edward Aglionby, Mayor of Carlisle, was expecting a visit from the new Deputy Warden and was ready for it when, belatedly, it came. The Deputy arrived on horseback and seemed to be in a tearing hurry, but he invited the young man into his solar for wine and wafers and even asked him to dinner.

'I'm sorry, Mr Aglionby, I'm bidden to my sister's table and in fact I'm going to be late. But I must talk to you first.'

Edward Aglionby stood with his arms crossed, waiting.

'You know, of course, that there was an attempt made on your packtrain by Wattie Graham...'

'And Skinabake Armstrong. Yes, Sir Robert. I also know that it was you who prevented it, thereby saving me a great deal of gold and trouble.'

Aglionby waited for the new Deputy's demand, but it seemed Carey wanted to shillyshally first, asking irrelevantly about Atkinson's inquest.

'Yes,' he answered the Courtier. 'The case does fall under City jurisdiction. In fact my lord Warden was quite willing for the Carlisle Coroner to hear the inquest, although my lord has empanelled the jury.'

Carey nodded. Given a very tight spot, with Lowther on the one hand badgering him to find Carey or his servant guilty and Philadelphia badgering him on every other hand to find someone else, Scrope would gratefully wriggle out.

'Who is the Coroner?' he asked.

Aglionby smiled. 'I am.'

'Excellent,' Carey beamed back. 'I have a favour to ask of you, Mr Aglionby, which I hope you will...at least consider.'

'Mm,' said the Mayor cautiously.

'We have a multiplicity of suspects for murderer,' said Carey. 'Among them, though I think no longer the most suspected of them, is my servant Barnabus. Now I have no way of being his good lord here—I have no influence with the jury and would not dream of insulting you by attempting to influence you yourself— excepting if I can put my case against the man I think truly did the deed, directly in open Court.'

'Are you a lawyer, Sir Robert?'

Carey coughed, not willing to lie directly. 'I have some small experience of law and lawyers, though I never was a member of an Inn of Court. I would like to act as *amicus curiae*, a friend of the Court, in an unofficial capacity.'

'Mmm.'

'It's the best way I can think of helping my unfortunate servant who was only accused as a way of attacking me. Obviously I can't hire him a barrister since he's accused of a capital crime.'

'Hm. *Amicus curiae*. Is that all?'

Carey's face was guileless, though in fact he was wondering how long Aglionby would take to decide and how furious Philadelphia would be when he was late.

'Yes,' he said.

Aglionby was very suspicious at such a cheap discharge of an obligation. There was no question that the Deputy Warden had saved him large sums of money. On the other hand, why look a gift horse in the mouth?

'I see no reason to deny you, Sir Robert; in fact, I'm happy to be of service in the matter.'

'Thank you very much, Mr Mayor,' said Carey, and then decided that since he was going to be late anyway, he might as well drop a little poison. 'Do you know who it was who passed on word of your packtrain to the Grahams?'

'No,' admitted Aglionby. 'Though I have suspicions.'

'It was Sir Richard Lowther.'

Aglionby did not look surprised. His square smooth-chinned face changed only slightly.

'He was at the cardgame where your lady sister…'

'Was indiscreet. Yes. And one of my men saw him at the Red Bull…er…later. Mick the Crow was certainly there too and I know Mick was the messenger to Wattie that brought in the raid.'

'Ah,' said Aglionby. 'Mick the Crow hasn't named Lowther?'

'Of course not. I deduced it.'

'It isn't enough to accuse him.'

It will be, thought Carey; when I indict him for ordering Atkinson's murder, it will. Aloud he said, 'No. But straws show which way the wind blows.'

It was obvious. Lowther needed money and would have got it as his cut from the packtrain profits. Also he would be undermining Carey in the City of Carlisle with the implication that commerce wasn't safe under his rule. Why had he let Carey take his patrol out? Simple greed, perhaps, coupled with the hope that if Carey came on Skinabake with Sergeant Ill-Willit Daniel Nixon behind him, that was Carey out of his way forever. And Atkinson was killed to keep him quiet about it.

'Mm,' said Aglionby again.

'Mr Mayor,' Carey said, making for the door. 'I simply must get back to the Castle or my sister will skin me alive. It's arranged for tomorrow?'

'Ay,' said Aglionby. 'You can be *amicus curiae* for the inquest, no bother. Good evening to you, Deputy.'

weðnesðay, 5th July 1592, early evening

It was a quiet little supper party, with only Philadelphia, Scrope and Carey himself, eating his way voraciously through five covers of meat and a number of summer sallets, sharp with herbs and nasturtium flowers. Philadelphia forgave him for being so late and exerted herself to keep the conversation going; she was worried by Carey's rather remote politeness. She even asked Carey's advice about her son who was away south at school and perpetually in trouble, but with typical masculine obtuseness all he would say was that she should worry more if the boy didn't get into scrapes now and then.

Eventually, Scrope wandered over to the virginals in the corner. He opened it and began plinking the notes gently, head cocked, listening for sourness, face dreamy. After a moment of struggle, he sat down and began playing.

'My lord,' said Carey tactfully, watching the spider-like hands move. 'What can I do or say that might convince you to release Barnabus...'

'My dear fellow, I know perfectly well that you didn't have anything to do with Atkinson getting his throat slit; it isn't your style at all.'

'Lowther thinks different.'

'Yes, he does, doesn't he? Now isn't that interesting?'

'Interesting, my lord?'

'Fascinating, in fact. At one time I was quite sure Lowther himself had done it, for some reason, or at any rate, paid somebody to do it. When he came to see me yesterday morning he was in such a rage and was so certain it was you, I was almost convinced he was simply overdoing things a bit.'

'My lord,' Carey interrupted. 'Surely you see that whoever actually did the killing, it *must* have been Lowther who ordered it.'

'Must have been?'

Scrope had stopped playing. Carey lifted up one finger. 'Imprimis, he was the last man to see Atkinson the night before he was killed. He was at the Red Bull when Atkinson was paying Long George and his friends for beating up Andy Nixon.'

'Oh.'

'He was also, by the way, the man who sent Mick the Crow to Netherby with the information that not only was my Lady Widdrington on the road, but so was a large packtrain from Newcastle. Unfortunately, I've no way of proving it.'

'How did he know about the packtrain?' put in his sister. Carey looked at her.

'You let it slip at the card party,' he said, careful to keep accusation out of his voice. 'Remember?'

Philadelphia flushed and fell silent.

'Ah,' said Scrope, trying to look wise. 'You know you did have a little too much wine that evening, my dear. I have often said...'

'No doubt Atkinson was threatening to tell Aglionby,' Carey trampled on, hoping to distract the Scropes from a quarrel. 'Perhaps he was no longer so useful since I'd sacked him from the Paymastership. Perhaps they quarrelled. And I'm not at all sure Lowther didn't have a hand in Andy Nixon's attempt to frame Barnabus and me for it. He wanted to get rid of me. A man like Lowther does it the indirect way...'

'Mmm,' said Scrope, unhappily. 'But then there's his offer to you.'

Carey paled and then flushed. 'You mean his suggestion that if I took myself back to London, he would stop with Barnabus?'

'Yes. Very unlike him.' Scrope started playing at venture again, warming his hands up.

'My lord?'

'Sorry, got caught up in the music.'

There was a clattering as Hughie, John Ogle's eldest son, cleared the dirty plates and Philadelphia followed him to supervise their scouring and locking away. Scrope's long fingers were at home and at ease on the rosewood keys; they moved by themselves and gave expression to his thoughts in a tangled elaboration of a haunting tune Scrope had heard sung by one of the local headmen's harpers.

'Where was I?'

'We were speaking about Lowther, my lord.' The smooth voice was thinning with impatience.

'Um...yes. You see, he's not a man to let his prey escape. If all of this was some elaborate trap to catch you, he'd not rest until you were beheaded or at the horn.'

'No doubt that is what he wants.'

'Oh, no doubt at all. But offering you a way out and keeping hold of your servant...I'd almost say he genuinely thinks Barnabus is the killer and will settle for losing his chance of you, if he can have his way with Barnabus.'

'Or he's cleverer than you think him and offering me a way out is a trap as well, a means of getting me to admit my guilt by running away.'

Scrope looked sideways at him. That was the irritating thing about the Careys; sometimes they were sharper than they seemed.

'Yes, that's also a possibility. If so, then you must have disappointed him.'

Carey looked away and swallowed, still clearly furious at Lowther's imputation that he was threatening little Mary Atkinson in order to maker her mother confess to the murder.

Scrope stopped playing, stood and started digging in the casket of sheet music.

'I'm sorry, Robin, I don't believe it. The whole thing is far too elaborate and complicated for Lowther. Oh, he's capable of it, but if he'd been the man behind the killing Jemmy Atkinson would have wound up in your bed with his throat slit, not his own or Frank's vennel or wherever it was. Lowther's simply grabbing at an opportunity he sees to oust you. While I'm not at all surprised about the packtrain, I doubt very much he made that opportunity himself.'

Philadelphia had come back into the room and sat down quietly.

'But that leaves only Mrs Atkinson as the murderer.'

'Quite,' said Scrope complacently. 'I think she did it, just as she confessed.'

Carey held onto his temper.

'My lord, I'm sorry, but I think she was lying to save Andy Nixon's skin, just as Andy Nixon lied to save hers. I have to admit I think Lowther was right about that; cutting someone's throat is not a woman's means of murder. And Mrs Dodd has pointed out to me that doing the deed in her own bedchamber let her in for a great deal of work in washing the sheets.'

Philadelphia nodded vigorously.

'Janet Dodd is talking good sense,' she said. 'And in any case, what on earth could Mrs Atkinson hope to gain by it?'

Scrope smiled at her kindly for her womanly obtuseness. 'She wanted to marry Andy Nixon,' he explained. 'So of course she had to kill her husband.'

Philadelphia glared at him for some reason, then turned and picked up her workbag, delved in it, pulled out some blackwork and began stitching with short vicious movements.

'Let's make up a fairy tale,' she said at large. 'Let's pretend, Robin, that you wanted to marry someone who was married to another man.'

Carey gave her a glare of warning but she wasn't looking at him, she was squinting at a caterpillar made of black thread, which was eating a delicately worked quince.

'Now let's suppose that you and this other man's wife plot together and you decide to solve your problems by killing the woman's husband. Would you cut his throat?'

Carey harumphed. 'What are you getting at, Philly?' he asked in a strained voice.

'Robin, I'm not accusing you of anything improper. I'm playing let's pretend. Go on. Would you cut his throat?'

'Probably not.' Carey's voice was wintry in the extreme.

'Do you think Eli...the woman would cut her husband's throat?'

'Er...no.'

'And why not?'

'Well, obviously, you would want to make his death look like an accident so no one would be blamed. If his throat was cut people would look around for the murderer and unless his wife had an excellent alibi, they would think of her.'

'She would be risking a charge of petty treason?'

'Yes.'

'And burning for it?'

'Er...yes.'

'So do you think Mrs Atkinson *wanted* to die at the stake?'

The question was actually intended for Scrope, although it was aimed at her brother. Neither man answered her.

'I mean, burning to death is a very painful way to die,' Philly continued thoughtfully as she elaborated on the caterpillar's markings, 'I'm not sure hanging, drawing and quartering is that much more painful. Think of the Book of Martyrs and Cranmer and Latymer burning for their faith under Queen Mary—half the point is that they faced a much worse death than just hanging or the axe. Isn't it?'

'I was intending to order the executioner to strangle Mrs Atkinson at the stake,' said Scrope gently, 'before the fire was lit.'

Philly didn't look at him. 'Well, she couldn't know you would do that. Nobody bothers with witches, do they? Do you really think Mrs Atkinson is stupid enough to kill her husband by cutting his throat in bed, where the blood alone is likely to accuse her, never mind the corpse? I mean, there's nothing much less accidental than a cut throat, is there?'

'Well, she might not have thought of it…' said Scrope lamely.

Philadelphia found her snips and cut her thread peremptorily.

'Oh, my lord,' she cooed. 'Every woman knows the loyalty she owes her husband as her God-given lord. Every preacher makes it clear, every marriage sermon tells her. It's not a secret. Mrs Atkinson isn't half-witted. Cutting his throat would have been idiocy for her.'

'But Philadelphia,' wailed Scrope. 'Who did it then? If it wasn't Barnabus and it wasn't Andy Nixon and it certainly wasn't Lowther and it wasn't even Kate Atkinson, who did it?'

His wife was stitching a cabbage quite near the caterpillar. She stopped and looked up at Carey.

'Ask the question nobody seems to have thought of yet,' she said to him simply. 'You remember, Robin, Walsingham's question.'

'What's she talking about?' demanded Scrope, his brow furrowed.

It wasn't exactly the light of revelation, more the promise of it, the moment when Alexander the Great drew his sword when faced with the Gordian knot.

'She means the lawyer's question. *Cui bono*? Who benefits?' Carey explained slowly. 'It was what Sir Francis Walsingham always asked when faced with some complicated political puzzle.'

'Ah,' said Scrope, not sounding very enlightened. 'Well, you'd best be quick about it, Robin. The inquest opens at 11 o'clock tomorrow which is the earliest the jury can get here.'

And I've been wasting my time with damn silly letters about lodgings, Carey thought to himself.

'Plenty of time if you get up early enough,' said Philadelphia brightly, reading his mind. 'And my lord gives you leave.'

'Oh, ah, yes, of course,' said Scrope, his attention already diverted back to the music in front of him. He squinted at the close-printed notes and began playing again.

'Thank you, my lord.' Carey said nothing more, blinked past the candles on the virginals lid at the copper sunset light slowly seeping into the bright sky. He shook his head suddenly like a horse with a fly in its ear, as if he had almost fallen into a dream standing up.

Philadelphia was silent at last. Scrope looked sideways at him, saw the frustration and annoyance still in him and rambled into a madrigal accompaniment that he was sure Carey knew. For a moment Scrope wondered if his brother-in-law was still too tense to take the musical bait, but then he opened his mouth and began singing the tenor line to it, which happened to be a very graceful melody. Scrope closed his eyes: God had made a miracle in the human voice, there was no instrument like it, and Carey's tenor was very good, clear, like a bronze bell, entirely free of affectation. When he forgot the words in the third verse, he made some up and they came to a flourishing end with a cascade of nonny-nos which Carey miraculously managed to negotiate without getting his tongue tangled. Philadelphia had listened to the end without moving, her heart-shaped little face tilted to one side, and then she rose, kissed her brother on the cheek and silently left the room, went down the stone stairs.

Scrope sighed happily and turned a beaming face to him.

'Splendid. What it must be to be able to sing...'

The music had worked some of its accustomed magic; Carey smiled back and dug in the box of music.

'You're sure it wasn't Lowther?' he said, still sounding puzzled.

'Quite sure,' said Scrope. 'For the same reason I was sure it wasn't you either. Character.'

'Character?'

'I loathe the man as much as you do and I don't doubt you're right that he sent Mick to bring in the Grahams and lift Lady Widdrington. That's much more his style. In any case, why duplicate his effort? Presumably he wanted Lady Widdrington kidnapped so as to lure you into some kind of trap.'

'I suppose so.'

'Well, then, what's the point of it if you're in irons for Atkinson's murder and can't risk and break your neck trying to rescue her?'

Carey sighed. That was certainly logical, blast it. So now he had three suspects in gaol and not one of them the right person. He turned back to the sheet music and finally found what he had been looking for.

'This is the one the Queen likes.' He set the music before Scrope.

'Good lord, this is new.'

'All the rage at Court, my lord,' murmured Carey.

Scrope was running through the music, first right hand, then left hand, then both together.

'Here you go, two and one.'

Carey sang the Latin voice part to the end, knowing it quite well. Scrope turned the page, blinked hard at the close-tangled black notes, and carried straight on sight-reading, humming to himself and tapping his foot. It was a delicate pastoral piece, the kind of thing the Queen always liked to play. Carey sat down in Scrope's carved chair to listen until Philadelphia returned again. Despite the somnolence brought on by a heavy meal and the end of the day he was in no hurry to return to his bedchamber, the absence of Barnabus's snores and the ridiculously short truckle bed to which Buttercup and her family had relegated him. If he closed his eyes he could imagine an Arcadia of shepherds, shepherdesses and Elizabeth Widdrington, as constant in his phantasy as the Queen at Court, and quite as formidable, despite being generally mother-naked in the Greek style. He smiled a little.

'Oh, look at him,' said Philadelphia when she returned at last, leaning over her sleeping brother. 'Poor thing.'

Scrope was lost in the lands of music and only said 'Eh?', before carrying on with a complex variation on the notes before him. Philadelphia called John Ogle and his eldest lad. They carried Carey to the guest chamber where Scrope's own bodyservant, Humphrey

Rumney, undressed him and put him to bed to the complex strains from the nearby dining room, and through it all Carey smiled.

thursday 6th july 1592, before dawn

Carey awoke with that feeling of dislocation that comes from sleeping in a different bed than the one expected. At least it was just long enough for him. The curtains drawn around his bed were half-open and the darkness had that faint pearly greyness of false dawn. For a few seconds he blinked and picked his way through fragments of dream and memory. There was snoring in the room, as usual coming from a truckle bed by the door, though on a subtly different note from Barnabus. No, he was not in fact in bed with a woman; unfortunately he was alone. For a moment he dwelled on his unnatural and pitiable womanless state; in Carey's opinion, if God had meant men to live without women, He wouldn't have created Eve.

But Court music was still flowing through his memory. Oh yes. He had been listening to Scrope's playing the night before and had dozed off; they must have put him to bed. Had he been drunk? No, his memories of the evening were too clear; he had simply been tired.

Memory filtered back. At the forefront of them all was Philadelphia's reminder of Walsingham's question: who benefits? If not Lowther, if not Kate Atkinson, who actually benefited from Jemmy Atkinson's very bloody death?

The answer had come to him from God while he slept: it lay in the fact that by English law, all the murderer's property went to the victim's family. Underneath all the complications, that was a simple beacon. Andy Nixon couldn't have benefited simply because it was so likely he would be accused; as Philly had said, that went double for Mrs Atkinson who was not at all martyr material. No, he was actually looking at an attempt at double or even triple murder, with himself intended as the murder weapon.

He flung back the sheets and counterpane and jumped out of bed. Energy filled him; he loved this time of day and he was impatient to do what he should have done from the start. He knew where he was now, mentally and physically: who could mistake the virulent dragon and St. George on the tapestry hangings, and the strangely shaped pointy-hatted women of the last century? He wondered why Philadelphia had not sent for some better hangings from London for her guest chamber, as he used the chamber pot under the bed, found the tinderbox to light a taper, and looked about for his clothes.

In the truckle bed he found Simon Barnet, lying on his back and imitating his noisy uncle.

'Quicker if I dress myself,' said Carey, passed his hand over his chin and decided to shave now. He doubted he would have the time to go to the barber's later and he certainly didn't trust Simon with a razor yet. On the other hand he needed hot water.

He shook the truckle bed vigorously until Simon sat up on his elbow and blinked at him.

'Wha'?' Simon asked.

'Good morning,' Carey said brightly. 'Run and fetch me a pitcher of hot water to shave with and something to eat and drink, there's a good lad, Simon.'

Simon swung his legs over the side of the truckle bed and rubbed his eyes. Like most of the boys in the Castle he hardly ever bothered to take his clothes off. 'Yessir,' he muttered, got up, swayed, hauled his boots on and shambled out of the door.

'I said run,' Carey called after him reproachfully. 'I'm in a hurry.'

'Urrh,' sighed Simon and speeded to a tottering trot.

One of the boys from the kitchen eventually turned up with a pitcher of hot water, saying Simon was on his way. Stuffing his face again, Carey thought, as he worked the soap into a lather and nipped through to Scrope's chamber to borrow his razor; I'll have to get him new livery soon, the rate he's growing. It was a lot of trouble shaving himself, but life at Court had ingrained it into him that he couldn't appear in any official capacity with a chin covered in stubble. And he couldn't regrow his beard until the black dye in his hair had finished growing out, which he hadn't thought of when he did it. The Scropes were still fast asleep, along with their respective maid and manservant, their bedchamber a choir of snores. Amazing how people wasted the best part of the day lying in their beds.

Half an hour later he was in his green velvet suit and shrugging the shoulder strap of his swordbelt over his arm. As usual, Simon Barnet was taking three times as long as Barnabus to do a perfectly simple job and Carey soon got tired of waiting for him. He put his hat on, crept through the intervening chamber and his sister and brother-in-law's bedroom, and clattered down the stairs of the Keep. Nobody was stirring in the hall, where most of the servants still slept wrapped in their cloaks, on benches or in the rushes, and out into the cold morning air. There wasn't anybody about so Carey went across to the Keep gate and had a quick word with Solomon Musgrave. Then he went to his chambers in the Queen Mary Tower, greeted Buttercup, lit a candle and did some hurried paperwork. Finally he went to the new barracks, and knocked on the door of Sergeant Dodd's little chamber next to the harness room.

It took a while but eventually there were thumping sounds inside and Dodd opened the door in his shirt and hose, with his helmet in one hand and his sword in the other.

'What the hell is it...?' he demanded. 'Och, sorry, sir. Is there a raid?'

'Er...no, Sergeant,' said Carey, trying not to look past his shoulder at where Janet Dodd lay in the rumpled little bed. 'Only we have a lot to do and not much time to do it in.'

'Oh. Ah,' said Dodd, slowly catching up with this. 'There's no raid?'

'No.'

'Och God, it's still the middle of the night, sir; it's...'

'Dodd,' said Carey patiently, wondering what on earth was the matter with the man. 'It's a couple of hours before dawn and I want to start rounding up witnesses for the inquest, so I'd be grateful if you would get yourself dressed and come and help me.'

Dodd leaned his sword against the wall and then put his hand across his eyes and moaned like a cow in calf.

'Ay sir,' he said heavily at last. 'I'll be wi' ye.'

Dodd yawned and shut the door. Carey went outside the barracks building and stood in the yard, mentally making lists. Janet came out still lacing her kirtle and hurried past him with an amused expression on her face.

'Have they opened the buttery yet, do ye know sir?' she asked him.

'I don't know, Mrs Dodd.'

'Och,' she shook her head and hurried on.

By the time Dodd was ready, the stable boys were beginning to stir although the gate wasn't due to open for an hour yet. Solomon Musgrave opened the postern gate for them and Carey and Dodd went down past the trees and into Carlisle town. There were a few lights lit in the windows and a night-soil wagon clattered slowly down Castlegate ahead of them, while two men with shovels picked up the least unpleasant piles of manure and tossed them in the back.

'Now,' said Carey. 'Firstly, what did you find out last night, Sergeant?'

Dodd blinked and rubbed his eyes. 'Ay,' he said with great effort. 'Er…well, after I found Michael Kerr, I spoke to the men working on the roof by the Atkinsons' house and asked if any of them had seen aught, and the foreman said they hadnae but they had found a bloody knife stuck deep in the new thatch and they were going to give it to the master.'

'To John Leigh?'

'Ay. So any road, I got them to give it to me and it's in my room now.'

'Excellent, Sergeant, well done. Anything else?'

There were a few women moving about the streets, maidservants who didn't live-in going to their work.

'Ah…Janet went to speak to Julia Coldale again, but got nothing but cheek from the girl, so she came away. None o' Mrs Atkinson's gossips saw aught; it was too early in the morning and they were too busy. Janet says none of them save Mrs Leigh thinks Kate Atkinson did the murder. Maggie Mulcaster was wanting to know was there anything they could gi' ye to persuade ye to leave it.'

Carey sighed. 'What did she say?'

'She said she didnae think so and besides ye're a courtier and verra expensive, but in any case she thought ye had enough sense to see she didnae do it, but it was a case of convincing the jury and ye hadnae set that up, Lowther had.'

'Well, that's something. Though Lowther still thinks it was Barnabus. Anything else?'

'Then we went to Bessie's to see if anybody there had heard anything, but they hadnae except that Pennycook's left town and gone back to Scotland.'

'Very wise of him,' said Carey. 'And that was it?'

'Ay sir,' Dodd saw no reason to fill Carey's enquiring pause with the details of their evening in Bessie's. 'Janet says she thinks ye should arrest young Julia and frighten her into…'

'Speak of the devil,' said Carey softly. 'Look there.'

It was hard to miss the girl's wonderful fall of hair, even under her hat, as she walked quickly down the street ahead of them. Carey put his arm out to stop Dodd and then followed her cautiously. The girl went to the door of the Leighs' house and knocked softly. The door opened at once and she stepped in.

'What's she up to?' Carey said to himself, walking about under the spidery growth of poles and planks on the Leighs' house. The workmen had pulled up all their ladders when they left the night before. Carey whistled very softly between his teeth.

'Right, Dodd,' he said. 'Give me a leg up.'

'Eh?'

'Give me a boost. I want to get up the scaffolding.' He was already unbuckling his sword.

Dodd sighed, bent his knee next to one of the poles and Carey climbed from knee to shoulder, to an accompaniment of complaint from Dodd, caught the horizontal pole of the first platform and heaved himself up.

Carey's legs were kicking, so Dodd backed off a bit. It was the Courtier's padded Venetian hose that were causing the trouble; they had caught on the edge of one of the planks. No doubt they were well enough for a life spent parading in front of the Queen, though Dodd with sour pleasure.

At last Carey was onto the first platform, a bit breathless. He let down one of the ladders and Dodd climbed up after him, bringing the sword belt, then he pulled the ladder back up to use it for getting to the second platform. Once there, Carey went to the boundary with the Atkinsons' house and called Dodd over. He nodded at the place where Carey was pointing.

'Ay,' he said, suppressing a feeling of sickness at being so high over the street. 'I was wondering about them marks.'

Carey went along the platform again. 'Where did they find the knife?'

'Just about here, sir.'

'Right. Help me make a hole.'

'But sir…'

'Don't argue, Sergeant. I don't need a warrant.'

'But they just had the roof done, sir.'

'So they did, Sergeant.'

Carey had drawn his poignard and was digging away among the rushes. Reluctantly Dodd took out his own knife and helped. The hole was rather large when the Courtier finally hissed softly through his teeth and started pulling something from the thatch.

It was a man's linen shirt, crackling and stiff with brown crumbling stains.

'Och,' said Dodd and then. 'The silly bastard.'

Carey looked at him quizzically and gave him the shirt.

'Why?'

'Should ha' burned it, that's why. What's he want tae keep it for?'

'Couldn't bring himself to waste a shirt. Or was going to but hasn't had the chance yet.'

Dodd shook his head. Carey led the way back along the platform and started down the ladder, but Dodd stopped by the small window and peered in between the shutter slats.

'Sir,' he said softly. 'Come and look at this.'

Carey came back, peered between the shutters as well. It was hard to be sure in the half-light, but there were two people standing in the little room. One was John Leigh, the other the girl with long red curls. They were murmuring too low for Carey to hear. The girl shrugged and spoke sharply. John Leigh nodded and held out what looked like a heavy purse. The girl reached to take it and in that moment, John Leigh dropped the purse, grabbed her wrist and hit her hard on the jaw. She reeled back and slumped. Then John Leigh was on her with his hands round her neck, silently squeezing the life out of her.

Dodd's mouth was open. Carey stepped back, lifted his boot and kicked the shutters hard, kicked again. Dodd remembered something, left him to it, and slid down the ladder to the next level.

It was a horrible shock to John Leigh when a boot suddenly started splintering the wood of his window shutters and then burst apart the lead flushings of the expensive little diamond window panes.

Foolishly he let go of Julia Coldale's neck, and started back, staring wildly. The head and one shoulder of the Deputy Warden shoved through the tattered window, causing glass to fall and shine in the rushes.

'Get away from that girl,' ordered Carey.

He can't get through the window, thought John Leigh; it's too small for him. Without really thinking things through, he reached for Julia Coldale again. There was a loud hammering downstairs. She was making crowing noises and blindly trying to crawl away from him; he grabbed her shoulder, pushed her back, clipped her jaw again and started strangling her once more. Something hard hit his ear painfully, drawing blood. He looked up, saw Carey with two more diamond panes in his hand, taking aim to throw them at him, his dagger in his left hand. He did throw them, John Leigh ducked, but didn't duck fast enough and was hit on the cheek. He let go of Julia to put his hand up to the cut and another piece of glass hit him on the forehead.

There were footsteps on the stairs, but John Leigh had picked up his wife's sewing table and was using it as a shield against the rain of missiles from Carey. The door was booted open and there stood Sergeant Dodd, breathing hard, a drawn sword in each hand.

'Now,' said Dodd sadly between pants. 'Ye'd best do as the Deputy tells ye, Mr Leigh.'

Leigh's teeth showed like a cornered dog's. He drew his own dagger, dropped the sewing table in a mess of pincushions and thread spools, and picked up Julia, turned her about so he could put his blade to her neck. Her legs weren't supporting her and she didn't look as if she was breathing.

'Stay away, Dodd,' he shouted wildly. 'Or I'll cut her throat.'

Dodd stopped, partly because Julia Coldale was between him and Leigh and it was always hard to put a sword through two bodies at once. The girl made a loud snoring noise and then another, started coughing and gagging.

'Matilda,' roared John Leigh. 'Matilda, come and help me. Matildaaa!'

There was no answer. Dodd stood there, a sword in each hand and no way to use either of them while Leigh kept his knife to the girl's neck.

'Get back,' whispered Leigh hoarsely. 'Get back through the door.'

'Now listen,' said Dodd regretfully. 'Ye canna make it work. We both saw ye trying to kill the girl an' I dinna care why and nor does the Deputy. But ye willnae hang if ye dinna kill her, see, so why not let her go and save us all trouble and sweat?'

The girl was gagging and whooping pitifully, still not able to stand. She must be an awful weight on his arm, thought Dodd, taking one considered step back. Leigh followed, facing him, his hand with the knife trembling dangerously.

I wonder what the Deputy's up to, Dodd thought to himself.

'Where will ye go?' he asked Leigh reasonably. 'What will ye do? Ye'll be at the horn for sure and could ye live in the Debateable Land?'

'Other men have,' said Leigh desperately. Julia slipped against him and he hefted her up again, sweat on his face.

Dodd shook his head. 'Fighting men,' he said. 'Wi' all the respect in the world, sir, ye're not a fighting man. Have ye a sword? Harness? A helmet? D'ye have horses? Can ye use a lance? My brother-in-law Skinabake Armstrong has his pick o' men to join his gang, sir, and he'll no' take a Carlisle draper.'

The knife was shaking hard now. 'I can learn,' croaked Leigh.

'Ay, ye could,' said Dodd, consideringly. Behind Leigh something white appeared at the little window. 'But could ye learn fast enough? The prime raiding season starts in August, after Lammastide, and we're well into July already, sir.' He raised his voice. 'Ye'd have a lot to learn, ye ken. Are ye in one of the Carlisle trained bands, or did ye pay another man to take your place? Ay, I see ye had a substitute—and why should ye no', ye're a busy man, a prosperous merchant, an' there's nae reason in the world why ye should waste yer time out on the race course playing about wi' pikes and arquebuses and the like...'

Carey barked his shoulders painfully, easing them through the window, then snagged his shirt on a piece of glass and had to free it. He caught the beam above the windowseat with the tips of his fingers and hefted himself through as quietly as he could, with his knife in his teeth and his tongue and lips as far back from its edge as he could grimace. He sucked his stomach in as far as it would go and prayed devoutly as he hauled his hips through past the points of the broken window panes. And then his knees were in, he could drop to the ground quietly, while Dodd droned impassively on about civic duties and Leigh's own children. Carey was a head taller than Leigh. So with the back of John Leigh's neck and his expensively furred brocade gown only a pace in front of him, Carey took his dagger lefthanded from his mouth, reached over the man's shoulder to clamp Leigh's wrist in his right hand

and brought the hilt of the poignard down as hard as he could twice on the back of Leigh's head.

Leigh grunted and collapsed, dropping his knife as well. Julia Coldale fell too, then picked herself back up onto her hands and knees and was sick. She looked up at Carey, past his hairy calves and his bare knees and his now ragged white shirt to his face, made a soft croak and fainted.

Dodd looked at him impassively and handed his sword back. 'I'll go and fetch in yer suit, shall I, sir?' he asked.

'If you would, Sergeant,' said Carey.

thursday 6th july 1592, dawn

Mrs Leigh met them on the stairs, her swollen body entirely blocking them. Dodd had tied John Leigh's hands behind his back after the man had come mumbling and sobbing back to consciousness, and was pushing him down the steps ahead of him, his sword pressed against the man's backbone, and the bloodstained shirt they had found in the roof tucked into his belt. Carey was carrying Julia Coldale who was still coughing and cawing like a jackdaw.

'Wh...what are you doing with my husband?' Mrs Leigh demanded. She was in her smock and dressing gown and her hair in its nighttime plait.

'We're arresting him, Mrs Leigh,' said Dodd. 'Would ye kindly move away?'

'Wh...what for?'

'Trying to kill Julia Coldale,' came Carey's voice from above. 'He nearly succeeded as well.'

'That little whore,' sniffed Mrs Leigh. 'My husband has nothing to do with the bitch.'

That's what you think, mistress, thought Dodd, who could think of one reason why a man would give a woman money. He didn't say that, mainly because he didn't want to bring on Mrs Leigh's labour.

'We only just stopped him throttling the life out of her,' said Carey. 'Please, Mrs Leigh, out of our way.'

She did move back into the doorway of the shop. Jock Burn was standing there as well, licking his lips. As he went past, John Leigh looked desperately at his wife.

'Matilda,' he whispered. 'Do something.'

She looked away.

They had a full escort of small boys and dogs by the time they got back to Carlisle Castle and Carey was beginning to puff and blow a bit with Julia's weight. She had managed to stop whooping by then, so he put her down and she leant very prettily on his arm, trying to give him the occasional trustful smile. Oddly enough he didn't smile back.

They were running out of space for prisoners; there was only the Lickingstone cell left apart from the hole under the Gaoler's floorboards which was reached with a ladder. In the end they decided the hole was the least bad of the two.

'Chain him,' said Carey.

'But sir...' Dodd protested. 'He didnae actually kill her.'

'Only by the Grace of God,' said Carey coldly. 'And besides, haven't you worked out why? Chain him.'

'Ay sir.'

John Leigh sat down on the bench in the Gaoler's room with his head bowed while Dodd locked his feet together in the leg irons. When he had climbed down awkwardly, and the ladder pulled up again, Carey looked at Dodd.

'Fetch at least four men from the barracks and go and arrest Jock Burn. If you can't find him, tell the men on the City gates that they're on no account to let him out. And have the Crier give his name at the marketplace.'

'Ay sir,' said Dodd, wondering what on earth he was at but not inclined to argue with the expression on Carey's face.

Philadelphia had already taken Julia Coldale up to her stillroom, given her a dose of something unpleasant and painted her usual infusion of comfrey on the terrible bruises around her neck.

By the time her brother arrived looking grim and followed by a puzzled Richard Bell, Philadelphia had decided she should be put to bed.

'I have to speak to her first,' said Carey. 'I must know...'

Philadelphia drew him aside and whispered fiercely at him. 'The poor girl can hardly breathe, let alone speak; you can talk to her tomorrow...'

'It must be today,' said Carey implacably. 'Unless Scrope can get the inquest adjourned.'

'What's that got to do with...?'

'That's what I want to find out.'

He gently put her aside and went to stand over Julia who had started weeping quietly into her apron.

'Well?' he said. 'Will you talk to me now?'

'Ay,' she whispered.

It took an inordinately long time for her to croak out the story: Bell had no trouble writing down what she said and when she finished, she made her mark with a shaking hand. Philadelphia was less sorry for her by that time, as she signed her own name in witness to the mark with Carey himself. She agreed with her brother to bring the girl down to the inquest in her own litter.

By that time the jury for the inquest were assembling at the town hall and Scrope was putting on his black velvet court gown and his gold chain of office, while the prisoners were fetched out of their various cells. Carey sprinted up the stairs of the Queen Mary Tower to his own chamber to change his clothes to his good black velvet suit and found Simon Barnet asleep and snorting on the truckle bed.

Finally ready, Carey ran down the stairs again to join the tail end of the inquest procession, with his hat in his hand. Ahead, guarded by Sergeant Ill-Willit Daniel Nixon and Lowther's men, were all of the prisoners, including John Leigh: Barnabus shambled along looking frowsty and bad-tempered, Kate Atkinson walked with her head bowed and Andy was having trouble with his leg irons. It was a slow march. Dodd fell in behind him at the Keep gate with his four men and no prisoner.

'No sign of him?' Carey asked.

'Nay sir,' said Dodd mournfully. 'We were too late. He must have run as soon as we left. I did the rest of what ye said.'

'Damn, damn, damn,' muttered Carey. 'Why the hell didn't I think of it?'

'Well, sir,' Dodd was comforting. 'Ye couldnae arrest Jock Burn as well as his master wi' only the two of us and a half-dead maid to carry; Jock would ha' made mincemeat of us.'

'I suppose so.'

'And ye've caught the master good and proper, sir.'

'Have you got the shirt?'

'Ay sir, but no' the knife. I'll send Bangtail for it; he's a fast runner.'

Bangtail sprinted off from the end of the procession. Carey saw Janet Dodd among the crowd at the entrance to the town hall, a very formidable sight in red, black and brocade, surrounded by many of Kate Atkinson's gossips, likewise dressed in their Sunday best. There was no sign of Mrs Leigh, which was hardly to be wondered at.

thursday 6th july 1592, 11 am.

Edward Aglionby looked impressive in his budge-trimmed green velvet gown, black damask doublet and hose and tall hat. He stood on the steps of the hall as the Castle procession arrived and greeted Scrope with suitable respect.

'My lord,' he said in a carrying voice. 'There's nae room in the hall for all the folk that must be seen and examined and all the folk that wish to attend and so I have decided to hear the inquest at the market cross.'

'An excellent idea, Mr Aglionby,' beamed Scrope, who had been secretly dreading the heat and smell of a small town hall filled full of people in summer. 'Please dispose your inquest as you wish.'

Carey looked about him, wondering if Aglionby had considered security for the inquest. He needn't have worried. The Mayor and Corporation had called out the City trained bands and all three hundred of them stood around the cross, controlling the crowds, capped in steel, bearing halberds and billhooks and delighted to get such prime viewing positions.

Running his eye critically over them for the first time, Carey decided he liked the look of them. They were clean and so were their weapons and while they didn't stand to attention, they were orderly, paying attention and not one was picking his nose.

A large table had been taken out of the hall and set up by the cross. Aglionby sat himself down behind it in the Mayor's large carved chair, and indicated that Scrope should sit at his right at one end as a courtesy. The jury lined up on benches to his right. As they filed in Carey growled at the sight of them, for there at the front was Thomas Lowther, Sir Richard's brother. Sir Richard himself was of course present to give evidence, his heavy face only prevented from grinning with satisfaction by invincible dignity.

The Chancellor of the Cathedral came in solemn procession, bearing the large Bible from his lectern. Each of the twelve gentlemen of the jury stepped forward to swear that he would truly judge of the matter before him, so help him God.

Behind Carey the marketplace was packed with people, talking excitedly, held back by their sons, brothers and husbands, stern-faced with office. An inquest was not precisely a trial, but it could be very much more than simply finding what a person had died of. Since the Assize judge and his armed escort would not be coming from Newcastle until Lammastide at the beginning of August, and as there were suspects in the case—too many, in fact—the Coroner had wide powers to establish the identity of the man or woman who actually went before the judge as the accused. At which point, of course, the thing was pretty much a foregone conclusion.

'It is your duty, gentlemen of the jury,' said Aglionby sonorously, 'to decide how, when and why the deceased died and whether he died of natural or unnatural causes, by Act of God or by man's design. To this end you are charged by Almighty God and Her most gracious Majesty the Queen...'

It's still a bloody farce, Carey thought with disgust, looking at the two rows of assorted faces before him. Apart from Thomas Lowther there were Captain Carleton, his brother Lancelot and Captain Musgrave. He recognised another as Archibald Bell. One friend, eleven neutral or enemies. Their general hostility to Londoners was plain. His stomach tightened.

'Does the jury wish to view the body?' asked Aglionby and Thomas Lowther rose to answer him.

'It willna be...'

Archibald Bell pulled on his gown from behind and whispered in his ear. Lowther coughed.

'It seems it will be necessary,' he finished.

The jury filed up the steps to the hall where Atkinson's body, already smelling gamey, was laid out ready for them. They came back down, all of them impassive.

Aglionby asked Sir Richard Lowther to give evidence from the steps of the cross, since he had been called immediately and was the first gentleman to have seen the body. After swearing his oath loudly he gave evidence of where the body lay, in Frank's vennel, on Tuesday morning, with great emphasis. He then added that he had immediately known who must have done the deed, to wit, one Barnabus Cooke, late of London town, footpad, currently pretending to serve Sir Robert Carey. He had hurried back to the Keep, found the said Cooke, and arrested him. Although he, Lowther, had besought the vile Cooke to confess his crime with eloquent words, he, the vile Cooke, had refused with many foul oaths, thereby compounding his offence. Seizing his moment, Carey stepped forward and bowed.

'Your honour...' he said hintingly to Aglionby. Scrope looked at him, puzzled. Aglionby smiled and tilted his head.

'Yes, Sir Robert, please continue.'

'Just a minute,' snorted Sir Richard. 'What's he want?'

'He is acting as *amicus curiae*.' Aglionby told him repressively. 'He will ask supplementary questions to aid the Crown.' Scrope leaned over and whispered urgently, to which the Coroner replied with another smile and half-shut eyes.

Lowther snorted. He wasn't sure what an *amicus curiae* might be—nor clearly was Scrope—but he couldn't possibly admit to ignorance. Carey moved around so he was half-facing Lowther and sideways on to the crowd, and pitched his voice as if he were making a speech in a tournament with most of Whitehall Yard to reach.

'Sir Richard,' he said respectfully. 'Who came to fetch you on Tuesday morning?'

Lowther's face darkened. 'Some clerk or other.'

'Was it one Michael Kerr, factor to Mr James Pennycook?'

'It might have been. Ay, it was. So?'

'Your honour, I trust Mr Kerr is available to give evidence?' Carey said to the Coroner. Aglionby rifled through the papers in front of him and found the list of witnesses.

'Yes, Sir Robert. We can call him next, if you wish.'

'If your honour pleases.'

Aglionby turned aside to whisper to his clerk who transmitted the whisper to one of the trained band. Carey looked at Lowther.

'Sir Richard, can you describe what Frank's vennel looked like when you came to see the body?'

Lowther snorted again and said contemptuously that it had had a body lying in it and a powerful lot of people looking on and one o' the dogs being dragged off.

'Was there blood?'

'I dinna ken. There might have been.'

'But was there in fact any blood?'

'I dinna recall.'

'Did you notice anything else unusual in the alley?'

'No.'

'Er...Sir Richard, what made you think that Barnabus Cooke had killed Mr Atkinson?' put in Scrope helpfully. Dammit, thought Carey, whose side are you on? Aglionby let him get away with it.

'Oh, ay. I found Barnabus's knife and one of Carey's gloves on the body,' said Lowther, looking slightly embarrassed.

Carey smiled kindly at him. 'Where were these incriminating items?' he asked.

Lowther coughed. 'Laid on top o' the body.'

Now isn't that interesting, Carey thought. I did you an injustice, Tom Scrope.

'I'm sorry, Sir Richard,' he said, elaborately obtuse. 'I don't quite understand. Exactly how were they placed?'

'Well, the corpse was on its back, and the knife lay on its chest and the glove by it.'

Carey paused to let this picture sink in. 'Someone had carefully put them there, in other words,' he said.

'I dinna ken.'

'Well, they could hardly have dropped so neatly by accident, could they?'

Lowther shrugged. Carey waited a moment to see if he would say anything else, then continued.

'Now when you found my servant Barnabus Cooke, where was he?'

'In yer chambers.'

'At the Keep?'

'Ay.'

'What did he say when you accused him?'

'I didnae understand because he spake braid London,' said Lowther.

Probably just as well, thought Carey. 'Did he say anything you understood?'

'He lied.'

'What did he actually say?'

'He said he didnae do it. But he...'

'What did you do then?'

'I arrested him.'

'Barnabus, stand forward,' Carey said and Barnabus took a step out of the group of accused. 'Is this the man you arrested?'

'Ay.'

'Tell me, how did his face come to be so battered?'

Lowther shrugged and wouldn't answer. There was a certain amount of muttering among the public, none of whom were naive.

'Who else was in my chambers?'

Lowther shrugged again. 'A boy,' he said.

'In fact, Simon Barnet, Cooke's nephew.'

'If you say so, Sir Robert.'

'Is it true that you tried to get into my office and Barnet prevented you, so you beat him as well?'

'Nay. He was insolent.'

'Did Lady Scrope then come and order you out of my chambers which you were preparing to search?'

'Ay.'

'Did you in fact, threaten her as well?'

'Nay,' said Lowther. 'She threatened me.'

Scrope blinked gravely at Lowther. 'You hadn't mentioned this, Sir Richard,' he said reproachfully, which was why Carey had brought it up. Lowther cleared his throat and Aglionby put out a repressive hand. Scrope subsided.

'Now, Sir Richard,' said Carey. 'Apart from a knife and a glove laid carefully on the corpse, did you have any other reason at all for accusing Barnabus Cooke?'

'The man's throat was cut. Yon's a footpad's trick.'

'Is there no other man in Carlisle who can use a knife?' Carey asked, rhetorically.

'It's a footpad's trick,' repeated Lowther doggedly.

'So you actually had no other evidence or reason for thinking that Barnabus Cooke had killed Atkinson?'

Go on, thought Carey, I dare you; I dare you to say you thought I'd told him to do it. For a moment he was sure Lowther would say it, but in fact he did not, he simply stood there with his arms folded and a sour expression on his face.

'Thank you, Sir Richard.'

Carey made a gesture of dismissal and the Coroner nodded that Lowther could go.

Michael Kerr was ready to be examined next. He gave his evidence in a mutter that the jury had to strain to hear. He had happened to go through Frank's vennel that morning. No, he had not been sent. Yes, he did know he was on oath. No, he had not been sent, well, he had wondered if there was anything to find there. He couldn't remember why. Yes, he knew the dead man. Yes, he was Mr James Pennycook's factor and son-in-law. Yes, he understood Mr Pennycook had left town. He had gone to join the Scottish King's Court, he believed. No, he didn't know anything about anything else.

According to the list Carey had provided, the next to be called was Fenwick the undertaker who had come to fetch the body away.

He explained that he had done this but that he had been worried by many things about the body.

'Oh?' said Aglionby with interest. 'What were they?'

Fenwick's grave face was troubled and he put up one finger. 'Considering the man's throat was cut, there should have been blood in the wynd. There was none that I could see. There was blood on his shirt, but not his outer clothes, except the linings. He lay very straight, as if he had been arranged, quite respectfully really, and on his back which is not the way someone falls when they have been attacked from behind.'

'I see, thank you. Sir Robert?'

'Did you notice any tracks in the wynd, Mr Fenwick?'

He hadn't at the time, though now he came to think about it he thought there might have been marks of a hand cart in the softer parts.

The next was Barnabus himself, brought forward under guard to stand by the cross. Of course, as one of the accused he was not allowed a lawyer, even if there had been one available. The day was warm and Carey had already started to sweat under his black velvet: Barnabus was unwell and unhappy in the sunlight after so long in semi-darkness, with his battered round brimmed hat crushed in his hands, his bruised ferret-face with its collection of pockmarks and scars making him look an ugly sight even to Carey, who was used to him. The thin film of moisture on his skin didn't help either.

The Coroner looked at the unsavoury little man impassively.

'Barnabus Cooke,' he said after Barnabus had whinged out his oath with his hand on the cathedral Bible. 'Remember you are on oath and at risk of sending your immortal soul to hell if you lie.'

'Yes, yer honour.'

'Did you kill Mr James Atkinson?'

'No, yer honour. I didn't.'

'Why does such an important gentleman as Sir Richard Lowther think you did?'

'I dunno, yer honour. Only I didn't.'

'Where were you on Monday night?'

Barnabus's eyes darted from side to side making him look even shiftier.

'Well, see, yer honour, I was at Bessie's first, because my master was out wiv a patrol. Then I…I went to a house I know. Perhaps one of the girls lifted my knife while I was there. I never went nowhere near Frank's vennel.' Barnabus paused and then smiled slyly. ''Course it's funny in a way and serves me right,' he volunteered, while Carey winced inwardly. 'I've been teaching the girls to do tricks with dice and such, and I expect one of them used 'er lessons on me.'

Half of the people in the marketplace knew exactly where Barnabus had been on Monday night. The other half learnt it from them within a few seconds. They hissed and muttered at each other at the news that Madam Hetherington's girls had been taking lessons in cheating at dice. Carey fought not to laugh. That would teach Madam Hetherington not to betray her customers.

'Do you mean you were committing the sin of fornication on Monday night?' interrupted Scrope pompously.

Barnabus didn't look at him and nor did Carey. 'Yes, my lord,' said Barnabus, turning pointedly to the Coroner. 'I wouldn't say, if I wasn't on my Bible oath, yer honour, but I was. I'm a poor sinner, yer honour, and if I'm sentenced to do penance for the fornication, well, I can't gainsay as I deserve it, but I never murdered Mr Atkinson and that's a fact. I don't deserve to swing for a murder I never did, yer honour.'

Lowther leaned over from his place on the other side of the cross.

'Ye're a footpad, and that's a fact,' he snarled.

'Sir Richard!' snapped Aglionby.

'Well yer honour, 'e's right and 'e isn't, if you follow. It's true I was a footpad down in London, but since Sir Robert Carey took me on as 'is servant, I've left my evil ways behind, sir.'

More or less, thought Carey, smiling inwardly at the strained piety on Barnabus's face.

'Apart from passing on what small skills I have to Madam Hetherington's girls,' he added reflectively, making sure the audience got the point. 'Anyway, no footpad would make the mistake of cutting someone's froat, yer honour.'

Aglionby raised his heavy grey brows.

'Oh? Why?'

'Specially me, because I'm too short. I'm about four inches shorter than Mr Atkinson, yer honour. If I'd wanted 'im dead, which I didn't, I'd have stabbed 'im in the back. In the kidneys. S'much safer and less messy.'

Carey risked a glance over his shoulder to see how the people in the marketplace were taking this. A lot of them were nodding wisely. Even one or two of the jury were nodding. Barnabus, thought Carey, you don't need me at all, do you?

'Yes,' said Aglionby, impressively straightfaced. 'Thank you, Cooke.'

Barnabus stepped back among the other suspects and looked modestly at the cobbles.

Somewhere on the other side of the marketplace, Lady Scrope had arrived with the litter transporting Julia Coldale, who was helped down from it. Carey waited for the stir to die down a little, then nodded at Richard Bell to call the next witness.

That was Mrs Katherine Atkinson. She was shaking and as white as her apron. Compared with the other women watching, tricked out to the nines in their best clothes, she was a doleful hen sparrow, her blue working kirtle and her apron showing the signs of her imprisonment. She wasn't manacled; Carey assumed Dodd had quietly forgotten Scrope's order to chain her.

She swore her oath in a voice that was almost too soft to hear. Edward Aglionby stared at her solemnly and then said, 'Well, Mrs Atkinson, tell us how you killed your husband?'

There was a muttering from the people. Mrs Atkinson gripped her hands tight together, looked straight up at him and said clearly, 'I didna.'

This time there was a distinct gasp. Carey instinctively swivelled his head round to look at his sister's face and found her very pleased with herself.

'I beg your pardon?' said Scrope.

'I didna kill my husband, my lord.'

'But...but you confessed to it. Yesterday. You stood in front of me and you said you did it.'

Scrope was leaning forward, half-standing, forgetting himself in his outrage. Mr Aglionby had been very patient with him but now leaned towards him and whispered something sharp in his ear. Scrope coughed and sat down again. Carey was starting to like Mr Aglionby.

'Please, Mrs Atkinson,' the Coroner was saying to her. 'Address yourself to the Court.'

'Ay sir,' said Mrs Atkinson, quailing at his annoyance. 'My lord, I did say so. I'm very sorry. But I wasna on my Bible oath then, and I dare not put my soul at risk wi' perjury.'

'What's your story now?'

''Tisn't a story, your honour,' said Mrs Atkinson, two hot spots of colour starting in her cheeks. 'I lied to my lord Warden before, because I'm a poor weak-willed woman and I was frightened. But I've had time to think and pray to God and what I'm saying now is God's own truth, your honour.'

Scrope sniffed eloquently but said nothing.

With the Coroner pumping her with questions, Kate Atkinson told the tale in a stronger voice now Scrope had made her angry. She told the sequence of the morning's events, how she had left her husband sleeping in the dark before dawn and gone down to milk the cow and how Julia had come and finally brought herself to the moment when she took a tray up to her husband and found him dead in his bed.

'Your honour,' said Carey, stepping forward again. 'May I?'

'Yes, Sir Robert.'

'Mrs Atkinson, what did the bedroom look like?'

'Och, it was terrible, sir. It was all covered wi' blood, like a butcher's shambles. It was on the sheets and the blankets and the hangings and the rushes...It made me stomach turn to see.'

'And your husband?'

'He was lying on the bed...with...with...'

'With his throat slit.'

She swallowed hard. Her knuckles were like ivory. 'Ay sir,' she said.

'Tell me, when you got up that morning, did you open the shutters?'

She frowned at this sudden swoop away from the awful sight of her husband's corpse. 'I didna,' she said at last. 'I don't usually; Mr Atkinson likes to sleep a little longer and it would wake him.'

'Did you open them on this day?'

'Nay sir, I didna.'

'When you came up to see your husband dead, how did you see him. Was there a candle lit in the room?'

'Nay, sir, it had burned down. I saw by the daylight...Oh.'

'Were the shutters open by that time, then, Mrs Atkinson?'

She nodded at him. 'Ay,' she said in a surprised tone of voice. 'Ay, they were, and swinging free, what's more, not hooked back.'

'Now tell me what happened after you saw your husband.'

She looked at the floor again and mumbled something.

'Please speak up, Mistress,' said Aglionby.

'I said, I fainted, your honour. Then I couldna think what to do, so I went downstairs again and I sent my little girl Mary to fetch...to fetch my friend, Mr Andrew Nixon.'

Her brow was wrinkled now. 'When he came, what did he look like?' Carey asked.

'Oh, he was not well,' said Mrs Atkinson. 'He'd been in a fight, and lost it by the looks of him, and his right hand was in a sling and at first he said he didna want to meet my husband because he was angry.'

'Quite so,' said Carey hurriedly. 'What did you decide to do?'

'Neither of us could think of anything, sir, so Andy...er...Mr Nixon went to his master, Mr Pennycook, to ask his advice, and he took two pieces of silver plate from my chest wi' him, for a present.'

'And what did Mr Pennycook advise?'

'Well, he said we should borrow his handcart and put m...my husband's body in a wynd and he'd see to it that ye and yer London servant got the blame, not us.'

'How?'

'He said he could get hold of one of Barnabus Cooke's knives wi' a bit of luck, for the week before he'd left it in pledge at Madam Hetherington's, which is a house with a lease he owns. He sent Michael Kerr to Andy with it, as well as the handcart. I was busy at washing the sheets and blankets—it took all day—but I sent

Mary out and Julia Coldale too and that's when we brought his body down from the bedroom and into Clover's byre. Clover's my cow,' she added, in case there was any mistake. 'Andy got the glove.'

This recital was causing immense excitement in the crowd and Aglionby banged with his gavel. The noise died down gradually. Carey saw with interest that Michael Kerr had his face in his hands. Mrs Atkinson had fallen silent.

'And then?' he prompted.

'Well, I kept the children from looking out the window by telling them a story while Andy put the body on the cart under some hay and left it in the back so I could milk Clover before sunset, and then when it was dark, Andy took the cart away.'

'Why didn't you send to the Keep for Sir Richard Lowther and tell him what had happened at once, as your duty was?'

Mrs Atkinson licked her lips. 'I was too afraid to think straight. All I could see was he'd been killed; he was my husband, he'd been killed in his bed and I was about the place and so I was…I was afraid.'

'Why?'

'I was afraid…that I would get the blame for it, sir. I know what a terrible sin it is for a wife to kill her husband, sir, and I would never ever do it, but I knew people would say I had. And I was right, sir, they did. You did.'

'So you decided to try and hide the body and lay the blame on me,' said Carey sternly.

'Ay sir. I'm sorry. I've done many wicked things in the past few days, sir, but none of them was murder, as God sees me, sir. I never killed him.'

'One more thing. Exactly when was Mr Atkinson killed?'

'I told you, sir, it must have been around dawn on Monday, between the time when I got up to milk Clover and when I came back wi' his breakfast.'

'Thank you, Mrs Atkinson.'

Thomas Lowther was whispering to the man on his right, shaking his head. Carey could do nothing about that: truthfulness shone from Mrs Atkinson but the jury could refuse to see it if they chose.

To try and make sure that Andy Nixon made up no more foolish stories, Carey called Goodwife Crawe his landlady next. She stood small and stalwart under the cross before all the solemn men and repeated in a high clear voice what she had told Carey: she had found Andy Nixon in a bad state in her living room, when she went in before dawn on the Monday morning. She had nursed him, bound up his hand and given him food and drink and he had left after the gates opened. She didn't know where he had gone after that, only he had come home late that night.

Carey approached Andy Nixon with the feeling he might be a lighted bomb. He took his oath, stood straight and frowned with concentration.

Ay, he had been jumped in the alley on Sunday night by Goodwife Crawe's front door. Ay, they had been four men; he didn't know who they were or why they were there, or he wasna certain, and he had been too sore to climb the ladder to his own bed in her loft, so he had slept on Goodwife Crawe's fleeces. Ay, she had nursed him. Ay, he had gone out and met Mary Atkinson and against his will gone to see Kate Atkinson. He had been appalled when she showed him the body of her husband. After that, it had been as she said, he had gone to see Pennycook, who had recommended blaming Carey and to make sure of him, Andy himself had gone up to the Keep and inveigled one of Carey's own gloves from Simon Barnet his serving lad.

Ay, he had left Atkinson in Frank's vennel. No, he hadnae left him sprawled; he had laid him out proper, as was right.

'Why didn't you go and tell Lowther immediately as your duty was?' Carey asked. 'Instead of trying to get me blamed for it.'

Andy Nixon flushed. 'I wasnae thinking straight. I was afraid Kate…er…Mrs Atkinson would be blamed, and she was afraid too. We're no' important people, sir, we didnae think anyone would listen.'

'It was a disaster that Mr Atkinson's throat was cut, wasn't it?'

'Oh, ay,' said Nixon feelingly. 'It was.'

Scrope had learned the manners to look to the Coroner for permission to ask a question. Wisely Aglionby granted it. 'Mr Nixon, why did you tell me yesterday that you did the murder?'

Andy Nixon stared at the ground, lifted a foot to scrape his toe and was reminded of his leg-irons.

'I thought ye would think Mrs Atkinson did it,' he said. 'I didnae want her to burn, so I said I did it as hanging's an easier death.'

In France Carey had seen how hanged men could jig for twenty minutes if the executioner botched the drop and he doubted it was as easy as all that. There was a feminine buzz of approval from the audience behind him.

'But I'm on oath now and feared for my soul if I perjure myself,' Nixon added with commendable piety. Somebody had been coaching these witnesses and Carey knew it wasn't him. Out of the corner of his eye, he could see his sister nodding approvingly at Andy Nixon. Thomas Lowther snorted in a manner exactly like Sir Richard's.

'If you lied once, you might lie again,' said Scrope irritably.

'No my lord.' Andy Nixon was quite steady, for a miracle. 'Not on oath.'

Aglionby said he could step back now. Carey bowed to him.

'Your honour,' he said. 'May I address the jury?'

Aglionby nodded though it was highly irregular. Carey took a deep breath, paced up to the two benches full of jurymen and removed his hat, bowed to them.

'Gentlemen, you can see what perplexity I was in yesterday,' he said. 'Here were three suspects for a murder and the only one that could in any way have done it was a woman. Now if it had been a less bloody and violent murder, I would have been in less doubt. If Mr Atkinson had died by poison, for instance. But he did not. His throat was cut and in his bed. If you cut a man's throat from behind, you may avoid being soiled, but that was not possible because he was asleep in bed. It must have been done from the front. Now I myself have sliced open a man's throat in battle with a sword, and I may tell you, gentlemen, that I never was more dirty with blood in my life. Is it possible to do it without being sprayed? I doubt it.'

Most of the gentlemen in front of him had fought their own battles, perhaps one or two of the elder ones even with Carey's own father, during the Northern Rising. They were listening gravely, a couple of them nodding.

'Here we have the woman who might have done it, Mrs Atkinson herself. She is wearing now what she was wearing that morning, according to all witnesses. Can you see bloodstains on it?'

Their eyes swivelled to where Mrs Atkinson stood and took in the fact that although her clothes were dirty, there were no bloodstains.

'She is a woman, gentlemen. God made woman to serve man and accordingly he made her weaker, more timorous and less apt to violence. Is it believable she could have cut her own husband's throat, a dreadful crime and against all nature, and then gone downstairs immediately, spoken with her daughter, set a tray with breakfast, and gone up again? Of course not. Even if she could have done it, why should she? She is not mad nor melancholy. Even if she was such a wicked Jezebel as to turn against her rightful lord, why should she do it in such a way that she was bound to be suspected?'

Apart from Thomas Lowther, whom Cicero himself could not possibly have convinced, the other gentlemen were looking encouragingly puzzled.

'Well, gentlemen, although I cannot claim to be a learned lawyer, I did finally bring myself to ask the lawyer's question, *cui bono?* Who benefits? Who could possibly benefit from James Atkinson's death? And in particular, who could benefit from the manner of it? The very bloody manner of it which guaranteed that Mrs Atkinson would be accused of the crime of petty treason and would most likely burn.'

He paused impressively to let them think about it and a tiny thought darted through his mind like a silver fish that here was a surprise, the world could be focused down to an intoxicating point of intensity outside a card game or a battlefield. For a second he was intrigued and happy and then he turned his attention back to the jury.

'*Cui bono?*' he said again. 'Well, gentlemen, it's important you know that in a case of proven murder, the murderer's property goes to the victim's family.'

Lancelot Carleton was frowning at him. 'Yes, gentlemen. Mr Atkinson's death would normally mean that Mrs Atkinson inherited his goods and property, including the house where they lived. However, if she was arraigned and burned as his murderer, neither she nor her children could enjoy the gain. Instead, all the property would pass to Mr Atkinson's family. In this case, to Mrs Matilda Leigh, née Atkinson, his half-sister, and of course, her husband Mr John Leigh, draper, and their next-door-neighbour.'

It was terribly satisfying to listen to all the gasps around him. Carey swept his glance around the packed marketplace, took in

Scrope who had his fingers interlaced and a surprised expression on his face, and Edward Aglionby whose expression was very intent and then went back to the jury who were staring at him with their mouths open.

'Your honour,' he said to the Coroner. 'May I call first Mr Leigh, then Julia Coldale, maidservant to Mrs Atkinson, and then return to Mr Leigh?'

Aglionby wanted to hear the story too. He nodded immediately.

John Leigh reluctantly took the oath.

'Mr Leigh,' said Carey, pointedly putting his hat back on his head. 'Is it true that you have a long-running lawsuit in Chancery over the ownership of Mr James Atkinson's town house?'

Leigh looked from side to side and nodded.

'Speak up, please.'

'Ay,' he said with an effort. 'It's true.'

'Is it true that the case was costing you a great deal of money you could ill-afford, but you wanted the house in order to expand your business and your family into it?'

'Ay,' muttered Leigh.

'Your wife was estranged from her half-brother; the lawsuit made things worse, especially when the young lawyer the Atkinsons had retained then married the daughter of the judge in the case and might have gained from that a great deal of influence.'

Leigh nodded again, caught himself and said, 'Ay. I cannot deny it, sir.'

'Thank you, that's all for the moment. Mr Bell, will you call Julia Coldale?'

The girl came slowly forwards, leaning on Philadelphia's solicitous arm, and despite the obvious pain in her throat, enjoying herself. So was Philadelphia, Carey saw, despite her serious expression.

Carey had Julia stand close to the jury so they could hear her, and also see the marks on her throat.

Julia said she was a cousin of Kate Atkinson's and she was serving her to learn housewifery. The sun was high overhead by now and the heat causing sweat to trickle down Carey's spine.

'What happened early on Monday morning, Miss Coldale?' he asked the girl.

Julia coughed, took a deep breath. 'A man stopped me in the street when I was going to Mrs Atkinson's house—I live with my sister in Carlisle, sir—and he asked would I do him a favour for five shillings and I said I wasnae that kind of woman, and he said no, it was only to open a window shutter in the Atkinsons' bedroom, so he could throw a message in.'

She spoke slowly and huskily and leaned a little forward to Carey. 'Who was the man?'

As he asked the question there was a sound behind Carey, tantalisingly familiar and yet out of place, not quite the whip of a bow, more a...

The small crossbow bolt sprouted like an evil weed, a little above and to the side of Julia Coldale's left breast. She jerked, looked down and stared, put her hand up uncertainly to touch the black rod, then slid softly to the cobblestones.

The marketplace erupted. Over the shouting and screaming and the open-mouthed astonishment of the jury, half of whom instinctively had their swords out, Carey caught Aglionby's eye. The man was astonished, swelling with outrage, but he wasn't panicking.

'Mr Mayor, shut the gates,' Carey said to him, quite conversationally under the din, knowing the different pitch would get through to him when a shout would be lost.

Aglionby nodded once, was on his feet and up the steps to the market cross.

There was a thunk! beside him and Carey turned to see a crossbow bolt stuck into the table wood quite close by. Is he shooting at me or the Mayor, he wondered coldly, moving back. Scrope was also on his feet, sword out, looking about him for the sniper as aggressively as a man with no chin could. The trouble with crossbows was that they made very little sound, didn't smoke and didn't flash.

The towncrier's bell jangled from the market cross.

'Trained bands o' Carell city,' boomed the Mayor's voice and some of the noise paused to hear him speak. 'Denham's troop to Caldergate, Beverley's troop to Scotchgate, Blennerhasset's troop to Botchergate, close the gates; we'll shut the City. At the double now, lads, run!'

One of the jurors had already run up the steps and was ringing the townbell. Moments later the Cathedral bell answered it. Three bodies of the men-at-arms around the marketplace peeled off and ran in three different directions.

Another bolt twanged off the stone cross beside Aglionby and he gasped and flinched, but stayed where he was.

'Sir Robert,' he called. 'D'ye ken the name o' the man makin' this outrage?'

'Jock Burn,' said Carey instantly.

'Ay, a Scot. I might have known,' said Aglionby with hereditary distaste. 'Hue and cry for Jock Burn,' he bellowed. 'Mr Leigh's servant.' And he turned and glared at his erstwhile fellow guildsman.

Dodd had come up behind Carey who was still trying to calculate where the bolts were coming from. Most of the jurors had taken cover in the hall. The men-at-arms were commendably still surrounding the group of prisoners, though looking nervous.

'Shut the Castle?' he asked.

'Send up to Solomon Musgrave,' Carey began, 'but he's to let him in and...'

The tail of the bolt stuck in the table pointed directly back at the house covered in scaffolding. With a prickle in his neck Carey finally worked it out as a renewed shrieking broke from that direction, people streaming away from it in fear.

The woman with the withered arm—Maggie Mulcaster—came staggering through the crowd, bleeding and crying.

Behind her was a man on horseback, coming cautiously out of a yard-wynd, a crossbow aimed at her back. In front of him on the horse's withers sat Mary Atkinson, crying busily. Jock Burn cuffed her left-handed over the ear and snarled, and she choked back the tears.

'He's taken her,' gasped Maggie. 'He's got Mary. He says he willna kill her if ye let him through the gate.'

Jock had even found the time to raid Mrs Atkinson's platechest, judging by the clanking lumpy bag slung at the back of his saddle, no doubt while he was lying low in the locked house.

In the distance they heard the booms as the Scotchgate and Botchergate were shut and barred. Carey could see the whiteness of Jock Burn's teeth.

'If ye think Ah willna kill the little maid, Ah will,' shouted Jock. 'Ye cannae hang me mair than once.'

The boom was softer from Caldergate because it was furthest away. The lift of Jock's shoulder showed he had heard it.

Carey stepped forwards, his hands held away from his sides, away from his swordhilt.

Jock turned a little, so the bolt was aimed at Carey's chest now. He didn't need to explain what would happen if anyone tried to rush him. At the back of his mind Carey wondered why his stomach muscles were contracted so hard when they couldn't stop a bolt.

'Come nae closer, Deputy,' Jock warned.

Carey stopped. He has one shot, he thought, he can't wind up a crossbow on horseback, but he can break the little girl's neck with one blow. She was staring at Carey with enormous eyes. Somebody was shouting, screaming from the bunch of men-at-arms and suspects behind him, a woman's voice. He wasn't sure what she said; he thought it might be Kate Atkinson's voice.

Then another voice reached him, sharp with London vowels and lost consonants.

'I got a cuttle for the co; you get the kinchin.'

Some part of him which had picked up a smattering of thieves' cant from Barnabus got ready to move, the tension tightening in his chest and back. Jock kicked his horse, one of the jurors' no doubt, and moved sideways away from them, the horse prancing and shifting nervously, as its rider put pressure on ready to gallop to the Scotchgate.

Carey watched, praying Barnabus wouldn't leave it too late, waiting, changing his mind about what to do.

The horse pecked and at once there was a cry of 'Gip!' from Barnabus and a soft sound in the air.

No time to see where the knife went.

Carey launched himself across the cobbles, heard the metallic twang of the crossbow, no time even to know if he'd been hit because he was at Jock's stirrup, catching Mary's kirtle with his left hand, the stirrup and boot with his right, jerking down with one hand, up with all his strength with the other, Jock going over the horse's back one way, little Mary falling squealing towards him, catching her by his fingertips tangled in her kirtle and hair, putting her behind him, shouting, 'Run to your mam!'

Still squealing, she ran. Jock had hit the ground on the other side of the horse, which swayed back and forwards, panicking, in

Carey's way and finally reared and galloped off away from the crowds, nearly kicking him in the face as it did so. Then he saw that Jock was up again, sprinting for the Scotchgate, long knife in one hand, eating knife in the other, a bright splash of blood on his arm, not serious—not like Barnabus to miss, but it had been a fiendishly difficult shot.

Carey was already after him. Jock's short legs were a blur; he had a good nippy speed on him, but Carey had height and was using his greater length of stride now he had got moving. Dodd was on the chase as well, guttural shouts of 'Tynedale!' behind him, and the men at the gate running down towards them yelling 'Carell' in return.

Suppressing the urge to call 'T'il est haut!' as if he was on the hunting field, Carey dodged after Jock down a narrow alley between houses...

And almost charged straight onto Jock's knife, lying in wait. He dodged at the last second, felt cloth part along his ribs, cannoned into a wattle and daub wall which gave alarmingly and then used its spring to launch himself back at Jock who was distracted by Dodd thundering in his wake.

He caught the little man by the shoulder and punched him hard enough in the face to send pain lancing all the way up his own arm. Jock staggered, shook his head and came back at him. Dodd swung with his sword, tearing a long gash down Jock's arm. Jock was snarling, the alley crowded behind them with enthusiastic helpers, especially now Jock was wounded, and a sudden voice said inside Carey, 'No, this one's mine.'

Later he claimed he would have preferred to hang the man but had thought that a living prisoner was always a danger to others who could be made hostage by his family. He might be bought out. He might escape. He might be torn apart by the crowd.

In fact, Carey had a cold white rage in his heart for a man who could shoot a redhead like Julia Coldale and use a little girl as his shield. That coldness carried him past the stabbing knife in Jock's hand, knocking it unconcernedly aside, catching him by the front of his jerkin and pulling hard as he stabbed up leftwards into the man's chest under his breastbone with the poignard he wasn't even aware of drawing.

The blood came from Jock's mouth, not the slender wound caused by the poignard. Carey found himself supporting the man's weight one-handed and let him crumble to the muddy ground, twisting and pulling his blade out with that distinctive sticky sound.

Then the blood came, but mostly on the ground, not him. Carey stood there, hands bloody, lace cuffs bloody, knife bloody, chest heaving, and Dodd came over and watched dispassionately while Jock's heels drummed and his eyes turned to frogspawn.

'Ay,' said Dodd with satisfaction, wiping his sword on a clean bit of Jock's jerkin. Carey bent and did the same, feeling remote from his own hands and very tired, the way a killing rage always left him. He had never before knifed a man in an alley, though.

The Carlislers who had come to help cheered and slapped his back approvingly as he pushed his way out into Scotch street again. He smiled back, wishing they wouldn't get in his way, picked up his hat which had fallen from his head as he ran and as he did so felt the cold draught and sting on his ribs which told him where Jock's knife had passed and ruined his brand new (unpaid for) black velvet suit.

That brought him back to earth a little.

thursday 6th july 1592, afternoon

Aglionby had adjourned the inquest for two hours and when the jury reconvened it was in the Mayor's own bedroom, to which Julia Coldale had been moved. The surgeon came, saw, shook his head and went himself to fetch a priest.

The jurors gathered around her along with the Coroner himself, Scrope and Carey, while Philadelphia sat by the bed and looked curiously like a small sphinx in her gravity. It turned out she was the one who had given Barnabus her knife in the confusion when Jock rode out with Mary Atkinson. Now she was holding Julia's hand. Julia's back was arched, her breath bubbled and her red curls were dark with sweat: the surgeon had said he could not get the bolt out without cutting and as it was so close to her heart, he didn't think she had a chance of living if he did.

Even in such extremis, even with his eyes stinging for pity at the pretty girl turned to dust so soon, Carey couldn't help noticing how Julia's eyes looked around at them, pleased they were there.

'Do you want to give your testimony?' asked Philadelphia. 'Are you sure?'

The girl nodded, winced and began to speak breathily.

'Jock Burn gave me five shillings for opening of Mr Atkinson's shutters...' whispered Julia. 'An' I did it. I didn't know why he wanted to; I thought he might want to thieve the plate chest because he's a Scot...' She spoke arrhythmically, in long bursts of words interspersed with slow gasps as she caught up breath for the next effort. '...When the mistress came down wi' all the sheets bloody I was afraid as I understood it then...but then I thought perhaps I could get my dowry by it, so I asked Jock if I could talk to...Mr Leigh and when I went to see him this morning, he tried to kill me rather than pay me...and now he's done it, the stingy bastard.'

The next set of gasps for breath pained his ears to listen to them. Carey wondered remotely if there were any sort of death that didn't hurt and then put the thought from him deliberately as undoubtedly leading to madness and melancholy. It occurred to him for the first time that she was a brave lass, for all her foolishness in trying to blackmail John Leigh.

'Ay well,' she whispered. 'I'll get a dove on me grave...'

A dove was the sign of a girl who died still virgin, and it seemed some girls found the thought romantic. Philadelphia had tears in her eyes. Sniffles sounded from a couple of the jurors.

Aglionby faced the jury.

'I doubt she'll say any more, gentlemen,' he rumbled.

They took the hint and left her.

The inquest was reconvened at the market cross again, after Fenwick had come with his litter to collect Jock Burn's body. Julia Coldale had not died yet, but was sure to do so that night or the next day, depending on how strong she was.

The jury filed soberly into their benches. Aglionby declared that the inquest was reopened; Carey faced the jury feeling unutterably weary, and called Mr John Leigh.

He said nothing and would not take the oath. Carey reminded him that the penalty for failing to plead at his trial was pressing to death and then, at the Coroner's nod, began to speak.

'John Leigh wanted the house next door to his own to expand into. Unfortunately, not only had his brother-in-law Jemmy

Atkinson inherited it wrongfully, as he thought, he also refused to sell it. The Chancery case, as Chancery cases will, was taking years and costing a fortune. John Leigh was having money problems in other ways and he came up with an idea which was probably inspired by seeing the thatchers working on the scaffolding round his roof.

'Mr Leigh decided to kill Jemmy Atkinson in such a way that Kate Atkinson was sure to be accused and convicted and so he and his wife would get her property. After she burned at the stake. For in fact, this is an attempt at a double murder, with his honour the Coroner and you yourselves, gentlemen, used as the weapon in the second, judicial murder.'

Carey paused and cleared his throat. As he had said to Elizabeth, he could orate if he had to: thank the Lord there was hardly any law involved here.

'At first I misunderstood. I had seen the window to the Atkinsons' bedchamber and I thought it impossible for a man to squeeze through it unless he were very slim. John Leigh is not a small man, though Jock Burn is. Was. On the other hand, Leigh couldn't trust a servant to do the killing for him without laying himself open to blackmail. Another thing you no doubt already know is that the Leighs' house is next door to the Atkinsons' and as alike as two peas. Certainly the upper windows are the same size. You can see them over there and inspect them later, if you wish.

'This morning I climbed the scaffolding on the Leighs' house and dug about in the thatch. My Sergeant had found a knife hidden there the previous afternoon.'

Dodd stepped forwards smartly and held out the knife so the jurymen could see it. Thomas Lowther took it and passed it along, and Archibald Bell rubbed his thumb on the crumbs of brown at the place where the blade met the hilt.

'We found a bloody shirt,' said Carey, gestured. Dodd took the shirt out of a small bag and handed it to Thomas Lowther. He passed it on with the combination of distaste and prurience that seemed right for a bloody shirt. Nobody argued about the identity of the stiff brown stains on it, although Captain Carleton sniffed at them sceptically.

'As you can see,' Carey continued, 'it's a gentleman's shirt, fine linen and well-stitched. There were no other clothes. At first I thought he might have put it over his clothes to protect them from the blood, but I admit I was still puzzled. Then when I saw John Leigh through his own upper window attempting to kill Julia Coldale, I kicked the shutters and glass in and tried to get through. I couldn't, my shoulders wouldn't fit. I was reduced to throwing bits of window glass at him and I don't mind telling you, gentlemen, I was very annoyed.'

The barrel-like Captain Carleton was leaned back and smiling understandingly at him.

'Sergeant Dodd went round by the stairs and managed to distract John Leigh. By that time God had inspired me to the answer. I took off my doublet and Venetians and so lost an inch or two from each shoulder and a couple of inches around my girth. In my shirt I climbed through the window, just as John Leigh had done to kill Jemmy Atkinson, and so I was able to arrest him.'

'The only problem he had—how to make sure the shutters were open to Jemmy Atkinson's bedchamber—we have just heard how he solved it. At the cost of Julia Coldale's life, she has told us the truth of what she did that morning. And so the mystery is solved. John Leigh waited until he heard Julia opening the shutters and going down the stairs again, and then climbed out of his own window onto the scaffolding and across. There was some risk he would be seen from the street, but it was early in the morning and not light yet. He climbed in through the window, cut Jemmy Atkinson's throat, climbed out again, took off his shirt and hid it with the knife in the thatch, and then climbed back in by his own window. He could have done it in five minutes, washed and dressed and gone downstairs. Then all he had to do was sit back and wait for someone to find the body.

'He must have been worried when Andy Nixon and Mrs Atkinson conspired to move the body and blame the killing on me. In fact, they were trying to pervert the course of justice, which is in itself a crime, although I hope his honour the Coroner will be lenient with them on that score. However, in the end, he must have been sure he would gain all he wished after the Lammastide assizes, when Mrs Atkinson surely would have been convicted of petty treason and executed. Perhaps Andy Nixon would have died with her, as her accomplice, perhaps not. Evidently, he didn't care one way or the other.'

He wondered if he should mention the fact that the Atkinson children would thus be left fatherless, motherless and homeless, but he didn't. The jury could work it out for themselves. Mary herself had been allowed to cling amongst her mother's skirts, sucking her thumb and watching.

'There you have your verdict, gentlemen of the jury: Jemmy Atkinson was murdered most foully; his throat was cut by John Leigh and the reason was only so that John Leigh and his wife could eventually inherit his property as the nearest relatives of the victim. That is what you must find.'

Aglionby summed up briskly and the jurymen went up the steps into the hall in order to deliberate. A few of them went over to look at the houses in question. A short sharp argument between Thomas Lowther and Archibald Bell floated out at the windows which ended in Thomas Lowther's sullen agreement. They filed back down the steps again.

Without looking straight at his brother, Thomas Lowther delivered himself of the jury's majority verdict in a loud chant, like an old Mass priest.

'The jury finds that Jemmy Atkinson was murdered by John Leigh his brother-in-law.'

There was a scattered cheering and an approving buzz of talk from the stoutly watching public. Barnabus, Andy Nixon and Kate Atkinson were released immediately. Carey felt too wrung out to be triumphant, although he shook Barnabus's hand and congratulated him on a fine shot. The next inquest would be for Julia Coldale and Jock Burn. No doubt Jock had been paid to kill her by Mrs Leigh herself, but they could never prove it now unless Mrs Leigh confessed.

The procession formed itself again to travel back to the Castle and some of the crowd booed at John Leigh. Mrs Croser the midwife stood in his doorway to see him. He lifted his head at the muffled sound of shrieking from within, and then shook it despairingly and plodded on.

Relief and fatigue made Carey's perceptions unnaturally sharp, like glass. He had glimpsed Kate Atkinson weeping over the red marks the manacles had left on Andy Nixon's wrists and Nixon stroking her neck awkwardly as they walked. He had also seen Mary Atkinson swept up in her mother's arms and covered with kisses. Barnabus had disappeared in a hurry behind the hall and come out fastening his codpiece and looking green about the gills.

John Leigh kept trying to take longer strides than his ankle chains allowed, almost pitching forwards on his nose. Philadelphia Lady Scrope was nowhere to be seen—perhaps she had slipped away to visit Julia Coldale. Carey wondered if he should go, and thought perhaps he shouldn't. It was partly cowardice: he didn't want to see a pretty girl in such suffering.

Lord, what a waste. To Jock Burn he gave no further thought, except a mild regret that the man could not be hanged.

A happy idea suddenly struck him. He had a quick word with Dodd and then strode over to where Andy Nixon was still scandalously entwined with Kate Atkinson by her own front door.

'Andy Nixon,' he said and Nixon let go and looked worried. 'I've a proposition to put to you.'

Nixon looked even more worried. 'Ay sir?' he said warily.

'I need another man for my troop of men in the garrison. Would you be interested in the place?'

'Och,' said Andy, thunderstruck. 'But d'ye not mind the trouble we put ye to, sir?'

'I'm blaming James Pennycook for that,' Carey smiled. 'I hardly think you came up with the idea, did you?'

'Nay sir. Well…'

'I doubt very much if Pennycook will be coming back south of the Border again. He'll certainly not be purveying to the garrison any more.' Why Scrope didn't have his victuals supplied by a powerful local man like Aglionby was a mystery to Carey, which he intended to put right as soon as he could. 'And so you're in need of a new master.'

In his delight at Kate's freedom and his relief at his own, Andy hadn't thought of that and his square face clouded.

'Ay, sir, you're right.'

'Well, then? I want good fighters, which you are, and you've shown yourself faithful, at least to your woman. The pay's one shilling and thruppence a day and perks, including some of what we get in fees for rescuing cattle and such. And it's steady work based in the Castle.'

'But is there not a fee for the place?' Andy asked with puzzlement.

'You can owe it.'

Andy whispered quickly to Kate and then turned back to Carey.

'I'll do it, sir.'

'Excellent. Talk to Sergeant Dodd in the morning.'

He left them wrapping themselves round each other again, and tried to suppress his burning envy of them as he hurried back to the Castle.

thursday 6th july 1592, afternoon

Carey's feet were heavy on the stairs to his chambers in the Queen Mary Tower. When he opened the door he found Simon Barnet there with Young Hutchin Graham, playing dice. Young Hutchin scooped up the dice guiltily but Carey couldn't be bothered to tell him off for gambling, especially as he was so heartily relieved to see him. Young Hutchin gave him a sidelong look. The boy was very dirty and dusty and looked tired, so Carey sent Simon off to fetch small beer and food for both of them, plus water and soap so he could wash his hands properly. Barnabus had said that perhaps his suit could be rescued by taking out the slashed panel of velvet and replacing it with another whole one which had cheered him a little. The shallow gash in his skin would mend with much less trouble, despite Philadelphia's insistence on putting green ointment in it and bandaging it. It was burning sore now but not throbbing.

'What happened to you?' he asked Young Hutchin.

Young Hutchin grinned. 'It was verra interesting.'

'No doubt.' Carey looked around for Barnabus, remembered he was in the Keep, waiting for Philadelphia to give him a draught of something cleansing and foul from her stillroom. He took his sword belt off and leant it against the wall, opened up the top buttons of his black velvet doublet in the approved melancholy style, so he could at last breathe properly. He gestured at the still-curtained bed.

'Have you seen the pups?' he asked Young Hutchin.

'Ay. The kennelman came and moved Buttercup and all down to the pupping kennel where she should ha' been to start with,' said Hutchin. 'But your counterpane's in a terrible state.'

Carey wandered over, looked at it, and closed the curtains again. He went restlessly to the flagon standing on one of his clothes chests and found that without Barnabus about, nobody had refilled it. Curbing the impulse to throw it at the wall, he sat down on the chest and blinked at Young Hutchin.

'Well?' he asked.

'I couldnae get through to Thirlwall Castle, sir, for my uncle had put too many men about it, and they had dogs forbye. So I slept under a bush and when she came out on the road, I went along wi' her, to the north a bit.'

'I thought you'd been caught by your relatives.'

'Nay sir,' said Hutchin, cheekily. 'Not me, sir.'

At the end of that day's travelling, Lady Widdrington and her small party had come in sight of Hexham without any incident, which had rather surprised Hutchin.

'I stopped your uncle at the Irthing ford,' Carey said shortly. 'Sent him back to Netherby with his tail between his legs.'

'Ay, I thought something like that had happened. So I rode down and joined Lady Widdrington and told her all about it and she went red but she didnae say nothing. Then she had me ride behind, and when she got to Hexham, there was the Middle March Warden and he had...'

'Sir John Forster?'

'Ay sir.'

'How is he?'

'Very old and a mite forgetful, but well enough. Anyway, he was there and so was her husband.'

'What?'

'Ay, Sir Henry Widdrington.'

Carey's mouth had gone dry. 'How did he greet her?'

Young Hutchin shrugged. 'She curtseyed, he nodded at her. They went in. A while later, I was called for and gi'en a letter for ye. Then I come back wi' the dispatch rider from Newcastle. The ordnance carts from Newcastle was there too, sir, and we passed a powerful lot of packtrains by the road. The Newcastle man said that Sir Henry was for Scotland, although he didna ken why.'

Silently Carey put out his hand and Hutchin laid the letter on it. If I don't open it, he found himself thinking, then I won't know what it says and can ignore it.

Meanwhile his fingers were breaking the seal and unfolding the paper. It was Lady Widdrington's handwriting, her spelling as wild as most women's.

'*From Lady Elizabeth Widdrington, to Sir Robert Carey.*

Sir, I must ask you to have no more dealings with me in any shape or form and what friendship we may have had is now at an end.

Please honour my request as a knight of the Queen should.'

That was simple enough. Impossible to tell whose brain had framed the words: was it Elizabeth herself, or had she written at her husband's dictation? She had made it plain enough she thought his courtship of her was foolish.

Carey looked up unseeingly. He was amazed to find he could not feel anything. Perhaps it wasn't so amazing: after a fight or a football match he often found bruises and grazes he had not felt at the time.

'Sir,' came a boy's alien voice.

'What? You still there, Young Hutchin?'

'Ay sir. She had a verbal message. She whispered it to me when she give me the letter, sir, under cover of straightening my jerkin.'

Young Hutchin shut his eyes tight and frowned. 'It was in foreign, sir. She said to tell ye, ah mow tay, Robin, ah mah bow simper.'

Carey thought hard to rearrange the sounds. '*Amo te*, Robin, *amabo semper*?' he asked.

Young Hutchin nodded vigorously. 'Ay,' he said. 'That was it. Is it French?'

'No. Latin. Please forget it, if you like Lady Widdrington.'

Young Hutchin nodded again, a mixture of cunning and an attempt at forthright honesty on his face.

Simon came back with the small beer and some pieces of ox-tongue pie. Carey had lost his appetite. He told the boys to strip the ruined counterpane off the bed and see if they could find Goodwife Biltock to get another one for him. Then he wandered unseeingly down the stairs again.

By a kind of habit, he found himself in the stable yard where the Head Groom was at evening stables with Scrope. Carey went to Thunder's stall, went in and started picking up Thunder's feet to see how the farrier had done his work. Not bad. Not bad at all. But Thunder should go back to London. He had no use for a tournament charger here in the West March.

Amo te, Robin, *amabo semper*. She didn't know much Latin. Perhaps she had persuaded Young Henry to tell her the words, or a tiny bit of schooling had stuck as it had with him. She had obediently written her letter cutting off their friendship at her husband's dictation and then, being as honest as she was, she had quietly defied him. The words were curt but sufficient.

I love you, Robin, she had said, promising no more than that, risking God knew what kind of persecution, I will love you always.

Patricia Finney has been writing since she was seven and getting paid for it since she was 15. Her first book, *A Shadow of Gulls*, was published when she was 18 years old, and won the David Higham Award for Best First Novel. She studied Modern History at Wadham College, Oxford.

Since which time she has accumulated an American husband, one daughter, two sons, a dog and three cats, plus assorted rodents theoretically owned by her offspring. Her husband's work as a barrister (an English lawyer, specialising in litigation) has given her fascinating insight into real-life crime and her children have taught her more than she wanted to know about human nature. She has had a variety of jobs which have included editing a medical journal and writing a weekly column in the *London Evening Standard*.

She presently lives in Cornwall, and is working on the next couple of Carey stories, and some screenplays. She is planning a contemporary novel as well, whenever her fulltime work as nanny, chauffeur, handywoman, administrator, accountant and legal secretary gives her a chance to write it.

CPSIA information can be obtained
at www.ICGtesting.com
Printed in the USA
LVHW031610081118
596436LV00001B/200